DUST IN THE WIND

<u>Germany:</u>
Das Schiff
Der Stier und das Madchen
In Schwarzen Spiegeln (Grímsson Series)

<u>Denmark:</u>
Skibet
Ödeland

<u>Sweden:</u>
Skeppet

<u>Poland:</u>
Statek

<u>Italy:</u>
Nero Oceano

DUST IN THE WIND

STEFÁN MÁNI

Dust in the Wind

CONTENTS

Behind the Walls of Nightmares

Spider

Sitting on a footstool in a dark, dilapidated building is a booted miscreant. Behind him, a narrow stream of water runs from a tap into an overflowing concrete tub. The only light comes through a small window. The glass in the window is cracked and dirty, and the wooden frame is rotting. Two bluebottles buzz against the glass, wanting to get out into the light and freedom. The building is silent apart from the low gurgle of the water and the buzzing of the flies. Yet the silence is interrupted now and then by a singing, slightly piercing sound. The miscreant is sharpening old sheep shears with a damp whetstone. The shears are large, primitive scissors whose blades resemble knives. The miscreant draws the stone quickly along the edge of the sharp blades, first one and then the other. In the window is a spider web. The spider is lying in wait up in one corner. Suddenly, one of the bluebottles gets caught in the web. The miscreant stops sharpening and looks up. His eyes are resolute and cold. The spider, black and fat, crawls out of its hiding place. It trips quickly over its web, attacks the fly, and wraps it in silk. The other fly continues buzzing, unaware of the fate that awaits it.

The miscreant raises the sheep shears and snips at the air with them. Their cutting edges gleam and the razor-sharp steel sings…

Frosty the Snowman

The Day before Ascension Day

By the time Hörður starts from sleep, Bíbí has already left for work. He's sweaty and his heart is pounding in his chest. He woke to a chilling, piercing noise. Had he dreamed of knives? And a spider? He heaves a sigh, relieved that the night is over. The spring light illuminates the white curtains; outside, amorous passerines chirp as they busily build their nests. The cycle of life goes on and it's spring again, almost summer. It has doubtless been summer for quite some time in Europe, where spring begins in early April, even in March—a *real* spring with colorful flowers, warm breezes, and fragrant air. In Iceland there's no real spring, just wind and rain for a few weeks while the snow melts, and then the eternal Arctic light takes over, without, however, being necessarily accompanied by heat and sun— maybe just more rain, and the same wind. There are generally several reasonably warm days, and then it begins to darken in August, and in a short time, winter sets in—long, dark, and gloomy.

Soon afterward, Advent will have begun again. He hasn't looked forward to Christmas since his childhood. Now he fears it like a death sentence, and it's still only May.

How will he be in November? If only he could break the negative thought pattern that seems to be carved in stone in his brain. The fear is like a heavy rock in his stomach. If only he could divert his mind, find something interesting to do—something to *investigate.*

If only he could go to work like an ordinary person…

Hörður heaves a sigh, then pulls himself together and rises from bed in all his glory. He's about two meters tall, wide-shouldered and big-boned. His skin is pale, and he's long-limbed and heavy. Hörður is a robust man, but he's put on a few kilos this winter, being mainly inactive and on indefinite leave from his job since the Feast of St. Þorlákur at the end of December. His face is as if sculpted in granite. His shoulder-length hair is rust-red and tousled, while his eyes are emerald green, deep, and intelligent.

He starts the day with a cold shower. Then he dresses in black—black trousers, a black shirt, and black socks. His breakfast is black coffee. He turns on the radio, which is tuned to Gullbylgjan—the Golden Wave. The day begins with "Carry On Wayward Son," by Kansas. Could be worse. At his third cup of coffee, he gains a bit of an appetite and toasts a slice of bread, which he eats with butter, cheese, and mixed-berry jam. He turns off the radio when the ten o'clock news starts. At one time, he always listened to the news, but stopped when he himself wound up in them, day after day. What a roller coaster ride that was. A death march, more like it.

Hörður growls in frustration. Damn reporters. Damn gullible public. Damn spineless society.

He takes his fifth cup of coffee with him into the living room. There, he switches on his stereo and flips through his meager album collection. The Kansas song has inspired him a bit. His dad, Grímur, had had a few albums by this likable prog band. The moody ship engineer's favorite song by the boys in Kansas was the ballad "Dust in the Wind". Which is precisely the song that Hörður wants to listen to just now. But he doesn't have it, unfortunately, neither on vinyl nor CD. And of course he doesn't have Spotify or any of that other cash-grabbing app bullshit. He neither listens to music on his phone nor downloads it to a computer. That's just for stupid kids and people with poor taste, as those degenerate methods offer no good sound quality, besides the fact that he prefers to look at an album's cover while he listens, read the lyrics and appreciate the design and such. He wants to enjoy music, not *consume* it like some non-nutritious fast food. Hörður Grímsson from Súðavík may be a dinosaur, but he's not a neurotic *snowflake* like everyone else nowadays.

He breaks into a cold sweat, because as the word *snow-flake* comes to mind, a certain song gets stuck in his head, amped to the max, as if his skull is a powerful speaker. It's a song that has stuck to him like a nightmare day and night for the past weeks and months. The song that was playing in the Smáralind shopping mall when he ...

Hörður plunks down onto the living-room sofa and hides his face in his hands while that bastard Frosty the Snowman tramps around in his brain with that damn corn-cob pipe and a button nose.

It's Wednesday, for which Hörður is grateful because he and Þóra Sverrisdóttir, a friend of his from the police academy, have met for lunch every Wednesday for the past few months. These lunch meetings of theirs have been the highlight of the week in the recent life of the red-haired giant, as he has few female friends—in fact, none besides Bíbí and Þóra. This time, they've arranged to meet at

Haninn on Suðurlandsbraut Road, the best chicken place in the country. Hörður parks his black Ford Explorer work SUV in a parking space a short distance from the restaurant and steps out into the cool spring air. It's cloudy and a little less than seven degrees. The sidewalks in this cold-looking service and shopping district are dusty, the road's shoulders are lined with all sorts of rubbish, and visible here and there are the grimy outlines of piles of snow that have melted and run into the nearest gutter.

Þóra is waiting for him outside Haninn. She's wearing her uniform, as she's still a rank-and-file police officer. She's short and slender, and smiles warmly at the red-haired giant, who plods over to her in his combat boots, wearing his black leather coat and sunglasses on his pale face.

"Hi, big guy!" She smiles widely.

"Good to see you," Hörður replies, giving her a clumsy hug before they enter the crowded, noisy restaurant. They get in line behind repairmen and office workers, order their food at the counter and pay for it. Then they find a free table and hang their coats on the backs of their chairs.

"So how are you doing?" Þóra asks after they've settled in.

"Just, fine, thanks." Hörður squeezes out a smile.

"I see," says Þóra, who knows full well that her gigantic friend has been feeling miserable for a long time. After Hörður was promoted and became a plainclothes detective in the Criminal Investigation Department, things became a bit chilly between them, as Þóra felt she had just as much business being in that department as he did. Naturally, she was happy for her friend, but at the same time, it hurt her not to have been given the same opportunity. But after the incident at the Smáralind shopping mall, they became close again—and Hörður desperately needed friends.

"No change in your situation?" she asks gingerly.

He shakes his head. "Nope. It seems as if this indefinite leave will never end. It's been almost five months. That blessed *independent* committee is probably still at it, the gun permit is still in the drawer, and I don't know what will happen next, let alone when. I could lose my job or be demoted. It's the uncertainty that's the worst. It's driving me completely nuts."

"I can believe that," says Þóra. "But you're still getting paid, aren't you? And you get to keep using the car."

He heaves a sigh. "I'm on base pay, yes. But it's barely possible to get by on it. We'd just bought an apartment! And, yes, I still have the SUV, at least for the time being. Maybe they just forgot to take the keys away from me?"

"I'm sure you'll get some answers soon," says Þóra, just to say something.

Hörður shrugs. "Or not. What do I know? Maybe I'll cruise around aimlessly every day for the rest of my life, in between seeing that psychiatrist. Damn it, I'm tired of doing nothing!"

"You're seeing … ?" Þóra stops when an employee shows up with their food. Hörður ordered half a fried chicken with fries and strong piri-piri sauce, Þóra a quarter chicken with rice, salad, and lemon and herb dressing.

"Ah, this looks good!" says Hörður, licking his lips. "You were saying?"

Þóra lifts her fork and knife. "I don't remember. Unless I was just wondering if you could use all this down time for something constructive. You know, take the opportunity to do something instead of being bored. Take a class, take up a hobby, you know?"

Hörður nods, his mouth full of food. "I've actually been reacquainting myself with the guys in Easy Company. That never gets old. Damn, I admire them!"

"Easy what?" asks Þóra.

"Easy Company," Hörður repeats. "Easy for E, which was E Company, 2nd Battalion of the 506th Parachute Infantry Division of the 101st Airborne Division of the US Army, better known as The Screaming Eagles. It was a highly trained volunteer force that was formed in 1942 at a training camp in Toccoa, Georgia. Not far from the camp was Mount Currahee, which is an Indian name meaning 'we stand alone,' which became the motto of the Toccoa paratroopers. Didn't you see the series *Band of Brothers?*"

"Oh, right," Þóra mutters with sincere indifference. "No ... I didn't see it."

"Great series," says Hörður devotedly. "I'm watching it now for the eighth time. It's based on a book of the same name by the historian Stephen Ambrose. I've read it five times, as well as other books on the same subject, about the same men. They're *legends,* Þóra! Hardboiled heroes who parachuted into France on D-Day itself, June 6, 1944. They disabled a gun battery at Brécourt Manor, liberated Carentan, fought in the Netherlands, and nearly froze to death in Bastogne, where they held off an unexpected German offensive through the Ardennes. Men like Dick Winters, Babe Heffron, Shifty Powers, and "Wild" Bill Guarnere, who's my favorite, though my admiration of Dick Winters is unlimited. I could talk endlessly about these men!"

"I have no doubt about that," says Þóra, giving Hörður an indulgent smile.

"Like when Shifty shot the sniper who had hidden in the church spire," says Hörður, who's on a roll. 'One shot, around a corner, from long range ... and bang! This Nazi sniper had picked off his comrades, there being little shelter where they were and the shooter way up in the spire. Then it was the turn of our man, the low-key country boy who ..."

"Now I remember!" Þóra says suddenly, interrupting the red-haired giant.

"Huh?" he says, confused.

"What I was just about to ask you when the food came," says Þóra triumphantly.

"Okay," says Hörður, half-offended, before taking a big bite of food. "What was it?"

"Did I hear right?" says Þóra. "Did you say you're seeing a psychiatrist?"

Hörður rolls his eyes. "I *have* to. Because of what happened. They want him to evaluate me or something. Those guys on the independent investigation committee. Guys and gals; maybe there are women there too—what do I know."

"And?" she asks anxiously. "How's it going? Are you being cooperative and open?"

Hörður grunts, his mouth full of food. "Yes, yes, I suppose so. In a way. But I don't tell that monkey everything. I just tell him what he wants to hear. Whatever will help me keep my job. The rest is irrelevant."

Þóra puts down her fork and knife. "Hörður, you've got to be careful. You mustn't underestimate your psychiatrist. He's undoubtedly good at his job and will see through you if you try to deceive him or play games with him."

"Maybe," says Hörður, with a hopeless expression. "But the problem is just that *if* I tell him the truth, I'll definitely fail his assessment."

"Why do you say that?" she asks.

He clicks his tongue. "I killed someone, you see. I shot him in the head in the presence of witnesses. His head exploded and blood splattered everywhere."

Þóra pales and pushes her plate away, having lost her appetite. "Yes, right, and?"

Hörður shrugs and lowers his voice. "I dream about it every night. I hear the gunshot and the fucking song playing over the speaker system. 'Frosty the Snowman' at full volume. I wake up every morning drenched in sweat. But the thing is, I don't feel bad about what happened. I don't have a trace of guilt or feel as if I did anything wrong. I don't dream about the incident because it haunts me, like a bad conscience. I dream about it because it's the craziest thing I've ever experienced. I feel miserable about not having a job, but I couldn't care less about that Muslim I shot. I think it's because I'm a psychopath and if the psychiatrist realizes that, I'm in deep shit."

Þóra thinks this over but then shakes her head. "Your situation doesn't really sound good, but I don't think you're psychopathic. I know you better than that, and besides, it doesn't occur to a psychopath that he's psychopathic. That would be contrary to psychopathy."

"Really?" Hörður asks interestedly.

She nods. "You know what? I think you don't have a guilty conscience because those people you stopped at Smáralind were about to blow themselves up. In other words, they were dead no matter what. Dying was their choice. It could even be argued that you saved the life of one of them, because if you hadn't stopped them, they both would have died, along with a number of innocent civilians. *You* would have died, too, as well as Bíbí, who was there by coincidence."

"Interesting," says Hörður, distracted. He realizes immediately that Þóra has hit the nail on the head. But what she doesn't know is that he knew in advance that only one of the men would die. He saw a death shadow before he fired the first shot—*one* death shadow, not two or a hundred. The shadow he saw could certainly have belonged to anyone in the mall, even himself, but deep down, Hörður knew that one of the terrorists would die. He didn't *think* so; there was no time for that, but thinking back on it, he felt it—or *hoped* it, rather. Which is why it didn't shock him when the bullet ended up in the head of Iskandar Khara, despite his having aimed at the man's right shoulder. This is why he doesn't feel guilty about killing him. The Muslim was dead before Hörður pulled the trigger. The dice had been cast. Hörður isn't responsible for the cruel fate of that unfortunate man; he was only a cog in the invisible mechanism that the Witches of Fate had assembled and set in motion.

Hörður feels somewhat relieved. "I think you're right."

Þóra smiles. "Well?"

He nods. "I've been called a racist, a Black Shirt, a murderer and worse on social media and in comment sections online, but if you look at it coldly, I was just a cop doing my job—*to serve and protect,* as they say in America. Doctors remove malignant cancers from patients, engineers build bridges, and police officers either solve crimes or prevent them. I was just the right person in the right place at the right time, and did what needed to be done. I actually didn't intend to kill anyone, but…"

Hörður shrugs.

"It happened," Þóra concludes.

"Something like that," Hörður mutters. "But the investigation committee probably won't agree. After all, you can't say or do anything anymore. We live in a time of passionate emotions and violent reactions. Everyone is offended, sensitive, and hurt—mainly on behalf of a third party. Everyone is a bleeding victim, full of righteous anger that in recent months has, among other things, been directed at a big, ugly police officer who shot an innocent little terrorist. Apparently, I'm both unscrupulous and bloodthirsty. A soulless giant with heart of ice."

"Frosty the Snowman?" she suggests, with a mischievous look.

"Þóra!" says Hörður, offended and hurt. But then he can't help but burst out laughing, because it was just too funny and he doesn't want to be like the *snowflakes* he was describing—the *good* and thin-skinned people who can't bear anything.

"Sorry," says Þóra, laughing. "But you'd just become too dramatic for my taste."

"You're all right," says Hörður as he wipes a tear from the corner of one eye. "It's been a long time since I've laughed like this. I needed it."

"It's good to be able to help," she says.

"That's what friends are for, right?" says Hörður. Þóra nods.

That evening, Hörður is sitting on the living-room sofa at home, watching television with one eye. The news has finished and tonight's episode of the *Kastljós* talk show has just begun. This time it's about gender reassignment and homosexual people. On the screen is a blurry image of a young woman who wishes to remain anonymous.

"What girl is that?" Bíbí asks as she sits down next to her common-law partner and hands him a steaming cup of coffee.

"Thanks, sweetie," says Hörður, taking the cup. "Oh, I wasn't really listening. I think she wants to be turned into a guy but didn't pass her assessment."

"Oh, I see," says Bíbí. "The poor girl."

"Or the poor guy," mutters Hörður.

"I got the hormones myself; that in itself wasn't a problem," says the girl on the TV screen, in a distorted male voice. She sounds very bitter, and doesn't seem to be well balanced.

"But if I want to change myself completely, I've to go to Thailand or something. Maybe I will, maybe not. But until then, I'm just a trans man, not a real man."

Hörður gets a knot in his stomach. He himself has this hanging over him: that some stupid committee is going to decide that he's not qualified to do what he was born to do. If he can no longer be a cop, what is he going to do?

Tuesday after Pentecost

It's time...

Hörður Grímsson is numb from stress. He could hardly feel worse even if he were being led to his execution, with a hood over his head and his hands tied behind his back. He would probably even feel a bit better if he knew that he was going to be executed—then all his hope would be gone, and with it, any gnawing uncertainty. It's the hope that's worst. He's convinced that he'll lose his job, and therewith, the will to live. But within him flickers a faint light of hope, like candlelight in a storm. And it's this weak hope that's giving him nausea, headaches, and anxiety. He desires nothing more than a happy ending, but doesn't believe in them, because in his heart he's always a villain, not a hero. He sincerely hopes that his nearly six-month-long walk in the desert is at an end, but feels as if he's on the verge of plunging over a huge precipice.

Fucking bloody hell...

He parks his black Explorer in the lot behind the police station on Hverfisgata Street, inside the sturdy iron fence. This is where he used to park the SUV every morning, finding it as natural and ordinary as brushing his teeth or putting on his shoes. It's not until something happens that we realize that everyday activities such as going to work are worth their weight in gold, literally. Even more precious than gold, because it's impossible to buy honor, security, or happiness for money, even if some people think so.

Hörður shuts off the SUV's powerful engine, takes a deep breath and tries to slow down his heartbeat and calm his mind, without success. His mouth is dry, his stomach hurts, and he has a pain in his chest. He opens the glove compartment in the hope of finding cigarettes or whiskey there, but has to settle for mint-flavored nicotine gum. Could be worse. He opens the door and steps out into the temperate morning air. Cloudy, eight degrees, a slow, cool easterly breeze. It's June, but summer is long overdue.

It's a quarter to ten in the morning. Just over twenty-four hours since Axel M. Axelsson sent him an e-mail and asked him to come see him. Why this formality? Why didn't he call? Hörður walks dejectedly to the back door of the police station, which towers over him like a sea stack. As usual, he's dressed in black and is wearing his leather coat, which has practically merged into its owner. He hopes he won't run into anyone and actually manages to make it unseen through the basement and then by elevator up to the third floor, on the west side of which is the Criminal Investigation Department. He hasn't walked this way since being put on fucking leave and is uncomfortably aware that he may be doing so for the last time.

How miserable would that be?

Hörður swipes his ID card through the reader at the door of the Criminal Investigation Department with his card, simultaneously expecting it not to work. He's relieved when he hears a familiar beep and the soft click of the door unlocking. It opens into the long workspace better known as The Cave, where detectives sit working sit working in their cubicles, tapping on computer keyboards. The air is heavy and smells of aftershave, sweat, and coffee. Hörður hurries to his boss's closed door and knocks three times before opening it into the air-conditioned, humidity-controlled office.

"I'm not accustomed to having people just rush in here," says Axel M. Axelsson coldly. He's sitting behind his large desk with reading glasses on his nose, stocky, bald and tanned, dressed in an elegant suit and with a folded cloth in his breast pocket.

"You asked me to come," says Hörður, his voice hoarse with stress. "Best just to get it over with, right?

"Easy there, Hamlet," mutters old Steppenwolf. He closes the file he was reading and takes off his glasses. "Have a seat and cheer up."

"Cheer up, huh?" Hörður isn't amused. He plunks down in one of the visitor chairs and tries to relax, though he knows from experience that it's completely impossible.

"How have you been?" Axel asks in a fatherly tone.

Hörður grunts moodily. "Can't we skip the chit chat and get right to the point? Do I get to keep my job or not?"

"Yes and no," Axel replies stoically.

Hörður fidgets in his chair. "What do you mean, yes and no?"

"I was reviewing the committee's conclusion." Axel reopens the file he was reading and puts on his glasses.

Hörður tries to swallow, but his throat feels clamped shut. He goes numb and would doubtless collapse if he stood upright. So Steppenwolf wasn't just reading any old file, but the file on *him*.

"The psychiatrist considers you to be in denial," Axel says without looking up. "He believes that the consequences of what happened in Smáralind will break through the armor you've hidden yourself behind—to quote directly from the conclusion of his assessment. In other words, he feels that at some point, you'll have to face what happened, but at the same time, he doubts that you'll do so. He fears that you'll suppress all of your emotions regarding this incident, and that doing so will have harmful consequences for you, including affecting your work performance in the future."

Hörður's face reddens with anger. "You're not actually going to let such bombastic psychiatric bullshit influence you!"

Axel shrugs. "I've got to take it into account, at least."

Hörður sighs. "What does that mean? Am I in or out?"

Axel leafs through the file. "Your gun permit will remain on ice, probably until next year."

Hörður blinks. What's that? There's still hope? "Oh?"

Axel clears his throat and takes off his glasses again. "I'm somewhat between a rock and a hard place. Of course I want you back, but there's a, how should I put it … something of a political backlash at the moment. Certain people in certain places are very concerned about the image of the police; they're worried about public opinion and so on. The media hasn't exactly been helping. But it will all go away. The waves are subsiding, sort of little by little. Right now may not be a good time to rock the boat. But by the autumn … "

Steppenwolf tilts his head and puts on an expression that is difficult to read.

"Will I be returning this autumn?" Hörður asks hopefully. It would be better than nothing. Though he doesn't know exactly how he'll spend the summer.

"It's not out of the question," says Axel. "But I can't promise anything, unfortunately."

"Okay, okay," Hörður mutters. He's relieved; there's no denying it. But the uncertainty is still there.

Axel clears his throat. "But until then, you'll be reassigned."

"Huh?" Hörður leans forward. "I think I misheard you. Did you say I'd be reassigned?"

"Temporarily, yes," replies old Steppenwolf. "It's either that or being away from work until the autumn—on unpaid leave."

"Unpaid?" exclaims Hörður.

Axel nods. "The committee has made its decision. Your indefinite leave is expiring. You'll be given a reprimand for the careless use of a firearm in public, but won't lose your job. But I don't think it's advisable for you to return to the CID at this point."

"Reassigned. What does that mean?" Hörður asks anxiously. He goes over every conceivable possibility, but the only thing that comes to mind is that he'll be put back in a uniform and do summer temp work for the Patrol Division. Being at home on unpaid leave would be the lesser of two evils.

"A small position has opened up in the countryside," says Axel gingerly. "The lieutenant there, Steingrímur Róbertsson, had a stroke. He'd just turned seventy and was going to finish the year before retiring, but then just…boom, *game over*. His position will be advertised, but it needs filling until someone can be hired full-time."

"In the countryside?" Hörður asks in surprise.

Axel nods. "In the village of Kirkjubæjarklaustur."

"Klaustur," mutters Hörður. Looking pensive, he blinks several times. "Isn't that a complete backwoods? I didn't even know there was a police station there. How many subordinates did the lieutenant have?"

Axel smiles awkwardly. "Police headquarters for the South is located in Hvolsvöllur. Then there's a *lieutenant* in both Kirkjubæjarklaustur and Vík. The lieutenants report to the chief of police, but work independently, of course."

"Okay, okay," says Hörður, as he tries to digest all of this. "But how many subordinates does the lieutenant have?"

Axel clears his throat. "The lieutenant in Klaustur is the only police officer in the area. But he can deputize locals to assist him if need be."

"The only one?" exclaims Hörður. "Am I supposed to be the only cop out in some craphole somewhere?"

"You'll have a house and car at your disposal," says Axel.

Frowning, Hörður digests this for a moment or two. To call this a *reassignment* is, of course, a distortion. He's definitely being *reassigned,* no question there, but the position of lieutenant out in the countryside is nothing but a demotion for a detective in the CID. On the other hand, he'll be independent, almost a king in his own kingdom, like a sheriff in the Wild West.

But there's something about this *solution* that bothers him. Even if he's completely willing, per se, to go live in the countryside for a few months, the lead-up to all of this can best be considered bizarre. Clearly, they're attempting to kill two birds with one stone: temporarily rid the CID of the great *enfant terrible,* Hörður Grímsson, and at the same time, man some backwoods post that no one in his right mind would have any interest in. A position that opened up simply because some old man kicked the bucket. So what happens if no one applies for this blessed position of lieutenant? Will he be forced to remain there, even indefinitely?

Maybe he would never get the chance to return to the CID!

"What do you say, Hörður?" Axel asks condescendingly. "Isn't this just an excellent solution to our problem?"

The red-haired giant's temper flares. "Our problem? Just to be clear, *I* have no problem. You come unglued over some damn political stink and decide just to send me to the countryside. All I want is to be able to return to my previous job."

Axel sighs. "And you can do that. But not until the autumn. Until then, this lieutenant's position is yours for the taking."

"Thanks but no thanks," Hörður snaps. He gets up in dramatical fashion, both sorely offended and angry. "You can find someone else for that shitty job."

"Fine," says Axel coldly. "But before Prince Hamlet leaves the stage, I would like to ask him to leave his police ID card and car keys with me."

Hörður's face reddens and balloons out, like that of a powerlifter preparing for a heavy lift. He's on the verge of losing his temper, but manages to take a deep breath before the volcano inside him erupts violently.

"Here you are," he mutters ashamedly as he tosses his ID card and keys onto Steppenwolf's desk.

"Should I ask someone to drive you home?" Axel asks in a slightly warmer tone.

Hörður shakes his head stubbornly, then storms out and slams the door behind him.

What now?

Hörður is sitting at his kitchen table, staring trance-like at his plate, upon which, lamb goulash in brown onion gravy and homemade mashed potatoes are slowly cooling down. His anger had quickly subsided, leaving behind a void, numbness, and paralyzing anxiety. He'd left the police station in a huff and ended up at the bar and restaurant Vitabar, without necessarily having intended to. There, he'd swigged beer and whiskey, yet managed to stop himself before walking over the brink of oblivion and intoxication. Instead of plunging once again into the darkness, he'd pulled himself together, drunk a few cups of coffee, taken some painkillers, called a taxi and crunched some mints on his way home. Bíbí had of course realized that he'd had a bit to drink, but didn't scold him for it, despite all the beautiful New Year's resolutions he'd made. He'd drunk a great deal in the autumn and then again between Christmas and New Year. So much that he'd actually stopped and looked himself in the mirror, after having suffered *delirium tremens.*

But suddenly, drinking isn't his main problem. Now he's virtually unemployed, at least until the autumn. He has nothing to do, and no income. Idleness is doing him in, and if he can't make his house payments, they'll lose their nice apartment.

What would Bíbí say then?

She would be devastated and even leave him, and then he would definitely plunge off the precipice—it was no more complicated than that. He hasn't told her about his meeting with Axel. He can't. It's like he's paralyzed, and can't imagine reliving the meeting by putting it into words. His anger would flare up again and the rejection and humiliation would pour out over him once more, like pitch black, suffocating tar.

"Are you okay, darling?" Bíbí says suddenly. "You haven't touched your food."

Hörður blinks, looks up. How long has he been silent? He squeezes out a smile, stabs a piece of meat with his fork and forces himself to chew it. "All fine here. I was just thinking a bit."

"Okay, good." Bíbí seems to take his words at face value.

Hörður swallows the nearly unchewed piece of meat and takes a drink of water. Will it be like this in the coming weeks and months? With her going to work in the morning and him hanging around at home all day, in between roaming the streets of the city? Hörður breaks into a cold sweat. Now he has no car, meaning he can no longer drive around at the taxpayers' expense. If he wants to be able to drive around, he'll have to just grin and drive Bíbí to work in her compact car and pick her up again in the afternoon.

That's not what he wants at all. He can barely squeeze into her car, and he can hardly afford to buy gas, despite spending practically nothing.

Won't he just have to find himself a summer job? But doing what? He would prefer to work on a fishing boat, but summer is the most lackluster time for fishing. Maybe he should take the bus to Súðavík and stay by himself in his childhood home until the autumn? In *Future,* as the house is called. The old building probably needs some repair work done on it, its lawn mowed and so on, and who knows, he might even get the chance to go to sea now and then, even if only for some coastal fishing or angling.

Or would he just spend all his time drinking at home?

"Actually, I was also thinking," says Bíbí after several moments.

"Oh?" Hörður grows restless. When Bíbí *thinks,* it usually means an expenditure of some kind. What do they *need* now? A sofa, a bed, a new car?

"Will you still be on leave?" she asks.

He gets a knot in his stomach and loses whatever's left of his appetite. "Why do you ask?"

"Oh, just," she says, with a thoughtful expression. "If you've got nothing to do, I was just wondering if it might be a good idea for you to paint the apartment?"

"What?" says Hörður, horrified. Did she say *a good idea?* Painting is the most wretched thing he knows. Painting an entire apartment, which has, *nota bene,* two floors, would be double the godawful wretchedness. There's nothing good about it. The mere thought of it gives him a pain in his back and his soul. He would need to move the furniture—*all the furniture*—cover the floor with plastic, put tape around the doors and windows and then stir foul-smelling paint and brush and roll endlessly. And clean brushes and rollers a million times.

Day after day after day…

Hörður takes a big drink of water. "But, listen…we've barely just moved in. And I can't see that it needs painting. Not yet. Maybe in five years?"

Bíbí scowls. "It all looks so deadly dull and boring. Plus, I've had enough of the colors in the living room. Wouldn't it just be nice to have something to keep you occupied?"

Hörður wipes beads of sweat off his forehead. "Yes, but…"

"But what?" Bíbí exclaims suspiciously.

"I met Axel today." Hörður clears his throat. "My leave of absence from work is over. I forgot to tell you."

"Oh?" Bíbí says in surprise.

"Yes, I'll be starting in the CID again in the autumn," he says.

"In the autumn?" Bíbí repeats in a hopeful tone.

He nods. "But first he's going to send me to the countryside. To Kirkjubæjarklaustur. The lieutenant there kicked the bucket, and…"

Hörður shrugs embarrassedly.

"Axel's going to send you all the way to Klaustur?" Bíbí asks indignantly. "To fill some lieutenant's position?

He sighs. "Yes."

"And can't you just say no?" Bíbí asks with tears in her eyes.

"Unfortunately, no," says Hörður sheepishly. "He simply wouldn't budge on this, old Steppenwolf."

KLAUSTUR

June

It's going on nine o'clock on a Thursday morning. Outside, the sky is sunny and clear; the temperature is twelve degrees. Bíbí parks her compact car in front of the capital's main bus station, BSÍ, in the Vatnsmýri area. Buses are parked in their spaces behind the building. Hörður is sitting in the passenger seat, hunched up and so miserable that he feels nauseated. The last thing he wants to do is spend the summer in Kirkjubæjarklaustur, but it's too late to bow out now. Axel would be so angry that he would doubtless fire him. After all, Hörður had called him, tail between his legs, and asked if lieutenant's position was still vacant.

"Well," says Bíbí, just to say something. The silence in the car had become oppressive. She shuts off the engine and pulls the handbrake.

"Yes," says Hörður, hoarse with anxiety. At heart, he's a loner, and therefore often finds it difficult to be living with someone—in the constant presence of another person. But now he suddenly fears being alone. Bíbí has a positive effect on him. She has a good, constructive presence, besides being warm and often funny, and an excellent cook. And they love each other.

He sighs, opens the door, and squirms his way out of the car. He's wearing combat boots, green army pants, and a tattered denim jacket over a black T-shirt.

"Aren't you taking your leather coat with you?" Bíbí asks as she shuts the driver-side door behind her.

"No," says Hörður dryly. He'll miss the leather coat, but it's the coat of police detective Hörður Grímsson. For the next few months, he won't be an investigator, but a lieutenant, and lieutenants don't wear civilian clothes.

Hörður goes to the back of the car and opens the trunk. In it is his old army-green duffel bag, stuffed with clothing, books, and CDs. He lifts the heavy bag and hangs it on his left shoulder, then slams the tailgate shut.

"Are you sure you don't want me to drive you out there?" Bíbí asks tenderly. "I could take time off work."

He shakes his head. "It would be much harder saying goodbye to you there. To watch you drive away."

She nods. "Yes, probably."

They hug and kiss each other. He's all stiff and heavy, empty inside, and has a knot in his stomach. Tears well in her eyes.

He clears his throat. "Well then."

"Yes," she says.

"I'll call," says Hörður.

Bíbí squeezes out a smile. "Be careful."

"Awful, absolutely awful," mutters Barbara Hoffman in German. She shudders, despite the weather being sunny and perfectly still, almost fifteen degrees.

"I know, I know," says Hertha Meier, her childhood friend from Augsburg in Lower Saxony.

Barbara is blonde, while Hertha is dark-haired; both are slender and tall. They're twenty-two years old and are on a backpacking trip around Iceland. Today is their third day on the green island in the north. They're standing near the car-wash area at the gas station and shop in the village of Hvolsvöllur, trying to recompose themselves following the last ride they accepted. Or, it's Barbara who's upset, being a vegan and all. Hertha understands her to a certain extent, but has become a bit irritated by the drama. The man who picked them up in Selfoss was driving an empty truck, an old Mercedes Benz with a wooden grate around the bed. The truck was old and smelled of animals. Barbara had asked the driver if he was a horseman. They both love Icelandic horses and want to try to ride as often as possible during their hitchhiking trip around the country. But as it turned out, the man's job was transporting livestock to the slaughterhouse, both lambs and pigs. In fact, he'd just delivered a load of pigs to the largest slaughterhouse in the country.

Barbara's face had turned pale and she'd remained silent until the man stopped the truck at the gas station in Hvolsvöllur, where he needed to fuel up. Then she thanked him matter-of-factly for the ride, despite their having originally said they would accept a ride from him all the way to Vík in Mýrdalur, where he was headed. From there it wasn't far to Kirkjubæjarklaustur, where they were planning to camp for the night.

Hertha hadn't been happy about these sudden decisions of Barbara's, which she made without consulting her friend. It isn't always easy to hitch a ride; time is passing and they aren't even halfway to their destination. But that's how Barbara can be. When she's had enough, she can't be budged.

"Shouldn't we just try to forget about this and maybe get something to eat?" Hertha asks, trying to sound positive and encouraging.

Barbara shakes her head. "I'll never forget this. But yes. I'd really like something to drink, at least. But what I want most is a cigarette."

"You stopped smoking, remember?" Hertha asks gingerly.

"Yes, I know," Barbara mutters irritably. They lift their backpacks and saunter over to the gas station.

The bus cruises eastward along the highway, with flourishing countryside to both sides. The lowlands of the South are flat and green and almost entirely cultivated, completely opposite to the rugged, dramatic Westfjords, the home ground of the red-haired giant, where the imposing mountains and turbulent sea square off every day, all year round. Hörður is sitting in a window seat toward the back of the bus, with headphones on his head, resting his pale forehead against the cold window. He stares out the large window, at everything and nothing, as he listens to an old cassette on his Walkman—the greatest hits of Lynyrd Skynyrd, the psychedelic Southern boys who nearly all died in a plane crash years ago. His rusty-red hair frames his face like greasy curtains. He lets his mind wander as time passes and his destination draws slowly nearer.

Kirkjubæjarklaustur. Has he ever been there? He doesn't think so, but it's not out of the question that his mom and dad stopped there at some point in the past, in their white Ford Falcon on a camping trip with the kids. Back then, the highway wasn't paved—it was just a dusty gravel road— the bridges were single-lane and the Ring Road hadn't been opened—the expansive Skeiðarársandur sands, east of Kirkjubæjarklaustur, hadn't yet been bridged. Hörður doesn't remember much of those yearly camping trips, but he'll never forget the smell in the car—a combination of dust, motor oil, and tobacco—the old tent from the sail-making company Ægir and the simple yet tasty food that his mother cooked on a Primus stove. On those trips, his father was either silent or irritated, while his mother was lighthearted, constantly joking and singing. Recalling these things, he feels a sad twinge of nostalgia. The memories warm him a little, but first and foremost, they evoke painful regret that eats at him from within and leaves behind a hole in his heart.

Hörður sighs and looks around. How far have they come? He isn't sure, but knows that Selfoss is behind them, and probably Hella, too. The other passengers are staring either out the windows or at their phones—all of them avoiding eye contact and interaction with the other passengers. Won't the driver be stopping soon? Hörður craves coffee, and is hungry. Most of all, though, he wants a cigarette. Too bad he's promised Bíbí he would never smoke again. He blinks and tries to orient himself by the landscape outside the window. There's nothing to see, however, but unmown fields, straight ditches, and farms in the distance.

He has no idea where he is.

Hörður walks directly into the Hlíðarendi gas station and service center without paying particular heed to the village—and in any case, there's pretty much nothing to see there. Hvolsvöllur is a flat, featureless village, but still, it's probably more populous than Kirkjubæjarklaustur. Somewhere in it is the police station, where Hörður's current boss is in charge—Björn Bragi Björnsson, chief of police in the South. Hörður should maybe go and say hello to him, but he hardly has the time for it, besides having limited interest in doing so. Hvolsvöllur is far from the sea, like Hveragerði, Selfoss, and Kirkjubæjarklaustur. So there's no harbor, let alone a freezing plant or other fish-processing facilities. Hörður has no idea how the people here earn a living. Life in places like this is probably based mainly on services and the like—selling whoever passes through it gas, sandwiches, and coffee.

Hardly what he'd call exciting.

Hörður buys two hot dogs with all the fixings and a bottle of Coke, sits down at a window seat and wolfs down the hot dogs, which he washes down with a few swigs of the carbonated sugar water. Then he burps, feeling slightly sick to his stomach. He ate far too fast, and junk food like this doesn't exactly agree with him.

Hörður looks around. The other people from the bus are scattered around the shop and cafeteria, either drinking or eating or browsing the items on the shelves. Two tables over from him sit two young women in light outdoor wear, hardly more than twenty years old—foreign girls on a backpacking trip. One is dark-haired, the other blonde. It sounds to him as if they're speaking German. The blonde has a cup of coffee in front of her, and her dark-haired friend is eating a sandwich and drinking a non-alcoholic beer. They're pretty girls, very much so. He doesn't remember them being on the bus. They're probably hitchhiking, seeing as how they have backpacks with them.

The blonde girl suddenly turns her head and looks straight into Hörður's eyes, as if she sensed that he was watching her. Hörður looks away and blushes. Had he been staring? He isn't sure, but suspects that he was.

Hörður looks intently out the window and tries to act as if nothing happened—and in any case, nothing *did happen*. A truck is driven onto the shop's parking lot, a dark blue Volvo with yellow stripes. The engine grunts and the air brakes hiss. The truck's driver parks it at one of the gas pumps, then steps down from the cab. It's a man in his thirties, Hörður guesses, wearing steel-toed work boots, dirty jeans, and a dark blue work jacket over a dirty Budweiser T-shirt. The man has black, tousled hair and thick sideburns, his face is tanned and he has a noticeably large mouth, a bit like Mick Jagger's. He kicks his truck's tires, which is something Hörður has never understood. What do people pretend to be checking? Then the man walks out onto the lot, stretches a bit, and lights a cigarette—he's smoking a red Prince. Longing flares up in Hörður. Damn, he wants a smoke. Just one fucking drag!

The driver ambles around, smoking and peering in all directions, as if looking for something. Or maybe waiting for someone? Hörður watches his every move, just to kill time and divert his attention from the German girl who thought he was staring at her. Suddenly, the man reacts, takes one more quick drag from his cigarette, tosses it onto the pavement, and steps on it. At the same instant, a Subaru Impreza passenger car drives quickly onto the lot, bright green on low-profile tires, with a spoiler and a noisy exhaust. The truck driver walks quickly toward the Subaru, which disappears from Hörður's view. Shortly afterward, the truck driver reappears, now holding a package under one arm. He tosses the package into the cab of his truck before filling its tank with diesel fuel.

He has apparently promised to pick up a package, Hörður thinks to himself. He grimaces, having the taste of grease in his mouth from the hot dogs, while the sugar in his throat is making him nauseated. He's got to have a cup of coffee to perk himself up. So he goes back to the counter and orders a black coffee.

"For here or to go?" asks the cashier.

"To go," says Hörður, not remembering how many minutes ago the bus driver stopped and therefore having an unclear idea of when the bus will be leaving. He also doesn't want the German girls to think that he's stalking them or something like that.

The woman hands him a steaming coffee in a paper cup. "Anything else?"

"A pack of Camel Filters, please," says Hörður, without actually having planned to do so. Or had he decided to, but forgotten it? Maybe just old habit. He wants a cigarette … yet not. Or, yes, he wants one. His conscience is just gnawing at him a bit.

"And matches," he adds, slightly sheepishly.

After paying, Hörður goes out onto the lot and places his coffee cup on the lid of a garbage can before peeling the cellophane off the pack of cigarettes. Then he tears a hole in the pack, shakes out one of the cigarettes, and pulls it from the pack with his lips, carefully, like a horse taking a sugar cube from an outstretched hand. The cigarette tickles his lips and he smells the aroma of the tobacco. The anticipation of lighting it and inhaling the bitter smoke trickles like a small stream through his nervous system.

"Maybe we should ask that guy?" Hertha says, pointing out the window at a dapper truck driver who is pumping gas into his truck. "If he's going east, that is."

"Yes, maybe," Barbara mutters distractedly, still watching the red-haired giant who was staring at her a few moments ago. Now he was at the counter, paying for a coffee and cigarettes. Then he walks out, probably to have a smoke.

"Let's go, then." Hertha gets to her feet and slings her backpack over her shoulder. "Before he leaves."

"Okay." Barbara follows her friend out of the shop, but then asks her to wait a second.

"Wait?" exclaims Hertha, who has come out onto the parking lot.

Barbara doesn't answer, but goes straight over to the red-haired giant, who is about to touch a flaming match to the first cigarette out of his pack.

"Sorry," she says in English, with a strong German accent. "Could I bum a cigarette from you?"

The red-haired giant is so flustered by the question that he burns himself with the match, instead of holding it to the tip of the cigarette between his lips. He tosses the match away and lets the cigarette drop as he blows on his fingers.

"Uh, yeah … of course," he then replies in stiff English, handing her the pack. In the same breath, his cell phone starts ringing.

"Thanks," Barbara says as she takes the pack.

The red-haired giant pulls out his phone, looks at the screen, and turns pale.

"Do you have a light?" Barbara asks, after fishing a cigarette out of the pack.

"Just keep the pack," says the red-haired giant, before striding away and answering his phone.

"What was that?" Hertha asks annoyedly as Barbara walks back over to her.

"I asked him for a cigarette and a light," Barbara replies bewilderedly. "But he let me have the whole pack, and no light."

"Come on," says Hertha, before marching over to the truck. The driver is done filling his tank, and wipes a few drops of fuel off his trousers after hanging the nozzle back on the pump.

"Sorry," Hertha says in English, smiling her sweetest smile. "But are you heading east?"

"Maybe," says the driver, somewhat gruffly and suspiciously. He smells of diesel fuel and sweat.

"If you are," Hertha says politely. "Then I'd like to ask if we could go with you, me and my friend. We're on our way to Kirkjubæjarklaustur."

"Two, huh?" says the driver, grinning, before winking at Hertha. "Usually one girl's enough for me, but I certainly won't refuse two, ha ha!"

"Hi, sweetie," Hörður says into the phone. As soon as he saw Bíbí's name on the phone's screen, he chickened out on lighting his cigarette. Sometimes it's as if she has eyes in the back of her neck, or a sixth sense. She would somehow have heard it in his voice that he was doing something wrong. Or sensed it. She's more sensitive than the devil himself, having descended from sorcerer-folk in the Strandir district.

"Where are you now?" Bíbí asks cheerfully.

Hörður turns halfway around on the parking lot. He'd walked a short distance from the shop to give himself some privacy. "At Hvolsvöllur, outside the service station. There's at least a two-hour drive left."

Hörður sees that the next building over from the shop houses the village's liquor store. His throat goes dry. Would there be a liquor store in Kirkjubæjarklaustur? He actually hopes not. He should probably use this stay of his in the countryside to change his lifestyle a bit, eat healthier and take a break from alcohol and other toxins.

"Did you get something good to eat?"

"Yes, yes," Hörður answers dryly. He sees the bus and the truck. The German girls are talking to the truck driver, maybe asking him for a ride. There's something about this driver that gives Hörður an uncomfortable feeling about the backpacking girls getting in his truck. He's gives off a bad vibe. He's boorish, made of coarse stuff.

"Hopefully something besides a burger. There's no nutrition in that shop food."

"No, definitely not," says Hörður without taking his eyes off the girls and the driver. He sees that the driver is trying to joke with them. The girls start slightly, as if the lummox said something inappropriate, and then they turn on their heels and walk quickly away from him. The driver appears to find this funny; he bursts out laughing, yells something at the girls and then sticks out his tongue, like a snake testing the air.

Hörður's temper flares. Fucking pervert!

"You're so quiet. Is everything okay?"

"Yes, of course," Hörður splutters. He tries to focus on his conversation with Bíbí, but then sees the bus driver leave the service station and head straight over to the long-distance buses. "Listen, my bus is leaving. I'll call you later, okay?"

"Fucking pervert!" says Hertha contemptuously.

"Yes, not the first and probably not the last," says Barbara. They watch the dark blue truck exit the parking lot and head eastward out of Hvolsvöllur. Shortly afterward, a bus takes the same route. Barbara notices the red-haired giant sitting in a window seat toward the back.

"Well, there's only one thing to do," says Hertha. She puts on her backpack and walks off. "Thumb up and a fake smile on your face."

"Exactly." Barbara follows her. On a sign by the road are some words and an outline figure of a rider on a horse. "You think this means a horse rental? I saw a pickup truck with a horse trailer earlier. Maybe we should stay here for the night?"

"Let's stick to the plan," Hertha says without stopping or looking over her shoulder. "As soon as we divert from it, everything gets messed up. We'll see about it on the way back, okay?"

"Okay," Barbara mutters. She's pretty tired of that blessed plan they put down on paper before the trip, not least because almost none of her ideas were taken into account. It was as if Hertha had planned the trip a long time ago and just expected Barbara to agree to everything that she'd already decided—which Barbara did.

"Try here?" asks Hertha on the outskirts of the village. She doesn't wait for an answer, but stops, turns halfway around, and sticks out her thumb.

Barbara stops beside her. She wants to light a cigarette but knows that it will get on Hertha's nerves, who will assert—probably rightly—that no one ever picks up a smoking hitchhiker. Besides, she has no way to light it.

"This one's slowing down … isn't it?" says Hertha.

Barbara looks up. The approaching vehicle is a big, covered American pickup truck. A white Ford F-150 with a crew cab. It slows down, but definitely a bit hesitantly. The driver looks at the girls, seemingly making up his mind. In the back seat is a furry dog that sticks its snout out the open side window. There's plenty of space in the truck; that much is certain.

Barbara doesn't feel like hanging around there at the side of the road anymore. So she steps in front of Hertha, smiles her sweetest smile and puts her hands together as if in prayer. A moment earlier, the driver of the pickup truck had revved its powerful engine, but suddenly, its roar slackens; he steps hard on the brakes and swerves to the road's shoulder a short distance from the girls.

"Let's go!" Barbara says triumphantly as she hurries off.

"That was a bit weird," says Hertha, in less of a hurry to get to the truck. "Was he going to stop or not?"

"He stopped, didn't he?" Barbara calls out, shrugging. When she reaches the truck, she sees that the driver has rolled down the front passenger-side window. The truck is dusty, and she notices that it's rusty in places. Its engine rumbles in idle, pumping smoke out the stout exhaust pipes.

"Are you going east?" she asks cheerfully in English. The man in the driver's seat nods. He's in his thirties, she guesses, tall and light-complexioned, wearing a blue checkered work shirt. There's a tool bag in the passenger seat.

"Hello," Hertha says to the dog, which sticks its head out the rear window to greet her. It's a Border Collie, black and white.

"Could my friend and I get a ride?" Barbara asks.

The man sighs. "Yes, I suppose so. But I'm not going very far."

"Thanks!" says Barbara. She opens the back door, but sees that there's a cardboard box full of groceries in the back seat, directly behind the passenger seat. The dog had put its front paws up on it.

"Only one of you can fit in the back," the driver says in English, before shooing the dog out of the way and moving the tool bag from the passenger seat to the floor behind it.

"Cute dog, huh?" Barbara asks Hertha.

"Yes, yes," says Hertha, who is much fonder of dogs than the cat-loving Barbara.

The driver steps down from the pickup, revealing that he's a giant in stature—at least two meters tall. His hair is blond and his eyes blue. He walks around behind the car and opens the tailgate to the truck's covered bed, which holds various tools and equipment used by plumbers. "You can put your backpacks in here."

"Thanks." Barbara takes off her backpack and hands it to the man. Hertha does the same. He tosses their packs in through the opening and shuts the tailgate.

"Are you a plumber?" Barbara asks after they've taken their seats in the car. She's in front and Hertha in back, busy fondling the dog.

"Something like that," the man mutters as he drives off. "Where are you going, by the way?"

"To Kirkjubæjarklaustur," Barbara replies, hoping she's pronounced the name of the village correctly.

The man seems slightly startled. "Oh? Why there?"

Barbara shrugs. "Why not? Isn't there a canyon there, Hertha?"

"Yes, and a lake above the village," says Hertha. "A very beautiful place."

The man shakes his head. "I would go to Vík in Mýrdalur, if I were you. The black beach—haven't you heard of it?"

"Of course," Hertha says from the back seat. "We'll stop there on the way back. First it's Kirkjubæjarklaustur, then Höfn in Hornafjörður. And on the way back, Vík in Mýrdalur and the Seljalandsfoss waterfall."

The man shakes his head. "I would skip Kirkjubæjarklaustur. Just a waste of time, believe me."

"All right," says Barbara. "But can you take us there?"

"I guess," the man mutters. "But only to the gas station. I'm not going into the village."

"Is there an information center there?" Hertha asks.

"No, I don't think so," says the man.

"Oh?" says Hertha. "That's what I gathered from what I saw online."

"I'll drop you off at the gas station," the man mutters.

"Thank you," says Barbara. "What's your name, by the way?"

"Björgvin," the man mutters.

"My name is Barbara," says Barbara, "and my friend's name is Hertha."

Björgvin nods, but says nothing.

"What's your dog's name?" Hertha asks.

"Aesop," Björgvin answers dryly.

"Thanks for picking us up," Hertha says as she scratches Aesop behind the ears.

"Whatever," Björgvin mutters in Icelandic.

"What did he say?" Hertha asks in German.

"I don't know," Barbara replies in her native language. "But this country seems to be full of depressed giants. First that redhead who gave me the cigarettes, then this blue-eyed plumber."

"Is he depressed?" Hertha asks softly.

"Almost suicidal, I'd say," Barbara replies with a grin, before glancing at the blond giant in the checkered shirt. He steers the pickup truck with one hand while shaking a cigarette from a pack of filterless Camels with the other, then lighting it with a Zippo.

"Do you mind if I smoke?" asks Barbara in English, showing him the pack she got from the red-haired giant.

"Not at all," mutters Björgvin, the burning cigarette clamped between his lips. He steps on the gas and passes a bus.

"Could you give me a light, please?" Barbara asks.

In the back seat, Hertha sighs.

Hörður is gnawing on a match from the box that he bought. His lower back, neck, and legs ache badly. Sitting like this on the bus is doing him in, mentally and physically. But they must be nearing their destination. Behind them are the Reynisdrangar sea stacks, the village of Vík in Mýrdalur, and the Hjörleifshöfði inselberg, and for the last twenty minutes, the lower part of the Mýrdalsjökull glacier has been visible in the distance to the left, cracked, dirty, and imposing, its upper reaches covered by clouds. Otherwise, the route between Vík and Klaustur is quite homogeneous, in fact void of landmarks. On both sides are the expansive lava fields from the terrible Skaftá eruptions, covered with thick moss that turns the otherwise uneven lava into a dull green carpet that stretches to infinity.

The landscape is more like a dream than something real. Somehow, it has neither a beginning nor an end, like the highway that divides it. The bus cruises onward, but doesn't seem to be moving at all…

Hörður closes his eyes for a while. When he opens them again, the view has changed. On the left are grassy mountainsides, with a farm or two at their feet. Here and there, waterfalls pour from the crests of cliffs, and elsewhere, ravines cut deep into the heaths.

"Finally," sighs the red-haired giant when he sees a massive crag standing separate from another escarpment in one place. He'll be damned if it isn't Systrastapi, one of the main landmarks of Kirkjubæjarklaustur.

He fidgets in his seat and stares intently out the windows. And yes, sure enough, at the foot of an approximately two-hundred-meter-high escarpment appear more houses, either half-hidden among trees and bushes or highly noticeable on the treeless banks of the Skaftá river, which stretches between the escarpment and the highway, heavy and brownish-colored. The glacier river appears slow and calm at the moment, but during thaws, it can transform into a frightful monster that shows no mercy.

Ahead is a long bridge over the river, and then a roundabout, where the road branches in three directions. The highway continues eastward, toward the Vatnajökull glacier and the village of Höfn in Hornafjörður; the other road leads into a valley, it looks to Hörður, while the bus turns out of the roundabout onto the third, Klausturvegur Road, which leads into the village beneath the escarpment. The bus, however, doesn't follow the road all the way into the village, but instead turns immediately left and stops at an old, weathered gas station and shop called the Skaftá Shop, standing next to the bridgehead. The driver shuts off the engine.

Hörður has reached the end of his journey. He gets up from his seat and steps out onto the paved lot, where he is met by muted sunshine and a pleasant warmth. The glacial river flows with a slow, heavy murmur, but otherwise, the area around the roundabout is quiet.

The driver opens the bus's luggage compartment and tosses Hörður's duffel bag onto the parking lot.

"You're the only one getting out here," the driver declares.

Still holding the match between his lips, Hörður grunts, as he doesn't know what to say. He hangs his duffel bag over one shoulder and looks around the spacious lot. Axel had said that someone would pick him up, but as far as he can see, no one has come to do so. He shields his eyes with one hand and looks toward the village, which is a few hundred meters away, but sees neither a car on its way nor a single soul out and about.

"Figures," mutters the red-haired giant. He decides to go into the shop. Maybe someone's waiting for him there. The shop is very typical. In it, one can buy burgers and ice cream, various automotive items and a few groceries, mainly cookies, candy, and dry goods such as dried fish, but also skyr and milk.

Two girls are standing at the counter, talking to the man behind it. Then they turn around, and to his horror, Hörður sees that it's the German girls from Hvolsvöllur. How did they get here before him? As they pass each other, the blonde girl smiles at Hörður, who gets completely flustered and scowls instead of smiling back or just pretending not to notice her.

Damn tourists! He tosses the heavy duffel bag onto the floor, throws the match into a garbage can, and goes to the counter.

"Hello!" says Hörður. "I took the bus here. Someone was supposed to come pick me up. Was anyone waiting for me here?"

"No," replies the cashier. "Who was it supposed to be?"

"Damned if I know," says Hörður dryly. "Where can I find the village offices?"

"The district manager's office is on the upper floor of the Skaftá Visitor Center," replies the man.

"And where the hell is that?" Hörður asks irritably.

The man smiles faintly, as if he's amused. "Just follow those backpacker girls. They're on their way there."

Hörður grunts sullenly, lifts his duffel bag and leaves the shop without another word. Outside, the silence actually seems to have deepened. A car or two drives past on the highway, but otherwise, only the calm murmur of the river is heard. In fact, it's impossible to call it *silence*; it's more like something is *missing*. The red-haired giant has apparently lived in the capital for far too long, where the commotion is non-stop.

Hörður sees the German girls walking into the village. He ambles off with his duffel bag on one shoulder. He has the road, the riverbank, and the glacial river on his left. Soon, the first houses appear on the right, newly built semi-detached houses on unfinished lots. The village is apparently experiencing an upswing. The residential areas are all to the right of the road, it appears to Hörður. The streets are neither numerous nor long; the houses are all single-story, and most are partly concealed behind trees. In the heart of the village, under the green mountainside, the vegetation is densest and the trees tallest.

How many people live here? Hörður thinks to himself. Three hundred? And how do they make a living? He has no idea.

The German girls have stopped at the intersection west of the local grocery store. They whisper together and take pictures with their phones. Hörður slows down, but in the end, can't avoid catching up with them. They get on his nerves without him knowing exactly why, and because of this, he has no desire to be in their presence, let alone to have to interact with them any further.

The blonde girl is lighting a cigarette from the pack he let her have. She probably bought a lighter at the shop, where they stopped to ask for directions. When she sets eye on Hörður, she holds out the pack to him, offering him a cigarette.

Hörður stops, tongue-tied with irritation and shyness. That's his pack! Is she actually offering him his own tobacco? His temper flares, but he quickly calms down. He gave her that pack, didn't he? Yes, he certainly did.

"Thanks," Hörður mutters sheepishly, fishing a cigarette out of the pack. He notices that the girl is wearing a necklace made of light-blue turquoise stones that go well with her skin color and hair. She's pretty, in fact quite beautiful, and it's probably *that* that gets on his nerves. Puts him off balance, rather. He's always been something of a klutz in the presence of cute girls. They make him feel bad about himself, as if he's ugly and stupid and has no business paying such princesses any attention.

But of course, it's not cute girls who make him feel idiotic. *He's* the one who makes himself feel idiotic, by thinking like that. Girls are just people, whether they're cute or not.

"Need a light?" the girl asks in English. Her friend has set off again, clearly impatient and tired of this loitering.

"No, I've got it," says Hörður. He puts down his duffel bag, then takes out his box of matches and gives it a shake, as if to prove his point.

"Okay," the girl says with a smile, before walking off and catching up with her friend after a few meters.

Hörður lights a match, shields the flame with his palm, and is about to hold it to the cigarette when his cell phone rings.

What the hell! He tosses aside the flaming match, takes out his phone, and looks at the screen. Once again, it's Bíbí. He sighs, takes the cigarette out of his mouth, and answers.

"Are you there?"

"Yep," says Hörður. He hangs the duffel bag back on his shoulder and sets off walking. On his right, a stone's throw from the road, is a two-story building with large windows, light blue in color. Some sort of institution, he guesses. A little further on is a small church on a low hill; rather newish-looking, it appears to him. At least modern. In fact, it's so small that it's probably more like a chapel.

"And? What do you think?"

"I've just gotten here, sweetie," says Hörður wearily. "No one has come to pick me up. I'm walking around here, trying to find someone who can help me. I don't know where the police station is or the house I'm supposed to live in, let alone whether there's a car here for me."

"Oh, I see. Aren't there any offices there? You know, the mayor and such."

"I'm on the way there," says Hörður, half-annoyedly. "Shouldn't I just call you after I've gotten to my place?"

"Do that, babe. Bye until then."

"Bye." Hörður sticks his phone in his pocket and continues on his way. He sees that the German girls have crossed the road and are walking toward a white, elongated building with more or less of a barrel roof. The building is located higher up the riverbank and there's a spacious parking lot next to it.

Is that where the village offices are?

Hörður moves the duffel bag from one shoulder to the other. A garbage truck comes from the opposite direction, from within the village—loud and smoke-spewing. The driver slows down as he approaches the building that might house the village offices, then turns almost spontaneously onto the lot in front of it, with such a commotion that the two German backpackers stop and step back. Suddenly, the driver slams on the brakes, which screech loudly, causing the heavy vehicle to jerk forward and its axles to creak.

Hörður watches this from a distance, then looks over his shoulder before crossing the street.

The driver of the garbage truck rolls down the passenger-side window, leans over and calls out something to the German girls, who are standing on the sidewalk at the building's southern end. They say something in reply, and the driver smiles broadly and says something in parting before driving off again with an accompanying commotion and a cloud of smoke.

Hörður watches him drive by. The garbage truck is both old and worn and is clearly seldom or never cleaned. He doesn't get a very good look at the driver, but the man appears to be in much the same condition as the vehicle. The stench of garbage follows the car like a shadow, mingled with black diesel smoke.

When Hörður comes to the building with the barrel roof, he sees a sign on it reading *Skaftárstofa—Skaftá Visitor Center*. A few cars are parked in the spaces nearest the entrance, including an old dull-green, longer-style Land Rover and a white Ford F-150 with a covered bed. In the back seat of the pickup truck is a dog, staring out the windows. The sign doesn't mention village offices. Hörður curses under his breath; he's tired, sweaty, and irritated, and wants to rid himself of his burden and take a hot bath. He realizes that he's still holding the cigarette he accepted from the German girl and had almost lit. He tosses it into a garbage can standing against the wall of the building. Then he goes in through a windowed vestibule and enters the Skaftá Visitor Center, which turns out to be a kind of information center for tourists.

Hörður looks around in the rather narrow space, which opens up slightly on the interior. Besides him, there are probably seven or eight tourists in there, or even more. On the left side of the room is a short reception desk, behind which stands an elderly woman, on either side of seventy, Hörður guesses, energetic-looking and dark-haired, dressed in a red fleece jacket bearing the community's logo. On top of the desk is a stand with brochures and a pile of maps of the area, intended for tourists. The German girls are standing at the desk, talking to the old woman. On the room's right side is a low table with various merchandise on it, including books for tourists, handicrafts made of wool and wood, and cheap mass-produced souvenirs.

"It's very easy to hike up to the lake," says the old woman in English. She puts on glasses hanging on a cord around her neck and scribbles with a pen on the map on top of the pile on the desk. "But camping there is not allowed, even though some people do anyway, of course. The short name for Kirkjubæjarklaustur is simply *Klaustur*, the Icelandic name for a convent, because there was a convent here in olden times, in Kirkjubær. And the lake is named after the nuns or *sisters* – Sister's Lake."

"Is that so?" says the blonde-haired girl.

"What about the canyon?" asks the dark-haired girl. Hörður sees that she's wearing a pink wristwatch with a black dial. He's never seen another watch like it.

"It's here, see," the old woman points to the map and then draws something on it.

Hörður leaves his duffel bag near the exit and elbows his way past a foreign couple looking at an illustrated book on hiking trails and pushes his way further into the room. Behind the reception area is a wide wooden staircase that runs up to the building's second floor. The only thing that separates the staircase and the reception area is a thin wooden wall. At the top of the stairs is a closed door. Hörður feels like walking up the stairs and finding out what's behind the closed door, but he decides not to. Just then, the door opens and a man in work clothes appears in the doorway. He closes it behind him and walks down the creaking staircase. The man is the same age as Hörður, blond and blue-eyed, a little bit hunched and with a depressed demeanor. He's wearing hiking boots, dark blue work trousers with numerous pockets, and a blue-checkered work shirt. But what Hörður notices first and foremost is his height. The man is giant of stature, as tall as the red-haired giant from Súðavík, if not a sight taller.

When the man reaches the ground floor, he and Hörður's eyes meet momentarily. It's not every day that such tall men run into their equals. They say nothing but nod curtly to each other, like comrades in some sort of secret order. Then the blond giant steps out in front of the reception desk, and the red-haired one follows him.

The German girls are still talking to the old woman, who beams when she sees the blond giant.

"Oh, here's my son Björgvin," she says proudly, in her stiff tourist-English. "He just brought his mother her glasses. They were being repaired in Selfoss. I can't see a thing anymore without them, ha ha!"

Hörður looks at Björgvin, who appears startled for some reason.

"We've met him," mutters the dark-haired girl.

"Oh?" asks the old woman in surprise.

"He gave us a ride," says the blonde. "He picked us up in Hvolsvöllur."

Björgvin blushes and fidgets embarrassedly.

"Is that right?" says the old woman, before laughing out loud, looking at her son, and switching to Icelandic. "Is that true, Bjöggi? Have you started transporting whole truckloads of girls here to Klaustur?"

"No," Björgvin answers coldly, before marching out like an irritated teenager.

"My, aren't we sensitive!" says the old woman in Icelandic, looking at the same time at Hörður, as if she expects him to agree with what she says.

"How do you say thank you in Icelandic?" the blonde girl asks in English.

"*Takk*," says the old woman, loudly and clearly.

"*Takk*?" asks the blonde.

"Very good!" says the old woman, laughing theatrically.

"Thanks for the information," says the dark-haired girl in English.

"And the map," the blonde adds.

"You're welcome, girls," the old woman replies. "Just remember what I said, and be careful!"

"We will." They move to the souvenirs table. Looking sheepish, Hörður nods at them and inches his way in the opposite direction, to the desk where they'd been standing.

"Icelandic?" the old woman asks spiritedly. She's rather tall for a woman of her generation, around eighty-one centimeters high, slender, and healthy-looking. Her hands are calloused and sinewy, her face is wrinkled and scored, even harsh-looking; her dark-brown eyes shine with power and her thick hair is deep black but with gray at the roots, meaning that she probably colors it.

"That's right," says Hörður.

The woman regards him carefully.

"I feel as if I recognize you," she then says. "Have you been on TV?"

Hörður's face reddens. He'd almost managed to forget that he's been on people's lips more or less since December. His name has appeared many times in print, and both *dv.is* and the *Fréttablaðið* daily have published photos of him.

"No," he says. "You've got me confused with someone else."

"Oh, all right. My name is Sigrún," says the woman with a smile, revealing teeth that are clearly decades younger than their owner. "Tourist Information Officer here at the Skaftá Visitor Center. What can I do for you?"

"Well…" The red-haired giant clears his throat. "I'm apparently your new police lieutenant. Hörður Grímsson. I took the bus here, but no one came to pick me up at the shop."

Sigrún scoffs. "What are you saying? Didn't Adam come?"

Hörður shakes his head.

"Listen," says Sigrún firmly. "I'll call Adam and ask him to come here right away!"

"Thank you," says Hörður.

"You're welcome," says Sigrún. She lifts a cordless phone and taps in a number from memory. Then she looks at the red-haired giant and smiles apologetically. "I hope you'll like your lieutenant's job. But you might get bored. Nothing ever happens here."

Hörður is standing in front of the Skaftá Visitor Center, waiting for this Adam who was supposed to pick him up. His duffel bag is lying at his feet on the sidewalk. Sigrún suggested that Hörður go and greet the district manager, but he said he would do that later. In contrast to the old woman, the district manager doubtless knows precisely who Hörður Grímsson is, what he did, and why he's been sent to Klaustur. Going into *that matter* is something he doesn't have the energy for at the moment. Besides, he's met more strangers today than he would have liked. Getting to know new people and having conversations about everything and nothing isn't his strongest side. After this Adam has driven him home, he's going to take a bath and then go to bed. There's no way he can skip calling Bíbí, but still, he doesn't really feel like doing so.

Isn't that bastard coming? Hörður sighs and looks at his watch. It's half past three. He sees a car approaching at high speed. It's a Toyota Hilux pickup truck, beige in color and lifted. To Hörður's great relief, the driver turns into the parking lot of the Skaftá Visitor Center, parks the truck, and steps out. He's a chubby man of around forty, dressed in beige camouflage outdoor clothing and combat boots. The man has short, dirty-blond hair and a well-groomed beard and mustache, and is slow-moving and red-cheeked.

"Hörður?" the man asks in a deep voice.

The red-haired giant nods.

"I'm Adam Knútsson," says the man. They shake hands. "Teacher, exterminator, police deputy, and your new neighbor. Sorry for being late, but I unexpectedly had to take my daughter to Reykjavík. Something came up and … "

"Spare me your life story," says Hörður coldly. He lifts his duffel bag and walks over to the pickup. "I've been traveling all day and would really like to get to my new home, if you don't mind."

He feels a bit strange talking about some house that he's never even seen as his new home, but at the moment, he desires nothing more than to get to it, wherever and however it might be. In any case, when he thinks of *home*, he always thinks of the house *Future* in Súðavík, and not the basement dump in 101 Reykjavík where he lived before he met Bíbí, nor the apartment they bought together in the capital's Grafarvogur district.

Adam's cheeks redden even more. "Of course, sorry again. But as I said … "

He stops when he sees Hörður giving him the evil eye. The red-haired giant tosses his duffel bag into the Toyota's bed before getting into the front passenger seat. In the truck's back seat is a child's car seat, in addition to a gun in a specially made protective bag in camouflage colors, most likely a powerful rifle. Adam gets in behind the wheel and starts the engine. He looks so much like a guilty puppy following the new lieutenant's chidings that it's as if his ears are drooping.

Hörður's anger has subsided and he feels a familiar pang of guilt. Why does he always have to act like an oaf?

"Tell me," he says, as if to make up for his brusqueness. "That little church there across the street. What can you tell me about it?"

"It's the memorial chapel for Reverend Jón Steingrímsson, the fire priest," says Adam, who returns to his low-key, cheerful self. He backs out of the parking lot, and then drives slowly toward the highway. "He's said to have stopped the terrible Skaftá lava flows by means of his religious conviction alone. It was in 1783, if I remember correctly, and … "

"Right, right," says Hörður impatiently. Adam speaks so softly and slowly that it tries the red-haired giant's patience, on the one hand, and his hearing, on the other. This teddy-bearish, camouflage-clad rustic appears to be one of those blessed wiseacres who think they know everything and from whom everyone greedily laps up the completely soulless and uninteresting factual swill that trickles out of them in a rhythm that's more akin to a contrived radio spiel than any ordinary way of talking.

"And what place is that?" asks the red-haired giant, pointing at a light blue, two-story building with large windows standing a short distance from the road, close to the intersection nearest the grocery store.

"That's the Klausturhólar Nursing Home," Adam replies dutifully. "Our old people live there, as well as a few patients. A very good institution and well run. In fact, you might be interested to know that… "

"I see, right," Hörður interrupts, and Adam stops in the middle of his story—as the red-haired giant intended. He notices that the truck he saw at Hvolsvöllur, the dark blue Volvo with yellow stripes, is parked at the receiving door of the grocery store. The truck is open at the back, but he doesn't see the driver who was rude to the German girls.

Where might they be? Probably hiking up to the lake.

"How long does the store stay open?" asks Hörður, who will no doubt have to buy some groceries for his new home.

"Until eight o'clock on weekdays, four on Saturdays," Adam replies. They drive past the village's liquor store, which is a short distance from the gas station and shop and the roundabout on the highway. "Should I show you where the police station is before we go to Meðalland?"

"What the hell is Meðalland?" Hörður asks irritably. "Isn't the lieutenant's house here in Klaustur, or…?"

"Actually not," Adam answers. "It's just a bit south of the highway, in Meðalland, behind Hotel Laki. It's only about five or six kilometers from here."

"Five or six kilometers?" exclaims Hörður. "By some hotel? Is it way out in the countryside, or…?"

"Yes, actually," Adam replies. He drives into the roundabout and turns out of it to the east, where the highway continues over the Skeiðarársandur sands and onward to Höfn in Hornafjörður.

"Don't tell me the police station is out in the boondocks somewhere, too?" Hörður asks, both angry and in despair. He feels a bit as if he's the butt of some prank.

To the right of the highway is a self-service ÓB gas station, and a little farther on are a few industrial buildings that house, among other things, the Icelandic Waste Management Company and a construction company called RR Woodwork.

"No, not exactly," Adam answers as he signals and turns south down a gravel road running parallel to a long industrial building before disappearing somewhere down on the sands east of the Skaftá river. "Our garbage is buried just a bit farther out, at the Waste Management Company's landfill site down in the Stjórnarsandur area. But the police station is here."

Adam turns down to the industrial building, which is newly built and clad in unpainted corrugated iron. The building is divided into different segments, with the police station in one of them, next to the fire department.

With an expression of hopelessness, Hörður looks out his window. The police station is very small, with only one door and one window. Above the door is a sign that reads *Police.* There is no fenced-off lot behind it or reception area at its entrance, with bulletproof glass and a locked inner door. No surveillance cameras or cafeteria or break room open twenty-four hours a day—let alone an elevator or Criminal Investigation Department on the third floor.

"Would you like to look around inside?" Adam asks. "I have the keys."

Hörður shakes his head. "Just bring me home. I need to take a bath and go to bed."

"No problem." Adam turns his pickup around, drives back to the roundabout and out of it as if he's heading to Reykjavík. For a few moments, Hörður hopes that he does. That this camouflage-clad teddy bear had been ordered to bring this red-haired giant back home, because he obviously had no interest in taking on the job of police lieutenant here in Klaustur.

But his hope is dashed when Adam signals and turns once more to the south, this time to the west of the Skaftá river. The road through Meðalland is paved and traverses green countryside. Hörður finds himself staring at the multitude of grassy hills that rise a bit like pyramids from the landscape on the right, as far as the eye can see.

"The Landbrot Hills," says Adam, as if he's read the newcomer's thoughts. "They were formed during the Skaftá eruptions. As far as I understand it, they're pseudocraters of some sort, but I'm not quite sure."

"Not sure, no," says Hörður. So the man might not be as much of a know-it-all as he feared. They drive through the countryside in welcome silence. But then Hörður remembers the gun bag in the back seat.

"Did you say you were an exterminator?" he asks.

Adam nods sagely. "My wife Ágústa and I took jobs here as teachers, originally. Which is why we live in the teacher's residence. Then I worked as a temp for the police for a few summers, in addition to being on standby if help was needed due to accidents or drunken gatherings. But then the department's funding was reduced and the summer temp jobs went by the board. So I started shooting foxes and minks for the community, just to earn some extra money. Still, it doesn't add up to much, but since I already had the gun, it was a no-brainer."

"What kind of gun is it?" Hörður asks.

Adam beams, and his voice deepens and slows by half. "It's German, a Blaser R8, 6.5 by 55 caliber. 6.5 is the diameter of the bullets, 55 their length. It's an old Swedish military caliber that I'm very fond of. The gun is absolutely *top of the line,* as they say, but it's the scope that makes the difference. It cost almost half a million krónur, a Zeiss, magnification 4.8 to 35. A 60-millimeter lens."

"Okay," says Hörður, who has only half an idea of what the man is talking about, and couldn't care less. He seriously regrets having asked him about this stupid gun.

"Pretty good accuracy at 500 meters," says Adam proudly. "Which isn't bad, but nothing really remarkable. For example, the longest confirmed sniper kill was 2.7 kilometers, but is now 3.5, as I recall, which is a bit farther than the distances I'm used to. The bullet would take maybe 5 or 6 seconds to reach its target. You can find it on *YouTube* if you want to know more. But I'm shooting small animals, of course, and not…"

Adam stops in the middle of his sentence and turns bright red.

And not *people,* Hörður thinks. In other words, Adam was recalling that the man in his car shot another man in the face from short range with a pistol. Great…

"I'm sorry," Adam mutters. "I didn't mean to…"

"Forget it," mutters Hörður. Of the two evils, he would rather listen to a long lecture on guns and their ranges than just sit there awkwardly, enwrapped in embarrassing silence and half-hearted apologies.

The rifle in the back seat is undoubtedly a fine piece of work, but Hörður finds himself instinctively thinking of the men in Easy Company, who had no such modern gadgets but still managed to hinder the Nazis' blitzkriegs.

"Shifty Powers didn't need a scope," says Hörður, mainly to break the oppressive silence.

"No indeed!" Adam becomes restless with excitement and nearly loses control of the pickup. "You know Easy Company?"

Hörður curses to himself.

"I know of it," he says hesitantly.

"Fucking brilliant, man!" says Adam, as excited as a little boy. "I've been waiting a long time to meet someone else who knows those guys. In fact, I've been watching *Band of Brothers* one more time. I'm at the episode when Dick Winters attacks the Nazis all by himself. Maybe we should watch it together tonight?"

"Umm, no…impossible," sputters Hörður as he squirms with discomfort. Like Adam, he's been waiting to meet someone who shares this interest of his. He finds few things more interesting than talking about World War II. But now, when it finally happens, he finds himself in a quandary, being, as he is, far from sociable and open. He has no desire whatsoever to hang around with a *new friend,* and least of all this camouflage-clad teddy bear who can't shut up and is sure to call him regularly or *pay him visits* over and over again.

Didn't he say they were neighbors?

"That's fine," says Adam, finding it difficult to hide his disappointment. "Naturally, you must be tired after your long day. Maybe later? I also have a decent collection that you might be interested in viewing. Various mementos from the Second World War, mainly from the Allies but a few Nazi items, including an excellent Luger. You can't actually shoot it, but still, you know."

Hörður nods. He *would* enjoy seeing these things, no question. But to go to a stranger's home for that purpose, he finds uncomfortable, to put it mildly. Almost as uncomfortable as if a stranger came to his home. The thought alone gives him a suffocating feeling.

"Maybe later," he says, just to say something.

"Sounds good," says Adam, before pointing out the windshield at a brown-painted wooden gate to their left— a high, wide gate big enough for trucks to drive through. "Here's the gate to Efri-Vík."

"Efri-Vík?" exclaims Hörður. "Is it where I live?"

"We both live there," Adam says as he slows down, turns onto the sideroad, and drives through the gate.

"We?" Hörður exclaims confusedly. Surely they don't live in the same house? He reads two signs at the intersection. One of them says *Hotel Laki,* and the other, *Efri-Vík.*

"They're more or less semi-detached houses, both owned by the community," says Adam. He drives along a potholed dirt road lined with tall poplar trees. "One is the teacher's residence, and the other the lieutenant's."

"I see," says Hörður, who doesn't really understand any of this.

"This is the hotel," says Adam. He drives through a muddy gravel parking lot. Hotel Laki is a two-story, L-shaped building that looks quite new. There are a few cars in the parking lot, and flags flap on flagpoles. "It doesn't look like much, but it's really nice. It's open all year round."

Hörður nods.

"Here back behind it is Efri-Vík." Adam drives out of the parking lot onto a narrow dirt road marked as private.

The road is very short and ends behind the hotel's north side. Standing there are two low-rise residential buildings. One is longer and stands a bit forward of the other, and has an attached garage. It's gray in color. In front of the garage is a camouflage-colored six-wheeler with a dump bed at its back. On the fenced lawn in front of the house are a sandbox and swing set. The smaller house, partly hidden behind the larger house, is farther from the hotel and surrounded by tall spruce trees that shadow it. It's dark brown or black and looks mainly like a summer cottage—a *depressing* summer cottage where it's ideal to stare into the void, lose one's mind, drink oneself to death, or commit suicide.

Adam parks the pickup in front of the larger house and shuts off the engine. "Well, we're here. What do you think?"

In the parking lot in front of the smaller house, under a giant spruce tree, stands an old Nissan Patrol police SUV.

Hörður sighs as he says a silent prayer. *Good God, don't leave me alone in this house of darkness and death.* "Tell me I live in the big house."

Adam laughs awkwardly. "Actually, you don't. That's the teacher's residence, where I, Ágústa, and our little Pállína live. Your predecessor was single, and from what I understand, you'll be by yourself during the months you're here, right?"

"Apparently so," mutters Hörður. He opens the door and steps out onto the parking lot. Adam does the same.

Hörður lifts his duffel bag from the truck's bed. At least he's made it to his destination; that's something, anyway.

Adam pulls out a key ring and hands it to the red-haired giant. "Here are your keys. The car keys, house keys, and the key to the police station."

"Thanks." Hörður takes the keys. He's now the police lieutenant in this backwoods, whether he likes it or not.

"Just let me know if you need anything. Whatever it might be," says Adam. He takes the gun bag from the pickup's back seat, apparently intending to bring his rifle in with him. "Technically, I'm always on call. The lieutenant can call me anytime if he needs me. But besides, I'm here as a neighbor, you know."

"Thank you," says Hörður. "And thanks for the ride."

"You're welcome," says Adam. "I'm going to be heating up some lamb soup for dinner. There's more than enough, and it would be fun to have you over."

"Maybe sometime later," says Hörður, before walking away. The sky is clear, the sun is high in the sky, and he squints under its strong rays. It's probably around seventeen degrees out—even twenty.

"See you!" Adam calls out to him.

"I suppose it can't be avoided," Hörður mutters irritably. As he walks beneath the spruce trees, everything darkens and cools. It's as if it's still autumn around the lieutenant's black-painted dwelling. The surrounding earth is barren and covered with old spruce needles. The house is dark; its windows are dirty. On the dilapidated deck is a flimsy-looking wooden lawn chair. Next to it is a flowerpot filled with sand, and in the sand are countless cigar butts.

Hörður shuts the door behind him and drops the duffel bag onto the floor of the vestibule. Without taking off his shoes, he walks into his new home and starts turning on all the lights, but soon discovers that every third lightbulb is out. All of the windows are closed, and the air inside is heavy and *dead*—it's muggy and there's a foul smell, as if something is rotting. The walls are white but haven't been painted for a long time and are therefore grimy, scratched, and pitted with nail holes. The cracked parquet crackles. The house feels empty, despite it's having the usual sorts of furniture, and in the living room is an old stereo set in a custom-made cabinet. There are no pictures or decorations, or anything giving a hint as to the home's previous inhabitants. Hörður feels a bit as if he's looking over a summer cottage that he's rented from a trade union. There's a tired old sofa and a coffee table, and a TV screwed to the wall. The bedroom has a decent bed, and an otherwise empty wardrobe holds clean bedding. The refrigerator is empty but is running and fairly clean, the stove is old but of a good make, and on the kitchen counter are both a microwave oven and a toaster. The pantry is empty, apart from a black garbage bag half-full of empty beer cans and three empty bottles of Jack Daniels. The door to one room is locked but Hörður doesn't have a key to it, and can't find it anywhere. The lock on it is old-fashioned. He can't tell whether the locked room is a closet or a small bedroom. He needs to ask someone about this. The bathroom is small and rather uncared-for, with a shower stall but no bathtub. He runs water into all the drains in order to get rid of the bad smell that occurs when the traps dry out.

Hörður opens all the windows that can be opened. Then he plunks down on the living-room sofa and sighs. His sigh echoes through the empty house. What now? He looks at his watch. It's nearly half past four. He doesn't feel like unpacking his duffel bag right now, and he's in no mood to call Bíbí. He can't take a bath as he intended, and doesn't want a shower—if he can even fit into that shower stall. He would prefer to go to bed, but then he would have to make it first.

In short, he doesn't feel like doing anything. But least of all does he want to hang around so much as one minute longer inside this empty, musty house that's supposed to be his home.

Maybe he should just go swimming?

Barbara and Hertha walk to the wooded ravine, where the old woman at the information center said they would find a trail to the lake. They take in the scent of the trees and bushes, listen to the birdsong and low murmur of flowing water. They hardly feel tired, not having walked much this day. Their backpacks are certainly heavy, but the two girls are in fine shape and the good weather, clean air, and beauty of Icelandic nature make everything easier for them. A beauty that is always either low-key or spectacular.

"It's more beautiful here than I expected," says Barbara, breaking the silence. It's so peaceful that disturbing it feels almost sinful.

"Did you find it strange with that man in the pickup truck?" says Hertha, who clearly has her mind on other things besides their hike and the surroundings.

"What do you mean?" Barbara asks.

"He said he could only bring us to the gas station and not into the village," says Hertha. "But then he was at the information center ahead of us."

"Yes, yes," says Barbara, with only limited interest. "But that doesn't change anything, does it?"

"He said he didn't think there *was* an information center in Kirkjubæjarklaustur," says Hertha indignantly. "But then we find out that his *mother* works there! He downright lied to us. The question is, why?"

"We'll never get the answer to that, will we?" Barbara asks ruefully in return, before stopping where a small stream runs alongside the road.

"Probably not," mutters Hertha. "Is it here?"

From the road, one can walk down to something of a clearing at the bottom of a steep ravine. The mountainside is covered with trees almost to its crest.

Barbara nods. "It must be. There's a sign, and that's where the trail starts."

They go down into the clearing, which is dark, damp, and smells of leaves and wet soil. The sign has a hand-painted illustration of the two hiking trails from which they can choose. One snakes through the woods, while the other leads uphill, straight to the lake. That trail is marked with red wooden stakes.

Water streams diagonally down the nearly vertical rock wall of the ravine and then runs through a gap under a huge boulder that once fell from the rock face higher up the mountain, and finally crosses the ravine at its bottom. The boulder is ogrish and mossy. Sometime in the distant past, it crashed violently down from the mountain, but now it's still and silent, like a sleeping troll.

"It's sooo beautiful here," says Barbara. They take photos of each other at the edge of the ravine, with the boulder and delicate waterfall in the background, and then a few of them together, smiling at imaginary followers on *Instagram*.

Then they head off along the narrow trail that winds through the woods. The trail is easy, almost free of rocks, and laid with wood chips, and there are steps where it's steepest. The woods are dense, but the trees are neither as stout or tall as in Germany. But the beauty is unique and it's absolutely peaceful. They walk in silence, almost as if in a trance, enjoying the passing moments.

Before they know it, they've reached the top. The woods are behind them, and facing them is the lush, green Klausturheiði Heath, stretching as far as the eye can see. They catch a glimpse of the lake, from which flows a stream that plunges over the crest of the rock wall, transforming for the most part into a fine mist. The catch their breath, smile at each other, and go on. The trail passes a small concrete shed next to a small man-made lagoon.

"What's this?" Barbara asks.

Hertha shrugs. They continue onward, away from the edge of the escarpment toward a blue-colored sign by the lake. To their right is the cliff above the village. A path leads toward it, with a small wooden bridge over the stream that runs from the lake. When they reach the sign, they finally see Systravatn Lake in all its glory. It's much bigger than they'd imagined.

"Wow!" says Barbara.

"Very beautiful," says Hertha, before turning to the sign. It says *Katla Geopark. Systravatn.* Beneath this heading is a story in Icelandic and English, an old legend about the lake and the nuns who lived in the convent after which the village is named. They read the English version in silence.

"Oo, how horrifying!" says Hertha cheerfully.

Barbara looks up and regards the placid, peaceful water. "Do you think the story is true?"

"Of course not, Barbs," says Hertha. She only calls her childhood friend *Barbs* when she wants to tease her and or let her know that she cares for her. No one else calls her by that old nickname. "Do you think the story of Hansel and Greta is true?"

"Probably not," mutters Barbara. She notices that there's a building on the heath at the far side of the lake. Rather large, probably some sort of outbuilding. "Do you see the building there on the other side? Isn't it strange that it's there?"

Hertha shades her eyes, then nods. "What do you say about walking around the lake? We can have a look at that building along the way."

"Let's do it," says Barbara.

They set off in a clockwise direction around the lake. The heath is full of rises and hollows, but is also uniform and plain in appearance—covered with grass and heather, with a moss-grown rock here and there. The heath stretches toward the highlands, where glaciers, sandy wastes, and rugged wilderness are hidden in the distance, behind wavering mirages. Systravatn Lake is blue and tranquil, its banks covered with damp moss, and in many places grasses grow out of the water where it's shallowest. Out on the lake there are dark shadows, as if large creatures lurk beneath the surface.

They walk on in silence; all that is heard is the rustling sound when they step on the delicate heathland vegetation. They've grown warm from the hike, and the uneven ground beneath their feet puts quite a strain on their legs. When they finally get to the building, sweat is dripping from their foreheads. They stop, take off their backpacks, and catch their breath.

The building, which is high and wide, is old and half-dilapidated, crooked and worn, like an old man. It's clad with corrugated iron that's both rusty and riddled with holes. They've seen enough farms to conclude that it's a barn and shed for livestock.

"A cowshed?" Barbara suggests.

"More like a horse stable or sheep shed," says Hertha, who, unlike Barbara, spent time in the countryside as a child. "There are no proper pastures for cows here, and it would be too problematic to do the milking up here on the heath."

They walk around the building, which seems not to be in use any longer. Its few windows have been boarded up, and there are practically no traces of humans or animals, apart from paths that meander from the house eastward, toward the heath's edge in the distance.

Barbara finds a door that opens onto the darkness within. "Should we?"

Hertha shrugs, then follows Barbara into the barn, which turns out to be empty, apart from a handful or two of old hay. The barn is high and wide, and it smells of mold and mildew. In the roof and walls are nail holes through which the sun shines—the narrow sunbeams cleave the darkness and form points of light on the floor. Hovering in the cool air are motes of dust that glow when the light hits them.

Barbara lights a cigarette. "If it rains, we could sleep here."

"Exactly," mutters Hertha. "But there's no rain forecast, so we won't need to hang around in such a cold, bad-smell-ing, haunted shack."

Their voices echo in the void.

Barbara grins and blows smoke rings. "Haunted shack? I find this building quite charming. A remnant from the past."

"I know what you mean." Hertha makes a face. "I may have just watched too many horror movies."

"Maybe," Barbara says thoughtfully. She smokes, letting her eyes wander around the room.

"Should we keep going?" Hertha says cheerfully.

Barbara nods, somewhat distractedly. Then she takes one more drag from her cigarette before dropping it on the floor and stepping on it.

"Is everything okay?" Hertha asks once they're back out in the sunshine, the warmth, and the pure air. They put their backpacks back on and fasten the straps.

Barbara shivers as she glances at the rusty outbuilding. "I felt a bit uneasy in there. Had kind of a bad feeling or something. It passed as quickly as it came, but I've still got the chills."

"Old buildings like that are undoubtedly breeding grounds for bacteria and the like," says Hertha as she walks off. "Cold and damp. Besides that, you might want to quit smoking again. It's poison, you know that."

"I know, I know," mutters Barbara. She follows closely on the heels of her friend. Then she looks over her shoulder, at the depressing outbuilding that grows more distant with each step—thankfully.

They walk briskly along the lake and don't stop until they've reached the edge of the escarpment above Kirkjubæjarklaustur. The stream flowing from the lake is a little farther to the right.

They stand side by side on the verge and look out over the village and the surrounding countryside.

"This is a small and peaceful community," says Hertha. "No traffic lights, let alone traffic jams. No apartment buildings or skyscrapers, no factories, no nightclubs and no nightlife, no criminal gangs, no vagrants, and no prostitutes—no alienation."

"No fun?" Barbara asks with a grin.

"Oh, my dear," Hertha says, laughing.

"I know what you mean," says Barbara, "but I think I'd get bored pretty quickly, living in such a small community."

"Maybe," Hertha mutters.

"Look. They do have cops," says Barbara. She points to an old police SUV that's driving slowly along a road running from a large white building on the riverbank to the village's main road.

"They hardly have much to do," says Hertha.

The police SUV stops at the intersection. The sun is reflecting off the SUV's windshield, yet Barbara gets the feeling that the person behind the wheel is watching them, looking back at them.

"Should we have something to eat?" Hertha asks.

Barbara nods. Just then, the SUV's left turn signal blinks and the vehicle drives into the village, toward the ravine and the trail to the lake.

They find a comfortable hollow beside the lake, take off their backpacks, and prepare a light meal. They fetch water, heat it on their Primus stove and have cups of soup and bread with butter and cheese. They eat in silence and allow the weariness to pass from their legs.

Hertha unfolds the map that the woman in the information center gave them and looks it over. "Maybe we should walk over the heath to Fjaðrárgljúfur Canyon? Instead of going back down and following the Skaftá river. It looks to me to be a shorter route. Maybe not easier, but hardly so difficult. We'd also have the view."

Barbara nods. "Sounds good. It's also funner to hike off the beaten path. More original, more demanding."

Hertha folds up the small tourist map. "Then it's decided. We'll cross the heath."

Hörður is finished swimming. Feeling refreshed, he walks out to the parking lot, which is just above the bank of the Skaftá river. His rusty-red hair is damp and wavy, and he's holding his wet swimming trunks in one hand and the car keys in the other. He hadn't found any towels in his new house, so he borrowed one at the pool. He breathes in the healthy countryside air and feels how much mellower he is, more relaxed, and much lighter of mood. He'd swum a few laps in the small but clean pool, then let himself float on his back for some time, or at least until he went and relaxed in one of the pool's two hot tubs. He'd really needed to rinse off the dust from his travels and recharge his batteries a bit.

It's a quarter to six. Outside, the sun is still shining and there's a comfortable warmth. It will soon be the summer solstice, when day and night merge into a reddish light around midnight and the birds are awake and sing in raucous choir of voices. After that, it's only two months until the autumn, with its cold, death, and darkness, but he prefers not to think about it. The incessant blinding brightness of the Arctic summer often gets on the red-haired giant's nerves, but that's a picnic compared to the pitch-black winter darkness, when the days shorten quickly and fade away like dying flowers, before finally changing into lifeless frostwork...

Hörður shakes his shoulders, as if to scare away these untimely thoughts. He unlocks the SUV and gets behind the wheel. The vehicle is almost ten years old and smells of road dust and cigar smoke. Hörður had started by emptying the ashtray, which was full of cigar butts. He would have to vacuum the car when he got the chance, rinse the floor mats, and clean the windows. Maybe he'll buy an air freshener for it, too. The vehicle has a powerful police radio, 35-inch tires, and a spotlight on the roof, as well as the traditional blue flashing lights. A real countryside car. In its trunk are a shovel and a box holding winter chains, as well as a first-aid kit and wool blanket. The space for the driver is a little smaller than in the Ford that Hörður had at his disposal in the CID back in Reykjavík, but if he slides the seat as far back as possible, tilts it a bit back and sticks his left elbow out the open side window, it's not so bad, really. The SUV has a radio and tape deck. There's only one cassette tape in the glove compartment: an ancient compilation tape—*Top of the Pops* from 1963, with a photo of a scantily clad model on the cover. Not exactly the red-haired giant's cup of tea—he won't be playing it anytime soon.

Hörður starts the SUV's diesel engine and drives calmly out of the lot and onto a narrow road that runs along the south side of the pool building and the elementary school and then curves gently up to Klausturvegur Road, to the west of the hotel. He stops at the intersection, leans forward and looks up the mountainside across the road. On the slope's rocky crest, two people stand admiring the view. It looks to him to be the two German backpacker girls, but he could be wrong.

The vehicle's engine hums idly. Hörður signals to turn right, in the direction of the grocery store, the highway, and his home in Meðalland. He has yet to buy groceries and then settle into the house standing there in the shade of the spruce trees. But he doesn't drive off immediately. Instead, he looks to the west, where several houses stand clustered beneath the wooded mountainside with its steep ravine.

He changes his mind, signals to turn left, and heads west. The houses in the heart of the village turn out to be old commercial buildings of some kind, concrete and nearly windowless, and on one of them is a large sign that reads *Klaustur Char.*

So this is how the villagers support themselves. By fish farming. He doubts that the farming itself takes places in these buildings, but it could very well be so. He thinks it more likely that the arctic char is slaughtered and processed here. Perhaps the building is an old slaughterhouse for sheep. At one time, there were slaughterhouses in all parts of the country, but today they're few and far between, but much larger, and the animals are driven long distances to be slaughtered, which can hardly be considered humane treatment.

Hörður turns the SUV, as it's impossible to drive farther in along the foot of the mountain—except perhaps on tracks or trails. He looks up at the ravine on the mountainside and sees what should be a high waterfall that isn't standing up to its name at the moment—branching out diagonally on the bare cliff wall is a thin streamlet that turns to nothing before disappearing behind a huge boulder at the ravine's bottom.

This is probably Systrafoss Falls, surmises the red-haired giant, who thought that the waterfall was both bigger and more impressive. He steps on the gas and drives back into the village. On the left, on a tree-lined street opposite Hotel Klaustur, he spots a low building that houses the village's health clinic and pharmacy. He drives past the hotel, the Skaftá Visitor Center, and the chapel. There are no parking spaces free in the lot outside Systrakaffi Café, Arion Bank, and the Kjarval grocery store, but the red-haired giant finds a vacant space in front of the liquor store. He looks at the clock on the dashboard of the SUV. It's three minutes to six.

I wonder when the liquor store closes, he thinks.

When Hörður parks the SUV in the gravel parking lot in front of the sky-high spruce trees at Efri-Vík, he finds the black-painted house standing in the shade of those same trees less depressing than when he first saw it, having left, as he did, a light on in every room, as well as above the front door. Adam's pickup truck is there where he parked it, but fortunately, Hörður sees no movement in or around his neighbor's house. He starts by carrying in the case of beer and two bottles of whiskey that he bought in the liquor store, and doesn't waste time doing so, as these purchases of his are his business alone. He hadn't planned on going to the liquor store, let alone buy anything there, but since it was still open, he decided he'd have a look at what was available here in the countryside, and once he was in the store anyway, it would actually be a bit silly to walk out of there empty-handed, so he just grabbed this case to have on hand at home—half-liter cans of Egill's Gull lager—and two bottles of White Horse, just if he happened to want a drop or two in his evening coffee now and then.

He sticks a few cans of beer in the empty fridge and goes back out to get the two bags of groceries from Kjarval. The selection in the store had surprised him, and he'd even been allowed to open an account there. He mainly bought microwave meals, but also eggs and bacon and baked beans, cereal and cookies, toilet paper, a few cleaning supplies, and lightbulbs, of course. He starts replacing the lightbulbs that are out, but then stops in front of the locked room, gives the door handle a good try, without result, and looks again for the key, but can't find it anywhere. Why is the room locked? And why doesn't he have the key?

It's seven o'clock and Hörður is hungry. He takes out one of the microwave meals, meatballs in brown gravy with mashed potatoes. He follows the directions, punches numerous holes in the plastic film covering the tray, puts the tray in the microwave and sets it at the highest temperature for five minutes. Then he takes a can of beer from the fridge, opens it, and takes a hefty drink. The beer is still warm, but he'll just have to deal with it. The house is dead silent, apart from the humming of the microwave oven.

What's missing is music!

Hörður takes his beer with him into the living room and opens the cabinet holding the stereo set. At the top is a turntable, below it is an amplifier, and at the bottom is a shelf of LPs. He turns on the amplifier, squats down, and flips through the LP collection. It turns out to be quite unexciting, yet he does find a few classics, including Bob Dylan's *Blood on the Tracks* and Tom Waits' *Rain Dogs*. He decides to put on Dylan. It's been a long time since he heard his favorite song by the old master, "Idiot Wind," which is on this album. He puts the glossy black vinyl on the turntable, lifts the arm and moves it inward, but the record doesn't start spinning as he expected. He checks to see if there's a switch on the device that needs to be flipped, but doesn't see any. Usually, such turntables don't need to be switched on—the arm just has to be moved inward.

Doesn't the turntable work?

Hörður sighs, takes the record off, and tries to lift the disc off the platter itself. There's usually a belt in such turntables, between the motor and the platter, and sometimes it breaks or comes off its wheels. If it has come off, it can usually be put back in place. But he can't lift off the platter. Maybe he needs to turn the whole thing upside down and do this from below?

Suddenly, his cell phone starts ringing, but Hörður doesn't remember where he left it. Never any peace! He polishes off his can of beer with one more gulp, crumples it and then goes to the vestibule, where his phone is ringing in his jacket pocket.

Hörður is about to answer the phone, but is startled by a bang from the kitchen, and then the electricity goes out. He hurries into the kitchen and sees that his microwave meal has exploded—brown gravy drips down the door's glass and foul-smelling smoke rises from the oven.

"No!" groans the red-haired giant. He's at a loss, but then he yanks the microwave's plug from its socket to prevent further disasters. He moves to open the oven, but stops—the gravy will no doubt spill out over everything and he can't imagine cleaning it up.

Hörður is so disappointed and irritated that he could scream. But instead, he goes to the vestibule, where the fuse box is, and switches the circuit breaker back on. Then he goes and gets another can of beer, plunks down on the living-room sofa, and takes a swig of the lukewarm liquid. The silence in the house is almost maddening, and the awful stench coming from the microwave makes him queasy. He gives the stereo system the evil eye. If he could sit here and listen to music, that would be better than nothing. But no, apparently, that's the one thing he can't do!

He chugs his beer as he thinks things over. What the hell should he do?

What can he do?

They've put the heath almost entirely behind them.

"I don't think it's too far now," says Hertha, wiping sweat from her forehead.

"Good," says Barbara, before frowning because of a cramp in her right calf. The two girls are sweaty and tired, and their backs and legs are sore.

It's going on nine o'clock. The sun is still rather high in the sky, yet it's starting to darken and the temperature is beginning to drop. They've walked along the edge of the heath from Systravatn Lake down to the mouth of a valley, which appears to mark the end of Klausturheiði Heath.

They come to a narrow, potholed dirt road that winds up the valley to the west.

"Should we go up this road?" asks Barbara, who is both hungry and half-lost. Their hike hasn't exactly been demanding, but it's still tiring walking off-road, including having to detour around ravines and riverbeds that cut into the heath.

Hertha looks at the map. "Not up, no. But back to the intersection where the road begins. Then we follow another road that leads to the mouth of the canyon. It's more of a main road."

They walk along the narrow road and soon reach the intersection. Hertha turns out to be right. The narrow road is a sideroad off a broader gravel road that isn't as potholed. At the intersection are two signs on a metal pole. The upper sign is yellow and points toward the valley that they just crossed. On it is written *Laki 45 km*. Below the yellow sign is a smaller one, white with one word in black letters—*Heiðarból*. From experience, they know that these white signs point the way to farms of the same name.

They stop and catch their breath.

"As I recall, Laki is a volcano," says Hertha. "It would be fun to go there, but we would have to do so by car."

"Should we go on?" Barbara asks.

Hertha nods. They walk over a hill, and then the road curves into a wide valley. Through the valley runs a river— no doubt the Fjaðrá river, whence the canyon takes its name. They speed up a bit, sensing they only have a short distance left.

"You see!" Barbara says excitedly. The road now leads downward and ends at a large parking lot. Below the parking lot is an old concrete bridge over the river, and above the bridge, they catch a glimpse of the mouth of Fjaðrárgljúfur Canyon.

"We've made it!" says Hertha cheerfully. They practically jog down the road. All their fatigue is gone.

There's only one car in the parking lot, a terribly dirty SUV. Three tourists come walking down a trail leading up along the verge of the canyon to the east, and head for the SUV. By the time Barbara and Hertha reach the parking lot, the tourists have gotten into their SUV and driven away.

"We're the only ones here!" exclaims Barbara, who can barely contain her excitement.

"I know!" says Hertha. They walk down to the bridge, stop in the middle of it, and look rapturously into the canyon, which appears before them in all its glory. The vertical rock walls on both sides resemble curtains that have been drawn open. The wide river meanders tranquilly through the canyon, which is so deep that its end can't be seen. The river doesn't quite reach the rock walls, but rather, bits of grassy bank can be seen here and there within the magnificent canyon.

"Incredible," Barbara whispers. They'd seen photos of the canyon online, but seeing it with their bare eyes is a sheer delight.

"I think that we can camp in it," said Hertha. "As we were hoping."

Barbara nods, smiling.

After his fourth beer, Hörður puts on his denim jacket and combat boots. He was going to shave, but decided to allow his three-day shadow to develop into a four-day shadow, and see how it looked before shaving it. But he did splash on a little aftershave, just to make an attempt. He carries the fire-damaged microwave oven out to the deck and then ambles over to his neighbor's house, rings the doorbell and waits. After waiting somewhere around a minute, he looks at his watch. It's half past seven and there are lights on inside the house, so the bastard must be at home.

"Just as I thought," says Hörður when Adam finally opens the door. He's wearing a black T-shirt, camouflage trousers and Birkenstocks. He seems absentminded and a bit sleepy; maybe he'd dozed off to the TV news. Hörður notices that he has little white paint splotches on his forehead.

"Have you come for some lamb soup?" asks Adam. "I was actually painting the master bedroom, and haven't started heating it up yet…"

Hörður holds out his hand, silencing him. He has no interest having dinner with an entire family. "We'll go get ourselves something to eat. You drive, I'll pay. We'll take the police car."

Adam stares confusedly at the red-haired giant, but then he blinks and nods. "Okay, then, I'm coming—I'll be just a moment."

As Hörður is waiting, he remembers that his phone had been ringing. He fishes it out and looks at the screen. It was Bíbí, as he thought. He's about to call back, but stops when Adam appears in all his camouflaged glory, having cleaned the paint off his face. Hörður will just call after they've eaten.

Less than a quarter of an hour later, they're sitting at a window table at Systrakaffi Café, having ordered food and gotten their drinks. Hörður ordered a large beer, and Adam a coffee and sparkling water. The restaurant is both roomy and cozy, with furnishings of dark wood, and half the place is something of a solarium, letting in plenty of light from outside. The sun is still high in the sky, though it's just beginning its daily descent. Almost every table is occupied, mainly by foreign tourists.

"This is a really cozy place," says Hörður before taking a drink of beer.

Adam nods. "And the food is very good."

"Do the locals come here much?" Hörður asks.

"Yes, yes, from time to time, I guess," replies Adam. "People don't always feel like cooking, or they might want a cold beer or glass of wine. You can also order pizza to go."

"Right," says Hörður. "How many people live here, by the way?"

"A hundred and ninety-six, last I knew," Adam replies in his deep, slow narrator's voice.

Hörður nearly chokes on his beer. "Not even two hundred?"

Adam smiles apologetically.

"What are the main duties of the police in a place like this?" asks Hörður, who fears having too little to do in the coming months.

Adam clears his throat. "Mainly highway patrol. Speed monitoring and the like. Of course, there are car accidents from time to time, sometimes serious. Then there's risk management: implementing various contingency plans for floods, glacial flooding of the Skaftá river, storms, or volcanic eruptions, done in coordination with search-and-rescue and the fire department. The plans are mainly designed to prevent or mitigate damage to structures and injuries to people, and to ensure a swift response when and if something happens. But apart from traffic accidents and natural disasters, not much happens here. No crimes or break-ins or anything like that. Here, people live for the most part in peace and harmony."

Hörður nods thoughtfully. It's not such a bad thought, being free of the drug addicts, thieves, and thugs in the capital. "When did anyone die here last?"

"Die?" Adam exclaims with a concerned expression. "One old woman here in the countryside was buried around three weeks ago. Before that, a foreign tourist died in a car accident. That was around six months ago, but the accident wasn't here in the village, but out east at Skeiðarársandur."

"Great," says Hörður, smiling to himself. Maybe he'll finally get some peace from those damn death shadows. They only appear when someone is suddenly doomed to die, and it might be many weeks or months before anyone here gives up the ghost. He may not exactly be on summer vacation, but maybe he'll be taking a break from death…

That wouldn't be so bad!

Hörður smiles widely. "Here's to small villages and low mortality rates. May the people here live as long as possible—hurrah!"

"Cheers," says Adam, with a mischievous look, and they clink their glasses. Just then, the waiter appears with their food. Hörður has ordered a steak with a salad and fries, and Adam a pizza with the dramatic name of *Exorcist*.

"I was going to heat up a microwave meal," says Hörður, as he cuts himself a piece of the juicy steak. "But the microwave just exploded. I don't know if it was broken or if I set it wrong."

"Sorry to hear that," says Adam. "I have no idea whether old Rock Grinder used the microwave at all. I'm guessing not. So it probably just malfunctioned; maybe it hadn't been used enough. Hard to say."

"Rock Grinder?" Hörður asks, his mouth full of food.

"Lieutenant Steingrímur," says Adam. "Your predecessor. He was a real strongman in his younger years, notorious for dealing quite harshly with brawlers and other trouble-makers. He practically went looking for conflict back then, but calmed down with age, as is usual. But it was apparently no laughing matter getting on his wrong side in the old days. By the time I met him, he was pretty worn down."

Hörður nods. He knows the type: strong, old-school cops who rely on strength instead of smarts. He himself is no weakling, but he's never sought out conflict with others.

"One other thing," says the new lieutenant. "Back in the house there's an old stereo system, kind of like the ones kids got as confirmation gifts back in the day. Actually just a turntable and an amplifier, but no tape deck or radio, as they usually had. The only thing is that the turntable doesn't work. Do you know anyone who can take a look at it for me? It sucks not to be able to play music."

Adam nods knowingly. "Our priest, Páll, is a genuine jack-of-all-trades. He repairs everything between heaven and earth. Mainly lawnmowers and the like, but also electronic equipment and anything else, really. There's no electrician in the village, so people often turn to Páll, who generally manages to fix whatever he's handed. He lives on Skriðuvellir; it's the street closest to the mountain. I don't remember the number, but the house is fiery red. You can find it easily."

"Sounds good," says Hörður. "I'll look in on the apostle Páll at the first opportunity."

"He'd enjoy it, the old fellow," says Adam. He eats his pizza slowly and calmly, one small piece at a time, like a pudgy thrush. He chews for a long time and rinses down each bite with a sip of sparkling water. He seems to be entirely in his own world, relishing the food.

Hörður, who usually devours everything like a hungry lion, secretly admires this almost poetic ingestion of the food at the same time as he doesn't get it. After all, he's much closer to being a fanged predator than a fluttering little bird.

"Is the pizza good?" asks the red-haired giant, munching his steak.

Adam nods slowly. "Very much so."

The door opens and the truck driver that Hörður saw in Hvolsvöllur walks in. The one with the sideburns that remind the red-haired giant slightly of Mick Jagger, and who took the package and was then rude to the German girls. Where might they be now? The driver doesn't wait to be shown to a seat, but instead, walks in a macho manner to the bar, leans against it like an outlaw in a saloon in a Western movie, grins and says something to the girl behind it. Shortly afterward, she brings him a mug full of frothy beer.

"Do you know that guy?" Hörður nods toward the bar.

Adam looks up and nods. "That's Hallgrímur Olsen, truck driver. He actually lives in Vík but comes here often. I prefer not to say anything bad about anyone, but Hallgrímur's a damn racist and not shy about advertising it. He's even prone to giving colored people a hard time, saying all sorts of bullshit to them."

"He definitely doesn't give off a good vibe," mutters Hörður. He watches Hallgrímur out of the corner of his eye.

The driver runs his hawkish eyes over the room, and narrows them when he sees the red-haired giant. He lifts his glass, grins coldly, and nods to Hörður, who looks away quickly and pretends not to have noticed.

"Has he gotten into trouble with the law?" Hörður asks.

"A while ago, yes," Adam replies. "Assault and battery and the like. A rape, too, as I recall. But nothing lately, as far as I know."

"Rape, huh?" exclaims Hörður.

Adam shrugs. "I vaguely recall having heard that. Maybe not much happens here, but what does happen is never forgotten."

Hörður nods. He grew up in a small village and knows what Adam means. In small communities, everyone knows everything about everyone, and whatever you do follows you forever—the good, but no less the bad. So it's very common for black sheep to leave such villages to escape the past and try to start fresh elsewhere, with an unblemished reputation.

This Hallgrímur is clearly not one of them.

Hörður glances again at the driver and sees that he now has company. Standing next to him is a short man in baggy trousers, a dirty shirt, and an old parka, and with dark eyes and tousled, dark but gray-tinged hair. He's past middle-aged, ugly but cheerful-looking, with a potbelly, and he rocks to and fro when he moves. He reminds Hörður of a dwarf, although he isn't small enough to be a real one.

He's served a full mug of beer, which he clinks with Hallgrímur's, who downs his in one gulp.

"That's Júlíus, our garbage man," says Adam, who clearly notices that Hörður is sizing up the man. "He's odd, but completely harmless, I'd say. Lives alone and has done so since his mother died. He's been in charge of garbage collection here in the area for as long as the oldest people can remember, as the saying goes. But apart from the garbage truck, he also drives an excavator and a livestock truck."

"I saw him today in the garbage truck," says Hörður. "He made a detour to say something to two German backpacker girls who were on their way to the Skaftá Visitor Center. What he said to them, I have no idea."

Adam smiles faintly. "He's very fond of young girls. But as far as I know, he's never been with a woman. He does appreciate them, though—that's for certain."

"I see," mutters Hörður. He pushes away his empty plate and polishes off his beer. Adam is barely halfway through his pizza.

Wanting another beer, Hörður starts looking around for the waiter when he notices a woman who has just entered the place. She's about thirty, he guesses, blonde, slim, and very pretty. Her long hair is hanging loose, and she's wearing a flowery summer dress and high-heeled, open-toed shoes. Like Hallgrímur, she doesn't wait to be shown to a seat, but walks straight to the bar—making him assume that she's a local and a regular visitor to Systrakaffi Café. Just before the woman reaches the bar, she turns her head and looks straight into the eyes of the red-haired giant, who becomes flustered, blushes, and quickly looks away. It's as if she sensed that he was watching her.

"She's the cat," says Adam as calmly as can be, with a mischievous look. "And you're the mouse."

"What do you mean?" Hörður asks, surprised and slightly offended. He gets the waiter's attention and gestures to him that he would like another beer.

"You're *the new man in town*," Adam says with a strong American accent. "A new face, fresh blood. Silja hits on any man who moves. You'll draw her to you like a magnet, whether you like it or not."

"Bullshit," says Hörður, who doesn't dare to look in the direction of the bar.

"Oh?" says Adam, struggling to contain his laughter. "Here she comes."

Hörður becomes agitated and feels his face heat up. He hopes that Adam is messing with him, but before he knows it, someone lays a hand lightly on his right shoulder, and then he catches a faint whiff of perfume and catches a glimpse of the flowery material and painted toenails in open-toed shoes.

"What do we have here?" asks a voice that was doubtless sugary-sweet at one time but now has a husky undertone due to smoking.

Hörður feels as if he's paralyzed.

"This is our new police lieutenant," Adam replies dutifully. "Hörður Grímsson from Reykjavík."

"From Súðavík, actually," mutters Hörður, before looking up and shaking the woman's delicate hand. "Hello."

"Pleased to meet you," the woman says. Holding a glass of white wine in her left hand, she looks flirtatiously into Hörður's eyes. "My name is Silja. Welcome to the most boring village in Iceland. Nothing ever happens here."

"So I'm told," says Hörður softly. He pulls his hand back and is hugely relieved when the waiter appears with a new beer.

"So, are you single?" asks Silja.

Hörður shakes his head, at the same time remembering that he still has to call Bíbí. "I live with someone. Or … not *here*, but in Reykjavík. I came here alone … out east, err … to Klaustur."

"I see, dear," says Silja, laughing. "Welcome to the east, err … to Klaustur!"

Hörður blushes; she's making fun of him.

Before leaving, Silja fiddles with the hair on the back of his neck. "See you at the hotel later."

Hörður sighs with relief, then takes a big gulp of cold beer.

"She's just like that," says Adam apologetically. "But she's not a bad person or anything. Just lonely, I suppose."

Hörður nods, without knowing exactly what he's agreeing with. Beautiful women always throw him off balance, for some reason. He glances at the bar. There they sit on their barstools, chatting and laughing: Hallgrímur, Júlíus, and Silja. She's probably telling them about the new lieutenant, who is as stiff as a driftwood log and says things in bad rhymes.

East… err… to Klaustur. Really? He curses himself in silence.

"Sigrún, the old woman who works at the Skaftá Visitor Center?" says Adam in an inquisitive tone. "She's Silja's ex-mother-in-law. They were married, she and Sigrún's son Björgvin, and they have one son. Björgvin Geirharðsson is a plumber, besides being the leader of the search-and-rescue unit Torch. Silja still lives in their old house, but Bjöggi moved to Hörgsárdalur Valley, just this side of Síða."

"Síða?" asks Hörður. He notices a self-conscious teenage boy who has just come into the café. The boy hesitates, as if he doesn't know whether he's coming or going.

"Síða is the area here to the east of Kirkjubæjarklaustur," Adam explains. "But the area to the west is called Landbrot."

Hörður nods. He watches the driver Hallgrímur and the teenage boy go outside. "That Björgvin, I think I saw him today in the Skaftá Center. Very tall and blond? Blue, melancholy eyes?"

"That's right," says Adam. "He drives around in a big Ford pickup."

"White with rust stains?" asks Hörður. "A dog in the back seat?"

Adam smiles faintly. "You're were obviously born to be a police detective."

Hörður shrugs, but is clearly flattered. "I don't know about that. But I always notice details in my surroundings. Sometimes it's a blessing, sometimes a curse. It can be tiring taking in information all the time."

"I can believe it," says Adam, who has finally finished his pizza.

Hörður takes a drink of his beer and licks his lips. "What did she mean, that Silja, when she said she hoped to see us at the hotel later?"

Adam looks at his watch. "The café closes at nine o'clock, in ten minutes. But the hotel bar is open until half past eleven. More often than not, those who are having a drink head over there."

"Oh, I see," mutters Hörður. He's feeling just slightly tipsy and should maybe be getting home. But he's also quite up for having another cold one. What would he do back at home but drink more beer and stare out at the void, alone in the silence?

Doesn't one say "into" the void?

At the bar, he would at least have company. And if he has one or two more beers, he would be able to go straight to bed and fall asleep.

"Maybe you want to go there?" Adam asks hesitantly. "To the hotel?"

"Maybe," says Hörður. "Unless you need to get home?"

"I'm in no big hurry," says Adam, in his nuanced narrator's voice.

"Well, then maybe we can stop by the hotel," says Hörður, and he polishes off his beer in one gulp.

The bar at Hotel Klaustur is on the ground floor, in something of an annex adjacent to a bright, spacious area that's a breakfast room for the first part of the day and a restaurant in the evening. Hörður and Adam are standing at the short bar waiting for their drinks—there's no table service so late. The evening sun shines through the curtains drawn halfway over the large windows. Pleasant jazz music is blended with the patrons' chatter. All but one of the tables are occupied. The atmosphere in the bar is both cheerful and relaxed. Most of the guests café foreign tourists who are doubtless staying at the hotel, which is newish and quite elegant, considering its size and location.

Hörður runs his eyes over the people's faces. There are some Asians and a few Europeans, as well as a group of Americans of both sexes, who have pushed two of the tables together and are laughing energetically and talking loudly in their artificial, nasal accents. A few of the Yanks have the American flag embroidered onto their baseball caps, patched onto their jacket sleeves, or printed on the fronts of their T-shirts, as if to emphasize their nationality and endless pride at belonging to the *land of the free, home of the brave.* The women are loud and the men are chubby, with trim beards and baby-soft skin. Hörður looks at Adam, and then smiles to himself at the thought that this teddy-bearish, camouflage-wearing neighbor of his could fit right into that group of clichéd Yanks without anyone noticing.

At one table sit Hallgrímur, Júlíus, and Silja. The two men are drinking beer and have already polished off a few shots of Ouzo, while Silja sips white wine in between glancing at Hörður, who pretends not to notice.

"Here you are," says the bartender as he places a large beer and a steaming cup of coffee on the bar. "Pay together or … ?"

"Keep a tab, friend," says the red-haired giant. "I'll pay up before we leave."

"Certainly," says the bartender.

Hörður takes a drink of beer, then nods toward the only free table in sight. "Shall we?"

Adam nods and they go and sit down at the table. Hörður notices Silja following them with her eyes, and then how she stiffens when her cell phone starts ringing. Hallgrímur says something with a grin, and Silja squeezes out a smile and lowers her phone's ring tone before draining her glass at one go.

Hörður breaks into a cold sweat; he hasn't called Bíbí back yet. Can he do that now? She'll doubtless be able to tell that he's drinking. He takes out his phone, taps in a message to his partner and sends it:

Sorry sweetie am on duty will call tomorrow good night

"Everything all right?" Adam asks gingerly.

"Of course!" Hörður laughs dryly. "It's really cozy here. Great bar."

"Yes, and the restaurant is outstanding," says Adam.

"Tell me," says Hörður, "this Hallgrímur, the driver, does he have a teenage son?"

Adam shakes his head, but seems distracted. "Those Americans at the next table. I think the men are in the military. Or were in the military. Are maybe retired. Many of them are able to take early retirement."

"I don't know," says Hörður doubtfully. "They look like real fatsos to me."

"Not the black one," says Adam.

Hörður knows which person he means, there being only one black man in the group. He's around fifty, maybe, average in height and extremely fit-looking, wearing jeans, running shoes, and a lined jacket. He's started gaining a bit of weight, but was obviously in good shape before.

"Maybe," says the red-haired giant. "But he could just as well have been an athlete."

"Do you want to bet?" Adam asks mischievously.

Hörður shrugs his shoulders. "Why not? A case of beer, or…?"

"Done," Adam says with a smile. They shake hands and Hörður can't help but smile. He's really starting to like this new neighbor of his. Maybe they can become friends after all?

Raucous laughter comes from the locals' table. Hallgrímur and Júlíus burst out laughing at something that one of them has apparently said, but Silja isn't amused. Her face is pale and she glances at her phone now and then, in between looking out of the large window facing the parking lot in front of the hotel.

Hörður looks at Adam, who is tapping a message into his cell phone, probably to let his wife know that he's late. Hörður feels a little pang of guilt. He looks at his phone and sees that Bíbí has answered:

Good night, babe. Call me in the morning

He frowns. That smiley is a bad sign. She's probably angry at him, but has tried to cover it over with that soulless, electronic smile. Or is he over-interpreting that yellow psychopath?

He could very well be. But he's calling her in the morning, that's for sure.

Hörður puts his phone back in his pocket. At the same moment, the noisy roar of an engine is heard outside and then a screeching of brakes, and finally a heavy car door is slammed shut. Hörður sees Silja literally stiffen in her seat.

"Bjöggi is here," says Adam softly.

Hörður nods, having put two and two together. The blond giant he saw in the Skaftá Visitor Center marches into the hotel bar, his movements stiff and his face like a storm cloud. He sets eyes on the mother of his child and signals commandingly to her to come to him. Hallgrímur and Júlíus act as if they don't notice him, but Silja gets up from her seat and follows Björgvin out, sheepishly, while trying, however, to maintain her bearing.

"They've been through a few things over the years," says Adam, as if to excuse this oppressive but silent drama.

"I'm going to get some fresh air," says Hörður, who fears that this blue-eyed hulk is actually going to rough up his ex.

"Be careful," Adam advises him.

Hörður hurries to the lobby but there's no one there, so he heads out of the hotel. The sun is finally setting; the sky is reddish and the air is agreeably cool. In the middle of the parking lot, a white Ford pickup truck is idling. Not far from it are Björgvin and Silja. Clutching her by the upper arm, he pulls her closer to the pickup truck, chewing her out at the same time. She resists and makes a few unsuccessful attempts to break free.

"…and you just leave him home alone?" Hörður hears Björgvin barking.

"Agnes is…" Silja groans.

"Agnes is just a child!" Björgvin snaps. "I'm this close to reporting this to…"

He stops shouting when he sees Hörður, who is standing under the eaves of the hotel entrance. The red-haired giant looks away, and then pats his jacket pockets as if searching for a pack of cigarettes.

Silja seizes the opportunity and tears herself free. "You don't own me!"

"Bitch!" growls Björgvin, pitch-black with malice. He tries to grab Silja but isn't quick enough. She escapes from him and walks a bit unsteadily toward Hörður. Björgvin could easily catch her if he wanted to, but the red-haired giant's presence holds him back.

They stare each other down, the two giants. Hörður is both calm and prepared for anything. He doesn't want to fight with the blond giant, but he's not afraid to do so. Björgvin is clearly in a fighting mood, yet manages to restrain himself. He blinks his icy eyes and spits on the street before getting into his pickup and speeding off with a ruckus.

"Thanks," says Silja, in a tremulous voice. She throws herself into Hörður's arms with dramatic flair.

"You're welcome," says Hörður, looking embarrassed. He's forced to put his arm around Silja so she doesn't collapse. She hangs on to him like an exhausted child. He pats her scrawny back lightly, like a bashful but reassuring father.

"He's a monster, that's what he is," says Silja, on the verge of tears.

"He's gone," says Hörður, just to say something. He looks across the street, at one of the houses at the foot of the mountain. The house is unassuming, standing a bit apart from the others and surrounded by untrimmed trees, but no real yard. Parked side-by-side on the spacious gravel lot in front of it are Júlíus's old garbage truck and an even older livestock-transport truck. The red-haired giant concludes that the house belongs to Júlíus, the dwarfish garbage man of around fifty, he'd guess, and who is fond of young women.

"Let's go back in," says Hörður. He frees himself from Silja's grip and helps her back into the bar. There he orders a new beer for himself and a glass of white wine for her, and asks the waiter to put both on his tab.

"You're awesome," says Hallgrímur as he appears at the bar. Grinning, he looks at Hörður and lifts his half-empty beer glass. "You're the man who shot that fucking sand-nigger in Smáralind. My man! Here's to you!"

Hörður's temper flares, but before he so much as opens his mouth, someone taps something metal against a glass, as if signaling for silence. The chatter stops and all eyes are directed at the garbage man, Júlíus, standing with his head held high in the middle of the room and basking in the attention.

"I'm a good old communist," says Júlíus in something of a squeaky voice, in stiff English. "And I protest the presence of these corrupt and malicious imperialists sitting here among us."

He points at the eight Americans who had combined two of the place's tables.

"The US military left Iceland, and rightly so," says Júlíus in his thin voice. "But it should also leave all other countries that it has defiled by its presence, and stop invading Iraq and Syria and other countries that it has nothing to do with."

The black man in the group of Americans has had enough. He gets slowly to his feet and points accusingly at the garbage man with the childlike voice. "Are you serious?"

The garbage man blinks before answering, loudly and clearly. "No, I'm Júlíus."

You could hear a pin drop—and then the whole room bursts into laughter, with no one laughing louder than the Americans. Looking confused, Júlíus bows and sits down again at his table.

"It's best that I take the little idiot home," says Hallgrímur with a laugh, before leaving Hörður and Silja.

"Sit down with us?" Hörður asks. Silja nods and they take their drinks over to Adam's table. He has finished his coffee.

"Would you like more?" Hörður asks.

Adam shakes his head, then points triumphantly at the Americans' tables. "Do you see what I see?"

Hörður follows the gesture. The black man has taken off his jacket, beneath which is a T-shirt. On the man's upper right arm is a tattoo of a screaming eagle, attacking with outspread wings and claws. Hörður knows as well as Adam what this tattoo means: that the man is a *Screaming Eagle*—a paratrooper of the 101st Airborne Division of the U.S. Army, like the boys in Easy Company.

"Fucking hell," Hörður mutters in admiration.

"Do you want to talk to him?" Adam asks, excited as a little kid.

Hörður gets butterflies in his stomach, as he desperately wants to. But he's too reserved to do so. Besides, Silja's waiting to get some attention. "No, but you go on and say hello to him."

Adam doesn't need to be told twice, but nearly leaps to his feet and approaches the paratrooper like a teenager approaching some idol of his—both zealously and respectfully.

Silja lays her delicate hand on the broad back of the red-haired giant's. "Thanks again for saving me earlier."

"It was nothing," Hörður mutters shyly. He takes a big gulp of beer and lets his eyes wander over the room. Adam is engaged in a lively conversation with the soldier, and Hallgrímur and Júlíus seem to have evaporated, fortunately.

Hopefully, there will be no more incidents tonight.

Midnight, and peals of laughter echo between the steep cliff walls that merge with the darkness in the canyon. The sun is setting but the sky is still deep red, like red wine in a dusty bottle in a dark room. The only light in the canyon comes from a butane lantern burning inside a closed tent standing on an oval, grassy patch at the foot of the eastern cliff. The tent is orange and glows like a dying sun.

Barbara and Hertha have taken off all their clothes and waded barefoot into the river. There, they shriek like little girls, splash cold water on each other, and pretend to bathe, having neither soap nor shampoo. The flowing water reaches up to their knees. In order to get this far into the canyon, they had to cross the river in three places. They had taken off their shoes and socks, tucked their socks into their shoes and hung them by the laces around their necks before tiptoeing over the rocky riverbed, through the river's heavy current. They had grown cold and their feet were sore from walking on the rocks, but when they found the right patch of grass, both the cold and the pain disappeared like dew before the sun. The place was nothing short of perfect. They were alone in the world; the canyon blocked any other view and over it was nothing but the sky—first blue, then apricot-colored, and finally blood red.

Soon darkness will fall, and they might as well be on the moon or somewhere beyond the solar system. Then there will be nothing but darkness, silent cliffs, and a gurgling, peaceful river. Who knows—maybe it will be a starry night?

"Maybe we should get out?" Barbara asks, laughing. She's hunched and shivering from the cold; her teeth are chattering and her arms are covered with goose bumps.

The sun has disappeared and a few stars appear in the black sky.

"All right," Hertha says, giggling. They tiptoe stiffly toward the bank, occasionally making exaggerated cries when they step on rocks. They act like they're twelve years old, enjoying themselves to the fullest. To act like a kid is to be free. No adult is there to scold them or boss them around. They're safe and do what they want, when they want.

Their towels are lying on the bank. They reach for them and start drying themselves. They're so cold that their muscles are stiff, but this was so fun that they can't stop giggling and laughing. Bathing in a cold river in the dark! What a crazy idea.

"Should we make hot chocolate?" Barbara asks, her teeth chattering.

"Yes," says Hertha. "And gobble down chocolate cookies."

"Do we still have marshmallows?" Barbara asks. They wrap their towels around themselves and walk across the grass to the illuminated tent.

"I think so. But if not, then …" Hertha falls silent and signals Barbara to stop. "Shh!"

"What?" asks Barbara, who doesn't dare make another move.

"I thought I heard …" Hertha stops mid-sentence when she hears the sound again. A faint splashing sound, like footsteps in water.

Barbara stiffens and her heart starts beating faster. "Is someone …?"

Hertha swallows and stares motionless into the dark. The splashing sound draws nearer, and then it's as if a shadow separates itself from the bottomless darkness.

"Who's there?" Barbara asks in English. She's so nervous that her voice breaks, like that of an adolescent.

Suddenly a flashlight switches on. The person who was wading across the river has come up onto the grassy patch and shines the light first on Hertha, then Barbara. Barbara lets out a cry, but Hertha covers her eyes.

"What's the meaning of this?" Hertha calls out in English. She's angry, but since she's cold and scared, as well, her voice trembles.

The person holding the flashlight points it downward. They see the legs of baggy jeans tucked into black rubber boots, like those used by farmers and fishermen. The boots are flecked with old grime, perhaps dirt, and are wet with river water.

"Hertha?" says Barbara, frightened. She tries to wrap the towel better around herself but her fingers are stiff from the cold. Her wet hair clings to her face.

Hertha doesn't answer, but just stares at the shadow holding the flashlight while her heart pounds hard in her chest.

Suddenly the beam of light is directed upward and the face of the uninvited visitor appears like a full moon in the night.

Barbara cries out again, this time louder.

Hertha's eyes open wide. "You!"

Storm

Friday

When his good old and completely unbearable alarm clock rings, Hörður is fast asleep. The clock is all scratched, broken, and glued together, after all the times he's dropped it on the floor or hurled it at the wall. He rises halfway, fumbles for the damn clock, finally finds it and manages to silence the annoying ringing. What inhuman devils design and make such sadistic devices? Through the lime-green curtains, an uncomfortable light shines, and birdsong carries in from outside. Hörður lies back down, shuts his eyes, and curses in silence. He has a headache, his mouth is dry and sour-tasting, and his stomach is a bit upset. He knows very well that he has to get up, that he needs to be getting going, yet doesn't remember precisely why.

Isn't he on temporary leave from work?

The gears in the brain are stiff and slow, almost rusted stuck—they're squeaking. He tries to remember, to think, but it's as if everything is floating, upside down. He's light-headed, dizzy, and even feels like he has to vomit.

Déjà vu…

Hörður is in a cold sweat. Had he been drinking yesterday? The answer doesn't appear as a memory, but as a hammer blow to his head, terrible nausea, and a foul, sickish taste in his throat. All of a sudden, the gears start turning and images start to flicker on the movie screen of his mind.

Kirkjubæjarklaustur.

Alone in his house.

Beer in the fridge.

The restaurant.

The hotel bar.

Then everything goes black…

"God-damn fucking fuck!" growls the red-haired giant as his stomach tightens and the nausea intensifies. He jumps out of bed in his underwear and socks, crashes into the door frame, rushes forward, doesn't remember where the bathroom is yet manages to hit on it by chance, lets himself drop to his knees and pukes with all his life and soul into the toilet.

Déjà vu…

Stomach cramps.

Bathed in sweat.

Queasiness.

Chills.

Yet again…

Hörður groans heavily, flushes the toilet, and heaves himself to his feet. He splashes cold water on his face and then looks at himself in the mirror above the sink. His face is pale and ghostly, covered with coarse spikes that will gradually become a full beard. His lips are cracked and his green eyes bloodshot, anguished, and sad. His hair, damp with sweat, hangs down to his shoulders and frames the miserable picture.

Oh, why is he always so stupid? On his way back to the bedroom Hörður supports himself with his hand on the wall. He has to lie down for a bit, sleep a little more. Work will have to wait. Everything is spinning, and queasiness simmers within him like poison in a witch's cauldron.

Hörður has hardly let himself fall back onto his bed when his cell phone starts ringing elsewhere in the house. His temper flares, but then he just feels most like crying. What has he done to deserve all this injustice? Why *him*? Why is the world trying to kill him?

He's wouldn't dream of going and answering his phone. But the ringing robs him of all peace. His heart pounds and he breaks into a sweat. He tries to relax, pulls the pillow over his head, and prays for just a little peace and quiet, so that he can get a little more sleep, even if only for a minute or two. But then he remembers Bíbí. He never called her. And if this is her, then he has to answer.

Doesn't he?

Yes…Hörður forces himself to his feet, almost overwhelmed with discomfort and self-pity. He hobbles into the living room, where his phone is ringing on the coffee table, amid countless empty beer cans.

Did he drink all this beer?

The air in the living room is heavy and rank. Hörður picks up the ringing phone, blinks and stares confusedly at the screen. It's Bíbí; he sees that now. He clears his throat and answers, and at the same moment, sees that someone is lying there sleeping on the living-room sofa, beneath a woolen blanket. It's a blonde woman in a flowery summer dress.

"Did I wake you up?" says Bíbí.

Hörður is rigid with fear. He stands there holding his phone to his ear and staring at Silja, who mumbles something in her sleep. What's she doing there? Did he invite her home?

"Hello? Are you there?"

Half-speechless from stress, he clears his throat again. "Yes, of course. No, I was awake."

"How's it going? Did you go straight to work yesterday?"

"Ye-eah." Hörður starts to lie, but is too light-headed to spin a credible one. He slinks off, out of the living room and back toward the bedroom. But he has taken only a few steps when another cell phone starts to ring—a red *iPhone* lying on the coffee table, in between an ashtray filled with butts and a pack of slender menthol cigarettes.

Hörður stiffens mid-step. Silja starts, gasps for breath, and opens her eyes. The red phone keeps ringing. On the screen is a lit-up name: *Agnes*

"And what do you think… ?" Bíbí is silent for a moment. *"What phone is that ringing?"*

"What?" says Hörður, just to say something. He starts to walk off again, but is so dizzy that he gets barely anywhere.

Silja sits up abruptly, tears off the woolen blanket, and answers her phone, her voice hoarse and gruff. "Hi, dear! What's that…? I'm just over at one of my girlfriends."

Hörður hurries out of the living room as best he can. He feels like he's stuck in a nightmare from which he can't wake up.

"What woman is that?" Bíbí asks in his ear.

"Woman?" says Hörður, to buy himself time. He stumbles out of the living room, sweaty and confused.

"Calm down, dear… calm down," says Silja behind him. "Bjöggi has just gone and gotten him, that's all. He didn't want to wake you up… I'm on my way… yes, just go home, it's okay… but not a word of this to anyone, okay?"

"I'm… I'm at work, at the station," says Hörður, who is so hungover and stressed that his voice trembles. He has made it to the bedroom, and plunks down on the bed. "There's a woman here. She wants to file a complaint. Something about … I don't know what it's about."

"Just crazy busy in the countryside?" says Bíbí cheerfully.

Hörður props his elbows on his knees and his fragile head in the palm of his left hand, and holds the phone to his ear with his right. He feels so awful that he wishes he could die. Not only is he badly hungover, he's also a loser and an idiot who forgets to call his partner, gets smashed and invites strange women home. What's wrong with him?

"Yes … something like that," he says, on the verge of tears.

"Is everything okay?"

From out in the living room, footsteps are heard, and then the bathroom door shutting.

"Bíbí, would you forgive me if I did something terribly stupid?" Hörður asks in a broken voice.

"Like what?"

He swallows sour-tasting saliva. What should he say? What *shouldn't* he say? "Just, I don't know."

"Have you started smoking again?"

Hörður feels slightly relieved. This was the straw he needed to clutch at. "Almost, Bíbí, almost. I bought a pack but then gave it away. I was going to light up, but it didn't happen."

"It's only natural to fall into temptation. But you resisted the temptation, that's what counts—not anything else."

"Yes, maybe," mutters Hörður. Did he smoke any of those menthol cigarettes? Does it matter? He hears Silja flush the toilet, and shortly afterward, she unlocks the bathroom door and walks toward the bedroom.

"You mustn't judge yourself too harshly, darling."

Hörður looks up. Silja, standing in the doorway, smiles apologetically. She's pale and unkempt, as hungover as he is. "I've got to go now. I need to find out what this woman wants."

"Have a good day, Hörður! Maybe we can talk tonight?"

"You too … yes." Hörður hangs up. He feels like the biggest jerk who's ever walked the earth.

"Hi," says Silja hoarsely. "I don't want to bother you and all that. But do you think you could give me a ride home?"

Hörður can't bring himself to look in her direction. "Be out in a sec. I just need to get dressed and stuff."

"Okay," she says. "Maybe I should make some coffee?"

He nods.

"I'll do that."

Silja leaves, and Hörður opens the wardrobe and takes out his uniform, freshly pressed and still in its plastic bag from the dry cleaners. He hasn't worn these clothes since he was in the Patrol Division. These are the clothes he was wearing that cold morning when he and Vigfús, his old partner, stood guard at the taped-off murder scene in front of the parliament building. Vigfús had handed him a file including witness descriptions of the young man who had stabbed a member of the Alþingi to death with a knife and then disappeared into the night. Hörður realized that he had seen that same young man at a sports bar the night before, only a few hours before the murder. He went to the detective who was directing operations on the scene and told him about it. A few days later, he became part of the investigative team, and after the investigation was concluded, he was hired on a temporary basis as a plainclothes detective, and finally on a permanent basis.

His long-held dream had come true—not overnight, just slowly but surely. He had put in a great deal of effort, been lucky, and seized the opportunities that providence had put into his hands.

But then …

Hörður bears up. He's in such a vulnerable state that he could simply break down and start crying. So he tries not to think about the bad luck that caused him to end up in this place—out in the countryside with his old uniform in his hands, far from his home, his common-law partner, and the job he believes himself born to do.

His hands trembling, he puts on the fucking uniform. It's made of some sort of degenerate synthetic material that's wash-and-wear and repels dirt, but is too damn warm in the summer and too cold in the winter. The uniform consists of black trousers with countless pockets, a black shirt and black jacket with the police emblem at the shoulders and the word *Police* on the left breast. And of course the good old peaked cap that he always hated to wear and will hate wearing even more now, after having been free of it for a few years.

"The coffee is ready!" Silja calls from the kitchen.

Hörður takes a deep breath and then ambles to the kitchen, where he is met by a strong aroma of coffee. Silja has already poured him a steaming cup. He sits down at the kitchen table and lifts the cup tremblingly to his lips. The coffee is hot and strong and truly invigorating.

"Thanks," he mutters.

"You're welcome," says Silja warmly. She rummages through her purse and pulls out a blister pack of some tablets. "Want some, too?"

"What is it?" he asks.

"Parcodin forte," she replies.

"Oh, right," says Hörður hoarsely. Silja smiles faintly as she squeezes two tablets out of the blister pack, then rinses each tablet down with a sip of coffee.

He looks at his watch. It's half past eight.

"You look great in your uniform," says Silja with a shy smile.

Hörður sighs ruefully. He doesn't feel well, to put it mildly, and the last thing he cares for just then is flirtation. "Tell me, did anything happen last night? I mean, I probably invited you here … or what?"

Silja looks slightly embarrassed. "Yes, you did. But no, nothing happened. You told me you were pretty much married and that nothing would happen between us. And nothing happened. We just drank beer and listened to music."

Hörður frowns. "Listened to music? Did I fix the turntable somehow?"

Silja gives a little smile. "No, we just used my phone. *Spotify*, you know. You really wanted me to hear a song. 'Love You to Death,' it's called. We listened to it probably five times, and the entire time you talked about your partner and how much you love her."

Hörður blushes.

"I was really hitting on you, I admit it," says Silja. "But it was just because I'm lonely, you see. I'm no slut, as everyone says. I'm just unhappy; it isn't the same."

"I understand," he says.

"Do you hate me?" she asks.

Hörður shakes his head. He doesn't hate anyone but himself, after all. "Why should I do that?"

Silja shrugs. "I might have ruined your reputation. Probably everyone knows that I came home with you yesterday. This is that kind of village; everyone here knows everything about everyone."

He sighs. "I guess I'm capable of destroying my own reputation. Although there's not much left of it to destroy."

"Do you think we can be friends?" she asks.

"Maybe, I don't know," says Hörður dryly. "Finish your coffee. It's best that I take you home."

Twenty minutes later, Hörður parks the SUV in front of the police station. In the rear-view mirror, he sees Júlíus driving the garbage truck along the gravel road leading down to the sands south of the highway. Behind the garbage truck, a thick cloud of dust swirls up and combines with the acrid diesel smoke from the noisy vehicle.

Hörður sighs. He let Silja out of the car in front of her house on Skaftárvellir, a tree-lined, beautiful street close to the kindergarten. They had met two or three other cars in the vicinity of the kindergarten, and Hörður doesn't doubt for a second what the hottest gossip in the village is at the moment. He made a mistake, no question about it, but as long as Bíbí doesn't hear of this stupidity of his, he may be able to live with it. He'll *have* to live with it, that much is sure. The only consolation is that he didn't cheat on Bíbí. His reputation has been tarnished, but his conscience is as good as clean.

"I'm a stupid fool," Hörður mutters as he shuts off the SUV's engine. He steps out into the summer and the sunshine and walks to his new workplace with narrowed eyes and a grimace on his pale face. Still, he feels a lot better, which means that the painkiller has started to work—praise be to God and the pharmaceutical industry. He unlocks the door and goes into the dark police station.

When Hörður turned five, he was given a birthday present he'll never forget. It was a cowboy outfit—a hat, vest, and belt with a holster and cap gun. The vest had fringes and a tin star fastened to it. On the star stood the word *SHERIFF*. He had put on the vest and hat and buckled on the gun belt, so happy and excited that his feet barely touched the ground. Then came the days and weeks he spent in an endless cowboy game that took place on the one hand in and around their old house, *Future,* in the village of Súðavík, with accompanying shouting, running, and pops that smelled of gunpowder, and on the other hand, and maybe not least, inside his head—on the huge playground of the imagination. He was Sheriff Hörður, lawman in a dangerous gold-mining town in the United States, where migrant workers and bandits flocked all year round. Not to mention the Indians who rode bareback over the prairies and tried to drive the palefaces off their hunting grounds. The red-haired sheriff had his hands full, and often ran into trouble. He regularly locked up lawbreakers, and then sat guarding them with his feet on the table and his gun in his lap, and his hat pushed nonchalantly over his forehead.

These fond memories pour over the new lieutenant in Kirkjubæjarklaustur as he sits there in his tired old desk chair in his office, with his feet crossed on top of the desk and his peaked cap in his lap. The police station is small but well organized, in many ways reminiscent of sheriff's offices in the Wild West towns of old Hollywood movies, such as the classic *High Noon,* which is highly regarded by the red-haired giant. To his right are a small break room and bathroom. He had found ground coffee, and the coffee machine is making a pot at the moment. On the left is a dark-green filing cabinet and next to it is a wall-mounted, locked, steel gun locker, painted gray. Hörður opened the gun locker with a small key on his key chain. Inside the locker are a five-round pump-action shotgun and a .22 caliber, bolt-action rifle, as well as ammunition for both guns. Behind the desk is a short corridor with two jail cells on one side and a small, windowless interrogation room on the other. The jail cells have steel-grated doors, as was customary in the Wild West.

Hörður clasps his fingers behind his head and looks into the vestibule, which is separated from the office by a locked door, a tall counter, and bulletproof plexiglass. Between the top of the counter and the glass is a gap approximately the size of the back of a person's hand. Those who have business with the lieutenant enter the vestibule and can ring the bell if no one is visible. The lieutenant can chat with the person through the gap in the glass, write things down if he needs to, or hand something over. But if he has to take a report from the person in question, he can open the office door and invite him to come inside with him, to the interrogation room, where they can have privacy.

Hörður nods wisely, as if agreeing to his own speculations about the lieutenant's workplace and his imaginary working methods. On the lieutenant's desk is a desktop computer that he hasn't switched on, a calendar that still shows April, a closed diary, and an old-fashioned desk phone that suddenly rings noisily.

"What the hell!" shouts Hörður, starting in alarm and feeling slightly faint, with a pain in his chest. Do they want to kill him on his first day? He swings his feet off the table and takes a deep breath before answering the phone. "Yes, hello?"

"*Hörður Grímsson?*" asks a deep-voiced man.

"That's me," says the red-haired giant.

"*Welcome to your new job! It's your boss speaking, Björn Bragi Björnsson, chief of police in the South.*"

"Thanks, Björn," says Hörður tentatively.

"*I expect you've settled in and are ready to start?*"

"Yes, yes," says Hörður.

"The summer traffic is reaching its peak. The roads are filled with not-very-intelligent tourists in rental cars. So we could really use you to keep a close watch on the highway, keep people's speed down and so on. How about you and Lieutenant Yngvi in Vík go for a little drive this afternoon?"

"Sounds fine," says Hörður, who can't tell whether this is a friendly suggestion or a politely worded order.

"For example, you could meet at the intersection at Ytri-Ásar and compare notes. That's pretty much right in the middle. That's what Yngvi and Steingrímur usually did."

"Understood," says Hörður, without having any idea what the police chief is talking about. But hopefully, this intersection is somewhere halfway between Vik in Mýrdalur and Kirkjubæjarklaustur.

"It's settled, then. Bye for now!"

"Goodbye," Hörður mutters before hanging up. Was the bastard giving him an order? Why be the lieutenant in charge of a certain precinct if you're not even allowed to choose what to do?

The red-haired giant rolls his shoulders moodily. He feels like disobeying these instructions. Besides, he's hardly in any condition to be out driving the country's highways. What if this Yngvi smells alcohol on him?

Hörður looks at his watch. It's twenty minutes past nine. Maybe he should just go home and lie down for a bit? Then he'll feel right as rain by noon. Ready for everything and all that.

Yes, that's what he'll do. Hörður puts on his cap and gets to his feet. He's barely halfway out of the police station when the desk phone rings again. But the new lieutenant can't be bothered to answer it. Instead, he shuts off the light and locks the front door behind him.

Sunbeams pierce through narrow cracks and nail holes. The corrugated iron shifts with low pops when it warms up. Outside, a bird or two chirps, but otherwise, there's only gloomy silence.

It's a new day…

The night was long, horrific, and cold—so terribly cold. Fragile memories and vague images rush through the mind and provoke nervous twitches—darkness, blows, fear and anguish, ropes and a bag over the head, blood and bruised flesh. An ice-cold dunking in a concrete tub, the squeaking of hinges and clicking of a padlock…

Hertha isn't sure if she's awake or trapped in a nightmare from which she can't wake up. She's exhausted, confused, sore, and cold. She's lying naked in the fetal position on a hard wooden floor, on top of a thin layer of dirty hay and tufts of wool that she scraped together with her fingers. She's trembling from head to toe, her teeth are chattering, and she's whimpering like a baby. The building she's in is big and dark and smells of sheep dung. It's an old outbuilding, like the one they visited earlier in the day at Systravatn Lake.

Or maybe it's the same building?

They…Hertha blinks her eyes, swollen with tears. Suddenly she remembers Barbara's screams after she was dunked in the water. She had screamed and screamed, so loud and so long that Hertha felt she would lose her mind.

But then the screams must have stopped. At least she isn't screaming any longer. Could she be…?

It's as if an electrical current rushes through Hertha's cold body. No, it can't be! It *mustn't* be! Barbara isn't dead.

No, no, no!

"Barbs!" Hertha shouts, but her voice is little more than a pitiful whine, like a poor kitten. She sits up, but bumps her head against the top of the cage. A cage, that's right, she remembers it now.

She's locked up in a cage like an animal.

If anything is better than bacon, eggs, and baked beans, it's bacon, eggs, baked beans *and* coffee! It's going on twelve noon and Hörður is a completely different man, having managed to get one and a half more hours of sleep. He woke up extremely hungry, which was good—he knows from experience that hunger pangs are the first sign that a hangover is finally at an end. Before making himself something to eat, he emptied the ashtray in the living room, gathered the empty beer cans, tidied up a bit, and aired out the house. Again, he noticed the locked room, which he had to remember to ask someone about.

He's made coffee and is finishing heating beans in the pan in which he fried the eggs and bacon. The pungent smell of the fried pork fat combines with the fragrance of the strong coffee and whets the red-haired giant's appetite. He *loves* fatty bacon, he *loves* runny egg yolks and he *loves* hot, black, square-shooting coffee! He also loves Bíbí, who would never give her blessing to this meal. She's worried about cholesterol, blood sugar, heart disease, and everything else that could possibly shorten the life of her beloved partner.

But what Bíbí doesn't know won't kill her husband! Hörður laughs at his own humor as he pours the simmering beans onto his plate, then puts the pan in the sink and switches off the stove.

Done!

Hörður sits down at the dinner table, pours himself a cup of coffee, and licks his lips. But he has barely started eating when his cell phone rings. He curses silently, washes down his mouthful of food with hot coffee, and gets up in a huff. Is there *never* any peace?

The phone is in the pocket of his uniform jacket in the vestibule. He fishes it out, looks at the screen, and answers it, despite not recognizing the number.

"Yes?"

"Is this the lieutenant?" asks a male voice.

Hörður sighs. "Yes, it is."

"This is Sindri at Kjarval."

"Oh, okay," says Hörður. Is he supposed to know who that is?

"I called the station earlier but no one answered. I went to it, but no one was there. I got your number from the district manager."

"What's your business?" Hörður asks irritably. He's hungry and his food and coffee are cooling down.

"I want to press charges for vandalism. Graffiti has been scrawled on the store's walls, and I know who the culprit is!"

"Oh, okay," says Hörður apathetically. "What store is that?"

"Kjarval, I said!"

"Yes, of course," says Hörður. The grocery store in Klaustur is named Kjarval; how could he forget that? It's where he bought the bacon, eggs, and beans that are cooling down on his plate. "I'll stop by later."

"Thanks."

Hörður shakes his head and puts his phone back in his jacket pocket. Graffiti! Well, at least there isn't any violent crime here in the countryside. He finishes eating, then washes the dishes and pan and puts them away. After that, he puts on his shoes, jacket, and cap, and opens the door to the sun deck in front of the house—a deck that's actually so shady it's probably wrong to call it a *sun* deck. The microwave is still sitting there on it, burned and disgusting.

Shouldn't he throw it out?

Hörður opens the trunk of the SUV and puts the microwave in it, next to the box holding the winter chains. Then he remembers the defective turntable. Should he take it for repairs to the priest? Yes, why not. He goes back inside and gets the turntable, which he puts in the SUV's front seat. Before sitting down behind the wheel, he looks at the teacher's residence, where Adam and his family live. The curtains are drawn shut and there are no signs of life. The beige pickup truck is in the parking lot, but the camouflage-colored six-wheeler is gone.

It's warmer than the day before, and Hörður drives into the village with his side window open and his elbow sticking out of it, like a modern sheriff in a small American town. All that's missing is for him to be driving a real American eight-cylinder SUV, and wearing a cowboy hat and pistol. He parks the SUV in front of the Kjarval store and steps out onto the sunbaked parking lot. To the right of the store's entrance is a woman on her knees with a scrub brush in her hand and a bucket of soapy water beside her. She's busy scrubbing off graffiti scrawled on the dull-yellow concrete wall. Above the woman stands a man of around forty, thin-haired and skinny, wearing a red smock over jeans and a shirt, white socks, and Adidas house shoes.

"Have you seen anything like it?" the man in the smock asks unceremoniously when he sees Hörður approaching.

"I've seen more in my short life than I've cared to," mutters the red-haired giant, who deduces that the irritated man in the smock is Sindri, the store's manager. Hörður glances at the graffiti, which is a single word written in black marker:

METALLICA

"And people say that nothing ever happens here," says Hörður sarcastically.

"As I told you, I know who the culprit is!" says Sindri, with a look that's both gloating and spiteful. "He was spotted doing it, see!"

"Okay," says Hörður, who doesn't feel like filling out a report on such a trivial matter. "Then why are you getting the police involved in this? Can't you just contact the person and ask him to clean it up or paint the wall?"

Sindri scoffs. "Fannar will never see reason until the police shake him by the scruff of the neck! The boy is spoiled and has gotten away with too much for too long. It's enough, I say!"

"All right," says Hörður reluctantly. He squints in the sunshine. The painkiller has pretty much stopped working, and he has a headache and some sort of nervous irritation. He knows very well why he's irritated, and what he needs to do to get rid of it. "I'm going to talk to this Fannar. Do you know where he lives?"

"Of course," says Sindri indignantly. "He and his mother Sesselja live at the end of Túngata Street. The boy had no proper upbringing. It's certainly not ideal growing up fatherless, like him."

"Probably not," says Hörður, just to say something. He feels the good old irritation growing rather than the opposite, and knows from experience that the situation won't improve until he does something about it. What he wants most is a cigarette, but…

Hörður drives farther into the village, chomping strong menthol-flavored nicotine gum. He finds it neither fun nor tasteful to chew gum, but he's tired of the patches, and nicotine spray is just sort of…pompous, he thinks. So, chewing gum it is.

He parks the SUV on the sidewalk in front of a beautiful single-family house on Skerjavellir, the street at the foot of the mountain. It's a red wooden house with white eaves and white windows. Next to it is a large garage of the same color. In the yard are big, tall trees that are a part of the woods at the base of the mountainside. Based on what Adam said, this should be the home of the priest and jack-of-all-trades, Reverend Páll. Hörður decided to bring the turntable for repairs first and then see whether he feels like going and finding that graffiti-scrawling juvenile delinquent, who clearly has hopeless taste in music.

Hörður takes the turntable with him and walks up to the house. He's about to knock on the door but stops when he hears metallic blows coming from the garage. On the side of the garage, a door stands halfway open. The red-haired giant knocks on the door frame and peeks inside.

"Hello?"

"Come in," someone calls.

Hörður pushes on the door and strides over the threshold with the turntable in his grasp; his eyes open wide and he stands there staring in surprise and delight. The garage is definitely big, but is so full of machinery, various equipment, electrical devices, and other stuff that it appears barely possible to move around in it without running into something or knocking one's head on the things protruding from the shelves or hanging from the ceiling.

The long, wide workbench is covered with tools, cans, boxes, and various spare parts. On the wall above it is a large wooden board from which countless tools hang on hooks, each in its own place, with their outlines drawn on the board. Above and below the workbench are long shelves that hold the most unlikely of electrical equipment and all sorts of other things, from old toys to microwaves and computers. Covering the floor are lawnmowers, motorboat engines, motorbikes and snowmobiles, disassembled cars and one or two things that are hard to figure out. Hanging from the rafters are skates, skis, and sleds, very old utensils and tools, along with slabs of cured shark and unpounded hardfish. An old radio is playing Channel One and the air smells of coffee, motor oil, and gasoline.

In the middle of the room, an elderly man is bent over a grass trimmer. He is short and slim, with salt-and-pepper hair, glasses on his nose, and a tidy, full beard. Like Sindri at Kjarval, he's wearing a smock, but the old man's is blue, not red, and is so dirty that it's actually black.

The old man looks over the tops of his glasses at the red-haired giant, who stares inquiringly at him.

"You must be…?" Hörður stops mid-sentence, having almost said Reverend Jón Prímus, as the man and everything around him remind the policeman of the famous character from the Halldór Laxness novel *Christianity Under the Glacier.*

"My name is Páll," says the old man, before knocking several times on the grass trimmer with a small hammer.

"And do you repair Primuses, by any chance?" the policeman asks in a low voice.

"Huh?" Páll asks distractedly. "Who's a primate?"

The red-haired giant clears his throat. "I'm the new lieutenant. Hörður Grímsson."

"You don't say," says Páll. He puts down his hammer, wipes the grease off his fingers onto his smock, takes a step closer in his black wooden clogs and holds out his hand to the lieutenant.

Hörður shifts the turntable to his left arm and greets the priest, who shakes the huge paw of the red-haired giant firmly. The old man may be skinny and sinewy, but he's as vigorous as a Westfjords fisherman.

"Welcome to Klaustur," says Reverend Páll. "It's a really nice place to live. But…" He shrugs and smiles apologetically.

"But nothing ever happens here?" Hörður guesses.

Páll laughs softly. "Which is good for us residents. But maybe less exciting for a police detective from the capital."

Hörður blushes. Does *everyone know* who he is?

"But it rains here very often, which can be tiring, but 'good for the growth,' as the saying goes," says the priest. "Actually, I have a feeling it's going to rain this evening or tonight, and hard, too."

"Oh?" asks Hörður skeptically, as there's hardly been a wisp of a cloud in the sky since he came east.

"I can feel it in my bones," says the Reverend. "My rheumatism gets worse when there's a low-pressure system on the way."

"Is that so," says Hörður, who can't tell if the old man is messing with him or not.

"But what can I do for you?" asks Páll, who has the calm and gentle demeanor that's often characteristic of old priests—a demeanor that reminds the red-haired giant mainly of a castrated tomcat.

Hörður lifts the turntable higher. "It's this here. Something's wrong with it. I think the drive belt has fallen off or has simply broken. I don't have the tools to open this gadget, and was advised to talk to you."

Páll looks over the turntable, like a doctor evaluating a patient. Then he signals the policeman to follow him. "Let's have a look at it."

The Reverend walks to the workbench, makes space in the middle of it and then steps aside so that Hörður can put the turntable down. Páll immediately hunches over it, but the policeman lets his eyes wander curiously around the garage's interior.

"This place is a sight to see," says Hörður out loud, immediately getting the embarrassing feeling that he must have sounded just like Gísli Einarsson in *Our Countrymen*, the weekly television show in which people from all parts of Iceland tell about their lives. *This episode of* Our Countrymen *comes to you from a garage in Kirkjubæjarklaustur where the jack-of-all-trades and fire cleric, Reverend Páll, fixes equipment…*

"Yes, yes," Páll mutters, without looking away from the turntable.

Hörður shakes off his disdain for such a lame scenario and continues to look around, but at the same time, is careful not to bump into things or turn anything upside down. All his life, the red-haired giant has been like an elephant in a china shop due to his size. He sets eyes on a fine-looking sled that evokes nostalgic memories for him, even though he himself never owned such a sled as a child.

"Beautiful sled," says Hörður.

With a screwdriver in hand, Páll looks up. "Yes, and quite old."

Hörður turns his attention to several wooden cigar boxes stacked one on top the other on the workbench. He opens the topmost one to reveal a collection of badges, old coins, and medals. He rummages a bit through the contents and quickly finds a magnificent military decoration that he takes out and holds in his palm. It's a five-pointed star hanging on a white, red, and blue ribbon that has become crumpled and discolored. In the center of the star is a small diamond star within a gold laurel wreath. Hörður recognizes the medal from books on WWII. It's an American military Silver Star, awarded for outstanding bravery in combat.

"Where did these medals come from?" Hörður asks, holding up the medal.

Páll looks up again. "Those cigar boxes were part of the estate of someone from Höfn in Hornafjörður and ended up with me after some roaming. If you find something you like, you can take it."

"This is an important medal," says Hörður. "And valuable, maybe. You should maybe try selling it on eBay."

Páll shakes his head and continues working on opening up the turntable. "I'm not on the Internet and have no interest in any wheeling and dealing. And it isn't mine, either. It just ended up here, as I said."

"Up to you." Hörður sticks the medal in his pocket, then goes on exploring the great treasure trove that the priest's garage undeniably is. *Our Countrymen* should really come and visit this modern Reverend Jón Prímus, he thinks. On one shelf is an old Singer sewing machine, black with gold lettering, and next to it is a device that catches the red-haired giant's attention. It's a large, unwieldy Akai portable cassette player, silver in color. When Hörður was a teenager, some of his peers had such treasures, which could either be plugged in or run on batteries and taken anywhere.

"Where did this boom box come from?" Hörður asks. He lifts the player and blows dust off it. It's apparently been in the priest's garage for a long time.

"Boom-what?" Páll asks.

"This cassette player," says Hörður. He gives the device a good looking-over. On its bottom is a closed compartment for large batteries. On the front are two rectangular speakers behind wire mesh, and between them is the deck into which the cassette tape is inserted. Above the drawer, a red plastic strip with white, embossed letters has been affixed.

There's one word on the strip, presumably the name of the device's owner:

Johanna

"Yes, that," says the priest. "The late Geirharður brought the device to me shortly before he died. I don't remember if it was broken or not, but he at least wanted me to take it."

"Geirharður," mutters Hörður. Didn't Adam mention some Geirharður? Yes, but he doesn't remember in what context. "But the cassette player is marked Johanna. I remember those plastic labels. The little machine that you put a roll in, and then pressed letters into the plastic by turning the dial and squeezing the handle. Everyone used to label their stuff with those, but you never see it anymore."

"Johanna was a German girl who drowned in Eldvatn many years ago," says Páll. "Around 1970, as I recall. She worked as a farmhand for Geirharður and Sigrún, and had a huge interest in Icelandic horses."

Hörður tries to open the device's cassette deck, where the cassette tape is inserted. It's empty. "Are you telling me that this device has been here in your garage since 1970?"

Páll shakes his head. "Geirharður brought it to me in the fall of 1983. I still remember the date because it was shortly before he died, the poor fellow. He had found it in storage and couldn't bring himself to throw it out."

"I see," says Hörður, who is listening with only one ear. On the back of the device is a small socket for a power cord.

"You can keep the player if you'd like," says the priest. "It doesn't belong to anyone."

"Thanks," says Hörður, who definitely has his eye on this outdated treasure. "Didn't its cord come with it? You know, to plug it in. Devices like this are quick to drain batteries, if I remember correctly."

"There's a plastic bag over there somewhere, with some rubbish in it," Páll answers. "It came with the player. The cord could be in there."

Hörður immediately sees the plastic bag. It's old and discolored, and its handles have been tied into a knot. He opens the bag and peeks into it. The good old cord is in fact in the bag, but what makes the red-haired giant even happier are the cassettes that are there, too—ten or twelve original tapes in specially made cases. In the 1970s, music was widely recorded onto empty cassette tapes from records or the radio. Such *original* cassettes weren't a common sight when Hörður was a teenager.

"This is a treasure trove!" says Hörður cheerfully. The bag's tapes include not only classic rock like The Kinks, Jimi Hendrix, and Creedence Clearwater Revival, but also precious gems like *Wish You Were Here* by Pink Floyd, *Harvest* by Neil Young, and—he can hardly believe his own eyes—a greatest-hits collection of the prog band Kansas. "I'll take the cassette player for sure, no question about it!"

"Glad to hear it—then you'll make a small dent in the amount of junk in here," says Páll. "But I've opened the turntable and it's the belt, as you thought. It's broken. I don't have a new one, of course, but maybe I can rig something for it."

"It would be great if you could fix it," says Hörður as he brushes dust off the cassette player. "But if not, no worries. If this cassette player works, then my summer is saved."

"Okay, good to hear." The priest smiles at the giant newcomer. "It's always nice to be able to help. Check back in with me later, and who knows, maybe I'll have found a belt for the turntable."

"I'll do that." Hörður makes his way back toward the door. "I expect you know everyone in the village?"

"At least I know who everyone *is*," Páll answers sagely. "But when do you know someone and when do you not know someone? I've got the names and faces pretty much clear. Except for maybe the Poles who work at the fish farm. The Catholics don't attend my masses."

"Of course not," said Hörður dryly. He himself is something of a Catholic. He was raised in that religion, but the injustices of life have gradually turned him into a bitter skeptic, even an atheist. But deep within him there's always a small spark of faith that makes the darkness a little more bearable.

"Why do you ask?" says the priest.

"Hm?" says Hörður, who had *dropped out a little*, as he likes to call it when his attention wanders. "Oh, about you knowing everyone? Just, I heard about a kid who apparently scrawled some graffiti on the wall of the store. His name is Fannar."

Páll nods. "The son of Sesselja, Bubbi's widow. He's a decent kid, Fannar. But fatherless and a bit lost. His mother has raised him by herself, and naturally, has done her best. But she had the boy at a very young age and has had to do it all alone. She works at the fish farm—a very hard worker, from what I understand. Fannar isn't a bad kid. He's just gone a little astray, the poor dear."

Hörður parks the SUV at the end of Túngata Street, a short distance from a small, unpretentious single-family house standing a bit off by itself. He goes to the door and reads the label next to the letterbox before ringing the doorbell.

Sesselja Ásbjarnardóttir
Fannar Sesseljuson
When no one answers, he rings the bell again. After several moments, a teenage boy whom the red-haired giant

recognizes immediately opens the door. It's the bashful boy who stuck his nose into Systrakaffi Café the night before—the one who then stepped out with the truck driver, Hallgrímur. The boy has blond hair, and is pale and seems a bit on edge. He's wearing baggy trousers, socks with holes in them, and a hoodie bearing the logo of the *Trasher* skateboard magazine.

"Yes?" he asks, clearly startled.

"Hello. I'm the new police lieutenant." Hörður smiles faintly. "May I come in?"

"I suppose so," replies Fannar. He lets the red-haired giant into the hall and leads him into the kitchen. "Mom isn't home. But I can make coffee for you if you want."

"No need, thanks. I won't be stopping for long," says Hörður. He notices that both the boy's eyes are bloodshot and glossy, and has certain suspicions. The strong smell of incense strengthens those suspicions. "Would you mind if we go to your room?"

"All right," says Fannar hesitantly. Hörður follows him down a short hallway to a darkened room at its end. The room's window curtains are drawn shut and the air is stuffy, heavy with the smells of body odor and incense. Fannar removes a pile of clothes from a desk chair and offers the policeman a seat. He himself sits down on the edge of the unmade bed.

"Let's start with the reason why I came here," says Hörður in a fatherly tone. "Sindri at Kjarval contacted me about some graffiti. Might it have been you who put it on the store's walls?"

Fannar blushes and looks away.

"First of all, graffiti is vandalism—you realize that, don't you?" says Hörður in the same fatherly tone. "It needs to be cleaned off or painted over."

Fannar inhales through his nose. He tries to maintain his composure, but clearly feels nervous; he's all twitchy and breathes shallowly.

"Maybe you should offer to help with that?" Hörður suggests. "Just to calm Sindri down and smooth things over. Then maybe he won't press charges against you."

Fannar shrugs.

"I highly recommend it," says Hörður firmly. "And then there's the other thing. What you scribbled on the wall. Metallica, really?"

Fannar gives the policeman a puzzled look.

Hörður sighs. "How unoriginal can you be? Metallica is just one big fat cliché. You could just as easily have scribbled *Coca-Cola* on the damn wall. That overrated band hasn't released a good album since 1986! When Cliff Burton died, Metallica died; it's as simple as that. I mean, 'Enter Sandman' is like some brainless radio hit by Alice Cooper! If you want to listen to heavy metal, listen to something good, for example Danzig or Entombed. Do you know those bands?"

Fannar hesitates, but then nods.

"Anyway," says Hörður. "If you're going to keep doing that graffiti crap, show some ambition, huh? Otherwise, it's better just to let it go."

"Okay," says Fannar, his voice weak from stress.

"But then there's one other thing—more serious," says Hörður, before pausing for effect. "Are you in tenth grade?"

Fannar nods.

"And how's it going?" Hörður asks. "Do you think you can pass your exams and get into junior college?"

"I guess," mutters Fannar. "It doesn't matter. I'm not planning on going to any stupid junior college. Why?"

"So you're just going to get a job at the fish farm here?" Hörður asks. "Just go on living with your mom? Get stuck here?"

Fannar shrugs. "Maybe I'll just move overseas or something."

"How long have you been smoking weed?" asks Hörður in a gentle voice.

Fannar's face reddens. "What do you mean?"

"Don't try to argue or wriggle your way out," says Hörður. "You may be able to fool your mom, but I can see through you. Just answer the question."

"Just, kind of…a year, maybe," Fannar mutters, staring at the floor.

Hörður sighs. "That damn weed is brain-numbing rubbish. You use it as an escape route or anesthesia, but at the same time dig your own grave. It makes you apathetic, unambitious, and eventually brainless. Screws up your schooling and your future along with it. One day you'll look in the mirror and see a full-grown loser who has nothing, can do nothing, and knows nothing."

"What future?" Fannar asks, before finally opening up. "It doesn't matter whether I finish school or not. I don't matter, nothing matters—not in the big picture. The universe is endless, right, and therefore irrational, because nothing can be endless, can it? How could it be? So, maybe everything is just imagination, which means it doesn't matter whether someone goes to school or work or not. Don't you get it? Why have any ambition if nothing is really real and you've got nothing ahead of you but study, work, and then death?"

"Well…" Hörður hadn't expected such a speech, and is tongue-tied for a few seconds. "Let's say it's like that, as you said. But then isn't it best to try to do something sensible while you're here at Hotel Earth, instead of wasting the one life you have in pointlessness and nonsense?"

Fannar scoffs.

"It's your choice, of course," says Hörður dryly. "But I've got to ask you to hand over all your drugs."

Fannar sighs, and then opens a desk drawer and pulls out a small plastic bag containing a small amount of dark-green weed, along with rolling papers. Hörður takes the bag from him and sticks it his jacket pocket.

"Where do you get the drugs?" asks the red-haired giant.

Fannar shrugs before lying directly to the lieutenant. "Just, from tourists."

"All right," says Hörður. "But if I ever see you near the truck driver Hallgrímur again, I'll arrest you both. Do you understand?"

Fannar's face pales, and he nods quickly.

When Hörður parks his SUV in the shade of the spruce trees at the police lieutenant's house in Efri-Vík, he sees the six-wheeler in its place in front of the garage of the teacher's house, next to the camouflage-colored pickup truck. So Adam is probably at home, but the curtains are still drawn shut. Hörður gets out of the SUV, taking with him the Akai portable cassette player and the bag holding the power cord and cassettes. He catches a glimpse of something on the six-wheeler's dump bed, and Hörður notices that there's a smudge of some sort on its gas tank. He walks closer to the muddy vehicle. In the dump bed are several bloody carcasses: five minks and two foxes. Adam has apparently been out doing some shooting. The smudge on the gas tank is a brownish streak with a blurred fingerprint at its wider end; probably blood.

Hörður stands there unmoving for several moments, looking at the teacher's house, its front yard and the swing on which no one plays. Why are the curtains drawn shut? Where are Adam's wife and daughter? Why is the kid never out playing? It's not really any of his business, but why is the house so *quiet,* as if no one is home?

The red-haired giant shrugs and goes to the lieutenant's house, which is even quieter and more depressing than the teacher's house, looking more like a dilapidated cottage from a horror movie in which half-naked teenage idiots are killed one after another by a deranged murderer.

He opens the door, walks in, and kicks off his shoes.

It's only six o'clock, but Hörður has started making dinner, as he was getting bored and had nothing else to do. So he turned on the stove under the frying pan and has taken out bacon, eggs, and a can of baked beans, which was all he had apart from microwave food. I guess I'll have to go to the store again soon, he thinks. There was one can of Egill's Gold left in the fridge. He opens the cold can and takes a drink. He went swimming, changed clothes, and chatted with Bíbí, who talked for a long time about everything and nothing, as usual. It was nice talking to her, but it also made him feel a little lonely afterwards, and her, too, no doubt. Long-distance relationships aren't easy, that's for sure.

As the pan is heating up and the butter melting, he plugs in the cassette player, inserts a cassette into it, and presses play. The device kicks into gear, the cassette's wheels rotate, the speakers crackle softly, and then the first song on side one of Neil Young's masterpiece *Harvest* starts playing—"Out on the Weekend." The song is sweet, like the entire album and the artist's voice. Hörður smiles widely—it being a completely different life, having music there in his new home, filling the void. Whistling to the music, he goes to the stove and breaks three eggs on the edge of the frying pan. He takes another drink of beer. The eggs are just starting to fry in the simmering butter when he hears his cell phone ring.

Never any peace! Hörður turns down Master Young just a touch, then looks for and finds his phone. On the screen is a landline number that he recognizes immediately. Someone is calling from the police station on Hverfisgata Street in Reykjavík. Probably Axel M. Axelsson, checking in on *his man* in the countryside. About time, thinks Hörður, who is relieved, but is first and foremost grateful that old Steppenwolf hasn't completely forgotten him, as he feared.

"Hello, sir!" answers the red-haired giant, loudly and clearly.

"Sir?" says a woman's voice at the other end. *"I'm still a woman, the last I knew."*

"Þóra?" Hörður asks hesitantly as disappointment pours over him.

"That's me."

"I'm sorry," says Hörður. "I just saw the number and thought Axel was calling."

"Sorry to disappoint you."

"Ha ha, no no, not at all," says Hörður, with pretend cheerfulness.

"Okay. So how's life out east? Have you settled in and all that?"

"Yes, yes, kind of," Hörður answers. He goes back into the kitchen, squeezing the phone between his ear and shoulder so that he can remove the eggs with a spatula, but they've already stuck to the hot pan. "I didn't bring much with me and the house isn't big, either; no more than the police station."

"I see. And what, was today your first day of work?"

"Yeah." Hörður struggles to scrape the eggs, which have started to burn, free from the pan. "And I'm plenty busy, too, see—or kind of. But, you know, someone put graffiti on the wall of the store and I confiscated weed from the village's troubled teenager. It was actually him who scrawled on the wall, but still..."

Þóra laughs. *"Well done!"*

"Actually, I've pretty much uncovered a small dope ring," says Hörður. He's transferred the half-burned eggs to his plate, but not in their entirety—two yolks cracked during the operation, to his dismay. "The mule here in this area is named Hallgrímur, a truck driver who lives in Vík in Mýrdalur. He gets his stuff from someone who lives in Hvolsvöllur or thereabouts. That person drives a bright green Subaru Impreza. The only thing I don't know is whether the contact person at Hvolsvöllur is the ringleader or a middleman."

"All this in one day?"

Hörður gives a little smile as he arranges bacon slices on the pan. "Yes—I am a police detective, aren't I?"

"Yes, yes," says Þóra dryly.

Hörður pushes the sizzling bacon slices with the spatula. "How about you? Did you just come on an evening shift?"

"Exactly. Listen, I've got to go. Good to hear from you. We'll be in touch!"

"Likewise, and of course." Hörður puts down the phone and tuns the music up again. Was Þóra angry? He thinks so, but isn't sure. She can be difficult to read.

Hörður puts the bacon on his plate, opens a can of baked beans and pours the contents onto the pan. He quaffs cold beer from its can. The beans have just started simmering when the phone rings again. What's going on, anyway? Displayed on the phone's screen is a landline number that he recognizes, but can't place at the moment. He lowers the music again and answers the phone.

"Yes?"

"Hello, Hörður. This is Björn Bragi here again, chief of police in the South."

Hörður rolls his eyes. "Yes, hello."

"Am I interrupting?"

"No, not really," says Hörður. Again he squeezes the phone between his ear and shoulder, stirs the beans a little, and turns off the stove. "I'm cooking dinner."

"Did you leave work early today?"

Early? Hörður thinks. What was he supposed to do? Hang around the station and stare into the air? "No, no, just around five o'clock."

"It's customary for the lieutenant to be on duty until seven, and sometimes nine. Maybe not always, but from time to time, at least."

"Okay," says Hörður, who is now both hungry and irritated. He pours the hot beans onto the plate, over the eggs and bacon.

"You never went to meet Yngvi today. He waited for you at the intersection and made several attempts to call you on the radio."

Hörður puts his plate on the kitchen table and the pan in the sink. Is the bastard reprimanding him as if he were some kid? "Yes, something just came up. I had to deal with some of the locals. But I didn't hear anything on the radio. Maybe it isn't on; I don't know."

"You don't have your radio switched on?"

Hörður sighs. "As I said, I don't know. I just assumed it was on, but didn't actually check it."

"Having the radio on at all times is critical, absolutely critical!"

Hörður's face reddens with irritation. This yokel *is* reprimanding him! "Yes, right…I'll check it at the first opportunity."

"Call us up in the morning, me and Yngvi. We'll get synchronized via radio and organize the day. Right?"

"No problem," mutters Hörður.

"We'll say that, then—over and out!"

"What a fucking clown!" Hörður snaps as he hangs up. He feels like hurling his cell phone at the wall. Who the hell does this stupid country cop think he is? Doesn't he know who he's talking to? "Fucking idiot!"

There's a click when side one of the cassette ends, but Hörður is in a bad mood and doesn't turn the tape over. He grabs a fork and knife and sits down at the kitchen table, but is so upset that he has almost lost his appetite. What's more, the food doesn't look very good. The eggs are burned and the yolks broke, the bacon is soft, not crispy, and it seems that he hasn't heated the beans thoroughly. And he forgot the salt and pepper, of course.

He'd done much better at lunchtime…

The red-haired giant sighs, then finishes his beer in one gulp. It's half past six. What now? If only he had one, two more beers. And something other to eat than this crappy bean mush. If he hadn't already been drinking, he would drive into the village and eat at the shop or at Systrakaffi Café. Maybe he should call Adam again? Yes, why not. He looks up his neighbor's number on his phone and calls him. After six or seven rings, Adam answers.

"Hello."

"Are you busy at the moment?" Hörður asks as cheerfully as he can.

"No, not really." Adam doesn't sound cheerful at all, but maybe he always sounds like that. Hörður isn't sure.

"What do you say we go get a pizza or a hamburger?" asks the red-haired giant.

"Not now. I'm a little under the weather. I'm just going to take it easy."

"Oh, are you ill, or…?" asks Hörður, who can't really take much more disappointment this day.

"Yes, maybe. I don't know."

"No, yeah…right," says Hörður, before remembering something. "Listen, there's one room here in the house that's locked. Do you know what's inside it or where the key is?"

"No, but the key must be somewhere."

"Yes, one would think so," says Hörður. "But I still haven't found it, neither here nor at the station."

"It´ll turn up."

"Hopefully," says Hörður, who is so bored that he decides to stretch the conversation out a bit instead of putting a quick end to it, as he usually would. "What's up with your wife and daughter, by the way?"

"What's up? What do you mean?"

"Just," says Hörður. "I haven't seen them."

"They're just in Reykjavík at the moment. Did someone say something?"

"Did someone say what?" Hörður asks confusedly.

"Nothing. Forget it. Was there anything else?"

Hörður sighs. What a bizarre conversation! "No, not for now. Goodbye."

"Bye."

Hörður plugs his phone into its charger, then plunks down onto the living-room sofa and stares. What now? It's not just that he's bored. His ego has also taken a bit of a hit. The phone call from Björn Bragi in Hvolsvöllur didn't sit well with him. He felt as if the police chief was talking down to him, which was of course humiliating. He's irritable and has a bad taste in his mouth. Instead of being a king in his own kingdom here in Klaustur, he's just an errand boy for a little king who has probably never investigated a murder case, let alone arrested dangerous men.

He should never have accepted this damn lieutenant's position! Damn, he's pissed off at himself, but he's even more pissed off at that bastard Axel, who practically forced him to accept this damn act of charity, and then just acts as if Hörður doesn't exist!

Maybe Axel just wanted to get rid of him? Was that it? Hörður curses under his breath as he thinks of how he'll get his revenge on old Steppenwolf. He who viewed himself as a policeman by the grace of God, having become a successful detective in the CID itself. But no, it took only lousy accidental discharge for his boss to freak out and banish him, and only to appease some fucking pen pushers and politicians!

Hörður snorts. No, no one knows what he has until it's gone—so true. In continuation of these heavy thoughts, his mind turns to what Fannar had said earlier in the day. In what was in fact something of a soliloquy. What was it he said, again? *I don't matter, nothing matters—not in the big picture. The universe is endless, and therefore irrational because nothing can be endless, can it? So, maybe everything is just imagination, which means it doesn't matter whether someone goes to school or work or not. Why have any ambition if nothing is really real and you've got nothing ahead of you but study, work, and then death?*

Hörður nods thoughtfully. It was something along those lines, and there's a lot to what that idiot kid said—he has to admit.

Besides, the universe isn't just irrational, but non-existent, theoretically speaking. Before the Big Bang there was *nothing*, and then the whole universe came into being out of *nothing*. It's composed of matter and an equal amount of antimatter, so its total mass is *zero*—nothing.

If the universe is nothing, since it's created from nothing, then who is Hörður Grímsson and what the hell is he doing in the turbulent sea of life? Does anything matter? Does anyone matter? *Is* there anything?

He ponders these questions a little, a bit as if tasting an expensive wine—letting them float around in his mind and tasting their effects with a spiritual tongue. Then he opens his eyes wide, because he suddenly remembers the weed he took from the boy. It's still in the pocket of his jacket.

Should he?

Hertha is lying naked in a fetal position in a wooden cage. She's trembling and staring blankly into the darkness. Her wrists are red and sore from the rope that was tightened around her hands before she was pulled crying from the cage. She has one hand over her left ear, which is bloody—it's missing a piece. There are dry streaks of blood on her chalk-white face. She's numb with cold, pain, and terror. Her sense of time is now just a nightmarish haze. Somewhere in the distance, Barbara screams. She was pulled out of her cage after Hertha was locked back inside hers. Hertha knows very well what torments Barbara is suffering. Another scream cuts into her ears, tears through her nervous system, and flashes like lightning in her mind.

It's dark outside, the wind is picking up and heavy raindrops hammer on the corrugated iron. Thunder shakes the earth.

Hertha rolls her eyes. Thunder? Was the lightning she saw real, and not imaginary?

It's evening, but the sky isn't apricot-colored; the summer sun is gone and the temperature is dropping fast. The rain hits windows and roofs and the wind is getting stronger and stronger. The priest was right after all. Hörður has drawn the curtains shut, lit candles, and put the Kansas tape in the cassette player. He's sitting at the living-room table, rolling a fat joint with the weed and rolling papers he confiscated on Túngata Street. Naturally, he shouldn't be doing this, but found no decent reason not to.

Yolo, as the kids say—you only live once.

Hörður rolls the joint between his huge fingers, then sticks it between his thick lips and lights it. The sweet smoke tickles his throat and lungs; he coughs gently and takes a drink of water. After a few more puffs, the weed starts working; the high flows like a cold stream into his limbs and up into his head, where there's a silent, numbing explosion. The red-haired giant smiles widely, stares sluggishly into space and sinks into the sofa, both heavy and light as a feather. He giggles, smacks his tongue, and relishes relaxing and melting into eternity and timelessness and getting lost in thoughts, fluttering words, random memories, and colorful feelings. One song on the cassette tape ends and another begins. It's his dad Grímur's favorite song, the touching ballad "Dust in the Wind." One of the best songs ever written, in the opinion of the crochety ship's engineer, and his grown-up son can't help but agree. The song is sweet, the performance is outstanding and the singing is clear and beautiful. But it's the lyrics that elevate the otherwise simple and straightforward song to a higher level and transform it into timeless genius. Simple but beautiful lyrics that fit the melody so well and deal with the impermanence of existence, the sad fact that all we are is memories, thoughts, and the current moment, that everything will fade, crumble, and disappear—the flowers, the mountains, and we ourselves.

I close my eyes, only for a moment, and the moment's gone. All my dreams pass before my eyes, a curiosity. Dust in the wind. All they are is dust in the wind…

Hörður shuts his eyes again, allowing the song to flow through his consciousness as he thinks of his father, who had good taste in music. Fragile memories of the red-haired giant's childhood and adolescence in Súðavík blow through his mind, like leaves in the wind. Faces, expressions, incidents, and scenes—even smells. He finds it easier to recall various things about his father than about others in his family, because they were never really that close. He looked up to the long-haired engineer and respected him, but Grímur could be distant, peevish, and brusque, except maybe when he drank. But when Hörður thinks of his mother, he feels a twinge of pain in his heart and his eyes fill with tears…

Same old song, just a drop of water in an endless sea. All we do crumbles to the ground though we refuse to see. Dust in the wind. All we are is dust in the wind…

The song ends and Hörður, sobbing, wipes away his burning-hot tears. How he misses his mother, the red-haired, cheerful Valkyrie. How he hates the cruel God who brought an avalanche down over Súðavík, killed half the village and robbed him of everything he loved. Or are deadly catastrophes maybe proof that there's no God?

He pulls himself together, sits up, and takes another hit from the joint. He holds the smoke in for a long time, desperately needing its anesthetic effects. He lets the heavy smoke flow over his thoughts and feelings. He longs to sink into oblivion, disappear like a whale into the depths of a dark sea. The cassette's wheels revolve and the music continues, like time and life, and the red-haired giant manages to let the beautiful sounds of the instruments and singing capture his attention once more. Kansas is a fantastic band that creates and plays original, high-quality music, different than all the brainless crap that the modern world has to offer. Nowadays, it's all about fame and popularity, at the expense of content and quality. No one has real skill or talent or is willing to put in the work, but everyone longs to become rich and famous, preferably overnight.

When did things change? When the music world stopped being a disjointed collection of ambitious, creative, and unpredictable artists and became a money-driven big business? Hörður thinks this over carefully, letting his mind travel with him back in time. He finally stops at the sugary, brainless, and hugely popular pop hit "Sugar Sugar" from 1969, the same year that the rock band Led Zeppelin released their first two albums. The band The Archies performed the hit "Sugar Sugar," but there was no real band by that name, just made-up cartoon characters in the spirit of Fred Flintstone. The song was written by two people who got this and that musician to play and sing it. In other words, the song was just a manufactured product like breakfast cereal or chewing gum, and in fact a new type of music was created with the advent of this sugar-sweet pop song—*bubblegum pop*. The song was played almost endlessly on the radio and raked in the cash. Publishing companies saw their opportunity. Why spend time cajoling eccentric artists and doped-up bands when you can just hire session musicians, record one pop song at a time and release them on a conveyor belt? The music industry was born and capitalism took over a world that was previously characterized by fertility and creativity. The result was castration, spiritual death…

Hörður nods, as if to agree with his own thoughts. But he could of course be wrong. Maybe the decline of Western popular music isn't the fault of "Sugar Sugar". But he finds it damn likely, in addition to it being so bloody symbolic because in his mind, *sugar* is neither more nor less than a symbol of all the evil plaguing Western society. Sugar is cheap and addictive; it distorts and damages the taste buds and makes us turn our backs healthy foods and crave the unhealthiest ones. It makes us fat, stupid, and greedy.

Greed, exactly, thinks Hörður thinks. Sugar is assuredly a symbol of all that is degenerate, but the root of evil is money and greed. We hunger not only for sugary crap and fatty foods but also for money, toys, and other junk. More money, more expensive toys, and newer junk. Greed is wanting more than you need. Greed is fishing with a trawl and not a line. We work longer and demand higher wages to be able to buy a new car, a bigger house, and more electronic equipment—and of course flights abroad, nicer vacations! But because everyone works so much to be able to acquire more, everyone is so tired, irritated, and stressed that they can't relax and enjoy what they do have, and besides, they don't have time to do so. Inside of us is an emptiness that we can't fill. We spend our lives in a race that can't be won.

"Chasing shadows," Hörður whispers with his eyes half-closed. Wow, awesome phrase! Maybe he should write it down? Yeah, man. But he's too heavy to get up from the sofa. Too stoned to write. He smiles faintly. His eyelids sink all the way down.

He nods off, he falls asleep.

Outside, the wind is still blowing hard, the rain is pouring down and lightning illuminates the night. Shortly afterward, there's a peal of thunder.

Hörður is walking through dark and gloomy woods. He proceeds carefully, because he's scared, perhaps lost.

He isn't familiar with his surroundings, in any case. But he has the feeling that he's wandered in these woods before. A flash of light blinds him, and he hears a crackling noise.

Ahead of him is a clearing. Hörður inches his way closer. His heart is pounding in his chest. The darkness in the clearing is wavy, as if it's a liquid. The clearing is a black hole, a vertical vortex that gradually turns into a long tunnel. Someone is limping out of the tunnel. It's a young woman, dressed in a nun's habit that's torn and tattered. The nun stares at Hörður with wild eyes. Her face is white as wax; in her clear eyes something is reflected, but what? She opens her mouth in a silent scream, stretches bloody hands toward him and …

"No!" The red-haired giant is startled by a loud booming noise that shakes the sky. He blinks several times as his consciousness re-grounds itself in reality. Are there really thunderstorms? Hörður is still on the sofa; his mouth is dry and he's terribly hungry. The candles have burned down, and the living room is dark. He smells something bitter, like burned plastic. He gets to his feet and feels his way toward the kitchen. Does he have anything to eat? He finds the light switch and clicks it, but nothing happens. Is the electricity out?

Hörður can hardly tell up from down anymore and decides just to go to bed. Half-dazed, he bumps into a door frame, but then finds the door to the bedroom and throws himself face-down on the unmade bed.

DEATH SHADOW

Saturday

He'd really wanted to sleep in …

Hörður drives into the village, with the SUV's window wipers and heater on full. It's more or less autumn weather, seven degrees Celsius and rain, but the wind has died down. The red-haired giant isn't at his best this morning; he slept badly, his head is fuzzy, and he has something of a black eye, left side, from running into one of the door frames sometime during the night. He started from sleep around half past seven when his cell phone started ringing for the third time in less than ten minutes. It turned out to be an employee of the Department of Civil Protection and Emergency Management. An unforeseen summer storm had formed in a warm pool in the Atlantic Ocean, and had then made its way quickly northwestward and hit Iceland's southern region. The fire department and search-and-rescue teams had been called out in response to flooding in Kirkjubæjarklaustur, and consequently, the local police station had to be contacted and the lieutenant summoned to the scene to direct operations and write reports on property damage and other such things if necessary. All according to the official contingency plan, the employee told the unsuspecting lieutenant.

To Hörður's surprise and considerable frustration, the house was both cold and without power when he was forced to get up. So he couldn't make coffee, let alone have a hot breakfast. So he just got going and drove straight to the police station, where he warmed himself over an electric heater while the coffee trickled into the coffee machine's pot. He simply *had* to get caffeine into his body before doing anything else, regardless of all else. Breakfast, on the other hand, would just have to wait. When the coffee was ready, he downed two hot cups of it before pouring the rest into a thermos that he took with him to the SUV, along with half a packet of cookies.

The SUV's tires kick up rainwater, the windshield wipers beat in quick rhythm, and the heater whines softly.

Something is happening, anyway, thinks the red-haired giant as he sits hunched behind the steering wheel, driving along Klausturvegur Road, past the chapel on one side and the Skaftá Visitor Center on the other. He notices broken tree branches and all sorts of debris and rubbish that the wind has left behind here and there. The road is covered with leaves, and rainwater flows in a strong current along the western edge of the sidewalk, as the drains can't handle the volume of water. Hörður drives past the hotel and then turns onto the sideroad leading to the school and the swimming pool. There he sees a fire truck and two large search-and-rescue vehicles, all three of which have their lights flashing. A few people are bustling around the vehicles, firefighters wearing beige-colored protective clothing and helmets on their heads, and search-and-rescue personnel in red and blue uniforms. As far as he can tell, they're all men. They're busying themselves with a portable water pump that runs on gasoline and is extremely noisy. From the pump, two yellowish hoses run in different directions. The shorter hose disappears through an open window and is sucking up water from the basement of the school building, while the longer hose winds down onto the field below the pool, where the brownish meltwater splutters into a huge puddle that then merges with the churning Skaftá river, which is a formidable sight to see, and is overflowing its banks in many places.

Hörður parks the SUV at the shoulder of the road but doesn't shut off the engine. He steps out into the rain and opens the vehicle's driver-side back door. In the seat is a folded black raincoat that he found at the police station. He puts the coat on over his uniform and turns up the collar. He likes the feel of this long rubber coat, as it reminds him of the gothic leather coat he always wore in his days in the CID.

Hörður puts on his cap and walks over to the firefighters and search-and-rescue personnel, who nod at him. All of them are locals, and volunteers, to boot. He greets them all with a handshake. The fire chief's name is Áki, a friendly man of around forty who works as a machinist at the fish farm, and Björgvin Geirharðsson is the leader of the Torch search-and-rescue unit. Hörður expects the temperamental Björgvin not to be too friendly toward him, considering their previous dealing and the fact that the blond giant doubtless thinks that the red-haired one has slept with his ex. But if Björgvin is considering taking revenge on the new lieutenant, he's surprisingly good at hiding it. Maybe the locals put aside all disputes and differences of opinion and join forces when their small community is in danger?

"What's the situation here?" Hörður asks in a loud voice, so the noise from the water pump doesn't drown him out.

"The school has flooded, as you can see," says Áki. "We've repeatedly pointed out that permanent measures need to be taken, because this has happened before and will happen again. But we aren't being listened to."

Hörður nods. "But it's going well pumping it out, isn't it?"

"Yes, yes," says Áki. "As long as the pump doesn't give out. It's old, the poor thing."

"Right," says Hörður. "The power's out at my house. Did it go out everywhere last night?"

"In some houses, yes," Björgvin answers. He's wearing a blue balaclava that makes his eyes look both bigger and protruding. "But in all instances, it was just a tripped circuit breaker or blown fuse. I think that your house still has old-fashioned ceramic fuses. You probably just need to replace them. Lightning struck high-voltage lines, causing overvoltage, but no masts burned and the power supply never went out. Not that we know of, at least."

"A thunderstorm, huh?" says Hörður. He vaguely recalls having seen a flash of light during the night.

"Yes, indeed," says Björgvin. "One of the worst anyone here can remember. One or two trees burned here on the slope. The woods would doubtless have caught fire if it hadn't rained so hard."

"You mean up there?" Hörður turns and looks toward the escarpment. The woods are hidden behind a hazy rain and it's difficult to imagine lightning and burning trees in this lush and peaceful environment.

"Otherwise, there's some property- and water damage," says Björgvin. "Our people are checking out the situation as we speak. Roofing came loose in two places, fish crates were tossed about down at the fish-farm lot, and a few country roads were ruptured by overflowing streams and rivers."

Hörður nods distractedly. His eyes are fixed in more or less of a stare as he continues looking at the mountain and its wooded slopes, without noticing anything in particular. He sees Klausturvegur Road and its single-family houses, including the gloomy house of the garbage man, Júlíus, and the red house of Reverend Páll. The rain falls silently like a gray curtain, landing on his cap's visor with a rhythmic drumbeat; now and then cold drops run down under the neckline of his raincoat. The noise of the water pump fades and becomes a strange, low hum. It's as if time is standing still—and then what the redheaded giant should have known was going to happen, happens. He goes completely numb, and simultaneously, becomes perfectly focused. He grows cold and stiff, but his consciousness opens wide and goose bumps spring up. The road moves closer, as if through a zoom lens, and then a flickering haze appears in the middle of it, a kind of smoke that condenses until it becomes a vertical shadow...

Oh, no... Hörður feels paralyzed—but then manages to blink his staring eyes. The death shadow disappears as if at the click of a finger, the noise of the pump hits his ears, and the icy rain makes him shudder.

"...so I guess we can wrap it up for today," he hears Björgvin say, but Hörður wasn't listening. He walks toward the empty Klausturvegur Road and glances in both directions.

"What's...?" Björgvin calls out after him, before looking at Fire Chief Áki, who shrugs.

Was it a hallucination? Or is someone doomed to die? Hörður practically starts running as he glances in all directions. His heart is pounding and his mouth has gone dry. He approaches the road but notices no movement anywhere.

"Is something wrong?" the fire chief calls out after him, but the red-haired giant doesn't answer or look back over his shoulder.

Hörður is around two hundred meters away from the road when car headlights appear in the rainy haze to his right. Someone drives an old Land Rover SUV past the chapel and the Skaftá Visitor Center. The SUV is pale green with a white roof, and of the lengthier type.

Hörður dashes off to try to stop the driver before he or she reaches the spot where the policeman saw the shadow hovering in the air. The visibility is poor and who knows, maybe someone is about to stray into the road, maybe a child. As he runs, he doesn't take his eyes off the SUV.

"Hey, stop, stop!" Hörður waves his hands to try to get the driver's attention, and finally succeeds. Without slowing down, the driver looks to the side and stares in surprise at the black-clad giant who comes running up the sideroad to the swimming pool.

It appears to Hörður that the driver is the old woman who works in Skaftá Visitor Center, Sigrún, Björgvin's mother. She's wearing glasses, and is sitting very far forward and holding the steering wheel with both hands.

Isn't she going to stop? Hörður is winded and has a pain in his left side. He's about a hundred meters away from the road when he sees the girl. She's just suddenly in the middle of the road, as if having fallen from the sky—naked, snow white, and limping. Her black, rain-soaked hair hangs like a veil over her face.

"Stop!" shouts Hörður. At the same moment, Sigrún hits the brakes. The old disc brakes squeal and the old Land Rover creaks as it slides to a stop on the wet asphalt.

The vehicle's headlights cast a cold light on the naked girl standing motionless in the middle of the road, less than two meters from the SUV's metal bumper. Hörður is relieved, but only for a brief moment.

What girl is this; where has she come from and why is she naked? Hörður takes off his raincoat as he runs the last few meters, and then he wraps the coat around the girl and manages to grab her just before she collapses helplessly onto the rain-soaked asphalt. He takes the girl in his arms and feels immediately that she's ice cold. Her bare feet are dirty and scratched, as if she'd walked a long, long way, and dirt can be seen clearly beneath the tips of her fingernails. Her face is pale; there's clotted blood beneath her left ear, a black streak on her right cheekbone, and a feverish sheen in her half-open eyes.

The door to the Land Rover opens and Sigrún steps out, dressed in a blue raincoat over a gray fleece sweater. "Oh my god! I almost ran over her. What poor girl is this?"

"Do you have a phone on you?" Hörður asks gruffly.

"Yes, I do," Sigrún sputters.

"Call an ambulance, immediately," Hörður orders.

"Yes, of course," says Sigrún. She fishes out an old-fashioned push-button cell phone, taps in a number, and walks a little to the side.

"Hello?" says Hörður to the girl, but he receives no answer. She's trembling all over, her teeth are chattering and she seems to be in shock or delirious. Hasn't he seen her before? He isn't certain, but then a light comes on for him. Yes, this is one of the backpacker girls who came to Klaustur the same day as him. Not the blonde who bummed a cigarette from him, but the other one, the dark-haired one. Above her right ankle is a small black tattoo. It's the symbol for the zodiac sign Pisces.

The red-haired giant is an Aries.

"The ambulance is on its way," says Sigrún breathlessly.

"Good," Hörður groans as he tightens his grip on the girl and holds her closer. He has pain in his arms, back, and legs, as it's easier said than done to hold an unconscious person up. Björgvin and Áki come running to them.

"What's going on?" asks Áki.

"What woman is this?" asks Björgvin.

"I almost ran her over!" Sigrún answers agitatedly, before telling them in short what happened.

"Where the hell is the ambulance?" Hörður asks impatiently. He fears for the girl, who is breathing very shallowly. Her eyelids twitch as if she's dreaming. He notices that she seems to be missing a small bit of her left ear, and that her right wrist is chafed. The girl is still very cold, as the raincoat is only thinly insulated. "Can anyone bring me a blanket?"

"Of course, of course!" Sigrún hurries to the back of the Land Rover and opens the trunk, and then comes rushing back carrying two folded blankets. People in blue and red search-and-rescue clothing come walking up from all directions, drenched after hours of rescue work in the rain. Among them are the garbage man, Júlíus, and Hörður's neighbor Adam.

"How do you want these?" Sigrún unfolds one of the blankets, then looks alternately at the unconscious girl and the red-haired giant. "Oh, God."

Hörður feels a chill at the same time as he becomes somewhat numb and weak. He looks at the girl's face, which has turned white as wax. Her mouth is half open, as are her eyes. They stare into space.

"No!" cries Hörður in despair. He lays the girl down and starts trying to resuscitate her. He compresses her chest five times, then blows into the girl's mouth. He repeats this several times, but without success. Finally, he gives up.

Hörður takes the girl in his arms and holds her tightly. She is cold and bluish—dead. The search-and-rescue team members form a silent circle around the lieutenant, who cries, head hanging. Sigrún spreads the blanket over his shoulders.

The rain falls and in the distance the lights of an ambulance flash as it comes tearing down the road.

Hörður lifts his head, bears up, and wipes away his tears before giving the dead girl last rites. Then he crosses himself and says a silent prayer. He asks dear God to welcome this bedraggled soul—if he in fact exists.

Hörður is sitting at his desk in the police station, a wet lock of hair hanging down on his forehead and a sheet of paper and pen in front of him. He's pale and feels horrendous, but his expression is focused. Opposite him sit the two people he asked to be there with him as he decides the next steps. It's the mother and son, Sigrún and Björgvin, who watch him silently, waiting for him to say something.

The red-haired giant takes a deep breath. What happened lies heavily on him, like a nightmare. Seeing a death shadow is always an uncomfortable experience. But to have someone give up the ghost in one's arms is miserable, to put it mildly. He feels as if he has gone to Hell and back, but that part of him was left behind in the realm of the shadow. It's as if the Grim Reaper steals a piece of his soul every time their paths meet. In any case, he feels as if the emptiness within him has both grown and deepened.

"Thank you for sitting down here with me," says the lieutenant.

"You're welcome, friend," says Sigrún, but her son remains silent.

Hörður clears his throat, then reads the little that he's scrawled on the paper. At the top is the date and time of death. The doctor at Klaustur had declared the girl dead at the scene. The cause of death is unknown, but the doctor didn't rule out the possibility of hypothermia. The body had then been placed in the back of one of the search-and-rescue vehicles and was now on its way to Reykjavík. Next, the lieutenant wrote two important questions:

Who is the deceased? Where is the other girl?

"The reason that you're here, Sigrún," says Hörður, "is that I believe the deceased visited you at the Skaftá Visitor Center on Thursday, together with her friend."

"She did?" the woman says in surprise.

Hörður nods. "I'm almost completely certain, as I was there. The girl was on a backpacking trip with her friend. They spoke with German accents, which means that they're probably German, but could just as well be from Switzerland or Austria. They spoke to you and you gave them a map of the area and pointed out a few things to them on it, including the trail up to the lake."

"Is that so," says Sigrún, thinking this over. "Of course I remember *you*. But so many people come to me, and everyone gets the same map of the area. But goodness me, you may be right! Could the other girl have been blonde?"

"Yes, in fact," says Hörður, with a worried expression. "But where is she now? What are they? Where did they camp? What has happened and why did one of them wander naked into the village?"

"Good questions," says Sigrún, before glancing at her son. "Weren't these the girls who got a ride from you?"

Björgvin blushes and shrugs. "Maybe, I don't know."

"They said they got a ride from you," says Hörður coldly. "I was there and I heard them say it."

Björgvin throws up his hands. "I picked up two girls, that's true. The girls who were at the Skaftá Center. But whether the girl my mom almost ran over is one of them, I have no idea. I didn't get a very good look at her."

Sigrún nods. "I would say the same. I vaguely remember the girls I talked to. But whether…"

She stops and shudders.

"It was an unpleasant experience, that's for sure," says Hörður in a low voice. "But more likely than not, the girl who appeared here in the rain earlier is one of the girls we saw on Thursday. In any case, it would be foolish to assume that that *isn't* the case. Which means the other girl is probably in serious danger. Do you know anything about the girls who hitched a ride from you? Where they're from? What their names are? Anything?"

Björgvin blinks. "No, not really. I hardly talked to them. But one of them might have been named Barbara."

Hörður writes down the name. "Very good. Do you know which of them it was?"

Björgvin shakes his head. Sigrún pats his mother's forearm, but the touch appears to make him uncomfortable. It's as if his whole body stiffens.

"It doesn't change anything," says Hörður. "But I consider it extremely important that we start looking immediately for the other girl, the blonde. You're the leader of the search-and-rescue unit, right?

"I'm the leader of Torch, that's right," Björgvin answers.

"That's why I asked you to attend this informal emergency meeting," says Hörður. "Is there anything stopping you from organizing an extensive search?"

"Not at all," says Björgvin. "Since all available rescue personnel in the area have already been called out, an organized search can get underway at short notice."

"Exactly what I was hoping to hear," says Hörður. "But how would such a search be conducted? I mean, what areas would we search, how many searchers do we need, and how would we divide up the teams? I assume that the girls camped somewhere in the vicinity of Klaustur, but at the moment, we naturally know little or nothing about their travels after they left the Skaftá Center."

Björgvin thinks the matter over. "I would search around Systravatn Lake and up on Klausturheiði Heath, on the banks of the Skaftá river to Fjaðrá River, and of course up Fjaðrárgljúfur Canyon."

"They asked about the canyon, didn't they?" Hörður asks.

Sigrún hesitates for a second. "Yes, that could be. I'm not sure, but lots of people want to see the canyon. But I remember them asking about the hiking trail up to Systravatn Lake. I told them, like everyone else, that it was forbidden to camp there. But many still do."

"Exactly," says Hörður.

"I would also search around Stjórnarfoss Falls and at Geirland," says Björgvin.

Hörður nods as he writes this all down. "Very good."

"So it's three contiguous areas we're talking about," says Björgvin. "It would therefore be a good idea to assign one area to each of the three available search-and-rescue units."

"*Three* search-and-rescue units?" exclaims Hörður.

"Torch is here in Klaustur," says Björgvin. "The Star is in Skaftártunga, and Lifesave in Álftaver. Skaftárhreppur County is not only vast, it's also the most dangerous in the country. We have glaciers and glacial rivers, highland roads, countless bridges, dangerous coastlines, and sandy areas the size of deserts. We struggle with swelling rivers and glacial floods, volcanoes and sandstorms that show no mercy.

There's also an endless stream of tourists year-round. They get lost, wind up in car accidents, drown in the sea and rivers, and get stuck in the snow."

"I see," says Hörður impatiently. "And how do you want to divide up the tasks?"

Björgvin clears his throat. "Lifesave would go from here to Geirland and then cover the area to both sides of Stjórnarfoss Falls. The Star would go around Systravatn Lake and over Klausturheiði Heath. I'll take my people to Fjaðrá River, where we'll divide up. One group will head up the canyon, and I'll lead the other group up along it all the way to Heiðarból."

"My Björgvin knows the heath like the back of his hand," says Sigrún proudly.

Björgvin blushes and looks down.

"Then it's settled," says Hörður. "I'll go have a look at the campsite here in Klaustur, besides keeping in radio contact with the leaders of the search groups."

Björgvin nods and gets to his feet. "Anything we're missing?"

"No," says Hörður as he looks at his watch. "It's going on nine thirty. Time is working against us. The sooner we start the search, the better."

Hörður has put back on his raincoat and cap. It's still raining, though not quite as much now. He's standing apart in the police station's parking lot, watching the search-and-rescue teams prepare for the search. Their two vehicles idle as the team members have something to eat and drink and use the bathroom before setting off. A number of them are munching flatbread spread with liverwurst and drinking hot chocolate from paper cups, but Hörður has no idea where the refreshments have come from. He hears some of the others talking about the girl who died.

"Maybe they were lesbians and got in an argument," says the garbage man, Júlíus, in a gloating tone to two bearded men who act as if they aren't listening to his bullshit.

This pisses Hörður off, but he decides to follow the example of the search-and-rescue team members and ignore the garbage man. Júlíus seems to be a bit abnormal—maybe he's even mentally challenged.

Adam comes walking up to the lieutenant.

"So you're a member of search-and-rescue," says Hörður, just to say something. Although he likes this teddy-bearish neighbor of his, he hasn't quite yet figured him out.

With a serious expression, Adam nods. "What do you think about the girl?"

"I don't really know what to think," mutters the lieutenant.

"She just shows up all of a sudden," says Adam. "Naked in the rain. Apparently having walked a long distance. Did you see her feet?"

His brow furrowed, Hörður nods.

"What do you think hap…?" Adam stops mid-sentence when Björgvin claps his hands and orders everyone to get going.

Hörður is relieved, as he's still digesting what he saw and is unprepared to discuss it with anyone.

"Well, more on that later," says Adam, before climbing into the vehicle bearing the logo of the Torch search-and-rescue team. The other vehicle is marked The Star. As soon as everyone is in, the vehicles are driven away. Remaining in the parking lot is a six-person group from Lifesave, four men and two women. They set off on foot to the east, toward the Geirland area.

The unit's vehicle is on its way to Reykjavík with the girl's body aboard.

Hörður looks from side to side as he drives his SUV along Klausturvegur Road. It's eleven o'clock. No one is out on the streets, and the village seems deserted. He's searched along the banks of the Skaftá river, at the RV campground at Geirland and the village's campsite. The backpackers who'd been camping in Klaustur the night before were cold and wet after the night, but none of them recalled having seen anyone matching Hörður's descriptions of the German girls. So he's fairly convinced that they didn't camp in a purpose-built site, but somewhere out in the wild, although it's forbidden.

The most popular tourist attractions in the vicinity of Klaustur are Systravatn Lake and Fjaðrárgljúfur Canyon. The lieutenant has high hopes for the search that's underway, and which will hopefully yield some results sooner rather than later.

He drives past the place where the girl appeared, and where she collapsed and died. Now, there's nothing there but rain-soaked asphalt. Where had she come from? The village itself? Or down from the mountain, through the woods, and straight out onto the road? He isn't sure, as he didn't see her come walking from anywhere. She'd just suddenly been there, in the middle of the road. But her back was turned to the heath and the highlands as she stood there in front of Sigrún's old Land Rover, which of course indicates that she'd been walking away from them. But maybe she just turned toward the car's lights when she spied them in the cold rain?

Hörður sighs and drives onward, finally parking the SUV on the shoulder of the road close to the ravine and the trailhead to Systravatn Lake. He munches cookies and sips black coffee through the opened lid of his thermos before shutting off the engine and stepping out into the rain. He puts on his cap, sticks a map of the area in his inside rain-coat pocket and attaches a walkie-talkie that Björgvin let him have to his belt. The rain has actually slackened even more, and become more or less of a drizzle.

When Hörður walks down into the Fossgil ravine, he hears a heavy murmur. The Fossá river, which is usually a friendly village stream, has swollen, and Systrafoss Falls has turned into a foamy cascade plunging obliquely down the black rock walls. The red-haired giant peers through the rain, looking with admiration at the waterfall, the ravine, and the giant Fossasteinn boulder at its bottom. He really appreciates the magnificence of nature, and there's something fairytale-like and enchanting about Systrafoss and its surroundings. The waterfall is neither the highest nor most voluminous in the country, but it's beautiful, that much is certain.

The lieutenant sets off along the trail that winds up through the woods. The trail is a muddy mess and his shoes quickly become dirty and wet. He grows warmer as he walks and soon feels breathless. He knows that the search-and-rescue personnel have already hiked up the trail and searched both the woods and around the lake, but he finds it hard to wait and hope for the best while others do the legwork. The lieutenant's role in the search is to act as a *control center*, which means that he's supposed to receive messages from the leaders of the three search parties and pass them on to the others, instead of them getting all crisscrossed by calling each other. Each of the leaders concentrates on their own team and assigned area, while the lieutenant makes sure that no area is forgotten or that the teams proceed too slowly or quickly.

Did the German girls take this same trail? thinks Hörður as he inches his way carefully up the slippery steps at the topmost, steepest part of the trail. He thinks that it's probable, although he can't by any means be certain. Hadn't he seen two people on the crest of the escarpment on Thursday, after he went swimming? Yes, and it looked to him as if it was two girls. When Hörður finally gets to the top, he stops to catch his breath. The rain is at an end and a ray or two of sunshine breaks through the clouds. He looks over the edge, down toward the rain-soaked village. The Skaftá river is considerably swollen; it's brown and churning and rushes on at an alarming speed. If someone falls into a glacial river in such a state, he or she will not return—that much is certain.

Hörður shudders at the thought, but then turns his attention to the lake and the heath. He watches the Fossá river flow powerfully over the cliff's edge and transform into the waterfall he was admiring a few minutes ago. He feels dizzy from watching all that water plunge like that into the void. So he hurriedly moves higher up, closer to the lake and the small concrete shed standing on its bank. The shed houses equipment for opening and closing the reservoir for the small power plant that's in another small shed at the foot of the escarpment. He peeks into the shed and walks along the lagoon, all the way to the blue information sign for tourists. The sign reads *Katla Geopark. Systravatn Lake*, and on it is a drawing of two nuns standing at the bank of the lake, with a text in two languages, Icelandic and English.

Hörður reads the text:

The nuns came here often to bathe. Once when two of them were bathing, they saw a hand emerge from the water, holding a beautiful golden comb. When they seized the hand, they both disappeared with it into the water and were never seen again.

The hair rises on the back of the red-haired giant's neck, because this concise legend is like a creepy omen of what may have happened to the two German girls. He looks up and out at the big, rippling lake. Was this why the girl was naked? Did they decide to have some childish fun and go for a midnight swim? And then the storm hits; they can't find their tent, and the temperature drops. One of them drowns or dies of exposure, but the other manages to wander down to the village before succumbing to hypothermia.

Hörður looks in all directions but sees no searchers in the vicinity of the lake or on the heath beyond it. But he does see a building in the distance, a lonely outbuilding at the eastern edge of the mountain.

He pulls the walkie-talkie from his belt and presses the button. "Command calling The Star, command calling The Star. Over."

The walkie-talkie crackles loudly. *"The Star, we read you, Command. Over."*

"Have you searched around Systravatn Lake?" Hörður asks. "Over."

"We circled it, yes. Found nothing. Over."

"What about the building across the lake? Was it searched?" Hörður asks. "Over."

"The Sel outbuildings? Yes, there was nothing there. Over."

"Where are you now?" asks Hörður. "Over."

"We've covered the better part of Klausturheiði Heath. Over."

"Very well. Carry on, but not too quickly. Over and out." Hörður re-attaches the walkie-talkie to his belt, then sets off clockwise around the lake. He saunters over tussocks and looks around for places where it would be convenient to pitch a tent—a flat patch of grass or a sheltered hollow— while still glancing occasionally at the lake itself. He's somewhat stressed about finding what he fears most: the body of a blonde girl half-submerged. He's holding onto the hope that the girl is still alive, but the other possibility certainly exists. The Icelandic wilderness is not a safe place for any-one, not even in midsummer.

The hike has made Hörður hot and sweaty, despite his being in no hurry. He's just over halfway around the lake, but hasn't seen as much as one suitable spot for pitching a tent—making him start to doubt seriously that the girls camped for the night up here on the mountain. Around the lake are nothing but tussocks, gravelly areas, and marshes, and little to no shelter. But he's approaching the building, or rather buildings, there being two adjacent to each other, and which he now understands are called the *Sel outbuild-ings*. Next to them are fields where it would doubtless be possible to camp. It looks to Hörður as if these are typical outbuildings: a shed for sheep or horses with an attached barn.

Half an hour later, Hörður has searched everywhere in these outbuildings, which housed horses, but are in poor condition and clearly no longer in use. He walks around the fields near the buildings, searching for signs of the backpackers, but doesn't find as much as a square inch of trampled grass, let alone scorched earth from a campfire. He looks at the buildings and then out at the vast heath.

What has happened to the girls?

To the east is Stjórnargil Ravine. On the far edge, he glimpses search-and-rescue personnel on the move.

"Command calling Lifesave. Over," he says on the walkie-talkie.

"Lifesave, we read you, Command, over."

"Have you found anything?" asks Hörður. "Over."

"No, nothing. Over."

"Proceed. Over and out." Hörður re-attaches the walkie-talkie to his belt. He was going to continue onward, but then decides to check the barn again, just in case. It's big and empty, full of darkness and a musty smell. There are moldy tufts of hay here and there. He roots in the hay with his shoes, stirring up old dust. Hörður coughs and waves away the dust. He is on his way back out into the daylight when he spots something on the dirty floor.

Is that…?

Hörður bends down and picks up a cigarette butt that's been crushed. It's a Camel Filter. The same type that he smokes—the same type as the pack he gave the German girl. The hair rises on the red-haired giant's forearms. He hurries out of the barn and lifts the walkie-talkie.

"The Star, can you hear me?" He's too agitated to stick to formal radio lingo.

"The Star here, over."

"Where are you?" asks Hörður.

"We're nearing Fagrafoss Falls. The heath is pretty much behind us. We have about a half hour's walk to Heiðarból, where Torch will end their search, over."

"I want you to head back here. I've found evidence of the girls at the Sel outbuildings," says Hörður. "Search the heath more closely, and even better as you approach Systravatn Lake. Over."

"Acknowledged, over and out."

After Hörður has searched every last inch of the area in and around the dilapidated outbuildings, he goes on. He thinks it more likely than not that the girls were in this area, but whether they camped near the lake is harder to say. After around a twenty-minute walk, he's come full circle, back to the verge of the mountain above the village—from which, there's a magnificent view. He looks down at Klausturvegur Road and regards the sideroad to the swimming pool. He's standing in practically the same place as the two people he saw after he went swimming on

Thursday. What time was it then? Around six, if he remembers correctly. If it was the German girls that he saw at the top of the mountain, they would hardly have found a place to sleep right afterward.

Or what?

Hörður sighs. Maybe he should call Axel? Yes. In fact, he should have called him a long time ago. But it's Saturday, and not yet noon. He fishes out his cell phone and calls his old boss.

"About time." The head of the CID is unceremonious and brusque, as usual.

"So you've heard what happened here?" says Hörður, who should have known that nothing could get by old Steppenwolf.

"As far as I know, the body of a young woman is on its way to the capital. An unknown person, or what?"

"As of yet, yes," Hörður answers, before pacing aimlessly along the verge of the mountain as he summarizes what has happened for Axel, from the moment he spotted the German-speaking girls in Hvolsvöllur to the awful moment when one of them died in his arms, ice-cold and bedraggled, naked as a newborn baby.

"Did you notice anything unusual?" Axel asks.

Hörður shuts his eyes as he thinks. "The girl's left cheek was bloody. It was mainly dried blood softened by the rain. Her left ear was injured; it looked to me as if a piece of it was missing. And there was some kind of trauma to her wrist, chafing, it looked like."

"Maybe she fell?"

"Maybe," says Hörður. "Her feet were both dirty and cut; she'd clearly walked a long way. She had a tattoo on her right ankle, the sign of Pisces, which presumably means that the girl was born in late February or early March. There was also dirt under her fingernails. And there were dirty streaks on her."

"Streaks?"

Hörður nods, thinking. "For example, on her right cheek, near her jaw. And maybe elsewhere, too, I just don't remember. As if she ran into something sooty."

"Of course, an autopsy will be done on the body, this being an unnatural death. Then all of this will hopefully be explained better."

"Do you know when that will be?" Hörður asks. "I would give this case top priority. The other girl is still missing and I find it more than a little suspicious that the deceased was naked out in the storm."

"Maybe they were asleep when their tent blew down. Wasn't the weather crazy there last night? Thunder and lightning?"

"It was stormy, yes," admits Hörður.

"Unless they'd been swimming somewhere."

Hörður stops and looks out at Systravatn, which is big and deep enough to drown in. "I've also considered that possibility."

"Remember the women who fell into Bleiksárgljúfur Canyon?"

Hörður frowns. He's quick to recall the case, as it was highly publicized in the media. He was then in the Patrol Division. Various theories were circulated about the fate of the women, as usually occurs when the facts aren't clear. "Yes, they were staying in a summer cottage in Fljótshlíð and hiked to the canyon, or what?"

"Late in the evening or at night, yes. They were lovers, lesbians. Their bodies were naked when they were found. No one knows what happened, but it was probably some sort of accident."

"What does homosexuality have to do with it?" Hörður asks coldly. Had the garbage man Júlíus been referring to this event when he joked about the German girls being lesbians?

"They might have been arguing at the edge of the canyon; that was one theory. A lovers' quarrel that ended in disaster. But what I mean is that there can be countless explanations for people being naked in the night, and most of them are quite normal, so to speak."

"Yes, maybe," says Hörður dryly. "But we can't rule out anything at this point, can we?"

"Of course not. As lieutenant over that precinct, you have full control over the investigation of this case. But if any suspicions of foul play arise, I'll probably send someone from the CID out there. As things stand now, though, half of the department is on summer vacation and the other half has its hands full with cases."

Hörður grunts. "You don't have to send anyone. Aren't I a detective?"

"At the moment, you're a lieutenant. But as I said, you're in charge of the case. But I'll take care of the next steps."

"What steps are those, might I ask?" asks Hörður, irritated at how it seems as if Axel doesn't trust him to investigate the case.

"Number one, two, and three is to identify the deceased. Since she didn't have any ID on her, fingerprints and a DNA sample need to be taken from her, and we'll need dental records sent from abroad, if she's foreign. The Forensic Identification Unit handles cases involving unidentified bodies or remains."

"I see," says Hörður thoughtfully. "But hold on a second. How can you request the dental records of a person you haven't identified?"

"Naturally, we'll identify her first. We'll photograph her face and the Police Air Terminal Unit at Suðurnes will be asked to check arriving passengers at the Leifsstöð terminal during a particular period, with the help of a computer program that analyzes people's faces on footage from the surveillance-camera system. The tattoo that you mentioned is very important, if her relatives can confirm its existence."

"Of course, of course," mutters Hörður, who should have known all of this, having taken classes on these matters as well as countless others.

"If the girl is a foreign tourist, the International Division will be brought in to handle communication with the police authorities in her home country, the embassy of the country in question in Iceland, and so on."

"Then dental records would be requested and contact established with the girl's relatives," Hörður concludes, as he recalls the procedural policies.

"Correct."

"The search is ongoing, but I'm not too optimistic that the other girl will be found today," says Hörður. "It's as if the earth has swallowed her. But if she fell into the Skaftá river or something like that, I'm terribly worried she'll never be found."

"Could the girl who died have fallen into Skaftá?"

"It isn't out of the question," says Hörður. "But the river is in such a state that I doubt anyone could get out of it on his own."

"Nothing can be ruled out at the start of an investigation."

"True," says Hörður, who knows very well what old Steppenwolf means. A detective shouldn't assume one thing or another or jump too quickly to conclusions. He should work with an open mind, suspecting everything and everyone and asking questions instead of putting two and two together too soon.

"But I'll make sure that the Forensic Identification Unit starts its work right away and that the body is autopsied as soon as possible. Satisfied with that?"

"Of course," says the lieutenant. "Thanks…"

Hörður is unable to give the head of the CID a proper goodbye, as Axel M. Axelsson has already hung up. He puts his phone back in his pocket and looks once more at the lake and the heath to its north.

Where the hell is the blonde girl?

It's now three o'clock and the search hasn't yet yielded anything. Hörður Grímsson is sitting at a four-person table in the break room of the headquarters of the rescue squad Torch, along with Björgvin Geirharðsson and the leaders of the search-and-rescue units The Star and Lifesave, Magni Halldórsson and Úlfar Jóhannsson. On the table is a large map of the area around Kirkjubæjarklaustur, from the highlands down to the sea and from the Eldhraun lava field in the west to the Skeiðarársandur sands in the east. The areas searched first are shaded with horizontal pencil lines, and those searched twice are shaded with vertical lines crossing the horizontal ones.

"How are the search teams doing?" Hörður asks. He squeezes two Panodils out of a blister pack and washes the painkillers down with lukewarm coffee. All the stress and his worries about the girl who is missing having given him high blood pressure and headaches.

Magni looks his colleague in the eye and shrugs. "We've been working since six o'clock this morning and have hardly sat down the entire time. Because of the weather, most of us slept little, if at all, last night. So it's safe to say that everyone's tired."

Hörður nods sympathetically. "We'll try to give everyone a good rest tonight. But shouldn't we continue searching a bit more today? I'm mainly thinking about the banks of the Skaftá river and the area south of Klaustur."

"If the girl fell into Skaftá, she'll probably never be found," says Björgvin.

"The banks of the Skaftá river south of Klaustur are probably fifty kilometers long," says Úlfar. "And then the estuary area is many square kilometers of sand, as far as the eye can see in every direction."

"I know, I know," Hörður sighs as he rubs his temples. "But we've got to do something, right? We can't just sit here while the girl's still out there somewhere."

"No, of course not," admits Magni. "But can we be sure that the girl is lost?"

Björgvin fidgets in his seat and Úlfar inhales through his nose. If Magni hadn't asked this question, one of them would no doubt have done so.

Hörður grunts moodily. "Who should get the benefit of the doubt, the search teams or the girl?"

Magni reddens and looks away.

"Of course we'll continue the search," mutters Úlfar. "But at some point we'll be forced to call it quits. Unless any new information turns up, of course."

"The Forensic Identification Unit is working on the case," says Hörður heavily. "It won't be long before we know who the deceased is, and whether she was alone or not. Until then, I'll be working based on the information we already have."

He pauses for dramatic effect and looks directly at the three unit leaders before continuing.

"There were *two* girls on a backpacking trip here on Thursday. One blonde, the other dark-haired. The girl who died here this morning bears a close resemblance to the dark-haired one. I'm permitting myself to conclude that it's her friend who is missing. How often do I have to rehash this for you?"

Looking sheepish, Magni reddens even more, but Úlfar crosses his arms defensively.

"We'll find her," says Björgvin in his melancholy bass voice. "What do you say about us taking a two-hour break now, but meeting again at five o'clock and walking the banks of Skaftá? Our people have to have a chance to recharge their batteries before continuing."

"Sounds good," says Hörður. "But if the search still yields nothing, I want us to meet again here at nine tomorrow morning."

"With full crews?" asks Magni.

Hörður nods.

"That'll be no problem," says Björgvin firmly.

"Not at all," says Úlfar.

"Good to hear, boys," says Hörður. "But if everything goes according to plan, we'll find the girl tonight. Hopefully alive."

The fuse box was hidden behind the coat hanger in the hall. As Björgvin said, it turned out to be an old-fashioned setup, with ceramic fuses. One of them was blown and smelled awful. Had lightning really hit the distribution system? Probably so. But he found new fuses, and after replacing the blown one, he was able to reset the circuit breaker and *voila*—the lieutenant's house had power again!

As his radiators warm up, Hörður cooks himself a dinner of scrambled eggs and fried hot dogs, but his mind is not on his modest meal and he has no appetite to speak of. But he has to eat something, and since he doesn't have the peace of mind either to go to bed or read a book, he might as well kill time by frying up some food. He's taken a shower, changed his clothes, and spoken with Bíbí. He told her about the girl who died, but left out the part about the death shadow and the fact that the girl was naked and gave up the ghost in his arms. He simply told her that the girl had died of exposure, which was probably the truth. However, there's something about the girl's injuries that's troubling him, sort of deep down. But he pushes aside those unpleasant thoughts, at least to begin with. As things stand at the moment, he feels that all of his energy and focus should go into the search for the lost girl.

"If only we could find her," Hörður mutters as he turns over the hot dogs on the hot pan. He looks at his watch and sees that the evening news has begun. The girl's death will probably be reported there, but as far as he knows, no reporters have come to Kirkjubæjarklaustur because of the case.

But they will come—of that he's certain. He sighs heavily. All he needs is for the media to start bringing up the new lieutenant's old sins now.

Hörður turns off the stove, transfers the eggs and hot dogs to a plate and then rinses the pan in the sink. He squeezes a little ketchup over the half-burned food and sits down before the plate on the kitchen table. He's just started eating when his cell phone rings.

What now?

He searches for and finds the phone, and sees that it's Þóra Sverrisdóttir who is calling. "Hi."

"Am I interrupting you?"

Hörður sits back down at the kitchen table. "No, no, not really."

"I was just watching the news. A tourist died of exposure? What happened?"

"I don't really know," groans Hörður, before repeating everything he had told Axel. But since Þóra probably knows him better than anyone else, he doesn't leave out any details, not even the damn death shadow.

"Ugh, how awful. My dear friend."

"It wasn't exactly fun," mutters Hörður. Having completely lost his appetite, he pushes the plate away. He hasn't recovered at all after the day's events. He still senses the emptiness that the shadow left behind when it disappeared, and he can still feel the touch of the poor girl's cold body.

"Tell me more about her injuries."

He clears his throat, then rehashes what he saw. The congealed blood, the injury to the girl's ear, the chafing on her wrists, the black streaks on her jaw or cheekbone. "Her feet were cut and dirty, too, and she had dirt under her fingernails."

"Was the chafing on both wrists?"

Hörður closes his eyes, thinks about it. "I'm not sure. It was on one, in any case. It was like red streaks."

"As if from a rope?"

"Maybe."

"Do you suspect foul play? Do you think someone did something to her?"

He sighs. "I don't know. I hope not. But I have a kind of uncomfortable feeling that I can't shake. She was naked, of course, which is suspicious, you know. But maybe she just slept naked, or had been swimming. Who knows?"

"And her friend is still missing."

"Exactly." Hörður looks at his watch. The search is probably still ongoing, but will likely end soon. The searchers must certainly be tired after their long day.

"Do you think they might have had an argument or something? That her friend attacked her?"

"I find it unlikely," says Hörður. "But…"

"But what?"

Hörður clicks his tongue. "But if she'd been on a trip with a man who was now missing, he would be the first suspect."

"That's true."

"But if someone harmed the girl," says Hörður, "and if that person *isn't* her friend, then I'm up shit creek."

"Oh? How?"

He shrugs. "Because then, almost everyone in the village becomes a suspect. And I'm on my own here, a newcomer who knows no one. So I couldn't trust anyone, while at the same time, I need the help of a lot of people. For example, search-and-rescue teams are looking for the girl as we speak. What if a potential perpetrator is on one of them? Do you see what I mean?"

"Yes, of course. But hopefully it was just some sort of accident. Isn't that most likely?"

"Yes, absolutely," says Hörður.

"Keep in touch and allow me to follow your progress, okay?"

"I will," says Hörður. "Good to hear from you."

"Likewise. Bye, bye."

Hörður puts down the phone. Then he gets up from the kitchen table and throws his cooling dinner in the trash.

It's a quarter to nine, and the formal search is over for the day. Hörður was in almost constant radio contact with the leaders of the search-and-rescue teams during the search's final hour and is quite satisfied with the size of the area searched, but is terribly disappointed that the search turned up nothing. However, he can take comfort in the fact that no body was found, which means that the blonde girl is possibly and hopefully still alive somewhere.

But where?

The red-haired giant is too restless to sit still or hang around at home. He puts on his shoes and jacket and walks down to the banks of the Skaftá river, which is only about a half hour's walk from his house at Efri-Vík. The glacial river is still swollen, turbid and rough, despite the rain having stopped quite some time ago. It rolls along like a faceless monster. Everything is still sodden following the downpour, but the sky is clear; there's hardly a breeze and the evening sun is still high in the sky. The birds are singing, dashing around and plucking up worms that the rainstorm has lured to the surface. They have plenty to do, as their chicks are hungry all day and night and the summer in the far north is both short and unreliable—like life.

Hörður is downcast, his spirit as heavy as the current of the glacial river at which he stares. He knows that Björgvin is right. Anyone who falls into the Skaftá river in such a state is dead meat. He just hopes that that isn't what happened to the blonde girl. It would be incredibly tragic if they were both dead, the German girls who innocently left home to visit the green, innocent island in the north. The Icelandic wilderness has a strong attraction, being both varied and fascinating, but it's also tricky and treacherous—a gorgon beneath beautiful skin.

"It's not very inviting."

Hörður recognizes Adam's languorous bass voice, but still, it startles him and makes him stiffen up. The hair rises on the back of the lieutenant's neck, and it's as if an electric current runs through his nervous system. How could the bastard creep up on him like that?

Trying to conceal his agitation, he turns around slowly and exhales at the same time.

"Sorry. I didn't mean to startle you," says Adam, who is still dressed in the apparel of the Torch search-and-rescue unit. He's muddy up to his knees and his shoulders and back are still wet from the rain earlier in the day.

"You didn't startle me," says Hörður stubbornly. "I just didn't notice you."

"You don't ever take a break?" says Adam. The question sounds more like a statement.

Hörður snorts. "If I could, I would search day and night and not stop until the girl was found, alive or dead."

"I see," says Adam. He hesitates and gives a little sniff before continuing. "Áki mentioned something about there having been blood on the girl that died. Did she have any injuries, or … ?"

Hörður shrugs, feeling both tired of talking about what happened and suspicious of his neighbor, as well as everyone else in the village. But he's also a little curious. No one talks to him, the newcomer, but, naturally, the villagers talk to each other. "Are there any stories going around?"

Adam shakes his head. "If you mean whether someone hurt the girl or anything like that, then no … not really. But some people have mentioned the similarities to the tragedy at Bleiksárgljúfur Canyon. Most people believe that it was some sort of accident. That the girl had been swimming in Systravatn or even fell into Skaftá."

"She would hardly have been able to get out of the river again," says Hörður. "But what do I know? Anything can happen."

"After we had just moved here to the east, a body was found at the Skaftá estuary," says Adam. "It was of a young girl, a Belgian, as I recall. She'd disappeared earlier in the summer."

Hörður furrows his brow. "A tourist?"

"No, I think she lived and worked in Vík," says Adam. "At the Víkurprjón knitwear store. She was a pretty girl. Her name was Júlía or Júlíana or something. There were rumors that she was hooking up with Bjöggi."

"You mean, Björgvin, the leader of the Torch search-and-rescue unit?" asks Hörður in surprise.

Adam nods. "I don't know whether that had anything to do with it, but Bjöggi and Silja split up shortly afterward. Their boy was a newborn then."

"And?" asks Hörður. "How did that Júlía end up drowning in Skaftá?"

Adam shrugs. "No one knows. She just disappeared one day and was found a few weeks later, down at the estuary. Her name was Juliette, I recall now. Her last name was something odd."

"I see," mutters Hörður thoughtfully. "So a girl has disappeared here before?"

"Disappeared, fallen, died … this is a dangerous area," says Adam.

"Fallen?" asks Hörður.

Adam nods. "I don't know exactly when it was, but a girl fell into Hörgsárgljúfur Canyon ten or fifteen years ago. It was brought up again after Juliette disappeared. I remember that a search was conducted there, among other things."

Hörður's eyes open wide. "Didn't you say that Björgvin lives in Hörgsárdalur Valley?"

Adam nods. "But he didn't live there then. He was still living with his mother, being only a teenager at the time. Under twenty, in any case. It's happened a long time ago."

"Was the girl Icelandic?" Hörður asks.

"I don't think so," says Adam. "But you'll have to ask one of the locals about it. And as I recall, she worked at the fish farm."

Hörður grunts. Three dead girls in ten or fifteen years—and a fourth missing. Probably all foreign. It sounds strange, if not downright suspicious. Or is this just a normal statistic in a dangerous part of the country that's extremely popular with foreign tourists?

He isn't sure.

"Where is Hörgsárgljúfur Canyon, anyway?" he asks.

Adam points to the east. "On the other side of the mountain there. On the eastern side of the valley. Not far from the farm where Bjöggi lives."

"I see," mutters Hörður distractedly. He stares at the glacial river, but without looking at anything in particular, having disappeared into his own mind as he digests all this new information. He's glad that he came across Adam, because these unexpected facts are very interesting and potentially important.

But of course *he* didn't come across Adam. It was Adam who came across him. Or had Adam followed him down to the river?

Adam clears his throat. "If you need help or some sort of assistance, I'm ready and willing, of course. As I told you, I worked as a summer temp on the police force for a while and…"

Hörður holds out his hand to silence him. "Thanks, but no thanks. I don't need your help, or anyone else's."

Adam is startled by the lieutenant's rather condescending response. "Fine. But *if* you suspect foul play, it might be a good idea to have an assistant. Naturally, I'm pretty familiar with both the villagers and the local customs, and two eyes are better than one and all that."

Hörður looks coldly at his neighbor. "Do *you* suspect foul play?"

Adam reddens. "Since you ask, I think there's something strange about the girl's death. It was certainly bad weather, but not so cold that an adult would die of exposure in just a few hours. Not out of the question, but unlikely, I would say."

With a stern expression, Hörður nods. "I wish to say as little as possible at this point. But if the slightest suspicion arises that something criminal has taken place, then quite a few people automatically become suspects. Including you."

"Me?" The redness disappears from Adam's cheeks in an instant.

"Yes, you," says Hörður. "A man in his prime who drives around the wilderness on a six-wheeler with a gun at his side. Who says he has a wife and daughter, yet whose curtains are always drawn shut over his windows at home, and in whose yard no child plays or swings on the damn swing."

"Yes, but…" mutters Adam, before breaking into sobs.

"What the hell is wrong with you, man?" Hörður asks in shock. "Do you have something to confess?"

"Yes, I…" Adam stammers through his tears. "My wife left me. She went to Reykjavík and took the girl with her. We're probably going to get a divorce."

Hörður feels awkward, as always when someone shows emotion in his presence. "Oh, well… I'm sorry to hear that."

"Sorry," Adam says. He takes a deep breath and does his best to try to control his emotions. "It's just been difficult. Fucking hard, you know? I can't sleep anymore and don't know what to do."

"I wouldn't know," mutters Hörður. He clears his throat and looks out into the blue, then pats Adam on the back, probably a bit too hard. "Should we head back home?"

Adam nods. They walk back up the slopes without uttering a word for some time.

Hörður is deep in thought. Among other things, he's pondering the next steps in the search for the lost girl.

"Weren't you painting your house the other day?" he suddenly asks Adam.

"Yes, I was," Adam replies in surprise. "I painted both the master bedroom and my daughter's room. Just to have something to do. It felt so empty after they left. I'm thinking of pulling up the parquet in the living room and ... "

"Do you have any paint left?" Hörður interrupts. "And maybe a brush? Even three?"

"Yes, I think so. Why?" Adam asks.

"Nothing special; I was just thinking," mutters Hörður, who seems lost in thought again.

"Okay," Adam says, bewilderedly.

They continue walking in silence.

"Well," says Hörður when they come to the lieutenant's house.

"Yes, it's the end of a long day," says Adam wearily. He raises his hand in farewell, and, the very picture of misery, continues on to the teacher's house.

Hörður watches him, and can't help but feel a little sorry for this teddy-bearish fool. But he still doesn't know if he trusts him.

Hörður sits down in the living room, opens his notepad, and writes down everything that Adam told him. Then he leans back on the sofa and reads his notes, over and over again. He needs to find out more about these two accidents. But as things stand at the moment, he's too tired, mentally and physically, to do anything. He's had little sleep, has bad nerves, and still feels half empty after what happened that morning. In short, he's exhausted. He feels helpless because of the lost girl and is extremely worried about her. Each time he closes his eyes, he imagines her smiling face when she asked him for a cigarette. Her dark-haired friend is in the background. The same friend who lay dead in his arms less than two days later.

Hörður heaves a great sigh. Adam was right. He desperately needs an assistant. Someone to talk to and think aloud to. Someone who could take on various tasks and in doing so, relieve the burden on the lieutenant. The search for the blonde girl should be occupying his entire mind, but it isn't. The fact that the girl is missing is the consequence of some unknown cause. He can't get rid of the uncomfortable feeling that someone may have harmed the girls.

Or is it all just the storm to blame?

Maybe.

He isn't sure.

Hörður picks up his cell phone and calls Þóra.

"Hi, hi!"

"Am I interrupting you?" he asks.

"Not at all. Is there anything new?"

"Not really. The search is over for today, but will continue tomorrow," says Hörður.

"So she's still missing?"

"Yes. But as it turns out, girls have gone missing here before," says Hörður, before telling Þóra what Adam told him.

"Her name was Juliette?" asks Þóra.

"He said he thought so, yes," says Hörður. He can hear that Þóra is writing all this down.

"I'm going to look this up in the system and see what I find."

"Thanks, my friend," says Hörður. "I would do it myself but I hardly have the time or the focus for it."

"I'll let you know what I find. It will also be interesting to know what the autopsy reveals."

"Yes, I hope to get some news on that tomorrow or the next day," says Hörður.

"Aren't there reports on those older disappearances at the police station in Klaustur?"

"Good question," says Hörður. "I'm going to check on that tomorrow morning. I'm at home now."

"Yes, do that. Talk to you tomorrow."

"Absolutely," he says. "Good night."

"Good night, buddy."

Hörður puts down the phone and leans back on the sofa. Suddenly he notices evidence of his own doings the night before—the bag of weed is still on the living-room table, the curtains are still drawn over the windows, and there's a faint smell of marijuana in the air. At first, he was overwhelmed with embarrassment and shame. Had he really gotten high on weed and sat there feeling sorry for himself, pondering the universe and the purpose of life? And at the same time as something horrific was happening to the German girls. But the shame doesn't last long. He'd just done what he wanted to do—and so what? He even feels like doing it again. There's still some weed in the bag and he would have nothing against anesthetizing himself a bit and *just zoning out* or whatever it's called. But no, this is neither the place nor the time for carelessness.

Instead of rolling another joint, he throws the bag of weed and rolling papers in the garbage, then opens a window to let in clean air and tidies the coffee table a bit.

It's half past ten. He wants most just to go to bed, as he needs a good, long night's sleep. But there's some unrest in him and he knows that he wouldn't be able to fall asleep immediately even if he tried, but would just lie there awake with his thoughts and eventually become so irritated that he would get back up. So it's better to stay up a little longer and try to calm down a bit, and in doing so, become even more tired and more sleepy.

Maybe he should listen to music?

Hörður takes the cassette tape of Kansas from the Akai portable player, replaces it with a Neil Young tape and pushes play, but nothing happens. He notices that there's no light glowing on the player, so it's clearly not getting any power. He checks to make sure the power cord is securely connected, both to the wall socket and the device itself. It turns out to be so, but he thinks he catches a burned smell from the device, precisely where the narrower end of the cord is inserted into it.

He heaves a sigh. Is he managing to destroy every electronic device he touches?

There's a small screw next to the power socket on the device. He goes and finds a small screwdriver in a drawer in the kitchen that's full of small tools, screws, nails, and all sorts of booklets, and loosens the screw. Then he loosens the socket itself and pulls it out. It's a rectangular plastic box hanging on two wires, positive and negative. Like most smaller electronic devices, the portable cassette player isn't grounded. Inside the plastic box is a little fuse, a slender glass cylinder with metal at the ends. The glass cylinder is full of soot, as the fuse has blown. When the lightning struck the distribution system, it caused an overvoltage that blew the little fuse. Which means that the device itself is undamaged. But it also means that it can't be used without replacing the fuse.

"What a pain," says Hörður, who can't imagine finding such a small fuse in the next drawer or cupboard. However, there's a possibility that the priest might have one, or that they're sold in the shop.

He's almost given up on the idea of listening to music before going to bed when he remembers the battery compartment on the back of the device. It's a *portable* player, which means that it runs on both ordinary electricity and batteries. He turns the device over and snaps the lid off the elongated compartment, which turns out to be neither empty nor full of batteries. In it is a rolled-up plastic bag with something in it.

Hörður pulls the plastic bag out of the compartment and looks into it. The bag contains a strange collection—two small locks of hair in an elastic band, two silver earrings, a gold ring with a diamond pattern, and an old black and white photograph. He arranges the things on the living-room table and takes a closer look at them. The locks are both blonde, yet one is a little lighter than the other. He's seen hair clippings like this before, but usually under glass in framed children's photos. In such cases, the parents have cut a lock of hair from their child's head to keep as a memento—but why, he doesn't know. The earrings are plain rings, and one of them is missing its clip. The silver is burnished and as dull as lead. But the gold ring glints; it's clearly well-crafted and expensive, and therefore probably valuable. Hörður weighs it in the palm of his hand, and immediately thinks of the *Lord of the Rings* and the sinister creature Gollum, who was obsessed with the ring. The photograph, however, is of most interest to the red-haired giant. It's very old and has white-borders, as was customary for a time. Except that this is only half a photo—someone has cut it in two. In the half that Hörður is holding, a little girl is seen standing in a farmyard. The girl is probably twelve years old, dark-haired, big-boned, and rather ugly. She has black curly hair that partly covers her protruding ears, and her nose casts a shadow on her face. She's squinting in the sunlight, and half-frowning at the person taking the photo. Where the photo has been cut in two, a glimpse of the shoulder of another smaller and presumably younger child is visible.

Hörður puts down the photo and runs his eyes over this little treasure trove that someone put in a plastic bag and hid inside the portable cassette player. What are these things? And to whom do they belong?

Dead Girls

Sunday

They're sitting again at the table in the break room at the headquarters of the search-and-rescue unit Torch, Lieutenant Hörður Grímsson and the three unit leaders, Björgvin, Magni, and Úlfar. On the table is the same large map that was there yesterday, but now the banks of the Skaftá river and the estuary area have been partially shaded with horizontal pencil lines. On the floor by the chair in which Hörður is sitting are three paint buckets, and on top of each bucket is one paintbrush.

"What I want you to do," says Hörður, as he munches on nicotine gum, "is to draw circles on the big map around all the huts, all the abandoned farms, and all the outbuildings in the area. Both those that are in full use and those that are no longer used. Then mark the same places on the maps you have with you."

"Very well," says Björgvin, grabbing a pencil. "I guess it's best for me to start."

He leans over the big map and starts drawing circles here and there. Magni and Úlfar draw corresponding circles on their own maps.

"I don't know the area well enough to add anything," says Magni apologetically.

Úlfar watches Björgvin, then points to a dull-green dell just north of the farm Heiðarból, above Fjaðrárgljúfur Canyon. "Isn't there a hut there?"

"Hm, yes, of course," Björgvin mutters as he adds another circle to the map.

"Have you gotten all of them?" Hörður asks when Björgvin appears satisfied with his work.

"I would think so, yes," says the blond giant.

"What I want you to do today is to search those places thoroughly," says the lieutenant. "If the girl is still alive, it's not unlikely that she sought shelter during the storm."

"It's a sensible conclusion," says Magni.

"I suggest that each of you search a different area than the ones you did yesterday morning," says Hörður. "Torch will take the area around Systravatn Lake and the heath north of it, The Star will search Stjórnarfoss Falls and its vicinity, and Lifesave in Fjaðrárgljúfur Canyon and on the surrounding heath. How does that sound?"

"Just fine," says Úlfar.

"Each of you take a paint bucket with you," says the lieutenant, "and mark the outbuildings that have been searched with a white X, so that others don't need to waste time later looking in the same buildings."

"Good idea," says Magni.

"If the search today isn't successful, I'll call for assistance from other, bigger search-and-rescue units," says Hörður. "Then we'll expand the search area and tighten our ranks. But I hope that we don't have to take it that far."

"That makes the two of us," Björgvin mutters.

"The Coast Guard helicopter will take part in the search today," says the lieutenant. "And the Air Search-and-Rescue

Unit will search with drones in the estuary area and up along the banks of the Skaftá River, as far as the highway."

"Hopefully this will yield some results," says Úlfar.

The lieutenant nods. "I can only hope so. But shall we say that's it for now?"

They all get up.

It's sunny outside and the temperature is fifteen degrees. Hörður sticks a new piece of nicotine gum in his mouth. He's standing in the parking lot in front of the headquarters of Torch, watching the search-and-rescue teams make themselves ready and get in their vehicles. Björgvin walks over to Úlfar, puts his arm over his shoulders and says something to him in a low voice. Úlfar shrugs and then nods. Björgvin pats him on the back and walks over to Torch's vehicle, a lengthy Ford Econoline, raised on 44" tires. The Star's vehicle is a giant Mercedes Benz Unimog, whereas Lifesave has a lengthy Land Rover that has been modified considerably. Its powerful diesel engines roar loudly and the air smells of acrid exhaust. After everyone is aboard, the vehicles are driven off.

Hörður is sitting at the lieutenant's desk in the police station, flipping through old police reports. His jacket is hanging on the back of his chair, and the coffee machine is brewing a fresh pot. He's halfway through the reports in the top drawer of the filing cabinet, and has gone almost seven years back in time. Each report is more banal and unexciting than the next—no organized crime or murder, anyway. Most of the reports are on traffic accidents that resulted in injury or death, mainly involving foreign tourists, but he's also noticed several reports on burglary and sheep theft, a few on rape and assault and battery, all involving non-locals, two on domestic violence and one on poaching. He has yet to come across a report of a missing girl or the discovery of a corpse.

Had Adam remembered things wrong? Or had the locals just been messing with him?

The red-haired giant gets up to have coffee. He has barely filled his cup when the desk phone rings. He sits down with his steaming coffee and answers it.

"Lieutenant."

"This is Axel."

Hörður instinctively straightens his back. "Hello! Do you have anything for me?"

"Yes. One or two things. For example, preliminary results of the autopsy. I haven't received a formal report, just a few important notes."

"Shoot," says Hörður, after readying pen and paper.

"The cause of death was likely cardiac arrest due to hypothermia. She also had severe pneumonia, a sinus infection, and meningitis, which could have led to her death. Meningitis isn't a direct result of hypothermia, but an infection caused by a virus, fungus, or bacteria."

"Okay," says Hörður. He squeezes the handset between his ear and shoulder as he writes these things down. "Could the pathologist deduce how long the deceased... how shall I word it... how long she was cold, so to speak. How fast or slow does a person die from hypothermia and meningitis?"

"Maybe the final report will say more about that, though I would think that it couldn't happen overnight, but what do I know? Of course, she was naked, and a few hours in cold weather can no doubt lead to death. If she fell into a river or lake, it would happen in a matter of minutes."

"Right," says Hörður. "What about her injuries, etcetera?"

"A lot of bruises and scratches, especially on her hands and feet, but also on her shoulders and knees."

"Is that normal?" Hörður asks. "I mean, she was walking barefoot, probably in the wilderness, but why were her shoulders and knees bruised?"

"Maybe she fell or rolled down a slope? As you mentioned, her left ear was injured. In fact, a piece of it is missing."

Hörður's heart starts beating faster. "Yes, and what? What sort of injury is it?"

"I'm looking for it, hold on…" Hörður hears a rustling of papers. *"Here it is. A triangular bit is missing from the top of the right ear. The wound is fairly clean. It could have been torn off, but it's impossible to rule out a blade of some sort."*

"A blade?" exclaims Hörður.

"It can't be ruled out, yes. Which is a very open interpretation that means almost nothing. A very typical sentence in an autopsy report."

"But how could she have lost a piece of her ear?" Hörður asks.

"She could have torn it on barbed wire? Crawling under or over a fence. If she fell, she could easily have injured her ear."

"Yes, maybe… I don't know," says Hörður. "Is there anything else in those notes they sent you? Anything about chafing on the wrists or the black streaks on the girl's face?"

"No, nothing about either. But hairs were found on the body. Other hairs besides her own, that is."

"Hairs?" asks Hörður in surprise.

"Animal hairs."

"Oh?" asks Hörður. "From what animal, then?"

"It doesn't say. Do you want me to find out?"

"Of course," says Hörður. "And ask about the chafing. Every detail matters. Girls have disappeared here before; did you know that? At least two, both foreign, to the best of my knowledge. "

"Hm, no. What do you mean?"

"One apparently fell into a nearby canyon fifteen years ago or so," says Hörður. "Another was found in the Skaftá river, after being missing for some time. It wasn't as long ago—maybe five years."

"I vaguely recall it—when the body was found in Skaftá. If I remember correctly, Forensics had to use dental reports to identify the deceased. Aren't there any reports on it at the station?"

"I've just been going through them, in fact," says Hörður. "I haven't found anything yet. It's as if those reports are missing. I don't quite know what to think."

"They weren't criminal cases. I would remember that. People die in accidents in all parts of the country, all year round."

"Yes, I know, but…" Hörður heaves a sigh. Didn't Reverend Páll mention a girl who drowned in a lake? Was it the girl who owned the portable cassette player? Johanna? "There's something fishy about all this."

"Has the other girl been found?"

"No, but the search is still ongoing," says Hörður. "We have the helicopter assisting us all day today, as well as the Air Search-and-Rescue Unit. If she's not found today, I'll have to call in more searchers."

"What if no girl is lost? Are you sure that there were two of them?"

"Yes, rather sure … very sure," sputters Hörður, who has always doubted everything he does, believes, and thinks. "Maybe not one hundred percent, but *if* there were two, then I've got to search for the other one, right?"

"Aren't you just bored?"

"What do you mean?" Hörður asks, insulted.

"You'll have the opportunity to return to the CID, of course— don't worry about that. But until then, you're a lieutenant, not a detective. I know it's not exciting, but you can't just make up a criminal case to investigate."

"Make up?" Hörður reddens with anger.

"Relax, I'm just saying. If you want to investigate this death as a criminal case, then do so. But…"

Axel stops mid-sentence.

"But what?" Hörður asks irritably. "But don't let your imagination run wild? Is that what you were going to say? I'm not imagining anything! A young girl died in my arms after wandering naked in a major storm. She had various injuries, including missing a piece of her ear, and it can't be ruled out that it was taken off by a blade of some sort. And her friend might still be missing, even though you don't want to admit that possibility."

"Barbara Hoffmann."

"What?" asks Hörður.

"The missing girl is named Barbara Hoffmann. I just got an email from the Police Air Terminal Unit. They've identified the deceased. Her name is Hertha Meier. She and her friend Barbara came together to Iceland almost a week ago. They're twenty-two years old and are from Augsburg in Germany."

Hörður sighs. "So I was right."

"Yes."

"When will the media be given the girls' names?" Hörður asks.

"Sometime later today, I expect. But not until their relatives in Germany have been contacted."

"I see," says Hörður. "But I don't want anything else to leak out. Nothing regarding the injuries to the body or cause of death. Let alone that there's a suspicion of a criminal act. Is that understood?"

"Do you think anyone deliberately harmed the girl or girls?"

"I'm afraid of that, yes," says the red-haired giant.

"Who, then?"

Hörður thinks about it. "It may be difficult to imagine a criminal hiding in a small community like this. Yet that's what I find most likely. And whether you believe it or not, certain individuals come immediately to mind, more than two and even more than three."

"Would you like me to send a detective there, to help you out? You would of course lead the search as well as the investigation, but if this turns out to be a criminal case, which I consider unlikely yet can't rule out, it will be difficult for one person to keep track of every aspect of it."

Hörður grunts as he considers the situation. "Thanks, but no thanks. It's enough that I'm a newcomer here. But the locals know me, well, by sight, at least, and technically speaking, I'm one of them, that is, *their* police lieutenant. I think that a detective from the south would have a hard time getting the locals to talk. Gaining their trust isn't easy. In addition, the person in question would have to start by acquainting himself with all the circumstances, and who would end up having to fill him in but me—and I have no time for that."

"I understand, but you may not be able to lead both the search and the investigation. That's quite a lot of pressure on one person."

"I've put Þóra Sverrisdóttir on the case," says Hörður after a short silence. "She's working on data collection for me, and will most likely be of help. At least she's quite interested in the case."

"Isn't she in the Patrol Division?"

"Yes, but she should be in the CID," says Hörður stubbornly.

"I don't know about that. Doesn't she have duty shifts? What sort of time does she have for investigative work?"

"Maybe you could free her up from her duty shifts?" Hörður asks. "That's how I started in the CID, as a supernumerary from the Patrol Division. The Black Mirrors case, remember?"

"I remember. We'll see about this."

"No problem. I'll…" Hörður stops when he hears a rhythmic tone. Axel has hung up.

Hörður is driving along Klausturvegur Road into the village. It's a beautiful summer day, warm and bright. Everything is still more or less sodden following the storm, but the sun is baking the surroundings and warming everything, living and dead. The flowers straighten up and reopen, the grass turns greener, and both flies and birds dash across the blue sky. The villagers who aren't on a search-and-rescue team sweep the sidewalks, cut branches from trees, pick up debris, and clear drains.

Life definitely goes on, but there's a shadow over Kirkjubæjarklaustur. Up on the heaths and verges of the mountains, search-and-rescue personnel can be glimpsed, and from a distance comes the heavy droning of a helicopter flying at low altitude. The police radio is crackling and humming and the lieutenant has a mild headache and a knot in his stomach: he's sleep-deprived and has no appetite.

As he approaches the chapel, he notices an old man walking in the opposite direction on his side of the street. The man is probably on either side of seventy, tall and robust-looking, wearing a black wool coat over a red sweater, and black trousers. He's holding a cane and has a full head of gray hair, is clean-shaven, and has a cravat around his neck. When the old man sees the police SUV approaching, he stops and stares into the car with eyes that are blue and cold. Hörður notices that one corner of the man's mouth droops. It's as if that side of his face is paralyzed.

Hörður drives past the hotel, signals to turn right, and then parks the SUV in front of the priest's house and goes into the garage without knocking first.

"Is that you, yes," says Reverend Páll. He's standing at the long workbench, in his smock, but appears not to be working on anything. "If you were hoping I'd fixed the turntable, I haven't."

"No, that's not why I'm here," says the lieutenant as he takes off his cap.

With a sad expression, the priest nods. "Naturally, you have your mind on the lost girl, as we all do."

"Did you see them here on Thursday?" Hörður asks. "The girls with the backpacks? They stopped at the Skaftá Visitor Center and then probably hiked up to Systravatn."

Páll shakes his head. "Not that I recall. Unfortunately."

"But did you happen to see the one who died?" Hörður asks. "She came walking into the village yesterday morning, either from farther in, for example from the fish farm, or down from the mountain and through the woods."

"No," says the priest in a low voice. "Still, I was outside, up on the ladder, clearing leaves and other debris from the gutters. But I didn't see her. It was pouring rain; poor visibility."

"Very true," mutters Hörður.

"I'll be praying for her soul today, at Mass at two o'clock," says Reverend Páll. "For them both, of course."

Hörður grunts. "Listen, about that portable cassette player I got from you."

"Yes?"

"Did you say that Geirharður brought it to you?" asks the lieutenant. "The father of Björgvin, the plumber, and husband of Sigrún at the Skaftá Visitor Center?"

"That's right," says the priest.

"In 1983, if I remember correctly?" Hörður asks. "Shortly before he died, right?"

"Yes, your memory hasn't failed you. Why do you ask?" Páll looks curiously at the red-haired giant.

Hörður ignores the question, as it's for *him* to ask the questions and others to answer. "What can you tell me about that man, Geirharður?"

"Hm, good question." Páll smiles faintly, then sits down on a stool and narrows his eyes. "Geirharður Róbertsson was terribly broken and bent. Not that he was small or weak, far from it. He was more or less a strongman, like his father and brother, but his spirit was bent—even his soul."

"What do you mean by that?" Hörður asks.

"He was a quiet man, seclusive and depressed," says the priest. "He drank a lot, especially toward the end. But apparently, he wasn't always like that. Not as a young man. But I didn't know him then. He lost his fiancée, you see."

"How did he lose her?" Hörður asks.

"He was engaged to a German girl, Klara Zimmerman, who shared his interest in horsemanship," says Páll. "Geirharður was a great horseman and had German contacts who bought horses from him now and then. He met the girl through those contacts, I understand. She moved to Iceland and lived with Geirharður at Heiðarból, along with his parents. It was during the roundup in the autumn that the girl fell into Fjaðrárgljúfur Canyon. No one witnessed it; her horse just wandered back to the farm alone, and then her body was found in the canyon."

"What year was that?" Hörður asks.

"I'm not sure," the priest replies. "Around the mid-1950's, approximately. Geirharður was just over twenty when it happened, maybe twenty-two or three. Apparently he was so overwhelmed with grief that he became bedridden. Sigrún grew up on a smallholding, Heiðarsel, a small sheep farm—I guess you'd call it a croft, actually. She and Geirharður were childhood friends, even though he was a little older. She visited him daily, and gradually managed to get him back on his feet. But he was apparently never the same man afterward."

"I see," says the lieutenant thoughtfully. "You said he brought the cassette player to you shortly before he died. How did he die?"

"He was out in a sandstorm," says Páll. "He was the leader of the search-and-rescue unit Torch, as Björgvin would become. That autumn there was a huge sandstorm and an emergency call was received from foreign tourists stuck in a car somewhere on Skeiðarársandur. Torch went to get them. Geirharður disappeared mid-operation. He wasn't found until two days later, far out on the sands. No one knows how he became separated from his companions, but some people thought he'd just walked off."

"That he'd wanted to die?" asks Hörður.

The priest nods. "But no one knows what happened."

"Right," says the red-haired giant. "But regarding the cassette player, I pointed out to you that it's labeled 'Johanna.' You then said that a girl named Johanna had worked as a hired hand for Geirharður and Sigrún, and that this same girl had drowned, right?"

"That's right," says Reverend Páll. "She was German, came to Iceland because of her interest in Icelandic horses. She drowned in Eldvatn in the early seventies, seventy or seventy-one, around then."

"What happened?" Hörður asks.

The priest shrugs. "I don't know. One day, she was just gone, and then her body was found at Eldvatn. An accident, I presume."

"Where is this lake?" asks the lieutenant.

"Eldvatn is a glacial river, not a lake," Páll replies. "It's here, just a stone's throw to the west of the Skaftá river. A powerful river, especially during the thaws. Dangerous, like all glacial rivers."

Hörður lifts his notepad and makes a note of this, as well as a few other things. "Tell me, between us, was Geirharður a temperamental man? Even violent?"

The priest gets a sad look in his eyes. "Are people still talking?"

"Maybe," says Hörður, putting on a poker face. "What might those good people be saying?"

"Not everything that the raven croaks is true," says Reverend Páll. "But for a long time, the story went around that Geirharður had treated Sigrún badly ever since she was a child, and that nothing had been done about it because of her parents' situation. Sigrún supposedly let it slip herself, the only time she ever drank alcohol. She was just a teenager then."

"What was her parents' situation?" asks the lieutenant.

"Well, they lived on the croft and were therefore at the mercy of Geirharður's parents," the priest answers.

"I see," says Hörður. "When you say he supposedly treated her badly, what do you mean?"

"I don't know and I don't want to know, because I've never believed that gossip," says Páll firmly. "As I said, Geirharður was both depressed and drunk. But I never sensed any evil in him."

Hörður scoffs. "Maybe you don't believe that people can be evil?"

"Mankind can and has done many evil things," says the priest sagely. "But I believe that man is good by nature, having been created in the image of God."

"I thought so," Hörður grunts. "But let's say that Geirharður did decide to die. Could he have brought this cassette player to you for some specific purpose? As if he'd wanted to say something or leave behind a message?"

"To say what?" asks Reverend Páll. "What message? Was there anything on or in the player that could be interpreted as a message?"

"I'm asking the questions here," says Hörður.

"Yes, of course," mutters the priest apologetically. "But no, I couldn't and can't understand Geirharður's actions in any other way than that he just wanted to get rid of the device. He didn't want just to throw it out, as I told you. "

"Why should he have thrown it out?" Hörður asks coldly. "There's nothing wrong with it. Why not use it or give it to someone who wanted it?"

Páll shrugs. "Well, he gave it to me, didn't he?"

Hörður grunts, then puts his notepad back in his pocket. "True enough. But you didn't need such a device, and you didn't use it."

"No, no," mutters the priest. "I certainly didn't."

Hörður realizes that the man of God has become somewhat annoyed at this unexpected and informal interrogation. "I'm sorry if I've been brusque. But this wasn't meant to be a courtesy call; I'm investigating a death and a disappearance."

"I understand," says Reverend Páll. "But you don't suspect that someone did something to the girls?"

"What I suspect or don't suspect is my business," says the lieutenant as he puts back on his cap. "And everything we said just now is confidential. Is that clear?"

"Of course," says Páll. "You can trust me."

Hörður goes to the door, but turns around in the doorway when he remembers something. "Listen, there was an old man walking down the main street earlier. Tall, wearing a coat and using a cane, and with one of those cravats around his neck. It looked as if his face was partially paralyzed. Who is he?"

"I suppose it was just old Steini," the priest replies. "He has almost entirely recovered, the dear man. Maybe you should pay him a visit, when you have the chance? He's living at the Klausturhólar Nursing Home now."

"I have other things to think about now," mutters the red-haired giant before leaving.

As Hörður is driving back along Klausturvegur Road, he sees a car marked National Broadcasting in the parking lot in front of the Skaftá Visitor Center. Not far from the car, a cameraman is pointing a TV camera at a female reporter holding a microphone up to old Sigrún, who appears shocked. Hörður curses under his breath as he steps on the gas. Sigrún notices the police SUV and waves at it as if asking for help. But the red-haired giant neither slows down nor stops, not wanting to become the next victim of the newshounds.

Bloody vultures! Hörður parks the SUV in front of the police station, goes in and locks the door behind him. He takes off his hat, hangs up his jacket, and plunks down on the chair behind the desk. Piles of old police reports still clutter the desk. Hörður starts leafing through the reports from even farther back in time, from 1969 back to the mid-sixties, but finds nothing about this Johanna who is said to have drowned in Eldvatn.

What has happened to the reports on her? The lieutenant hides his face in his hands. Has someone removed them? Were no reports written? Or did no girls ever go missing? He doesn't know what to think.

Hörður calls Þóra on his cell phone.

"Anything new?"

"Yes and no," he says. "The search still hasn't turned up anything. But now I know for certain that it's the deceased's friend who is lost. The body has been identified and I have the girls' names: Barbara Hoffmann and Hertha Meier, and they're German. It's Barbara who's missing."

"You were right."

"Yes, unfortunately," says Hörður. "But regarding the girls who supposedly went missing here earlier, I can't anything about them in the filing cabinet here at the station. I'm starting to think that it's all just folklore."

"Well, it isn't. I found something in the system immediately."

"What did you find?" asks the red-haired giant.

"Juliette Vermeulen disappeared in the summer of 2001. She was twenty-three years old, from Belgium. She lived in Vík in Mýrdalur and worked at the Víkurprjón knitwear shop. She was found ten days after she first went missing, at the Skaftá estuary. One person was questioned about the case, but the investigation concluded that it was an accident."

"Who was questioned?" Hörður asks. "Maybe it was Björgvin Geirharðsson?"

"That's right. Do you know who he is?"

"Yes," says Hörður. "The story is that he cheated on his wife with this Juliette. But did he have an alibi?"

"He was questioned concerning his whereabouts the night Juliette was first reported missing. He said that he'd been drinking with Júlíus Angantýsson at the latter's house, and Júlíus confirmed this to the lieutenant."

"Júlíus, the garbage man," mutters Hörður as he writes this down.

"But since it isn't known for certain when Juliette disappeared, let alone whether or when she was murdered, an alibi covering a few hours one night doesn't hold much weight—neither for conviction nor proof of innocence."

"True enough," says Hörður.

"Who is this Björgvin?"

"A strange guy," says Hörður. "Blond, very tall, taciturn and ponderous. Temperamental, even violent. He does plumbing and that sort of thing. Lives alone in the countryside, is divorced and has a five-year-old son. Why do you ask?"

"That wasn't all I found. The girl who fell into Hörgsárgljúfur Canyon was Swedish and her name was Lena Nilsson, eighteen years old. It was in 1992. She worked at the fish farm in Klaustur and lived in temporary housing provided by the company, along with other foreign workers. She didn't show up for work one Monday morning, and hadn't been seen since that Saturday afternoon. She was found in the canyon on the Wednesday, after a systematic search. Her body was badly injured, especially her head. Several people were questioned in connection with the case, including Björgvin Geirharðsson—apparently he and Lena had been seeing each other. But according to his mother's testimony, he was at home sick with the flu all weekend. He was nineteen years old at the time. But the girl's death wasn't investigated as a criminal case. It was thought to have been an accident or suicide."

"You don't say," says Hörður.

"But, nota bene, others besides Björgvin were questioned in both instances, including locals as well as foreign workers. The girls were both single, and may have had more than one boyfriend or lover during their stay. In neither instance was there any suspicion of criminality."

"Maybe the cases weren't investigated thoroughly." Hörður sticks a piece of nicotine gum in his mouth and goes and refills his coffee cup. "Who was in charge of the investigation?"

"The lieutenant at Kirkjubæjarklaustur directed both investigations. Steingrímur Róbertsson. But both times, an investigator

came from Reykjavík, though not until after the bodies were found. It appears to me, however, that those investigators didn't do much besides speak again to the same witnesses that the lieutenant had already questioned."

"The deceased Steingrímur was the lieutenant here before me," says Hörður. "He'd had this job since the settlement of Iceland, or so it seems. But I haven't yet found so much as a single preliminary report here on these two cases, or the older ones."

"What older cases are those?"

Hörður takes a sip of coffee. "A certain Johanna drowned in the glacial river Eldvatn around 1970. She was German and had been working as a hired hand for Geirharður, Björgvin's father."

"Really?"

Hörður sighs. "So I'm told. And that's not all. Sometime in the fifties, Geirharður's fiancé fell to her death in Fjaðrárgljúfur Canyon, which is here to the west of Klaustur. Her name was Klara Zimmerman and she was also German, and they were both young."

"If this is true, then those girls died before Björgvin was born."

"That's right," says Hörður. "And Geirharður died in 1983 in accidental circumstances, but many believe that he wanted to die."

"What do you know about this Geirharður?"

"A horseman, depressed, a drinker, and so on," says Hörður. "And it seems that Björgvin is just a *copy/paste* of his old man. After Geirharður's fiancé fell to her death there that year, he married a neighbor girl. A girl whom the stories say he mistreated in one way or another since she was a child. Very romantic and beautiful all in all."

"Indeed! I've got to find these deaths in the system. Maybe there's a common thread in these cases?"

"There already is one," says Hörður. "Foreign girls, all young and single. They all die in the vicinity of Klaustur, either by drowning or falling. The only thing missing is a suspicious individual who is in the area in every instance … but I can't see at a glance who that might be."

"Maybe it's just a coincidence? We're talking about a pretty long period of time, around four decades. There have always been foreign workers and tourists in this country. And they don't know the countryside as well as the locals, and therefore often take risks. In addition, suicide can't be ruled out. Young girls who come to Iceland to work are perhaps fleeing something, more often than not."

"There's one thing I still have to tell you," says Hörður, before describing to Þóra how he got hold of Johanna's Akai cassette player and the little things he found inside the device. "So I wonder if Geirharður was trying to say something before he died."

"Even confess something?"

"That has occurred to me, yes," says Hörður. "But let's say he's connected to the two older disappearances. How could that be related to the disappearance of Barbara Hoffmann or the two girls, Juliette and Lena?"

"Like father, like son?"

"That Geirharður was a cold-blooded murderer and Björgvin followed in his footsteps, took the baton?" Hörður asks skeptically. "It sounds like a cliché from a bad crime novel."

"Clichés are based on facts. They seem similar, the fathers, according to what you've told me. Depressed, drinkers, and temperamental. Criminals' profiles are full of clichés, but they're all true."

"Björgvin is definitely high on my list of individuals that I'll be questioning in connection with the disappearance of Barbara Hoffmann, if she isn't found alive today," the lieutenant says heavily. "But he's not alone on that list, and

I've got to be careful not to jump to conclusions. I've got to investigate this case with an open mind."

"That's right. Prejudice is the enemy of reason."

"And speaking of prejudice," says Hörður with a cold grin on his face, "the undersigned himself is depressed, a drinker, and temperamental, isn't he?"

Þóra laughs. *"Well, now that you mention it… "*

Hörður clears his throat. "I mentioned to Axel that I wanted you to assist me in this investigation. Would you have anything against it?"

"No, of course not. Is he going to get me out of my duty shifts, or… ?"

"I don't know. Hopefully," says the red-haired giant. "Of course, he's damn unpredictable."

"Yes, yes."

"If you have the time, it would help if you could find those old cases in the database and go through them carefully and compare them with the later ones. For example, check if there's anything of note in the autopsy reports. I'd like to know if these cases have anything in common or not," he says.

"I'll find time for this and do my best."

Hörður clicks his tongue. "And since you'll be checking the database anyway, maybe you could do a quick background check on Adam Knútsson? I wonder if I can trust that man or not."

"I'll do that. But one other question. Can you send me the items that you found in the cassette player? At least the ring and the earrings. If they belonged to any of those girls, that may have been mentioned in the reports."

"Yes, of course," says Hörður. At the same moment, the desk phone starts ringing. "I'll put them in the mail tomorrow. I'll make a photocopy of the photograph first. Someone is calling the station; I've got to answer."

"Great. No problem. Talk to you later."

Hörður puts down his cell phone and answers the desk phone. "Lieutenant."

"Hello, this is the National Broadcasting news division," says a female voice. *"We're in Kirkjubæjarklaustur and … "*

Hörður gets so irritated that he hangs up on the woman without saying another word. Can't he get any peace from those god-damned … !

His thought is suddenly interrupted by someone grabbing the handle of the locked front door and then knocking on it, with three heavy blows.

"What is all this fucking commotion?" Hörður springs up from the table, storms into the vestibule, and opens the front door. Standing outside it are the reporter and cameraman from National Broadcasting—the same people who were interviewing old Sigrún in the parking lot of the Skaftá Visitor Center. The reporter is holding a cell phone. It was probably her who called a few seconds ago.

"Hello!" says the reporter. "We're from … "

"I know very well who you are!" growls Hörður. "Why don't you just piss off back to Reykjavík and leave us alone, huh?"

"We're working on a story about the girl who … "

Hörður cuts her off.

"There's nothing to report right now!" barks the red-haired giant, before slamming the door practically in the face of the terrified reporter. He snorts, clenches his fists, and feels like punching the nearest wall. But then his anger dissipates as quickly as it had flared up, leaving him feeling a bit ashamed.

Was it maybe too harsh a reaction? Hörður sighs heavily. Doesn't he have to talk to the media? Isn't that part of his job? Now he can't hide behind Axel as usual.

"Fucking hell," the lieutenant mutters, before opening the door again and looking sheepishly out. They're standing there discussing what to do next, the reporter and the cameraman. She's a respectable middle-aged woman who has worked in television for a long time and occasionally announces the evening news.

"Hello, again," the reporter says hesitantly. She switches on the microphone that she's holding, and the cameraman lifts the camera onto his shoulder.

Hörður steps out. "Sorry about that. I'm just pretty busy at the moment."

"No problem," says the reporter. She glances at the cameraman, who nods at her. "What can you tell us about the ongoing search? A young girl was found dead here yesterday morning, right? Is it her friend who is missing?"

Hörður clears his throat. "Yes, it is. They came here together on Thursday, two girls on a backpacking trip. We don't know where they camped that night or … "

He stops and frowns. If they camped somewhere near Klaustur, shouldn't their tents have been found already? Or their backpacks?

"Or what?" the reporter asks.

Hörður's recomposes himself. "Yes, or where they were on Friday, but then the storm hit late Friday night and it appears that the girls may have gotten into some trouble."

"Have they been identified?" the reporter asks.

"Yes, they have," says Hörður. He looks at the reporter, but then turns his attention to the area behind her and the cameraman. He looks southward, out to the sands east of the Skaftá river. Lying in that direction is a gravel road, but he doesn't know where it ends. What did Adam call that area? Stjórnarsandur?

"So who are they?" the reporter asks, when the lieutenant says nothing more.

"Huh?" Hörður blinks. What did Adam say was down there? The Waste Management Company? A site belonging to some waste management company?

"The girls," says the reporter. "Who are they?"

Suddenly Hörður remembers that he saw Júlíus driving his garbage truck in that direction on Friday. Júlíus works for the Icelandic Waste Management Company, which handles garbage collection in Kirkjubæjarklaustur and the surrounding area. The garbage is buried out there on the sands, in a particular area. That's it.

"Who are the girls?" the reporter asks once more.

"The girls?" repeats Hörður. He turns his attention back to the reporter. Didn't she publish a cookbook a few years ago? As far as he recalls, she did. What was her name again?

"You said it was known who they were?" asks the reporter, who has grown a little irritated. "Are they foreign?"

"Yes, exactly." Hörður clears his throat. "A press release will be issued later today. But I can't say any more at the moment."

Hörður says goodbye to the reporter and goes back into the police station. He calls the leaders of the rescue units on the radio, one after the other, and asks if they have anything new to tell him.

"Have you seen anything or found anything? Over."

"No, nothing. Over."

"No tent, no sleeping bag, no equipment…nothing? Over."

"Nothing. Over and out."

Hörður turns the radio back down and stares into space as he thinks. Isn't it strange that nothing was found? Their tent must be somewhere. And their sleeping bags? Their backpacks?

But where?

Hörður gets into the SUV, drives out of the lot in front of the police station and turns right onto the gravel road lying through the sands south of the highway. The road is bumpy, but isn't so bad. To both sides are sandy wastes, where lyme grass grows and seabirds nest. After a few minutes' drive, the lieutenant comes to the Waste Management Company's sorting- and landfill site—what's commonly called a garbage dump. The area is large and covered with heaps of all sorts of waste. Beat-up old cars have been piled up in several places, and scattered around elsewhere are newer looking junkers. In one spot is a huge pile of fishing equipment, all sorts of nets and floats, and hundreds of meters of nylon ropes. There are whole mountains of corrugated iron, scrap iron, and broken-down machinery and hardware. Between these mounds are roads pitted with large mud puddles. There's an old excavator parked there, and an even older bulldozer that Júlíus the garbage man presumably uses to move all the rubbish, pile it up, and move earth. A few seagulls are startled and fly off. Hörður drives slowly around the site and finally finds what he's looking for, the place where the household waste is landfilled. Júlíus apparently dumps out the garbage truck at the foot of a long sand dune and immediately piles earth over the garbage. It looks as if he started far out in the sands, months or years ago, but has now reached the middle of the area. During this time, a kind of man-made sand embankment full of decaying debris has formed, as if a giant earthworm has crawled there beneath the earth's surface.

Hörður steps out of the SUV, goes and opens the trunk and grabs the shovel. Then he sees that damn microwave, which is still in the trunk. He walks with the shovel over to the landfill area. There's a strong smell of garbage in the air and seagulls circle in the clear sky above the lieutenant. From a distance comes the faint drone of the Coast Guard helicopter. Finally, he walks up to the embankment, where earth has been pushed over the latest load of garbage. When might that have been done? thinks Hörður. The stench makes him grimace as he starts turning over the earth with the shovel. The seagulls have already scraped the sand off a few bags of household garbage and poked holes in them. Hörður starts digging toward the top of the mound, before spying a strange pile at the near end of the embankment, at the foot of the sand dune on which the bulldozer stands. It's as if someone has added this pile to the existing sand; it sticks out a bit.

The lieutenant walks slowly over to the pile. The soil there is covered with tire tracks from the garbage truck, making it difficult to see if there are any footprints there, too. He uses the shovel to scrape off the top of the pile, and soon drives the shovel blade into something within it. The red-haired giant's heart starts beating faster. The pile is large enough to hold a human body, and that's exactly what he's afraid of finding. However, something entirely different comes quickly to light.

"What the hell," says Hörður. He digs into the pile and doesn't stop until he's absolutely certain. Yes, there's no question about it. He has found the tent and the backpacks.

Hörður is behind the wheel of the SUV, which he parked across the road into the Waste Management Company's landfill site. The engine hums in idle and the driver's side window is down. He munches on two pieces of nicotine gum while tapping the number of the head of the CID into his cell phone.

"Yes?"

Hörður clears his throat. "I need at least two members of Forensics to come here, preferably more. I've found something. Ask the Coast Guard to fly two of them here to Klaustur immediately, and send any others by car. We've got no time to lose."

"What did you find?"

"Do as I've asked you and then call back." Hörður hangs up, sighs, and then looks at the two dirty objects lying in the SUV's front passenger seat. He had put on disposable gloves and partially unfolded the tent, and opened two side pockets on the backpack that came to light first. In them he found a tent stake and map that the girls had gotten from Sigrún at the Skaftá Visitor Center. The tent stake was a simple iron pin with a loop at one end, slightly bent and darker at its sharp end, indicating that it had recently been driven into the ground. The map was damp, dirty, and crumpled, but surprisingly intact.

Hörður puts back on the disposable gloves and takes a closer look at the map. He sees old Sigrún's markings on it. On the one hand, a curvy line indicating the trail up to Systravatn Lake, as well as an X at the lake. Having heard her tell the girls that camping at the lake was prohibited, Hörður thought that the X might have stood for this rule, as with Xs over objects on signs—no smoking or camping and so on. She had also circled Fjaðrárgljúfur Canyon after they asked her where it was.

Hörður is fairly certain that Barbara and Hertha hiked up to the lake. He saw two people resembling them at the top of the escarpment, and found the cigarette butt in the outbuilding. Did they then go to…?

The red-haired giant starts from these thoughts when Axel calls back. He puts down the map, takes off his latex gloves, and answers.

"Yes?"

"The Forensics personnel have been dispatched. Would you care to tell me what you found?"

"I started wondering why the search teams hadn't found the girls' tent or their backpacks," says Hörður. "People go missing, but usually someone finds traces of them or clues—a car, clothing, whatever. In the girls' case, with no such traces having been found, I began to suspect that someone may have disposed of the girls' belongings in order to hide their whereabouts. If so, where would that person get rid of the stuff? Of course, he could have done so anywhere, but the first place that came to mind was the most obvious. A garbage dumpster or landfill. As soon as something goes into the garbage, it's pretty much gone, and it's bloody hard to trace its path up to that point, if it's found. Do you understand what I mean?"

"What did you find, man?"

"I came to the landfill site here in Klaustur, where household waste is buried," says the lieutenant. "I found the girls' things—their tent and backpacks, their sleeping bags—everything!"

"How do you know it's their stuff? Are their names on it or did you find their IDs along with it?"

"No, nothing like that, but…" Hörður breaks into a sweat, as Steppenwolf's questions have made him doubt himself. "What other tent could it be? Two backpacks, sleeping bags, clothing. Of course they're theirs! And I found a map of the area in a side pocket of one of the backpacks. A map that they got at the information center in Klaustur."

"Are their names on the map?"

"No, but…"

"How do you know the map belongs to those girls?"

"Of course I don't know that it does," says Hörður angrily. "But *I know* they got a map like that because I saw it when they got it."

"Fine. But what? Did someone throw it in the trash, and it ended up in the garbage truck?"

"No," says Hörður. "Earth had been pushed over what was dumped from the garbage truck last. But someone had come here with the girls' belongings and covered them over by hand."

"So footprints or tire tracks could presumably be found there?"

"Hopefully," says Hörður. "I didn't touch much of anything after I found this stuff, and will keep watch over the area until the Forensics personnel arrive. No one here knows about this discovery, and I want to keep it that way."

"Understood. What are your next steps, then? Should I send you someone?"

Hörður takes a deep breath. "Wait with that. I'm putting together a list of witnesses and suspects. A few of them are in search-and-rescue and are therefore searching for Barbara as we speak, as ironic as that sounds. Tomorrow I'll be questioning those individuals, while search-and-rescue teams from elsewhere continue the search. But I'm not going to talk to those under suspicion as suspects, but as witnesses. After all, I have nothing to justify a request for a search warrant or the arrest of any particular person. But of course I hope to find the culprit by tomorrow night."

"I hope you do."

"That makes the two of us," says Hörður as he knocks three times on the dashboard of the SUV—knock on 'wood'.

It's six o'clock. Hörður is driving west along Highway One, with Kirkjubæjarklaustur across the Skaftá river on his right and the desolate Meðalland on his left. He's on his way to Fjaðrárgljúfur Canyon to look for signs of Barbara and Hertha. The Forensics personnel have finished their work at the landfill site and have set off for the capital with the girls' belongings, countless photographs of the scene, and casts of footprints and tire tracks. The search for Barbara hasn't yet yielded anything.

Hörður is heavy-hearted, as time is working against him, and his nervousness and stress are increasing with each passing minute. But he has in fact made a bit of progress. He now knows, for example, that this is a criminal case, which isn't exactly uplifting, but is certainly important. With this new information, however, his burden has doubled. He's not only looking for a missing girl, but also for the person responsible for her disappearance and the death of her friend.

Maybe he should ask for help from Reykjavík?

"We'll see, we'll see," mutters the red-haired giant. Maybe there's no help available—everyone on summer vacation and all that. After driving about six kilometers along the highway, he comes to an intersection and slows down. He signals and turns north, then drives down to the Skaftá river, which, in this section, flows through a deep ravine. There's a fine bridge over the ravine, and from there the gravel road curves upward to a wooded hill above the ravine. He drives to the top of the hill and past a sign pointing to another, worse gravel road extending some distance into the highlands between Klaustur and Fjaðrárgljúfur Canyon. The sign reads *Laki 49 km*. He drives onward, over the hill and past the farm Hunkubakkar, where it appears to him that tourist services are available. On the lush, green farmstead are cottages that are probably rented out. He drives onto the heath and soon sets eyes on the Fjaðrá river, and shortly afterward, arrives at the parking lot at the mouth of the ravine bearing the river's name. He parks the SUV in the empty parking lot and shuts off its engine.

Hörður walks down to the river, then stops and regards the canyon. It's truly impressive and picturesque, he has to admit. One of those so-called "tourist magnets." But not everyone knows about this canyon, it seems. The lieutenant is alone there at the moment, in any case. He walks off again, threading the riverbank to the east. Soon, he comes to the cliffs on that side and realizes that he'll have to cross the river if wants to keep exploring the canyon. Having forgotten to bring boots, he decides to take off his shoes and socks and fold up his trousers. He stuffs his socks into his shoes, ties their laces together, and hangs them around his neck.

The water is ice-cold, and the pebbles at its bottom poke at the red-haired giant's soles. But the river is neither very deep nor fast-flowing, so it's really no trouble at all to cross it. After reaching the opposite bank and entering the canyon, Hörður dries his feet on clumps of grass beneath the rock wall and puts back on his socks and shoes. The river gurgles amicably and a bird or two flutters between the cliffs. The canyon is a peaceful, enchanting place.

The river flows endlessly, clear and cold. It meanders gently through the canyon, slowly but steadily, like time through eternity. Or is eternity time and life the river that flows through it?

Hörður threads his way even farther up the canyon, until he finds a grassy riverbank that he feels would be a tempting spot for those wanting to camp in this wonderland. He walks around carefully, staring down and examining every inch of the bank—every rock and blade of grass. The riverbank is hard, there being almost no soil beneath the delicate grass. Soon he finds a particular area where the grass is pressed down, as if by a tent. He goes down on all fours and examines the area even closer, and sets eyes on something slender and gray just barely showing between the rocks. It's the top part of a tent stake that has been driven into the hard ground. He manages to loosen the stake and pull it up.

Hörður sits down and rolls the tent stake between his fingers. It's just like the stake he has in the car. Most tent stakes are doubtless very similar, yet he's sure that this stake was used to fasten down the tent he found at the landfill site.

"What the hell," mutters Hörður. He looks around. So the girls came here, probably late on Thursday, and made camp. That was the night he and Adam went and got dinner and stopped in at the hotel bar. Did something happen here that night? Or the next day?

Hörður takes out his cell phone to call Þóra, but there's no connection in the canyon, any more than elsewhere on the heaths. Which means the girls wouldn't have been able to call for help if someone has attacked them in this place.

The red-haired giant's heart sinks. Something evil is afoot in Kirkjubæjarklaustur.

Hörður gets into the SUV and starts the engine. Then he calls Þóra and explains the situation to her.

"Isn't it more likely that someone got to the girls on Thursday evening or that night? Then there would have been few people around, if any, since it was after dark, but on the day after, there was more chance of encountering tourists and other witnesses, right?"

Hörður agrees. "But what we don't know is whether someone assaulted the girls in the canyon or whether they went somewhere with the person in question, voluntarily or against their will. I didn't see any signs of a struggle, anyway... or something worse."

"Exactly. Hopefully, Forensics will find some clues in the girls' belongings. Though I'm not quite sure what they might be."

"We'll see," says Hörður. "But speaking of Forensics, I let one of them have the items I was going to send you. The locks of hair and the jewelry. His name is Ragnar, and he'll be in touch with you."

"Okay, great."

"But he immediately pointed out to me that the hair won't be very useful. Not as far as DNA is concerned, anyway," says Hörður. "In order to find genetic material in hair, the follicle has to be present—the roots of the hair. These locks were cut from someone's hair, so they're missing the roots."

"I see. But I've been rummaging through the files on the old disappearances a bit more, and have found out a few things. When Klara Zimmerman was found, she was wearing one earring. The other never turned up. And when the Forensic Identification Unit was working on identifying the body that turned out to be Johanna Schmitz's, one of the first things they did was check to see if she was wearing a gold ring that her mother said she never took off. It was a ring she'd inherited from her grandmother. Made of solid gold, with a diamond-shaped pattern. She wasn't wearing the ring when she was found."

Hörður whistles softly. "You're describing the ring that was inside the cassette player."

"This can't be a coincidence. But what does it really mean?"

"I think Geirharður had something on his conscience," says Hörður. "Something bad. Something really bad. I'm starting to believe the theory that he actually committed suicide. That he deliberately perished in that sandstorm back then."

"But what does that mean for the investigation into the death of Hertha Meier and disappearance of Barbara Hoffmann?"

"I don't know…not yet," mutters Hörður. "But tomorrow I'll be interviewing a few people, including Björgvin Geirharðsson. Did you do a background check on Adam Knútsson?"

"Yes, he's as spotless as a boy of confirmation age."

Hörður grunts, both with relief and suspicion. "I would like to be able to cross him off the list of suspects."

"He looks good on paper, at least. But that of course doesn't tell the whole story."

"No, it certainly doesn't." Hörður shuts his eyes again; he's tired in body and soul. The darkness inside his head is spinning, like a vortex. Little by little, the vortex changes into a long tunnel. Someone limps out of the tunnel. It's a young woman, dressed in a nun's habit that's torn and tattered. It's the nun he dreamed of the night that he was startled from sleep by thunder and lightning.

The nun stares at Hörður with wild eyes. Her face is white as wax, and in her clear pupils, something is reflected. Hörður squeezes his eyes tightly shut, stares in in his mind into the darkness and tries to dive deeper into the memory, into the dream…into the image that flickers in his head. The reflection is dark and distorted, but he sees the vague shape of a naked body lying huddled in a constricted space, a kind of cage. It's a blonde girl, bruised and battered. She's lying in a fetal position and shivering with cold. He catches a glimpse of one of her ears, which is bloody. She starts in alarm, looks up, and ...

"*Are you there?*" asks Þóra.

Hörður starts, like the girl. Barbara? He opens his eyes and at the same time, the vision disappears. Was he imagining this horror? Or did he see something real?

When Hörður steps out of the SUV in the parking lot under the spruce trees at Efri-Vik, he hears rhythmic blows coming from the teacher's residence, as if something is being built. Today's search is clearly finished. Without knowing exactly why, it crosses the red-haired giant's mind that his neighbor Adam is nailing together a coffin. But he doesn't really believe that; it's just something that flies through his fatigued mind.

Hörður goes into the lieutenant's house, kicks off his shoes, throws his cap onto the nearest chair and hangs up his jacket. He's tired and hungry, but since he doesn't feel like cooking anything and has no time for sleep, he decides to take a shower. He stands for a long time under the showerhead, watching the hot water flow down the drain. The water is time, passing uncomfortably fast while the girl is lost and the criminal walks free. When he finally steps out of the cramped shower stall, the bathroom is full of steam. He dries himself with a towel that he then wraps around his waist. He walks barefoot into the hallway and tiptoes toward the bedroom, but stops when he sets eyes on the locked door. Where the hell is the key to it? Why is it locked, and what's behind it?

The red-haired giant grunts annoyedly. He's had enough of questions that he doesn't know the answers to. He walks to the door, grabs the handle, lays his shoulder against the door and presses, pushing hard with his legs and feet for leverage. Of course, the door opens outward, not inward, but Hörður is too irritated to think clearly. Just now, he's using his temper and strength, not his intellect. First, a soft crack is heard, then a loud bang, and finally an abrupt pop as the lock gives way and the door breaks in two.

There!

The smell of cracked wood overwhelms him and old dust tickles his nose. Hörður takes the damaged door off its hinges and stands it against the wall of the hallway. Then he peeks in through the empty doorway. Inside it is a small room, full of darkness and stagnant, acrid air. Hörður tests the light switch, but nothing happens. The bulb in the ceiling light is probably out. He steps over the threshold, reaches for the chain on the dark-blue roller blind covering a small window, and, opening the blind, lets in the evening sun.

"Okay," mutters the red-haired giant. The room turns out to be more or less of a storage space. On one wall are shelves; opposite them is a stool, and on the floor next to it is an ashtray full of cigar stubs, dirty glasses, and empty beer cans. The shelves are full of books and all sorts of other stuff. All but one, the third from the bottom. It has noticeably less on it, but what is there contrasts drastically with everything else.

With his wet locks hanging on his forehead, Hörður sits down on the stool and takes a closer look at the shelf's contents. Farthest to the left are tubes with lubricants and a few dildos and other sex toys, mainly anal toys, it appears to him—plugs, beads, and other things to insert into the rectum. In the middle of the shelf are piles of pornographic magazines, and then pornographic films on DVD. He rummages loosely through the piles and discovers that it's gay porn, and on the coarser side, he allows himself to conclude. Farthest to the right is a shoebox with a lid. Hörður reaches for the box, lays it on his thighs, and removes the lid.

"Fucking hell," mutters Hörður, who is both surprised and not. In the box are the police reports that he was looking for, four in number, the oldest at the bottom and the most recent at the top. On the girls who either fell or drowned. Klara Zimmerman, Johanna Schmitz, Lena Nilsson, and Juliette Vermeulen.

The red-haired giant's heart pounds in his chest. He leafs quickly through the topmost reports, but sees nothing really new or remarkable. Þóra has gone through the records in the police database and told him the main details. But why are the reports here, and not with the other ones at the police station? What does this mean? When Hörður lifts the oldest report from the bottom of the box, he sees that there are some papers beneath it.

They turn out to be old clippings from the newspapers *Morgunblaðið*, *Tíminn*, and *Þjóðviljinn*. The clippings are all related to the disappearance of the foreign girls. Of these three newspapers, only *Morgunblaðið* is still being published. He looks at the yellowed clippings and glances over the headlines.

Þjóðviljinn, September 1966. *Name of the Woman Who Fell to Her Death*. The story is accompanied by a black-and-white photograph of a smiling blonde woman. Below the photo is a short text. *The woman who fell to her death in Fjaðrárgljúfur near Kirkjubæjarklaustur on Saturday was named Klara Zimmerman. Klara was German, 21 years old. She was a hired hand at the farm Heiðarból, and was taking part in the sheep roundup when the accident occurred.*

Tíminn, April 1971. *Extensive Search for a Young Woman.* He reads the beginning of the story. *Police, Scouts, and search-and-rescue units in the Southeast have been searching since 11 April for Johanna Schmitz, a twenty-four-year-old woman from Germany, without success.* The article is accompanied by a photo of Johanna, who has fair hair and skin. *Johanna is a hired hand on the farm Heiðarból. She went for a walk early that day, but when she didn't return in the evening, the police were alerted. There is heavy snow on the heaths in many places, and the weather has made searching difficult: a stiff southeasterly wind and sleet. Five years ago, a German girl fell to her death in Fjaðrárgil Ravine, which is south of the farm Heiðarból.*

The next clipping isn't about the discovery of a body in Eldvatn, but another lost girl, twenty-one years later.

Morgunblaðið, October 1992. *Alert for an Eighteen-Year-Old Girl.* Under the headline is a photo of a childlike blonde girl and a short text. *Police in the South are searching for Lena Nilsson, an eighteen-year-old Swedish girl. Lena was last seen in Kirkjubæjarklaustur on the 13th of October. She was wearing a blue coat and jeans. Those who have any information on her whereabouts are asked to contact the police lieutenant at Kirkjubæjarklaustur, tel. 444-2040.*

Morgunblaðið, October 1992. *Name of the Girl who Fell in Hörgsárgljúfur Canyon.* It was Lena Nilsson. Hörður sighs, then looks over the remaining clippings. Nine years have now passed.

Morgunblaðið, May 2001. *Search for a Young Woman.* Under the headline is a photo of a very attractive young woman with dirty-blonde or light-brown hair, shoulder-length. *Police and search-and-rescue units in the South and Southeast are still searching for Juliette Vermeulen, a 23-year-old woman from Belgium. Juliette was last seen at her home in Vík in Mýrdalur on the 15th of May, where she lived with other foreign workers. It is not* *known precisely when she left home or where she went. Juliette is of average height, slender and with dirty-blonde hair. She was probably wearing blue jeans, black sneakers, and a red, waist-length jacket. Those who have seen Juliette are asked to…*

Hörður stops reading when he sets eyes on a photograph at the bottom of the shoebox. The photo is in color, size A5. It shows three naked men having wild sex on a double bed. Above the bed is a map of Berlin; perhaps they are in a hotel room. One of the men is black. They're not entirely naked, but have leather collars around the necks and are dressed in strappy leather getups with metal rings here and there. These are clearly so-called "leather gays." The photo is probably not mass-produced pornography, but seems to be from a private collection, taken on a cheap camera, with corresponding poor quality. Hörður looks closely at the men's faces. One of them is blond, just over forty, maybe, robust and with fair, almost milky-white skin. Is he an Icelander?

Hörður turns the photo over. The following sentence has been written on its back: *The film is in safe hands*

The hair rises on the nape of the red-haired giant's neck. Is this a reassurance? Or a threat? The answer is fairly obvious. If the person who wrote the message had wanted to reassure whoever received the message, he would probably have sent him the film, and not a single photograph. So it appears to be a threat.

About an hour later, Hörður walks over to the teacher's house and pounds hard on the front door. The hammering stops, and Adam comes to the door. He's wearing a T-shirt and blue work trousers with countless side pockets. His face is red and there are sweat stains at his underarms.

The red-haired giant stares at him threateningly, but says nothing.

"Hello," says Adam, somewhat alarmed.

"May I come in?" Hörður asks rudely.

"Yes, of course." Adam lets him into the hall, then goes into the house and signals the lieutenant to follow him. "No need to take off your shoes. I'm laying parquet in the living room and everything's covered in dust. Would you like coffee or anything?"

Hörður grunts as he peeks into the living room, where everything is a mess. He hadn't really expected Adam to be constructing coffins for his wife and daughter, but still, he's glad the man is not. "Coffee would be nice, thanks."

Adam offers him a seat at the kitchen table, then takes two cups and pours coffee into them from a thermos. "Milk or sugar?"

Hörður shakes his head.

"Has anything happened?" Adam asks as he sits down at the table. "There was almost nothing new on the evening news earlier, but I heard at the shop, after the search was over, that some men had come here from Reykjavík. Were they police detectives?"

Hörður scoffs. "You people here in these small villages don't miss much, do you?"

"I guess not," says Adam.

Hörður knits his brows and takes a sip of coffee. Then he looks sternly into his neighbor's eyes. "Can I trust you?"

Adam half-freezes under the lieutenant's harsh gaze, but finally manages to nod. "Of course. Yes, you can trust me. Why do you ask?"

The red-haired giant inhales through his distended nostrils. "If you're hiding something from me, Adam Knútsson, you'll have hell to pay for it. Do you understand me?"

Adam becomes so frightened that he starts to giggle. "What's wrong with you, man? Come on. You can trust me, as I said!"

Hörður grunts, glances to the side and drums with the fingers of one hand on the kitchen table. "Right, then."

Adam looks at him inquiringly. "So you trust me? Is there anything you want me to do for you?"

"Lieutenant Steingrímur, who was here before me," says Hörður unceremoniously. "What do you know about him? Personally, I mean."

"The Rock Grinder?" Adam exclaims. "I worked with him often, as I told you. He's a great *legend*; was renowned as a strongman at one time—no one was a match for the lieutenant. Broad-shouldered, big hands, a back like a bull's. He was a bully and enjoyed taking on brawlers and drunks, crushing them and grinding them into the dust. But he was well over sixty when I came here. A serene man, taciturn but absolutely not dry, or something like that. Probably just bored with his job. And tired, you know. Not the same strongman he was. Why do you ask?"

"A wife, children?" Hörður asks in return.

Adam shakes his head. "He always lived alone, most of the time here in the house next door. Since when, I don't know, and until he had a stroke."

"Didn't you find it strange that he was single?" Hörður asks.

Adam shrugs. "I didn't give it any thought. Why do you ask?"

"You didn't know he was gay?" Hörður asks.

Clearly surprised, Adam's eyes open wide. But then he gives a little smile. "I didn't know that, no. But when you say it, it doesn't sound odd at all. But are you sure? Who told you that?"

"I'm sure," mutters Hörður. "But what I don't know is whether it was common knowledge or not."

"I see," says Adam thoughtfully. "If so, I think it would be one of those things that the villagers wouldn't talk about. No one has mentioned this to me, but I'm not originally from here, either. I don't get to know everything. Here, there's a definite but unofficial level of respect, you see. If you're at the lower end of the list, you can be made fun of, teased, and gossiped about. But if you're toward the top, you enjoy a certain immunity. Certain things about you are never discussed, others are covered over or overlooked when necessary, if you understand what I mean."

Hörður sighs. "I grew up in a small seaside village—so I know what you mean. And the lieutenant enjoyed immunity, didn't he?"

"Of that, I have no doubt," says Adam. "Because of his position, his earned respect, and simply because of his physical superiority. You don't slander someone who can crush your bones, and might be inclined toward doing so."

"Maybe not," says Hörður. "But people can know things without blathering about them at cafés and in sewing clubs. In places like this, everyone knows everything about everyone, the last I knew."

"True," says Adam. "But what are you getting at? Let's say Steingrímur was gay. What does it matter?"

"Never mind that for now," says the lieutenant. "But maybe everyone knew he was gay or that he might be gay or something along those lines. People probably didn't care as long as he didn't *act* gay or *do* anything gay, like dress weirdly or sleep with men. People's tolerance usually only goes so far; it's more in words than deeds. Right or wrong?"

Adam thinks this over. "I would guess you're right. No one would have cared as long as he behaved, yes."

Hörður takes a deep breath. "But if something juicy were to be reported, for instance, if a photo got around of the lieutenant sucking the dick of a muscular black man, might it change anything?"

Adam's face pales. "Uhh, yes. I mean, no one would look with the same eyes at the man again. As you said, prejudices don't lie deeply in society, particularly in such small villages."

Hörður takes a sip of coffee. "I thought so."

Adam clears his throat. "Where are you headed with this? You didn't find such a photo, did you?"

Hörður looks straight at him. "I've decided to trust you, to make you my deputy here in Klaustur during the investigation into the girls' disappearance. But I can't entrust you with everything. You have to understand that."

Adam's face reddens. "Okay."

Hörður pulls out a folded sheet of paper and hands it to his new deputy. "On this paper are the names of the individuals I'm going to meet tomorrow and take statements from. I'm talking about so-called witness interviews. Officially, I'll just be gathering information about the girls' disappearance. No one is a suspect, and no one will be arrested. I'm going to talk to these individuals in order listed, the top one first and the bottom one last. Some I'll interview at the station, others at their homes or at work. It's all marked on the paper. What you'll do is either summon these people to the station or let them know I'm on my way to meet them, about ten minutes in advance. When you call these people, do it from a cell phone, in your car parked near the person's home or workplace. If anyone refuses to come or to have me visit or flees the scene, I'll find them and arrest them. Are you up for this?"

"Definitely," says Adam immediately, his voice husky with excitement.

The lieutenant finishes his coffee in one gulp. "Talk to you tomorrow, deputy."

It's eleven o'clock. The sun is setting, the sky is dark red, and the mountains are black silhouettes. Hörður is so tired that he can barely stand, but he can't relax; he's laden with stress and worries and can't calm his mind. He feels half nauseated and has a headache. Having drawn the curtains shut and turned on the lights, he paces around his house. He goes over the events of the past few days and doubts everything he's done and said and not done or left unsaid. Was the search extensive enough? Manned well enough? Should he have called immediately for helicopters, dogs, and search-and-rescue teams from outside the district? He isn't sure, but in hindsight, yes, probably. But in order to use search dogs, the dogs have to have something to smell first, which wasn't the case. Should he have asked for the CID's assistance? Maybe, but Axel hinted that he couldn't spare any detectives. Besides the fact that there's little or nothing the CID could do at the moment. Hörður has a list of suspects, but no evidence that could connect them to the girls' disappearance or the death of Hertha Meier. He can neither arrest anyone nor obtain a search warrant. Tomorrow it will be revealed who has an alibi and who doesn't. But the problem is that he doesn't know exactly when the girls were attacked. So all the alibis will be more or less useless, no matter what. The suspects may be able to prove where they were from at such-and-such o'clock this day or that, but the police still can't prove when or where a criminal action took place.

Hörður heaves a sigh. But they *were* attacked, damn it! Probably in Fjaðrárgljúfur Canyon. He found the tent stake there. And he found the girls' tent, sleeping bags, and backpacks. Someone had buried the girls' things. Hopefully, Forensics will find something significant during its examination of them. At least proof that it belongs to the girls. Preferably, something that connects one of the suspects to the crime.

The lieutenant looks at his watch. Shouldn't he try to sleep? Yes, but he's actually too tired, too stressed, too worn-down to do so. If he only had a sleeping pill. Too bad Bíbí is so far away. She always has…

Bibi! Hörður breaks into a sweat. He still has to call his partner. He turns off the lights in the living room and kitchen, takes off all his clothes but his underwear, and hurriedly brushes his teeth and pees. In the mirror above the sink he sees the image of a man who is pale as a corpse and stiff with fatigue—his green eyes are like lifeless stones and his rough-hewn face is hidden behind a full red beard that is both thick and ragged. He looks like an exhausted giant.

Hörður lies down on the bed, pulls the duvet up to his chin, and switches off the lamp on the nightstand. He unlocks his cell phone and calls Bíbí.

"Hi, babe! I didn't think you would call this late. I'm sure you've been busy. Of course, they said on the evening news that the girl hadn't been found. Is she still missing?"

Hörður lies there in the darkness with his eyes closed, his phone to his ear, and a faint smile on his face. He likes hearing the bright, warm voice of the woman he loves. How she can talk, this angel! "There's nothing to report, sweetie. But I don't want to talk about work. What did you do today?"

"Oh, pretty much nothing. Just tidied up here at home, went to the store and so on. Baked a cake."

"What kind of cake?" Hörður mumbles.

"Oh, I decided to try the recipe that Jónína sent me the other day. Didn't I tell you about it? She found this great recipe for… " Bíbí goes on talking, but Hörður doesn't hear a word of what she says.

He's fast asleep.

Big Questions

Monday—First Part

It's half past seven in the morning. The sun is high in the sky and moorland birds flutter chirping through the sky. Hörður arrived at the police station at a quarter past seven, after sleeping like a rock for over six hours. Still, he started the day by going and getting a copy of the *Fréttablaðið* daily, which he took from a plastic-wrapped stack on the sidewalk in front of Kjarval. In rural areas, this free paper isn't delivered to every house, as in the capital area, but left in a large stack at a gas station or in a store. On the paper's front page are photos of Hertha Meier and Barbara Hoffman. *The Girl is Still Missing*, reads the headline. While freshly brewed coffee trickles into the coffee maker's pot, Hörður cuts the photos of the girls out of the paper and fastens them with thumbtacks onto the corkboard on the wall above the small table in the break room. He brought the newspaper clippings that he found in the shoebox at home, and has attached them to the board as well. The old police reports are on the lieutenant's desk. Once he has tacked the new newspaper clippings to the corkboard, he regards the outcome. The board now displays the faces of the six foreign girls who went missing and/or died in a tragic way in the vicinity of Kirkjubæjarklaustur in the last four decades. It's a long time, for sure, but six missing persons is a high number, at least by Icelandic standards.

The number of victims, of course, is not just six, but is almost innumerable, and the suffering never ends. Behind each of these faces are parents, siblings, grandmas and grandpas, relatives, and friends—a whole battalion of women, men, and children who are shoved without warning into a dark nightmare from which they never wake up. Anxiety, trauma, fear, panic, and finally anger. All-encompassing and suffocating grief that never disappears. The world is full of innocent people with invisible wounds that never heal…

The death of one is the suffering of many—Lieutenant Hörður Grímsson knows this best of all. He has a great deal of work to do, and the big questions he faces are these:

a) *Was the disappearance and/or death of these girls the result of criminal acts? If so:*
b) *Is the same party responsible for the disappearance and/or death of all of them? Or:*
c) *Are there two or more perpetrators?*

"Good questions," mutters the uniformed lieutenant after writing them down in his notepad. He reminds himself, however, of the fact that there are five dead girls, not six. Barbara Hoffmann is still just missing. He still holds the faint hope that she's alive. It's a hope he neither can nor wants to lose.

Hörður is pouring hot coffee into his cup when he hears the front door open.

"Hello?" calls a woman's voice from the vestibule.

"Just a moment!" Hörður calls out. He takes his first sip of coffee for the day and sighs contentedly. Then he writes the third big question in his notepad—a question that he'd almost forgotten:

> d) *Has he already met and/or talked to a potential perpetrator? The person who at least bears responsibility for the disappearance of the German girls and at the same time the death of one of them.*

Hörður takes a deep breath through his nose, then nods. He considers it very likely. The answer is yes. He closes his notepad and takes another sip of the strong coffee before going out and opening the door to the vestibule. Standing there are a girl and woman: Agnes Jónsdóttir, twelve years old, and Hildigunnur, her mother, who is thirty-two years old.

"Sorry to make you wait," says the lieutenant as he invites them in. "I was just finishing up some paperwork."

"No problem," says Hildigunnur. "But I still don't understand what *we're* doing here. Aren't you searching for a lost tourist girl? What does that have to do with my Agnes?"

"I'll explain it to you. But let's go in here first," says Hörður. He leads the mother and daughter into the windowless interrogation room.

"Fine," Hildigunnur mutters as she looks with a blend of curiosity and apprehension into the empty jail cells. She's red-haired and rather plump, wearing a light jacket over a summer dress with a floral pattern.

The interrogation room is plain and bleak. Actually just four white walls, an elongated table, and three chairs. The lieutenant invites the mother and daughter to sit down at one of the table's long sides and he takes a seat opposite them. On the table in front of him is a folder containing loose sheets of paper, a pen, and a small voice recorder.

"Thank you for coming," he says, smiling at Agnes, who looks away shyly. She's red-haired like her mother, thin as a reed and bony. She reminds the red-haired giant of his sister Lísa, which is both sweet and painful—mainly painful, as he hasn't seen his sister for more than a decade and will never see her again, or at least as long as he lives.

The lieutenant clears his throat. "Today I'm talking to a few people from the village. What I'm doing is mapping a specific time frame in order to get as clear a picture as possible of … "

He stops, clears his throat again. Then he looks straight into Hildigunnur's eyes.

"Of course, what we discuss here is confidential. I'm simply trying to find out where certain individuals were at a particular time. But I must emphasize that so far, no one is suspected of anything. Is that understood?"

Hildigunnur lays her hand on her chest. "God, yes … of course! Is this about Björgvin, maybe?"

Hörður smiles stiffly. "I need to ask Agnes a few simple questions. You're here as her guardian. Can I trust that our conversation won't go beyond the walls of this room?"

Hildigunnur nods quickly. "Of course!"

Hörður sighs, having no faith that she'll keep her word. He opens the folder, removes the top sheet of paper, and then turns on the recorder. Written on the paper are several questions, and below each of them is space to write the witness's answer. "Then let's begin."

He starts by reading particular information into the recorder—the date, time, and name of the witness.

"Agnes," says Hörður. He smiles at the girl, hoping at the same time that his smile is both friendly and reassuring. But also fearing that it looks like a psychotic scowl that will scare the dear child. He's always struggled to be what

Bíbí calls *congenial*. "This past Thursday, Silja asked you to babysit for her, didn't she?"

Agnes hesitates but then nods.

"Would you please answer out loud for me?" Hörður asks gently, before pointing at the recorder.

"Yes," says Agnes in a high-pitched voice.

"Thank you," says the lieutenant. "Do you remember what time you got to her house?"

Agnes looks at her mother and then at the red-haired giant. "Around eight, something like that."

Hörður nods. "And did Silja go out soon after that?"

"Yes," Agnes replies.

"What did you do that evening?" Hörður asks. "You and the little boy, I mean…" He looks at his notes. "You and Atli, Silja's son. He's what, five years old?"

Agnes nods. "Five, yes. We just watched cartoons and stuff. Had Cocoa Puffs and stuff."

Hildigunnur squirms awkwardly, perhaps unhappy about the Cocoa-Puff eating. Hörður signals to her to calm down.

"And then what?" he asks Agnes.

"Then Atli went to bed," she says. "But first he brushed his teeth and all that."

"Right," says the lieutenant. "Do you remember what time he went to bed?"

Agnes shrugs. "Around ten. Maybe a little later."

Hildigunnur makes a "tsk-tsk" sound.

"And what did you do after Atli fell asleep?" asks Hörður.

"Just, nothing," says Agnes. "Watched a little TV."

Hildigunnur sighs disapprovingly. Hörður glares at her.

"And then I fell asleep too," says Agnes, half-apologetically.

"Do you know what time that twas?" asks the lieutenant.

Agnes shakes her head. "No-oo. I fell asleep on the couch while I was watching."

"I see," says Hörður. "And did you wake up later that evening or during the night?"

Agnes shakes her head again. "I just woke up in the morning. But then Atli wasn't in his bed."

"What?" Hildigunnur asks in surprise.

"Agnes and I are talking, if you don't mind," says the lieutenant sternly.

Hildigunnur's face reddens.

"You wake up and see that Atli isn't in bed," says Hörður to Agnes. "What did you do then?"

"Called Silja," Agnes whispers sheepishly.

Hörður nods. He doesn't need to ask her what time it was, because he witnessed the call. Silja was at his house when the babysitter called. But he still has to ask her, on account of his report. "What time did you call Silja?"

Agnes thinks this over. "At eight o'clock, maybe."

Hörður nods again. He'd already recorded the time: 08:02. "But you neither saw nor heard Björgvin that evening or night? Atli's father."

"No," says Agnes.

Hörður writes down her answer. "Tell me one thing. You got to Silja's around eight o'clock. How long did she ask you to stay?"

"Until about eleven, something like that," Agnes replies. "But she always tells me not to wait up. I usually stay over when I babysit for her."

Hildigunnur sighs wearily but Hörður pretends not to notice. The sigh doesn't escape Agnes's notice, and she looks embarrassed.

"So you just expected Silja to come home late," says Hörður.

"Or not at all," Hildigunnur mutters annoyedly, but with something of a smirk on her face. She knows that Silja spent the night at the lieutenant's house, and she knows very well that he knows that she knows, because when three people know something, everyone does.

Agnes stiffens up, but Hörður blushes.

"Would you mind?" says the lieutenant to Hildigunnur, who scoffs before shrugging.

Hörður clears his throat. "Tell me, Agnes. Does Silja leave the door unlocked when she goes out? Or does Atli's father have a key to the house?"

"It's always unlocked, I think," Agnes replies in a soft voice.

"I see." Hörður smiles reassuringly at her. "That's all, then. I'd like to thank you both for coming."

One witness interview down, six to go. Hörður looks at the clock on the wall, and then goes and gets more coffee as he waits for witness number two. He's a bit restless, and paces the room as the minutes go by. Next is Silja Valdimarsdóttir; the divorced woman he invited back to his place after drinking at the hotel bar. Björgvin's mother. It's nine o'clock; she should be there at any moment. Hörður has compiled the most important points from his interview of Agnes and typed them up on his computer. He's going to make a short summary of the day's interviews and send them to Þóra, to make it easier for her to involve herself in the case—get a feel for the big picture.

"Hi, hi!" calls out Silja as she walks into the police station. She tries to sound cheerful, but her voice is forced.

When Hörður opens the door to the vestibule, he sees that she's holding a plate of something covered in plastic wrap.

"I made a sandwich loaf yesterday. My mother came to visit and I wanted to make her happy, "says Silja hurriedly. "It crossed my mind to bring you a piece. It's still very fresh; I kept it in the fridge last night."

"Umm, thanks," mutters Hörður. He takes the plate and places it on his desk. "Thanks for coming. Come with me back here."

He leads her into the hallway, and then stops at the door to the interrogation room.

"Ooh, so I'm immediately invited *back here*," says Silja flirtatiously, winking at the lieutenant. She's dressed in a pastel-colored tank top and wide linen trousers that are so thin he catches a glimpse of the waistband of her underwear through them.

"No fooling around," says Hörður dryly. He sees that Silja is far from being as relaxed as she wishes to appear. She's probably uncomfortable, but tries to cover over her insecurity by flirting and speaking quickly.

But why is she insecure? Because they nearly slept together? Because she knows the villagers *think* they slept together? Or is it something else?

What, then?

"Easy with the seriousness," says Silja, half-insulted. Her smile vanishes and her face darkens. At the same time, wrinkles form around her mouth and eyes. It's as if she's aged about ten years in an instant.

"Witness interviews in connection with a police investigation into a death and disappearance *are* a serious matter," says Hörður. He invites her to take a seat at the interrogation room's table, closes the door behind them, and sits down opposite her. He opens the folder and takes some papers from it—notes for the interview and a short summary of his latter conversation with Reverend Páll.

"My dear man," says Silja irritably. "You know as well as I do that I know absolutely nothing about those German girls! Wasn't I with *you* the night they disappeared?"

Hörður looks her straight in the eye. "Did they disappear?"

Silja reddens. "What do you mean? Isn't the search still on for one of them?"

"Yes," says Hörður, with a worried expression. He recalls his dream. A bloody nun in the storm. And the vision that he saw—the reflection in her eyes. A naked girl in a cage.

His mouth goes dry and his heart begins beating faster.

"Hello?" says Silja.

Hörður blinks. "What?"

"You dropped out," says Silja. "Are you okay?"

Hörður clears his throat. "Yes, of course."

He turns on the recorder and states the date, time, and name of the witness. Then he asks Silja about that Thursday night. What time Agnes came to her place, what time she herself went out, and what time Agnes called in the morning.

"You know that as well as I do," she mutters, half-embarrassedly. The lieutenant nods, but then points to the recorder.

Silja sighs. "It was about eight o'clock, if I remember correctly."

"Thanks," says the lieutenant. Silja's answers are in agreement with what Agnes said, almost to the minute.

"What did you do after you got home?" Hörður asks. "Did you call Björgvin? Did you go pick up your son?"

Silja fiddles with her hair. "I sent him a message. Said that I would pick up Atli around noon. Then I took a nap."

Hörður makes a note of this. "And did you do that? Did you pick up the boy around noon?"

Silja shakes her head. "Bjöggi brought him around ten o'clock. He had to go to work."

"I see," says Hörður. "So you didn't go to Björgvin's on Friday?"

"No," says Silja.

"Have you gone to his house since then?" asks Hörður.

"No. Why?"

"I'll ask the questions here," mutters the lieutenant. "Tell me, your house. Is it always unlocked? Or does Björgvin have a key?"

"It's usually unlocked," says Silja. "Always, actually. Few people lock their houses here."

Hörður nods. It was like that in Súðavík, too, when he lived there. "Let's talk a little about Björgvin. What kind of man is he?"

Silja sighs. "What kind of man? Terribly heavy and dreary. He's a damn brute. But not really more than that. I just don't understand why I was with him for so long. But I got pregnant, of course, and … "

Hörður holds out his hand, stopping her. "Is he temperamental? Did he lay hands on you?"

"He's temperamental, yes. Mainly depressed and grumpy; he gets into terrible huffs and the like," says Silja. "He never hit me directly, but grabbed me and pushed me and such. But never so that… "

She's stops, catches her breath.

"You don't think Bjöggi did anything to those girls, do you?"

Hörður grunts. "As I said, I'm investigating a death and disappearance. That means I speak to a few individuals, ask all kinds of questions and turn over countless stones."

Silja pales. "He would never do anything like that, I think. Good God, no. I mean, he had the boy with him that night, too!"

"I don't know any better than you whether or when something criminal took place," says Hörður in a grave voice. "I'm just feeling my way, ruling out one thing and another, examining this and that. To narrow the circle, if I can."

"Björgvin's a damn oaf, but he's no criminal," says Silja hurriedly. "He's had it difficult his whole life. His dad was really strange, distant, and depressed. He drank a lot and died when Bjöggi was only ten years old. His mother raised him alone. She's a tough woman; she's always had to fight to get by, grew up in poverty, and got stuck with a godforsaken husband. But she's not exactly the warmest mother there is. Bjöggi was never hugged or anything like that. That's why he's the way he is now. But he always got enough to eat, new clothes and all that, and when he was eighteen he got to go to Germany to study horse training even though his mother wasn't keen on the idea and could hardly afford it. But he's her prince."

Hörður makes a few notes from what she says.

"Didn't he once have a girlfriend who died?" he then asks. "A Swedish girl who fell to her death in Hörgsárgljúfur Canyon? Lena Nilsson."

Silja shrugs. "Girlfriend—I don't know about that. They'd been together for a while, yes. But she'd been with many others. Why do you ask? It was just an accident, wasn't it?"

"Then there was Juliette from Belgium," says Hörður. "She lived and worked in Vík. Drowned in the Skaftá river five years ago. Did he cheat on you with her?"

Silja's face reddens. "So goes the story. But she wasn't the only woman that Bjöggi cheated on me with. He completely flipped out after I got pregnant. But you don't think he had something to do with her death?"

"Good question," says the lieutenant.

Silja scoffs. "And for what reason? You're barking up the wrong tree, man! That slut just drowned; it was an accident. No one pushed her into the river or anything like that. And definitely not Bjöggi. He'd been on a binge with Júlli for days when it happened. They were drinking at Júlli's place."

Hörður nods thoughtfully. "Let's talk a bit more about your ex-father-in-law, Geirharður."

Silja shrugs annoyedly. "If you really want to."

"He once had a girlfriend who fell to her death, didn't he?" asks the lieutenant.

Silja frowns. "Back in the old days?"

"Yes, 1966," says Hörður.

"Why are you asking about that?" Silja asks. She sits up better in her chair, as if her curiosity is aroused.

Hörður smiles faintly. "I'm just gathering information; that's all."

Silja sighs. "I only know the little that Bjöggi has told me. It was a German girl, a cleaning lady for Geirharður's parents. They fell in love, as happens. Then she fell during the sheep roundup, probably having gone too close to the rim of the canyon. Her horse apparently returned home alone."

"Five years later, another German girl drowned in Eldvatn," says the lieutenant.

"Is that so?" asks Silja.

Hörður nods. "She'd also been working at Heiðarból."

"I didn't know that," says Silja thoughtfully. "Was it an accident?"

"It seems so," mutters Hörður.

"Why are you asking about those old deaths?" Silja asks curiously. "Do you think they *weren't* accidents? Is that why you're asking about Geirharður? Do you think *he* had something to do with this?"

"As I said …" Hörður stops when Silja laughs coldly.

"Is that your *theory*?" she asks sarcastically. "That Geirharður was a cold-blooded murderer and that Bjöggi is following in his footsteps?"

Hörður reddens; she has hit the nail on the head. "As a detective, I have to look at things from all angles and turn over every stone before I come to any conclusions."

"You're way off," says Silja. "Bjöggi isn't a murderer, and his father probably isn't, either. From what I understand, the old man barely got out of bed the last years of his life, except to drink himself senseless."

"Right," says Hörður distractedly, glancing over his notes on his and Reverend Páll's last conversation. "Listen, tell me … do you remember hearing something about Geirharður having treated Sigrún badly when they were children?"

Silja laughs sarcastically. "Do you mean about her ears?"

Hörður's eyes open wide in both surprise and curiosity. "Her ears?"

"Sigrún has deformed ears," says Silja in a confidential tone. "Apparently, she once said that Geirharður had cut them, but there's no way that's true."

"Hold on!" Hörður can hardly believe what he's hearing. A few other people doubtless saw the blood on Hertha's left ear and cheek, but no one outside the police knows that a piece of her was missing. "Deformed, how?"

"I haven't seen them myself; she makes sure no one can see her ears," says Silja. "But from what I understand, a mark was cut into them. Like they do with lambs."

"Her ears are marked? Really?" Hörður asks excitedly as he writes this down.

"Yes, I think so," says Silja.

"You said that someone cut her ears," says Hörður, "but that there's no way Geirharður could have done it. Why not?"

"Because of their age difference, Einstein!" says Silja angrily. "Geirharður was seven years younger than Sigrún. If it happened when she was a child, then it was hardly a much younger child who marked her, was it?"

"Hard to say," mutters Hörður. "But if not Geirharður, then who?"

Silja shrugs. "Maybe it was her mother. Bjöggi's grandmother. Apparently, she was completely nuts. But I still find it most likely that it was Steini. He's the same age as Sigrún and has always been a damn bastard. A sadist, really."

"Steini?" Hörður asks bewilderedly. Hadn't he heard that name recently? "What Steini are you talking about?"

"Oh, Geirharður's big brother," says Silja impatiently. "Steini the cop. Steingrímur Róbertsson. The Rock Grinder. Don't you know anything?"

Hörður gapes in amazement. "Lieutenant Steingrímur was Geirharður's brother?"

With a peculiar expression, Silja replies: "Uh, yeah."

Hörður whistles softly. So might it have been Steingrímur who murdered the girls here in the past? And is he Björgvin's mentor, so to speak, and not Geirharður's? "What can you tell me about this uncle of Björgvin's?"

"Other than that he's a sadist?" says Silja, smirking. "Hardly anything. Single and childless. I've always been convinced that he's gay. But maybe he was just asexual or impotent or something?"

Hörður seizes on this. "Why do you think he was gay?"

Silja shrugs. "Just a feeling, nothing special. But it can't be normal never to have been with a woman, can it?"

"Maybe not." Hörður clears his throat before asking the next question. "But how was the relationship between those cousins, Steingrímur and Björgvin?"

"Their relationship?" Silja sighs. "What do you mean? They were cousins, that's all."

"I mean…" Hörður looks aside. How should he put it? "Did they spend any time together? Did one visit the other? Were they friends, pals?"

"I don't think so," says Silja. "Of course, everyone here runs into everyone else, but Steini rarely ever came over to see Bjöggi while we were living together. But that doesn't mean they never met or weren't in contact. Why are you asking about this?"

Hörður smiles apologetically as he gathers his papers. "I'm just turning over stones, as I said. Sometimes you don't know what you're looking for until you find it."

"Some people sure are philosophical," mutters Silja.

After Silja has gone back out into the summer and the sun, Hörður notices the slice of sandwich loaf that she left behind, and at the same time, remembers that he hasn't eaten anything yet today. He fills his cup with hot coffee, takes the plastic wrap off the slice of sandwich loaf and eats it with a teaspoon while reading the notes he made following his conversation with Reverend Páll—he has the feeling that he's missed something the priest said.

"Mmmm," sighs the red-haired giant as he munches on the sandwich loaf. Silja hasn't spared the mayonnaise, and the bases are real sandwich-loaf bases, not crustless white bread as usual. This is a loaf as he remembers his grandmother and mother making on festive occasions. It's heaped with boiled shrimp, nice and plump, along with red peppers in thin strips, sliced hard-boiled eggs and finely chopped cucumber, all garnished with parsley, olives, and twisted lemon slices. But it's the bottom layer of the loaf that makes the difference—a thin layer of very finely chopped raw onion that's been mixed with ketchup. The strong onion flavor and sweet ketchup form a refreshing counterbalance to the fatty mayonnaise.

He gives this sandwich loaf a high grade—9 out of 10.

"She's got this down," mutters Hörður. He licks his lips, trying to reach the mayonnaise in his beard, and rinses the last mouthful down with a drink of coffee before turning his attention back to what he was doing.

The priest had mentioned Geirharður as having been a *strongman like his father and brother.* Hörður sighs. That's it. Reverend Páll said plainly that Geirharður had a brother, but Hörður clearly hadn't noticed it. In any case, that fact may not have been as important just then. He reads over his notes again, and feels as if something is missing. Hadn't he asked the Reverend something just as he was leaving?

Hörður scratches his beard. Yes! Suddenly he remembers it. The old man with the cane and cravat, the one who'd been walking along Klausturvegur Road. He'd asked Reverend Páll about that man.

But at the moment, he doesn't remember the priest's answer. Except that he'd suggested that…

Hörður starts when his cell phone rings. It's Adam, who has probably contacted the next witness. The lieutenant looks at his list. He has already crossed out the top two names.

The third is Hallgrímur Olsen, the truck driver.

He answers the phone. "Yes?"

"Hallgrímur is doing a run and doesn't really have time to meet you," says Adam.

"Either he meets me or I bring him in in handcuffs," Hörður growls into the phone.

"It won't come to that. He's hauling a load of fish from Höfn in Hornafjörður to Reykjavík and will be in Klaustur in half an hour or so."

"Then he can stop by the station," says Hörður. He actually would have preferred to speak to Hallgrímur at his home in Vík, just to be able to snoop around a bit at the same time. If Barbara Hoffmann is still alive, someone is holding her against her will, either at the captor's home or in another building to which he or she has access.

"He suggested that you two meet at the gas station. He needs to fill up there anyway."

"Is that right." Hörður is annoyed: he doesn't like being manipulated. But this witness's suggestion has certain advantages. "Okay, we'll do that. That'll give me a chance to talk to the kid at the shop before I interview Hallgrímur. What's his name again, the one working there?"

"Marteinn Gilsfjörð."

"Right," says Hörður. He scribbles the name in his notepad. "But since I can't talk to Hallgrímur at his home, I'm wondering if you could make a quick trip to Vík and snoop around a bit for me? Look in his windows and check if he has a garage or something. Just, inconspicuously. You understand what I mean?"

"No problem. I'm on my way!"

"Great, thanks. So we'll be in touch," says Hörður. No sooner has he hung up than he remembers that he was going to ask Adam about Geirharður and Steingrímur, if he knew they'd been brothers. But it's not so crucial that he feels the need to call his deputy back.

Hörður parks the SUV in the shop's parking lot and steps out onto the sunbaked asphalt. The sun is high in the sky, there's no wind, and it's seventeen degrees Celsius—more or less a heat wave by Icelandic standards. The sky is blue, clear and deep, like a lake, and the air smells of greenery, mingled with a faint odor of petrol. The Skaftá river flows heavily to the sea and cars rush back and forth along the highway. Life goes on as usual. There are hardly any visible signs of the summer storm; the locals are at work and tourists keep coming and going, like bees buzzing between flowers. No vehicles from television stations are visible, as the novelty has worn off the sensational story of the foreign girls, the one who came walking naked out of the rain, collapsed and died, and the one who's still missing. There's probably something new and exciting in the news now.

The red-haired giant takes a deep breath as he squints in the sunlight. There's nothing in the environment to suggest that anything's wrong, let alone that something terrible has happened. The small community of Kirkjubæjarklaustur is neither paralyzed nor hurt, seeing as how the lost girl is just a tourist and not *one of us*. Naturally, everyone wants the girl to be found, but in a short time, everyone will have forgotten that someone went missing—such a thing has happened before. If Barbara Hoffmann isn't found in the next few days, alive or dead, the search will be called off automatically and she'll simply be given up for dead. Without tangible evidence that a criminal act has been committed, her disappearance will be classified as an accident, or at best, an unexplained disappearance. Barbara's relatives will no doubt raise a ruckus with the authorities on both sides of the ocean over the case, but as long as neither a body nor a murderer is found, their despair and anger will end up in the same place as the police investigation, which is about to run into the sand...

Hörður stubbornly munches his nicotine gum. He tramps into the service station, as if attempting to escape his own doubts, dissuasions, and negative thoughts that follow him like a shadow—like a flock of ravens and pack of wolves. Inside the shop, a familiar smell greets him: a kind of blend of frying oil and cleaning agents. The lieutenant lingers as a young Asian couple pays for gas and refreshments, and then it's his turn.

"What can I do for you?" asks the cashier. He's in his twenties, with dark hair and eyes and peach fuzz on his jowls, wearing a fleece jacket labeled with the name of the service station.

"Are you Marteinn?" asks Hörður. He skips introducing himself by name and position, knowing that it's unnecessary. In a village such as this, everyone knows who the lieutenant is, even though he's only just started his job.

"That's me," Marteinn replies.

Hörður takes out his notepad and clicks his pen. "I'm investigating the disappearance of the German girl, as I'm sure you know. Were you on duty when the bus arrived from Reykjavík on Thursday?"

"Yes, I was," Marteinn replies.

Hörður notes this down, just for the sake of formality. He knows very well that Marteinn was working on Thursday. It was he who gave the new lieutenant directions when he asked about the town offices. "Do you remember the German girls?"

With a serious expression, Marteinn nods. "They came here shortly before the bus arrived. They asked if there was an information center here in the village, and I pointed them to the Skaftá Visitor Center."

"Did they buy anything?" Hörður asks.

"A lighter, that's all," Marteinn answers.

Hörður writes down his answer, then looks out the window. The ground trembles as a truck with a trailer drives onto the lot. It's Hallgrímur Olsen's blue and yellow truck, and it pulls up and stops at the pump farthest from the shop. The air brakes hiss, and the driver shuts off the noisy engine before climbing deftly down from the cab.

"Thanks," says Hörður to Marteinn. He clicks his pen again, then closes his notepad and sticks it in his jacket pocket before heading out into the sunshine. He notices water dripping out from under the closed door at the back of the truck and at the sides of the trailer, and catches a whiff of bad fish. The cargo is clearly iced fish that's suffering in the summer heat.

Hallgrímur stands wide-legged next to his vehicle as he pumps diesel fuel into its tank. He's wearing the same blue work jacket as on Thursday, but has changed his Budweiser shirt for a Marlboro one and has on dirty work gloves. He looks up as Hörður approaches and tries to squeeze out a smile that's little more than a scowl.

"How goes it, cop?" he asks nonchalantly.

"I'm the lieutenant," says Hörður bluntly, "and it's I who'll ask the questions, not you."

"Easy, man," mutters Hallgrímur, who doesn't like to be rebuked, judging by the sulky look that comes over his face. "What, I'm not allowed to say anything?"

Hörður ignores his fuss. He looks thoughtfully up at the truck's cab, which is large and bulky—probably with one or two bunks behind the seats. The truck is undoubtedly the driver's second home, what with the long distances he drives.

"Can we have a little talk in your truck after you're done filling up?" Hörður asks. The question is actually rhetorical, as he won't take no for an answer.

Hallgrímur shrugs. "If you want. But it's half-full of rubbish. We can also go sit in your car, or just in the shop—I want a hot dog and something to drink. But I don't know how I can help you."

"We'll chat in your car," says Hörður firmly. "The hot dog can wait."

"Okay, sir," says Hallgrímur irritably. Having filled his tank, he replaces the pump's nozzle. He takes off his gloves and puts them in one of his back pockets. Then he shakes out a cigarette from a pack of Princes that he keeps in the breast pocket of his jacket and grabs it with his thick lips.

Hörður grunts annoyedly as he munches harder on his nicotine gum. "Would you mind if we chatted first?"

"No prob, sir." Hallgrímur grins and sticks the cigarette behind one ear.

They climb into the cab; Hallgrímur on the driver's side, and Hörður on the passenger's side. The cab doors are big and heavy, and coarse stairs lead to the cab floor— three iron steps, the bottom one quite high. Hörður steps onto the bottom step, grabs a handle inside the door on the left side, next to the seat back, and the inside of the door with his right hand and pushes up into the cab. But then he stops in the doorway, with one foot on the top step, because there's both rubbish in the passenger seat and on the floor in front of it.

"Sorry about this," says Hallgrímur, now sitting in the driver's seat. He reaches for black rubber boots and a bag of clothes, both of which were on the mat in front of the seat, and tosses them into the back of the cab. In the seat itself is a red raincoat that goes the same way, along with a half-full two-liter bottle of Pepsi Max, a bag of snacks, and two sandwiches still in their packages.

"No problem," Hörður mutters as he sits down in the passenger seat and shuts the door behind him. He then peeks over his left shoulder. Behind the seats are two bunks, an upper and lower one, partly concealed by a burgundy-colored curtain. The upper bunk is full of stuff, mainly clothes, it appears to the lieutenant; Hallgrímur doubtless sleeps sometimes in the lower one. In it is a sleeping bag, along with the boots and a raincoat and the other things that were in the passenger seat.

"What can I do for you?" Hallgrímur asks gruffly. He's used to being alone in his truck and probably doesn't like the fact that someone is running curious eyes over this second home of his. Unless he's annoyed at being unable to get back out on the highway immediately.

"One or two things," replies the lieutenant calmly. He takes out the digital voice recorder and folded sheets of paper. He turns on the recorder and clears his throat before stating the customary information.

Hallgrímur rolls down the driver's-side window slightly; his face is sweaty. The sun is baking the truck's roof; it's boiling hot inside the cab and the air is heavy. The lieutenant takes off his cap and lays it on the dashboard, on top of old, yellowed receipts and other rubbish.

"As I'm sure you know," says the lieutenant, "a girl has gone missing. A German tourist. Her friend died on Saturday. It seems that they wound up in some trouble. Photos of them have appeared on television, in online media, and in the newspapers. Do you recall seeing those girls?"

Hallgrímur adjusts himself in his bouncy seat. "No, I don't. Why?"

"You don't, huh?" Hörður looks straight in the driver's shifty eyes. "But they asked you for a ride to Hvolsvöllur, on Thursday, right?"

Hallgrímur blinks and sniffs. "They did? I mean, was that them?"

"It was them," confirms the lieutenant.

"I didn't know," Hallgrímur half-growls. "How was I supposed to know that? They were just some girls! And what does it matter, whether it was them or not? I didn't even pick them up!"

"I'm the one asking the questions here," says the lieutenant. "Why didn't they get a ride from you?"

"I don't pick up hitchhikers," mutters Hallgrímur. "It's a violation of our rules. Plus, I'm no fucking taxi driver. Does this look like a bus to you, huh?"

"What did you say to them?" Hörður asks.

"What did I say?" Hallgrímur asks in return. "Nothing! Just that they couldn't get a ride from me. Something like that."

"You weren't rude to them or anything?" Hörður asks coldly. He remembers well how Hallgrímur had stuck out his tongue like a snake, and then burst out laughing when he saw the girls' reactions; how they shrunk back, disgusted and horrified.

Hallgrímur thinks this over before answering. He's probably trying to determine how much the lieutenant knows and how he knows it. "Not that I recall, no."

Hörður glances at his notes. "But did you see them again? Here in Klaustur or anywhere else?"

"No," Hallgrímur answers with conviction. "I did not."

"Where did you go after you filled your tank in Hvolsvöllur?" asks the lieutenant.

Hallgrímur thinks about it. "I made two deliveries in Vík, and then I emptied the truck here in Klaustur, at Kjarval."

Hörður nods. He remembers seeing the truck at the store on the Thursday. "After you emptied the truck, what did you do?"

Hallgrímur grins. "I jumped in the shower at the pool, went to the liquor store and then over to Júlli's. We had a few cold ones and cooked dinner."

Hörður jots a few notes on one of the sheets of paper. "And then what?"

"Then we went to Systrakaffi Café, and after that to the hotel bar," says Hallgrímur, smiling widely. "We met you there, remember? You and Adam and Silja, among others. You seemed to be having a good time. You and Silja seemed to get along well, didn't you?"

Hörður reddens with anger and shame. "How long were you at the hotel bar?"

Hallgrímur shrugs. "I guess I left the place around eleven, eleven-thirty, something like that."

"Where did you go then?" asks the lieutenant. He himself was so drunk and distracted that he can hardly remember when or how he went home, let alone any of the other bar patrons at the time. But Adam presumably does? He's got to remember to ask him about this.

"I went back to Júlli's place with him," Hallgrímur answers. "He was piss drunk, the old fellow. I hauled him into his bed and went to sleep myself."

"Did you sleep at Júlíus's house?" Hörður asks.

"No, here, in the car." Hallgrímur points with his thumb behind him.

"Where was the car?" Hörður asks.

"In the swimming pool parking lot," replies Hallgrímur. "I usually park it there when I stay here in Klaustur."

"I see," says the lieutenant. He notes this down. "Is there anyone who can confirm this? That the truck was at the pool and that you spent the night in it?"

Hallgrímur snorts. "It's not like the truck is invisible! Someone must have seen it; anything else would be ridiculous. But the other part's more complicated, isn't it? You'll just have to go around to all the villagers and ask if any of them saw me climb up into my cab that night."

Hörður watches Hallgrímur Olsen drive off in his truck, with the trailer and the stench of fish in tow. The diesel engine snarls loudly and black smoke gushes into the sky blue. Hörður doesn't like this lout of a driver; he's rude, a drug dealer, and a rapist. When Hallgrímur was nineteen, he was given probation for having had sex with a girl when she was passed out in his car after drinking too much one summer night at a dance. Hörður had found the case file in the filing cabinet at the police station.

Hallgrímur is a classic chauvinist pig. But does he have anything to do with the disappearance of the German girls? Hörður isn't sure. There's actually little to suggest this, but he isn't going to cross his name off the list of suspects, that much is certain.

He gets into the SUV, starts the engine, and calls Adam through the hands-free system.

"Where are you?" Hörður asks when Adam answers.

"I'm just leaving Vík."

"Did you find Hallgrímur's house?" asks the lieutenant.

"Yes. I rang the doorbell and looked through the windows when no one answered. I saw and heard nothing. I'm pretty sure the house is empty. There's a small garage there, but as far as I could see, it was full of junk."

"Did anyone see you?" Hörður asks anxiously. He half-regrets having asked Adam to spy for him. It's not for no reason that he himself hasn't been sniffing around the homes of those he's put on his list of suspicious persons. If he found something that connected the suspect to a criminal act, it might not be possible to present it as evidence in court, because without reasonable suspicion and/or a search warrant, such snooping would be a violation of the privacy of the person in question. In doing so, the evidence would have been obtained by dubious means, which could have a negative impact on the investigation—at least cast a shadow on the work of the police.

"No, I don't think so," Adam replies.

"Good," says Hörður. "Have you called Júlíus?"

"Yes, he's expecting you."

"I'm on my way to his place," says Hörður. He drives out of the shop's parking lot onto Klausturvegur Road. "Then call Björgvin in about five or ten minutes."

"I'll do that."

No sooner has Hörður hung up than his cell phone rings. He looks at the screen and recognizes the landline number immediately. It's that of the police chief's office in Hvolsvöllur. What does Björn Bragi Björnsson want from him now? Is he going to send him to do speed monitoring out in the middle of nowhere?

The lieutenant in Kirkjubæjarklaustur lowers the ring tone on his phone and sticks the phone in his pocket. He has more important things to do than the dirty work of this so-called boss of his.

Hörður parks the SUV in front of Júlíus Angantýsson's house, on the gravel lot where the garbage truck and the livestock truck stand side by side. Although Hörður Grímsson is a giant in stature and often gruff in demeanor, he's actually a rather sensitive soul. For example, he's always been a bit repelled by such livestock trucks. They're made to transport lambs and pigs from farms to slaughterhouses, and therefore have an air of panic and death. Not natural death, but mechanical slaughter that is calculated and organized. He thinks reflexively of the windowless, seatless transport trains of the Third Reich that brought Jews from the ghettos and prisons to concentration camps such as Auschwitz and Bergen-Belsen.

Júlíus's house is a sad sight to see, having been maintained so poorly. The paint on the concrete walls is drab and dirty, the woodwork is worn and decaying, and the roof is rusty. The curtains, which are stained, are drawn over all of the windows, whose panes are dusty. The lieutenant knocks on the pale gray front door.

From inside come the sounds of movement and muttering, and then the garbage man opens the door a crack and peeks out into the sunshine, squinting and open-mouthed, dressed in jeans and a shirt.

"So, it's you?" says Júlíus in his childish voice. He opens the door the rest of the way and signals Hörður to come in. The hall is full of coats, jackets, and other outerwear hanging on hooks, and footwear covers the floor—work shoes, boots, sneakers, rubber shoes, house shoes, and even dress shoes. The householder himself is barefoot.

The lieutenant doesn't take off his shoes, as it looks to him as if the floor hasn't been cleaned in ages.

"Would you like some coffee?" Júlíus asks. He plods down a hallway running the length of the house.

"Hm, yes, just a few drops, maybe," Hörður answers hesitantly. He follows the householder to the kitchen, which is on the left side of the hallway, across from the laundry room. To the right are two rooms. One is closed, while the other is half-open. In it, there's an unmade bed surrounded by piles of books, cardboard boxes, and plastic bags that have been tied shut. The garbage man's home is messy, and the air in it smells faintly of refuse. The living room is at the other end of the house, dark and gloomy.

"On the other hand, don't trouble yourself," says Hörður after going into the kitchen. He can't imagine drinking as much as one drop of coffee with the odor in his nostrils.

"No?" asks Júlíus, who was pouring water into an automatic coffee machine. He's so short that he practically has to stand on tiptoe to turn the kitchen faucet on and off.

"No."

"As you please." Júlíus sits down opposite the lieutenant, clasps his hands on the table, and looks wide-eyed at the red-haired giant.

"I'm gathering information on the girls who came here to Klaustur this past Thursday," says Hörður, taking off his cap. He places the voice recorder on the table and takes out his sheets of paper and pen. "The backpacker girls. One died on Saturday and the other is still missing. You've taken part in the search, haven't you?"

Júlíus says yes.

The lieutenant switches on the recorder, makes the usual preliminary remarks, and then turns his attention to the witness. "Did you see those girls here in Klaustur last Thursday? Barbara Hoffmann and Hertha Meier?"

Júlíus fidgets in his seat. "I didn't know their names."

"But you saw them?" Hörður asks again.

"Yes."

"Where did you see them?"

Júlíus blinks. "At the Skaftá Visitor Center. They were walking by there."

"And what?" asks Hörður. "Did you speak to them?"

"Yes, a little," Júlíus replies hesitantly.

"You stopped your garbage truck and said something to them through the window, didn't you?" says the lieutenant.

Júlíus clears his throat. "Yes, exactly."

"What did you say to them?"

"I just asked where they were from," Júlíus answers, smiling stupidly. "It interests me. To know where people are from."

"And what did they say?" asks Hörður.

"That they were from Germany," Júlíus answers.

"Did you talk with them about anything else?" Hörður asks.

"No," Júlíus replies.

"When did you see them again?" asks the lieutenant.

With an odd expression, Júlíus replies: "Did I see them again?"

Hörður throws up his hands. "I was asking you that! Either you saw them again or you didn't!"

Júlíus shakes his head sadly. "Only in the papers. I only saw them again in the papers. There were pictures of them there."

Hörður sighs. Is this man mentally challenged? "Do you remember the night at the hotel bar? Thursday night, the same day you saw the German girls. You went to the bar with Hallgrímur Olsen, didn't you?"

"Yes," Júlíus replies.

"When did Hallgrímur come to your place that day?" asks the lieutenant.

"I had just come home," Júlíus answers. "It was around six o'clock. Maybe half past six."

"What did you two do?" Hörður asks.

"We drank a few Faxe beers," Júlíus answers.

"A few beers?" Hörður asks.

Júlíus nods. "Then we had something to eat."

"Here, at home?" Hörður asks.

"Yeah," says Júlíus. "Hallgrímur fried hot dogs, mushrooms, and eggs."

"What did you do then?" asks the lieutenant.

"Drank more Faxe, watched the news," replies Júlíus conscientiously. "Then we went to Systrakaffi Café and the hotel bar."

"Do you remember coming home from the bar?" Hörður asks.

Júlíus smiles a crooked smile. "No-oo. I was so drunk."

"I see," mutters Hörður. He writes down the answer and then runs his eyes over his notes. "Tell me, do you remember when the Belgian girl disappeared? It was five years ago. Her name was Juliette Vermeulen."

Júlíus nods. "I remember it."

"Did you know her?" asks the lieutenant.

"No-oo," Júlíus replies. "But I saw her sometimes. I asked her where she was from. She was a friend of Bjöggi's."

"Is that so?" asks Hörður.

"She was also a friend of Hallgrímur's," says Júlíus.

"Oh?" asks Hörður.

With a dreamy expression, Júlíus replies: "She was very popular. She was cute."

"Do you remember that the disappearance of Juliette was investigated?" Hörður asks.

Júlíus blinks. "She was searched for, if that's what you mean. And Steingrímur questioned people, like you're doing now. He asked us when we last saw her and things like that."

"Us?" Hörður asks.

"Me and Bjöggi," Júlíus answers.

"Is it true that you and Björgvin were together when she disappeared?" asks the lieutenant. "That you two were drinking together? That you'd been drunk for many days?"

Júlíus scratches his head. "Yes, I guess so. I recall that. Bjöggi was drunk a lot at that time. Then he got a divorce. He and Silja had some difficulties."

"But Hallgrímur?" asks Hörður. "Was he with you and Björgvin? Was he also drinking with you?"

Júlíus thinks this over. "I don't think so. He may have stopped by, though. Hallgrímur never stops for long. He comes and goes. He's always driving."

"I see," says Hörður. He doesn't recall seeing Hallgrímur's statements in connection with Juliette's disappearance. It appears that Steingrímur's investigation into her disappearance wasn't very detailed.

"Moving on," says the red-haired giant after a short silence. "When was the last time you dumped garbage at the Stjórnarsandur landfill site?"

"Thursday afternoon," Júlíus answers. "I collect garbage on Wednesdays and Thursdays and bury it in the afternoon on Thursdays."

Hörður thinks back. "Last Thursday, when you stopped at the Skaftá Visitor Center to ask the German girls where they were from, were you on your way down to Stjórnarsandur with a load of garbage?"

"I still had one or two stops," Júlíus answers. "But otherwise, yes. I emptied the load around three o'clock and was done burying it an hour later. Why do you ask?"

"Have you been to Stjórnarsandur since then?" asks the lieutenant. "Since burying your load last Thursday?"

"No, I don't think so," says Júlíus, who now seems confused by all these questions. "Why?"

"No special reason," says Hörður dryly. He regards the short, stocky garbage man. There's something harmless about him. But that doesn't mean he's harmless.

When Hörður drives out of the lot in front of Júlíus' house, he has second thoughts. Maybe he should have had the geezer unload his garbage truck to prove that it was empty? Wouldn't that be the perfect place to hide a corpse, in the *stomach* of a vehicle that's visible to everyone every day and has therefore long since become invisible? In the lieutenant's mind, Júlíus is sitting behind the wheel of the garbage truck. He pulls a handle and the hydraulic jacks start raising the metal tank that holds all the garbage. The end of the tank opens like a giant, dirty mouth—the diesel engine roars loudly, the front of the tank is lifted higher and the mouth opens wider as it nears the ground. It's as if the garbage truck is a huge creature, snarling as it readies itself to vomit on the gravel lot. At first, nothing comes out of the creature's mouth except for a few pieces of plastic and a can or two, along with a few other things left behind in the tank. But then something starts rolling deep in the creature's stomach, before dropping out through the gaping mouth and hitting the gravel.

It's the naked body of a blonde girl, now purple and swollen, covered with grime and deep wounds…

Hörður shudders and tries to shake this tragic picture out of his mind. He steps on the accelerator and focuses on his driving. He'll ask Júlíus to empty the garbage truck in his presence. But maybe not at this point. And certainly not on the lot in front of his house.

The lieutenant intends to complete the interrogation before taking the next steps. The big picture, he reminds himself. He needs to determine what squares the black chess players are occupying before he moves the white queen. Investigative work, like chess, is a game of concentration, patience, and intelligence.

Just before Hörður arrives at the roundabout at the highway, he calls Adam through the hands-free system.

"Hello!"

Hörður drives into the roundabout and then out of it to the east. "Listen, I'm on my way to Björgvin's. Have you spoken to him?"

"Yes, he said he would be at home, but wasn't exactly happy about it. He was in the middle of something, I gathered."

"Where did you say that Hörgsárdalur was, again?" asks the lieutenant.

"You drive along Síða, east of Klaustur… "

"Yes, yes, yes," says Hörður impatiently. "I *am* driving east, as if to Höfn in Hornafjörður. I just don't know where or when I'm supposed to turn off the highway."

"It's about eight kilometers to Hörgsárdalur, something like that. You cross a river called Breiðbalakvísl, and then it's not so far from there. There'll be a sideroad on the left and then a turnoff to the right; the road leads northeastward and then turns up the western side of the valley. There's a sign by the road, but I don't remember what it says."

"Okay, okay," mutters Hörður. "I'm sure I'll find it."

"How did it go with Júlli, by the way?"

"Just fine," replies the lieutenant. "Listen, you might call him and ask him not to move the garbage truck until I give permission."

"Oh, why?"

"Just do as I ask you," says Hörður dryly. "I'll talk to you later. In the meantime, you can contact the last witness on the list."

Hörður drives along a gravel road through a valley that's both wide and deep—he hopes it's Hörgsárdalur Valley. Shortly before he turned off the highway, a cloud drew before the sun, and now it looks to him as if there's fog at the end of the valley, unless the clouds are so low that they've literally slid down the mountainsides. The valley floor is flat and grassy, for the most part, but here and there are patches and piles of gravel. At some distance ahead of him, he sees a sheep corral to one side of the road, and to the other, a fairly large auto graveyard where family cars, trucks, tractors, and haymaking equipment are quietly rusting away. Even farther, up on a hill across the valley, he glimpses a farm. There are no other houses visible. The lieutenant assumes that the farm is the home of Björgvin Geirharðsson. He drives farther along the road, down a sloping hill and diagonally across the valley floor. To the east he sees the mouth of Hörgsárgljúfur Canyon, which isn't as impressive as Fjaðrárgljúfur Canyon but is quite deep and cuts far into the heath. Leading to the canyon is an old track that is clearly difficult and slow-going.

When Hörður is about halfway up the slope leading to the farm, he drives into the fog that is creeping like a ghostly glacier down from the highlands. The temperature drops quickly and dainty drops of water settle on the SUV's windows. The lieutenant turns up the heater. He drives through a gate and into the farmyard. In front of a white-painted house with a red roof stands Björgvin's pickup truck—a white Ford F-150 with a crew cab and rust stains. North of the house are large and spacious outbuildings, half-covered in fog, also white with red roofs. Next to the outbuildings is a corral for animals, probably horses.

Hörður parks the SUV next to the pickup truck and shuts off the engine. He steps out onto the gravel with his folder in one hand, putting his cap on at the same time with the other. The voice recorder is in the side pocket of his jacket. He's just closed the door of the SUV when a barking dog comes rushing out of the fog. It's the black-and-white Border Collie that Hörður saw in the back seat of the pickup truck.

"Easy there," says Hörður, maybe more to himself than to the animal. The dog is menacing, but stays at a certain distance.

"Aesop!" calls a deep voice, and the dog stops all his growling and barking and puts its ears down.

Björgvin, brow furrowed, comes walking from the out-buildings, wearing a work shirt, jeans, and dirty rubber boots. "Excuse the mutt. He isn't mean, but defends his territory."

"No problem," mutters Hörður.

"You wanted to meet me?" says Björgvin.

Hörður nods. "I'm mapping the movements of the German girls and trying to find out what happened to them."

Björgvin looks into the fog and nods, as if distracted.

"Do you have any livestock here?" asks the lieutenant.

Björgvin shrugs. "A few horses, that's all."

"Could you show me?" asks Hörður.

"If you really want me to," Björgvin says wearily. He leads the lieutenant back to the outbuildings. The dog Aesop follows them like a shadow. Björgvin opens the door to the stable and invites the lieutenant to go in ahead of him. The doorway is so low that they both have to bend down.

The stable smells strongly of animals. It looks to Hörður like there are ten stalls, but there are only four horses in the stable at the moment.

"Most of the horses are in the pasture," says Björgvin.

"I see," says Hörður. He walks down the feeding aisle. At its end are doors to the barn. He peeks into the barn, but it's mostly empty.

"Should we go sit down in the kitchen?" asks Björgvin, who seems impatient.

"Sure," says Hörður, although he continues to look around a bit in the stable. He prefers to leave no stone unturned.

"I made coffee earlier," says Björgvin.

Hörður smiles politely. "I would absolutely love a cup of coffee."

They walk back out, where the chilly fog hides the view in all directions.

"Does it often get foggy here?" asks the lieutenant.

"On the heaths, yes," Björgvin answers. "Especially in the mornings, when the cold air comes down from the highlands. But it usually doesn't last long. It's been a long time since there's been such a dense fog."

"I see," says Hörður. He curses his luck at not being able to get a better look at the property. "Are there other buildings here besides the stable and the farmhouse?"

"No," says Björgvin.

The first thing the lieutenant does after Björgvin invites him in is to ask if he can use the bathroom.

"Down the hallway and to the right," says Björgvin, before he disappears into the kitchen.

"Thanks." Hörður walks down the hallway but doesn't go into the bathroom—it was never his plan. He just needs a bit of time to snoop around. Besides the bathroom, there are two bedrooms in the hallway, a children's bedroom and master bedroom. Hörður skips looking in the children's bedroom and instead peeks into the master bedroom, where Björgvin sleeps alone in a queen-size bed. The first thing Hörður notices is a metal gun cabinet bolted to one wall.

He didn't know that Björgvin had a gun permit.

Hörður knows that he doesn't have much time for snooping, yet decides to peek into the living room before heading back to the kitchen. In it is a huge TV, connected to a game console. On the floor in front of the TV are the covers of popular computer games. The living room has both a leather sofa set and two La-Z-Boy chairs with leather upholstery. On a shelf are several framed photographs, including one small black-and-white one that sticks out. The photo is of a young boy, five or six years old. The boy is standing in front of a white concrete house with a steep roof. The photo has been torn in half, which is clear from the partially missing white border.

The other half of the photo was in the battery compartment of the cassette player given to Hörður.

Hörður feels somewhat disconcerted. He has spent the day questioning people, drinking coffee, and driving from place to place, while Barbara Hoffmann is probably being held somewhere against her will—maybe even locked naked in a small cage. She may be dead, but hopefully not. But if she's cold, hungry, and in pain—hovering between life and death—she may be wishing for death.

If only he could find her…

"Let's begin," says the lieutenant wearily. He sits down opposite Björgvin at the kitchen table, opens the folder, and takes a few sheets of paper from it. Björgvin has poured coffee into two cups and laid a plate of crullers on the table.

The kitchen is homely and tidy, free of decoration and frills, like the living room. On the fridge are childish drawings by Björgvin and Silja's son, stuck on with colorful magnets. At the table are two ordinary kitchen stools and one wooden highchair that can be adjusted as the child grows.

Björgvin sips his coffee as Hörður turns on the recorder and states the place, time, and name of the witness.

"When did you first see them, the German girls?" he then asks. "Hertha Meier and Barbara Hoffmann."

Björgvin is about to answer, but is interrupted by his cell phone ringing. He looks at the screen and lowers the ringtone.

"Sorry," he says. "The girls, yes… exactly. Naturally, I didn't know their names. But they were thumbing a ride at Hvolsvöllur and I picked them up."

"Where did they say they were going?" Hörður asks.

"To Klaustur," Björgvin answers.

"And you drove them there?" asks Hörður.

"Yes," Björgvin answers dryly. "I let them out at the gas station."

"Where did you go then?" asks Hörður.

"Where?" asks Björgvin. "To the district-government office. I had business with the district manager. I do a lot of work for the community."

"So you went to the Skaftá Visitor Center?" Hörður asks.

"It's in the same building, yes," Björgvin replies. "The district manager … "

He's stops when his phone rings again. Hörður surreptitiously peaks at the lit-up screen, which appears to display the word *Mama*.

Björgvin lowers the phone's volume again. "Sorry, what was I saying? Yes, the district manager's office is on the second floor."

"Why didn't the girls go with you to the Skaftá Center?" Hörður asks. "Why did you let them out at the gas station?"

Björgvin blinks. "Why? Because they wanted to get out there. That's why. Why do you ask?"

Hörður looks inquisitively at the witness. "I ask because the only thing they did at the station was ask if there was an information center in the village. Then they went there, to the Skaftá Center."

Björgvin shrugs. "If they'd asked me, I would of course have brought them there."

"Did you and the two girls talk about anything?" Hörður asks.

"Very little," mutters Björgvin. "Just at the start, when they asked about a ride and such. Then they just spoke German together."

"They spoke English to you, didn't they?" asks the lieutenant.

"Yes," Björgvin answers, before cursing when his cell phone rings for the third time. He picks up the phone and turns it off. "Sorry, again. It's my mother. The fog probably has her a bit spooked."

"You can answer. Don't mind me," says Hörður.

Björgvin shakes his head. "She hardly gives me a moment's peace. If it's not fog then it's some noise or something is broken or some other crap. A person her age shouldn't be living alone on a heath. I'll call her back later."

"I see," says Hörður. "We'll go on, then. Where were you headed, anyway, last Thursday? Where were you coming from?"

"I went to Selfoss," Björgvin answers. "To buy groceries and such, and to pick up my mom's glasses. They were being repaired."

"Your mother is Sigrún Arnkelsdóttir," says Hörður. "And she works as an information officer at the Skaftá Center, right?"

"That's right," Björgvin mutters.

"And you brought her glasses to the Skaftá Center, last Thursday, didn't you?" Hörður asks.

"Yes, I did," Björgvin replies.

"So you had business at the Skaftá Center, as well as at the district-government office, right?" Hörður asks.

"Yes, you could say that," replies Björgvin.

"Why didn't you say that before?" Hörður asks. He looks straight at the blond giant, whose eyes are blue and cold. Björgvin is as pale and stiff as a driftwood log. It's as if he's frozen, or simply sculptured from ice.

"The glasses were irrelevant," says Björgvin, half irritated. "I just brought them to my mother along the way."

"It's I who decides what's irrelevant and what isn't," says the lieutenant.

"I just don't see how it matters," mutters the blond giant.

Hörður clicks his tongue. "What was it your mother said again when the German girls told her they'd gotten a ride from you to Kirkjubæjarklaustur?"

Björgvin's face reddens. "I don't remember."

"She asked you if you were transporting whole truckloads of girls here, or something along those lines, right?" Hörður asks.

"Maybe, I'm not sure," Björgvin says.

"Why did she say that?" Hörður asks.

"Isn't it best that you ask her?" growls the blond giant.

Hörður nods. "I'll do that, rest assured."

Björgvin sighs. "Aren't we about done here? I need to get working. I wasn't able to get much done this weekend because of the search."

"Just a few more questions." Hörður smiles reassuringly at the witness. It's always a good idea for him to make witnesses irritated and impatient. Most often, they quickly become irrational and blurt things out.

"Good," says Björgvin.

"Did you see the girls after you left the Skaftá Center last Thursday?" asks the lieutenant.

Björgvin shakes his head. "I didn't. That is to say, not until one of them appeared there in the rain on Saturday morning."

"Right," says Hörður sadly. It's been just over two days since Hertha Meier died in his arms, and he hasn't yet recovered from that life experience. "But let's talk a little about Thursday night."

"If you really want to," Björgvin grumbles.

Hörður knows perfectly well why the man is frustrated. He switches off the digital voice recorder. "Just so you know, nothing happened between me and Silja. Not that it's any of your business, but what you *think* might have happened is clearly bothering you, so it's right that you know the truth."

Björgvin scoffs. "I'm having a hard time believing you. But fine, then. Let's just say that. Nothing happened."

"Exactly. Nothing happened," says Hörður, before switching back on the recorder. "You and Silja, the mother of your child, were arguing outside Hotel Klaustur last Thursday evening around eleven. Where did you go after that?"

"I went and picked up our son," snaps Björgvin.

"From Silja's?" Hörður asks.

"Yes."

"Was it open? Or do you have a key to her house?"

"It was open," Björgvin replies.

"Was anyone at home, besides your son?" Hörður asks.

"The babysitter, Agnes," Björgvin answers. "She was sleeping in front of the TV. The boy was in his bed."

"And?" asks the lieutenant. "Did you wake him, or ...?"

Björgvin shakes his head. "I carried him sleeping to the car and drove him here."

"And did you spend the night here, with him?" Hörður asks.

"Of course!" says Björgvin indignantly. "I'm not an irresponsible fool like his mother. I would never leave him home alone."

"But he wasn't home alone, was he?" Hörður asks.

Björgvin scoffs. "Agnes is just a child. You don't leave a child with a child. Not overnight."

Hörður nods, as he understands Björgvin's view well. "But no one can confirm that you were here that night— Thursday night?"

Björgvin sneers coldly. "No, who should that be? Are you implying that I had something to do with the disappearance of those girls?"

"Did you have anything to do with their disappearance?" asks the lieutenant, looking straight at the witness.

"No," Björgvin answers without hesitation, but then he blinks and looks away.

Hörður shrugs. "Very well. I'm just trying to find out who was where within a particular time frame, that's all."

"But you don't know *whether* something happened to these girls or not," says Björgvin. "Let alone *when* something happened to them."

Hörður grunts, as usual when his temper flares. "As far as *whether* goes, it must arouse certain suspicions when a person falls dead in the middle of the street, naked in a cold rain, and another isn't found after an extensive search, right? And if the answer is yes, then *when* would be from the time the aforementioned individuals were last seen until the moment one of them dies. In other words, from last Thursday afternoon until Saturday morning."

"Which is around forty hours," says Björgvin. "And not just Thursday night."

"That's right," grunts Hörður. He knows best of all that this time frame is rather ample. But since Hertha was so bedraggled and cold when she died, probably after walking for a long time, he strongly suspects that *what happened* to the girls took place toward the time frame's start—on Thursday night, under the cover of darkness. But he's not about to share these thoughts with the witness. "And it's I who am asking the questions here and you who are answering, without having opinions about the questions I ask. Is *that* understood?"

"Yes, no problem," mutters Björgvin. Clearly very impatient now, he looks at his watch and sighs.

Hörður takes a deep breath. It's time for the big questions. "Let's go back in time a bit. You once had a girlfriend named Lena Nilsson, didn't you?"

Björgvin starts. "Lena? That was fourteen, fifteen years ago. Why are you asking about her?"

"What happened to Lena?" asks the lieutenant.

Björgvin blinks. His look of astonishment changes into one of contempt. "You know as well as I do what happened to Lena."

Hörður shrugs. "Do I? But I want to hear it from you."

"She just disappeared one day," says Björgvin angrily. "Then she was found, dead. She'd fallen to her death. It was an accident. This is a dangerous area."

"Where did she fall?" Hörður asks.

"A little south of here," Björgvin mutters. "In the canyon."

"In Hörgsárgljúfur?" Hörður asks.

Björgvin nods. "You know all about that accident. Why are you asking me this?"

"What was she doing in this area?" Hörður asks. "It isn't exactly within walking distance of Klaustur."

"She was probably just having a look around," Björgvin replies brusquely. "She often went for long walks. Sometimes alone, sometimes with me or someone else. It's actually a bit of a walk from here, but not too far. Maybe she hitched a ride or something, I don't know."

"Was it investigated?" Hörður asks. "Whether she got a ride from someone?"

"I don't know," mutters Björgvin. "Probably. I don't remember that time very well. It was a shock. Losing my girlfriend like that."

"I can believe it," says the lieutenant. "But five years ago, something similar happened. Your girlfriend from Belgium drowned in the Skaftá river. Juliette Vermeulen."

Björgvin reddens with anger. "What do you mean, something similar? Juliette wasn't my girlfriend; she was completely nuts and most likely committed suicide. I was with Silja at the time. We were expecting a baby."

"But you were seeing each other, weren't you?" Hörður asks. "You and Juliette. You cheated on Silja with her."

"What the hell sort of questions are these?" Björgvin's eyes shoot sparks of fury and he clenches his fists so hard that his knuckles whiten. He's clearly on the verge of losing control of his temper.

Hörður watches his every move, and is prepared for anything. "Hertha and Barbara aren't the first foreign girls to disappear here in this area. I can't investigate their disappearance without putting it in the context of similar, older cases."

Björgvin snorts, but appears to relax slightly. "First of all, those German girls were tourists on a backpacking trip, so it's pretty dubious to claim that they *disappeared*. They just kept hiking. They probably just got in trouble in the storm that hit without warning on Friday. Such things have happened before. As far as those two older cases you mentioned goes, they were investigated, and there were no indications that anything criminal took place—period!"

"Who investigated the disappearance of Lena and Juliette?" Hörður asks.

"Who?" exclaims Björgvin. "You must know that! It was the lieutenant who was here before you. Steingrímur."

"Your uncle Steingrímur?" Hörður asks.

Björgvin scoffs. "So his reputation is going to be tarnished too, huh?"

"Before we talk more about your uncle Steingrímur, let's talk a little about your father, Geirharður," says Hörður.

Björgvin throws up his hands. "Why?"

"There's a small black-and-white photo in your living room," says Hörður. "A photo of a young boy standing in front of a farmhouse. Is it of your father?"

"Were you snooping?" Björgvin asks angrily.

"Just answer the question," says the lieutenant.

"The photo is of Dad, yes," Björgvin snaps.

"Was the photo taken at Heiðarból?" Hörður asks.

"Yes."

"Do you know where the other half of it is?"

"The other half?" asks Björgvin in surprise.

"The photo was cut in two," says Hörður. "Only half of it is there."

"I know nothing about that," Björgvin says. "My dad gave me that photo. I got it like that, in the frame. Why are you asking about it?"

"When did he give it to you?" Hörður asks.

"Shortly before he died," Björgvin answers. "Why are you asking all these questions about my dad?"

Hörður shrugs. "He also lost his girlfriend when he was a young man. A German girl named Klara Zimmerman. Like Lena, she fell into a canyon. Fjaðrárgljúfur Canyon, not far from the farm Heiðarból."

Björgvin sighs. "Yes, so?"

"Five years later, a German girl drowned in the Eldvatn river," says Hörður. "Her name was Johanna Schmitz. Like Klara, she'd been living and working at Heiðarból."

Björgvin laughs coldly. "Where are you headed with all this? Four young women die accidentally over a period of what, forty years? Do you know how many tourists come here every year? Do you know how many German girls come to Iceland each year to work with Icelandic horses? They work for free, just to be able to spend time with our horses, take care of them and ride them."

Hörður turns a deaf ear to Björgvin's answer. "What sort of man was your father, Geirharður?"

"You don't quit, do you?" Björgvin snaps. "My father was depressed and a drinker, but he never hurt a fly, no matter what anyone says. If you think he had anything to do with those girls' deaths, you can forget it. He was with other people when Klara fell into the canyon. And when Johanna disappeared, my father was in Reykjavík."

Hörður's ears perk. The report on Klara Zimmerman's death states that Geirharður had been with two others on the heath to the east of Heiðarból when Klara fell, but since all the dates and times given in that investigation's reports were very imprecise, that alibi seemed rather unconvincing to the red-haired giant. But in the report on the discovery of the body in Eldvatn, there is no mention of the house-holder at Heiðarból being absent.

"In Reykjavík, you say?" asks the lieutenant.

Björgvin nods. "At the Kleppur psychiatric hospital."

"At Kleppur?" asks Hörður in surprise. "Your dad was admitted to a mental hospital?"

"He was there for a few weeks, yes," Björgvin answers.

"Due to his depression?" Hörður asks. He notes this down. This is definitely something that he'll ask Þóra to look into.

"Yes," Björgvin answers dryly. "Apparently, he tried to kill himself."

"I see," says Hörður. If this turns out to be true, that Geirharður was away when Johanna disappeared, then it must be considered unlikely that he had anything to do with her death or Klara's. But the same can't be said of his brother, the man who investigated these same cases. "Let's talk a little about your uncle Steingrímur."

"If you really want to," Björgvin mutters.

Hörður clears his throat. "Have you heard the rumor that he mistreated your mother when she was a child?"

"What do you mean?" asks Björgvin defensively. "Who were you talking to?"

"Was it Steingrímur who cut her ears?" asks the lieutenant.

Björgvin glares spitefully at him. "Why are you asking me that? Why not just ask him?"

"What do you mean, ask *him*?" Hörður asks. "Who?"

"Well, Steingrímur!" Björgvin retorts. "Who else?"

"Is he…?" Hörður blinks. Suddenly he remembers the old man with the cane and cravat, the one that Reverend Páll called Steini. "So he's alive?"

Hörður drives down the sideroad, out of the fog and down to the wide valley floor. The sun reappears, the temperature rises, and everything is back to normal. He puts on sunglasses and turns down the heater. To the left is the track that leads to the mouth of Hörgsárgljúfur Canyon. He'd planned on driving there after talking to Björgvin, in order to get a better understanding of the surroundings and conditions, but decided to wait on it. His interview of Björgvin took a lot longer than he'd intended; he's behind schedule, and now a name has even been added to the list of suspects.

"Steingrímur's alive," mutters the red-haired giant. He steers the SUV with one hand and keeps one eye on the road as he looks up Adam's number and calls him.

"Hello!"

"Why didn't you tell me that Steingrímur was alive?" Hörður asks.

"Why did you think he was dead?" Adam asks in return.

Hörður grunts. "I don't know! Someone must have said that he was dead. Probably Axel."

Or what?

"He had a stroke. But he has recovered, mainly."

"I'm on my way to Klausturhólar," says the lieutenant. "Doesn't he live there?"

"Yes, that's right."

"And I'll be going to speak to Sigrún at the Skaftá Visitor Center after that," says Hörður. He drives out of the valley on its western side and approaches the paved highway.

"She isn't there. I just spoke to her. She didn't trust herself to drive in the fog. She asked if you could just come to her place."

Hörður thinks this over. "Yes, of course. That's even better. I'm curious about that farm, Heiðarból. She still lives there, right?"

"Yes."

"I'll call you before I head out there. To get directions," says Hörður as he turns onto the highway. The sky is clear, the sun is shining, and it's as if the chilling fog had been just a dream. But the mountains and the heaths are still covered by a gray veil.

"No problem."

"Listen, while I remember," says the lieutenant. "Does Björgvin have a gun permit?"

"Yes, he has both a shotgun and a high-powered rifle. He hunts birds for food—geese, ducks, and ptarmigans."

"He doesn't hunt birds with a rifle?" Hörður asks.

"No, I suppose he would use it to kill horses."

"Yes, maybe," says Hörður. "Talk to you later."

When Hörður turns out of the roundabout and onto Klausturvegur Road, it's four o'clock. He finds time to be passing uncomfortably fast, but tries to think as little as possible about how Barbara is experiencing these same minutes and hours. She may be suffering sheer terror, even at this moment. Maybe Hertha was the luckier of the two.

Hörður feels sick with anxiety and overwhelming self-doubt. The more he investigates this case and the more people he talks to, the less he feels he's making progress. Yet, it's not quite so. He is in fact on his way to meet a man he thought was dead—a man who isn't all he seems to be.

Just before Hörður turns into the parking lot of the Klausturhólar Nursing Home, he sees that Fannar Sesseljuson, the village's troubled teenager, is snooping about the Kjarval store. The boy is wearing a hoodie, with the hood up in the sun and the heat.

He's not going to scrawl more graffiti on the wall, is he? thinks the lieutenant. He slows down a bit. Fannar looks up, and when he sees the SUV he turns on his heel and runs in the opposite direction.

"Very strange boy," mutters Hörður. He parks the SUV on the lot outside Klausturhólar and steps out into the good weather. He hears birdsong and the river's murmur, and smells the fragrance of trees and flowers.

Kirkjubæjarklaustur is peaceful. But in the lieutenant's mind and heart there's a confusing chaos, a kind of storm. He has a dull headache and a bad taste in his mouth, having drunk too much coffee and eaten too little.

The interior of the institution is rather bleak-looking, although attempts have been made to liven up the atmosphere with potted plants, most of which seem to be shriveling. Hörður comes across an employee, a young woman dressed in blue, and asks her where he can find Steingrímur Róbertsson. She points out the way to the man's room, but tells the lieutenant that he can't stop for long; it's rest time at the moment.

"No worries," says the lieutenant. He finds the room and knocks softly on the door before opening it.

Lying on a narrow bed in the room is an old man, the same one that Hörður saw out walking the day before. He's tall and broad-shouldered, but gray and haggard. The old man looks questioningly at the visitor and gets up halfway.

"Sorry for the inconvenience," says the red-haired giant. He pulls a chair over to the bed, sits down on it and takes off his cap. "You're Steingrímur, the former police lieutenant here, aren't you? My name is Hörður, and I'm the new lieutenant. Your successor."

The old man nods, then lies down again. He's clearly very tired.

"Do you mind if I ask you some questions?" says Hörður.

Steingrímur gives a kind of sigh, which the lieutenant allows himself to interpret as consent.

"I live in the house at Efri-Vík, where you lived before," says the lieutenant. "I opened the locked room, and found a few things in it. For example, a box with old police reports and a photo of you in, well … colorful company."

Steingrímur blinks his blue eyes but says nothing. Hörður isn't sure if the old man can hear him or understands what he's saying, yet has the feeling that he's not as out of it as he appears to be.

"Why did you keep those reports at home?" asks the lieutenant. "You know what reports I'm talking about. The missing girls."

Steingrímur swallows, but still says nothing.

"If you need to lighten your conscience in any way, this is the perfect opportunity to do so," says Hörður.

No response.

"That photo, of you with those…men," says Hörður. "Who sent it to you? Was it a threat? From someone who knew something? What about it?"

Steingrímur's dry lips twitch, but he remains as silent as before.

"Are you guilty of something criminal? Did you have anything to do with those disappearances?" asks the lieutenant firmly. "Or are you covering things up for someone?"

Steingrímur sighs heavily, as if he doesn't feel well.

Hörður has grown quite irritated. "Is it true that you hurt Sigrún when you were children? Was it you who cut her ears?"

Suddenly the old lieutenant comes to life. He blinks, rises to one elbow, and licks his lips.

"It was Hallbera," he says with difficulty. He's paralyzed on one side of his face and drools when he speaks.

"Who?" asks Hörður in surprise. "Hallbera? Who is that? What did she do?"

But Steingrímur doesn't answer. He sighs and lies back down, closes his eyes, and appears to sleep.

Hörður is on the highway, driving west. He's down-hearted after his conversation with Steingrímur, if a conversation it can be called. The old man is clearly in poor shape due to his stroke, more or less out of touch with the world. Hörður had felt a little optimistic after discovering that the old lieutenant was still alive. He allowed himself to hope that he would finally get answers to some of his questions, even a confession or other important information.

But no, just one more disappointment—another dead end in the maze he's stuck in.

He calls Adam.

"Hello! Did you meet old Steini?"

Hörður grunts. "Yes, but I got little out of him."

"I see. But why did you need to talk to him?"

Hörður clears his throat. He neither feels like sharing nor wants to share all his speculations with a man he barely knows. "I'll tell you later. But tell me one thing, who is Hallbera?"

"Hallbera? I don't recognize the name. Does she live hereabouts?"

Hörður heaves a sigh. "I don't know. Maybe Sigrún knows who she is? I'm on my way to see her. Where's the turn-off to Heiðarból again?"

"Where are you now?"

Hörður slows down and then turns right off the highway, at the same road he took to Fjaðrárgljúfur Canyon. "I'm coming to the bridge over Skaftá; the farm Hunkubakkar is on the hill opposite, if I remember correctly."

"Yes, exactly. But you'll turn right on the rise above Hunkubakkar. You'll see a sign for Laki. You drive along that road until you come to another intersection. Then turn right again. As I recall, there'll be a sign with the name of the farm."

"Okay, great," says Hörður. "I'll just call you back if I get lost."

"No problem."

The lieutenant drives over the bridge and up the hill. Shortly afterward, he sees a sign indicating a narrow road on the right. As before, the sign reads *Laki 45 km*. Hörður turns onto the road, which is bumpy and tough-going. The road leads into a large, wide valley that is part of the high-lands above Kirkjubæjarklaustur. Finally, he comes to the intersection that Adam mentioned. There he finds two separate signs, each pointing in a different direction. A blue sign points the way to Laki, and on a white sign is the word *Heiðarból.* That sign indicates an even narrower road that leads to the northeast. On the iron pole to which the white sign is fastened are two brackets, as if it there had been another sign beneath the one on the pole.

Hörður turns onto the road to Heiðarból and drives farther and higher into the homogeneous-looking heath-land, where there's still fog, although it's clearly receding. The road is very narrow, with deep wheel ruts. It's probably impassable for much of the winter. He drives past a dilapidated horse corral and racecourse that hasn't been used in years. Hörður sees the weathered foundation of a building and concludes that a stable had once stood there. The fog envelops the landscape colorlessly and mysteriously, and skews the imagination. Soon, though, the lieutenant notices something big and real within the ghostly fog. It's a farmhouse standing in a dell beneath a steep slope. The farmhouse is a stately white-painted concrete house with two gables and a red roof. Hörður recognizes the house immediately, despite not having seen it before in color. It's the same house that Sigrún and Geirharður are standing in front of in the black-and-white photograph, just much older-looking now. Next to the house are tall, stout trees, and in the farmyard is a pale green Land Rover with which the lieutenant is well acquainted. The area around the house is fenced off with barbed-wire fencing that's in rather bad shape. Hörður drives in through an open gate and parks the SUV next to Sigrún's Land Rover.

He shuts off the engine and steps into the farmyard, folder in hand. The fog forms a gray wall on the heath above Heiðarból. Leading northward from the farmyard is a faint path that disappears into the fog.

The door to the house opens and Sigrún hurries out. She's wearing her gray wool sweater, men's trousers, and weathered hiking boots. The hems of her trousers are tucked into wool socks that are pulled up to mid-calf. At first, Hörður thinks that the householder has come out to greet him, but Sigrún looks aside, at the gray bank of fog. Then she marches toward her car, but starts in terrible alarm and stops abruptly when she finally sees the giant lieutenant. He realizes that she had no idea a guest had arrived.

"Jesus!" shouts Sigrún, before putting on her glasses, hanging from a cord around her neck. "Have you just arrived? Goodness, how you startled me!"

"I didn't mean to frighten you," says Hörður.

"It's my fault!" the old woman half-shouts, energetically grabbing the lieutenant's hand. "I'm not wearing my damn hearing aids. I never use them at home, except when I talk on the phone."

"I see." Hörður smiles at her, and then points in the same direction as she looked, where the path lies. "Are the outbuildings there, in the fog?"

Sigrún shakes her head. "Just spirits and ghosts. There are no outbuildings at Heiðarból anymore. I don't have any animals. I've never liked them. Would you like some coffee?"

The kitchen at Heiðarból is old and cozy, like the home in general. The fixtures are original, painted white like the walls, and therefore fit it extremely well, being a continuous part of it. Where once there may have been a coal stove, however, there is now a modern electric one. Hörður is sitting at the cloth-covered kitchen table, while the house-wife makes coffee, sets the table, and lays out plates of cookies, rhubarb tart, and bread with butter, liverwurst, cheese, and the like.

The house is probably around a hundred years old, but has been well maintained. The walls are cracked here and there, and the woodwork is crumbling in places; the floors creak and smell faintly of mildew, but everything is clean, and it probably hasn't been more than five years since it was all painted. The walls are decorated with paintings and photographs, and from within the carpeted living room comes the soft ticking of an old clock.

Hörður manages to relax and forget time and place; this old farm reminds him of his childhood home, the house *Future* in Súðavík. The coffee smells delectable and the treats look very appetizing—for example the homemade bread with lamb paté awaiting him on a large plate.

"Were you at Björgvin's?" Sigrún asks as she pours cold milk into a beautiful clay pitcher. Apparently, she has put on her hearing aids, because she has stopped yelling at him.

"I was," says Hörður. He opens the folder, takes the papers from it, and places the voice recorder on the table.

"I was trying to call him but he didn't answer," Sigrún mutters regretfully.

"We were talking when you called," says Hörður.

"Oh, is that so?" says Sigrún. She sets the pitcher on the table and goes to the microwave to take out the crullers she was thawing in it.

"Don't go to any more trouble on my account," says the lieutenant. "I'm not stopping for long."

"I'm guessing you didn't get much in the way of refreshments from Björgvin," says Sigrún.

"Coffee and crullers," says Hörður.

Sigrún scoffs. "I'm sure those crullers weren't fresh. I should know, because I was the one who made them and brought them to him."

"I see," says Hörður, just to say something. He pours coffee into his cup, which is white porcelain with a blue pattern and a flowery handle, on a matching saucer.

"I just don't understand why he doesn't move in with me," says Sigrún. She puts down the plate of warm crullers and finally sits down at the table. "It's not as if there isn't enough room here! He just hangs around there alone with my grandson in that out-of-the-way valley, on a farm that's up to its ears in debt. Whereas I own my house and my land! I just don't understand how the boy can be so stubborn."

"No, I'm sure you don't," mutters Hörður. "Maybe we should start?"

"Yes, of course." Sigrún moves the plates and saucers a few millimeters and fiddles a bit with the tablecloth. "What do you need to know?"

"Just a few details," the lieutenant replies, before recording the customary preliminary information. "You were working at the Skaftá Visitor Center last Thursday, when the German girls stopped in. Hertha Meier and Barbara Hoffmann."

"Yes, you know that very well…you were there!" says Sigrún, with an awkward laugh. "But I didn't know who those girls were or where they came from. These were just tourists, you see. Girls on a backpacking trip. Terribly silly kids, I'd say. Seeing as how it went."

"How it went?" asks Hörður.

"Well, you saw her, the poor thing who came walking naked in the rain!" Sigrún says with a shudder. "They clearly got themselves in some trouble. Camped where they weren't supposed to camp, or went swimming in a river or lake. Did something *foolish*, and it turned out as it did because of it, I say. If they'd paid attention to the weather forecast and camped in an authorized campsite, we wouldn't be talking now, would we?"

"No, maybe not," says Hörður. He bites into a slice of bread spread with liverwurst and takes a sip of coffee. "But how do you know they didn't camp in a campsite?"

Sigrún scoffs. "How do I know? They wouldn't have gotten lost if they did, would they? What kind of question is that?"

Hörður smiles innocently. "Do you have any idea where they pitched their tents? Or where they went swimming, if that's what they did?"

Sigrún fidgets in her seat, as if irritated. "No, of course not. It could have been in a number of places."

"They asked you about particular places, didn't they?" asks the lieutenant.

Sigrún nods. "Yes, but that doesn't mean they didn't go elsewhere."

"What places did they ask about?"

Sigrún shrugs. "The usual ones. Systravatn Lake—how you get up there. And Fjaðrárgljúfur Canyon, where it was and the best way to get there."

"And you showed them both?"

The old woman nods. "Yes, I gave them a map and marked it. I do that every day. But I made it clear that they weren't allowed to camp wherever they wanted, so I did!"

The lieutenant nods as well. He was there, and most certainly recalls her doing just that. "Did you see the girls after they left the Skaftá Center?"

Sigrún shakes her head. "No, I didn't. Not until one of them appeared on the road, in the rain. Though I didn't realize that I'd met her before. I was in complete shock."

"Yes, right," Hörður mutters as he looks at his notes. "Speaking of that incident, when you nearly hit Hertha Meier with your car last Saturday morning. What trip were you on?"

"What *trip* was I on?" asks the old woman indignantly. "I wasn't on a trip, young man! I was bringing provisions to the search-and-rescue teams. I'm a reserve, you see."

"Reserve?" asks the lieutenant. "Provisions?"

Sigrún rolls her eyes. "Don't you know anything? The search-and-rescue units have a number of reserves, people like me who may not trust themselves to respond directly to calls and participate in searches, but can still do a lot of good. That morning, I was on my way with provisions for the people who'd been called out in response to the storm that night. Björgvin asked me to make coffee and prepare flatbread sandwiches for the teams. And that's what I did!"

"Yes, of course," mutters Hörður. He'd actually wondered where all those flatbread sandwiches that the search teams had been munching in the rain came from. Now that question had been answered.

"Here, everyone helps each other," says Sigrún proudly. "Not like in Reykjavík, where they all put themselves first."

"Right." Hörður clears his throat. The time has come for him to ask the old woman about the older disappearances. He isn't exactly looking forward to it, as those disappearances are directly or indirectly connected to her ex-husband. "Since I'm both new to the job and little more than a stranger here, I'd like to go back in time and ask you about some long-past incidents."

"Oh?" The old woman's voice is tinged with both suspicion and curiosity.

"Do you remember when Klara Zimmerman died?" asks the lieutenant. "She was twenty-one years old, blonde, German."

Sigrún sighs and looks aside. "That was quite a long time ago. But yes, I remember it. Why?"

"She was your husband's fiancé, right?" Hörður asks.

"Yes, that's right," says Sigrún dryly. "Her death was hard for Geirharður to bear. In fact, he never recovered from it. Why are you bringing up that tragic event?"

"I know that these aren't fun questions, but I have to ask them," says Hörður. "That's all I can say right now."

"Well, so be it," mutters the old woman.

"Five years later, another girl, Johanna Schmitz, died," says Hörður. "Also German. Twenty-four years old, blonde hair, blue eyes. She worked as a hired hand for you and Geirharður, right?"

"Hired hand? Well…she just helped with the horses," says Sigrún as she fiddles with the tablecloth. "I did the housework, the cooking, the laundry, and everything. I've never been interested in horses and don't bother with them."

"And she drowned, didn't she?" asks the lieutenant.

Sigrún nods. "In Eldvatn, yes. She was out there by herself. This is a dangerous area, especially for those who don't know it well. A huge search was conducted for her. The body wasn't found immediately."

"Right," says Hörður. "But weren't any rumors or suspicions sparked by Johanna's death? The second girl in five years to die in an accident. Both young and German, and living here at Heiðarból."

"Suspicions? Gossip?" asks Sigrún, clearly alarmed. "What do you mean? Are you accusing my deceased husband of having something to do with the deaths of those girls?"

"I'm not accusing anyone of anything," says the lieutenant. "I was just asking whether any suspicions arose. Whether people didn't find it all peculiar."

"I know nothing about any gossip," says the old woman haughtily, "but there was nothing *peculiar* about those deaths. Klara put herself at risk during the sheep roundup by going too close to the rim of the canyon on horseback—a local would never do that! And five years later, that so-called hired hand strayed into Eldvatn. What does that have to do with Geirharður?"

"I wasn't accusing Geirharður of anything," says Hörður gently.

"No, maybe not," says Sigrún.

"Who investigated those deaths?" asks Hörður, knowing the answer to that question.

"Steini had just joined the police force at that time," Sigrún answers. "Steingrímur, Geirharður's brother. But in both cases, investigators came from Reykjavík. One from the Criminal Investigation Department when Klara fell, and then two when Johanna's body was found. It was so battered that it took some time to identify it."

Hörður nods. "What sort of man is Steingrímur?"

"What sort of man?" asks Sigrún. "He's just the way he is. An old-school cop."

"Were they similar, the two brothers?" Hörður asks.

Sigrún scoffs. "Maybe in appearance, yes. But not in personality. Geirharður was always very delicate. He was big and strong, but his heart was small. Steingrímur enjoyed fighting and the like, but my Geiri never fought. He couldn't stand conflict."

"Was he depressed?" Hörður asks.

Sigrún glares at him. "I don't know who you've been talking to, or about what. Aren't you looking for a lost girl? Geirharður definitely had some psychological difficulties. But I don't see how that's anyone's business. In the old days, it was considered unseemly to speak so freely about the deceased."

Hörður tries not to let her statement affect him. "Is it true that he was at Kleppur when Johanna Schmitz disappeared?"

"That's right," mutters the old woman.

Hörður notes this down. It appears that Geirharður has a watertight alibi in Johanna's case. He just needs to have it confirmed. The same can't be said of his brother Steingrímur.

He gears himself up—now he needs to ask the old woman about an event she probably has no desire to discuss. He decides to speak a bit obliquely. "Tell me, is it true that Steingrímur was a bad-natured kid? That he hurt other children?"

Sigrún's face turns deathly pale. "What are you insinuating?"

Hörður smiles apologetically. "Nothing, really. I'm just trying to find out what sort of man Steingrímur is."

Sigrún shakes her head. "He's always been a bully. But I don't want to talk about that. He's just the way he is."

Hörður nods. She doesn't need to say more. The question upset her, as he'd expected. He assumes that it was Steingrímur who cut her ears when they were children.

"Do you think…" Sigrún blinks. "Do you think that Steingrímur had something to do with the deaths of those girls?"

Hörður looks at his notes. "I'm just trying to figure out this and that, and to put things in context, *if* there's any context to be found."

"They were just accidents," mutters Sigrún, as if talking to herself. "Weren't they? That's what I recall."

The lieutenant clears his throat. "There were other deaths. Fourteen years ago, a dead girl was found in Hörgsárgljúfur Canyon, the Swedish Lena Nilsson. And five years ago, a Belgian girl drowned in the Skaftá river, Juliette Vermeulen. They were eighteen and twenty-three years old. Lena's hair was blonde, and Juliette's dirty-blonde."

The old woman nods anxiously.

"Lena was your son Björgvin's girlfriend," says Hörður, "and some people are of the opinion that he and Juliette were seeing each other—that Björgvin cheated on Silja with her."

"I thought you might bring that up," says Sigrún. Her fragile voice betrays bitterness, and sorrow, as well. "I don't know exactly where you're headed with these questions. And yet…But if you're imagining that my Björgvin had something to do with the deaths of those girls, you can forget about it. He had an alibi in both instances."

Hörður nods. He's read the reports. But the man's alibis are rather weak.

"You were teasing him a bit, there at the Skaftá Center last Thursday," he says. "You asked him if it was true that he was transporting foreign girls by the truckload to Klaustur, or something like that. What did you mean by that?"

Again, Sigrún scoffs. "Like you said, just teasing. He'd given those German girls a lift. Can't I tease my own son?"

"Yes, of course," says the lieutenant. "I just felt it was a bit pointed. Björgvin didn't seem to find your remark funny."

Sigrún shrugs. "Since when do children find their parents funny? But it's all the same to me whether he picks up hitchhikers; it's none of my business. Maybe he just wanted to practice his German."

"Practice his German?" Hörður asks in surprise.

"Björgvin speaks fluent German," says Sigrún proudly. "He studied horse-training in Germany. A hugely expensive course that hasn't been of any use to him in life, any more than so much else."

"Of course," Hörður mutters as he notes this down. Silja had mentioned this, but he hadn't put two and two together. Björgvin had lied to him when he said that he didn't know what the girls were talking about in the car. Why?

He clears his throat. "Tell me, how has Steingrímur and Björgvin's relationship been over the years?"

"Unremarkable, I'd say," answers Sigrún, who is clearly surprised at the question. "Just like a normal relationship between an uncle and a nephew, I suppose. Why do you ask?"

"Did you know that Steingrímur is gay?" Hörður asks in return.

Sigrún scowls. "I knew and didn't know. How can *you* be sure of that? You don't know the man!"

"I know a thing or two," says the lieutenant, mysteriously.

Suddenly the old woman opens her eyes wide. "Is that why you're asking about the relationship between those two? Do you mean if Steingrímur had something to do with my boy?"

Hörður shrugs. "Yes and no. I'm just turning over stones."

Sigrún's face reddens, but the lieutenant can't tell if it's because she's angry or upset. "I don't know how I feel about your questions. You're insinuating that my son was sexually abused, and is therefore troubled—or what?"

Hörður swallows. He's well aware that these speculations of his are uncomfortable. But at the same time, he's quite convinced that they matter, in a larger context. "As I said, I'm simply trying to figure out what sort of man my predecessor in this job is. It's the person who investigated these older cases that I've been trying to get to know."

"You even think that Steingrímur has something to hide?" Sigrún asks in disbelief.

"What I think or don't think doesn't matter right now," says Hörður distractedly. He leafs through his papers, having the feeling that he was going to ask the old woman something specific, but can't remember what it was. Didn't he write it down?

"More coffee?" Sigrún asks suddenly. She doesn't wait for an answer, but fills the lieutenant's cup.

"Thanks, thanks, but I've got to get going," Hörður answers. "I have no further questions for now."

"Fine," says Sigrún. "But you're more than welcome to finish your coffee and have something with it. You've hardly touched the refreshments."

Hörður smiles faintly as he turns off the voice recorder, and then he taps the papers into order and puts them in the folder. "Maybe one slice of rhubarb tart."

"Yes, for sure!" says Sigrún, appearing cheerful once more. She pushes the plate holding the tart closer to the lieutenant and watches him cut a slice. "It was baked the day before yesterday—good as new. The jam is homemade, with rhubarb from the bed around back."

Hörður transfers the slice to his own plate. "There was a rhubarb bed behind the house I grew up in out west. And of course my mother used it to make jams and soups. As a kid, I used to eat it raw, sometimes, and I haven't forgotten how sour it was."

"You're from out west?" asks Sigrún.

The lieutenant's mood darkens. Why had he mentioned his origins, his youth? The bad memories wash over him— the avalanche that fell on Súðavík and snatched away his family, as well as numerous others. He gets a lump in his stomach, and has a sour taste in his mouth.

"Um…" He pretends not to have heard the question and finishes his coffee in one gulp. "May I use your bathroom?"

"Yes, of course," says the old woman. "It's upstairs, at the end on the right."

"Thanks," the lieutenant mutters as he gets up from the table. He's both managed to get out of talking about Súðavík and given himself the chance to take a little look around Björgvin's childhood home.

The staircase leading to the upper floor is in a small hall, in which there's a telephone table and chair. On the circular table is a crocheted cloth, a hardbound telephone/address book, a case for Sigrún's hearing aids, and a black telephone. The chair is high-backed, with an upholstered seat. The old woman doubtless sits there when she calls her son. Hörður is old enough to remember the world before the invasion of cell phones. Then, such telephone tables were found in every home.

He walks up the creaking stairs. The upper floor is rather low-ceilinged and the bedrooms have sloping roofs. An old rug covers the slightly bouncy wooden floor. The bathroom is at the far end, with a small storage room by the staircase landing. The old woman's bedroom is on the right, looking out onto the farmyard. On the left is another room that may once have been a children's room, but is now a kind of office or leisure room, even just a tidy storage room. Hörður peeks into it. On the floor beneath the dormer window is a wooden chest. He tries the lid, but the chest is locked, and there is no key in the large keyhole on its front. He pushes aside the window's crocheted curtains. Out the window, he has a view of the backyard and the heath behind it. On the yard's left side, large clotheslines hang over a patch of lawn, and on the right side is a defined patch of dug-up earth and vegetable beds, some under plastic and others not. In the corner of the yard is a small shed, where, perhaps, the old lady keeps her garden tools. Hörður continues to look around the room. In it are a desk and chair, a floor lamp, an old spinning wheel, folders on a shelf, an old double-barrel shotgun in one corner, boxes of books, and…

Hörður stiffens when he hears the stairs creak. Is the old woman on her way up? He hurries into the hallway, as quietly as he can. No sooner has he stepped out of the room than Sigrún's head appears at the top of the stairwell. They look each other a bit awkwardly in the eye.

"Did you find the bathroom?" asks the old woman.

"Yes," says Hörður.

"Well, that's good." Sigrún turns around and Hörður follows her down to the ground floor.

"Will you show me the rhubarb bed before I go?" asks the lieutenant.

"Of course," Sigrún answers. "I'll go out the back door. My boots are in the laundry room."

Hörður goes to the vestibule. He puts on his shoes and cap and opens the door onto the farmyard. The fog has receded but still covers the top of the heath, like whipped cream topping a slice of cake. It's bright outside, and the air smells of heather. The heath is noticeably silent. He throws the folder and the voice recorder into the SUV and then walks to the back of the house.

"This is my little vegetable corner," says the old woman when the red-haired giant appears in the backyard. "Look, there's the rhubarb. Isn't it big and beautiful?"

Hörður follows her gesture. Next to the garden shed is a bed of rhubarb that is certainly both tall and beautiful— the giant leaves are as green as the lieutenant's eyes, the broad stalks red and firm.

"Most definitely," he says, smiling.

The area behind the house is nicely sheltered. A paved path leads from the steps below the laundry-room door to the clotheslines, where white laundry is hanging to dry—sheets and bedding. On the wall behind the stairs is a tap, and beneath it, an old wooden bucket. Sigrún goes to the shed, opens it, and takes out a green watering can. The inside of the shed is dark, but Hörður sees the outlines of shovels, pitchforks, a grass trimmer, and all sorts of garden tools. There are also empty canvas bags hanging on nails.

"Very bountiful," says the lieutenant, just to say something. He knows nothing about gardening or vegetable growing. But there's no question that the old woman takes good care of her garden. There's not a weed in sight, and at the corner of the potato beds is a pile of sand and another of manure. In the shed can no doubt be found fertilizer, lime, dried seaweed, and everything else needed for growing vegetables.

"This is my little heaven," says Sigrún, who clearly has her mind on her garden, and not the lieutenant. She takes the watering can to the wall of the house and fills it from the tap. It's clearly time for watering something.

"Well, I won't bother you any longer," says Hörður. "We both have work to do. Thanks for having me. Thanks for the coffee and refreshments. We'll see each other again soon, I'm sure."

"You're welcome, friend," says Sigrún as she shuts off the tap, and then she plods with the full can over to the vegetable beds.

Hörður returns to the front of the house, gets in the SUV and starts the engine. He drives back along the narrow road. The SUV bounces and the undercarriage squeaks softly. When he reaches the intersection where the Heiðarból sign is, he suddenly remembers what he was going to ask the old woman about. It was the name that Steingrímur mentioned. He was going to ask her if she knew who this Hallbera was.

He stops the car, takes out his phone and taps in Sigrún's cell-phone number, but gets only an automated message informing him that the number he is calling can't be reached. He looks at his phone's screen and sees that there's no cell-phone connection on the heath.

"Figures," says the lieutenant. He sticks the phone back in his pocket and drives onward; he can't be bothered to turn around and go back. He'll just ask old Sigrún the next time he sees her. When he comes to the intersection on the hill above the Skaftá river, his cell phone rings in his pocket. He slows down a bit, and then answers the call by pressing a button on the steering wheel.

"Sigrún?" Hörður asks, as it crosses his mind that she saw he was trying to reach her and is now calling back from her home phone.

"This is Axel."

"Oh…" Hörður is slightly startled at hearing the deep voice of the head of the CID. He steps firmly on the brake pedal, heads to the side of the road and stops the SUV at the intersection.

"Is this a bad time?"

"Not at all," replies the lieutenant. He pulls on the handbrake and adjusts himself in his seat. "I was just driving, but have parked the car."

"How goes the investigation?"

Hörður suddenly feels mildly dizzy. He's spent the day questioning witnesses and suspects, but is nowhere nearer an answer. He feels as if he's wasted precious time on nothing. He's driven dozens of kilometers, drunk a huge amount of coffee, eaten bread and tarts while Barbara Hoffmann is still missing, maybe locked up somewhere in a cramped cage, naked, dirty, and cold…

"Hörður?"

The lieutenant blinks. Did he space out? "Sorry, I …" He clears his throat. "The investigation is moving forward, but rather slowly. I've been talking to witnesses and those on my list of suspects and have discovered this and that, but the girl is still missing and I have nothing sufficient for an arrest or a search warrant. But I think the circle is getting narrower, little by little."

"I see."

"And on your side," Hörður hurriedly asks. "Has Forensics finished its work?"

"Pretty much. One of the backpacks that was found was marked Hertha Meier, so the outdoor equipment most likely belongs to those girls."

"Good to have that confirmed," says Hörður, who has, however, been sure of this the whole time.

"The animal hairs found on the girl's body have also been identified."

"Really?" asks the lieutenant excitedly. "Let me guess. Is it dog's hair? From a Border Collie?"

"No, it's sheep's hair. Wool, that is."

"Sheep's?" asks Hörður. He vaguely recalls having written down the word *sheep farm* a short time ago, but doesn't remember in what context or who it was that mentioned this word.

"And the dirt under her nails turned out to be sheep dung. So she was probably in a sheep shed at some point, and very likely naked."

Hörður thinks of the buildings at Systravatn—the Sel outbuildings—and his dream comes back to mind. "Maybe Barbara is being held against her will in that same sheep shed?"

"Maybe. But soot was also found on the body. The streaks that were on the deceased's face and hands turned out to be soot, as from burned wood."

"Soot?" asks Hörður.

"But these results don't really matter at the moment."

"It all matters *somehow*," says Hörður determinedly. "I don't understand where the soot comes from. But if the hairs had been from a dog, as I thought, it would have strengthened a certain suspicion of mine. But since they're wool, that means the girls were in a sheep shed or somewhere where sheep are or have been, as you said. At least one of them. Which means we can narrow down the search and … "

Axel interrupts the lieutenant. *"This information doesn't really matter to* you, *Hörður. Not in the current situation."*

The lieutenant gets a knot in his stomach. "What do you mean? Why doesn't it matter to *me*? And what situation are you referring to?"

Hörður is halfway down the slope when the phone rings again. He glances at his cell phone, which is lying in the passenger seat, and sees that it's Þóra who is trying to reach him. He sighs and steps on the brake just before driving out onto the bridge over the Skaftá river. Through the side window, he sees the turbulent glacial river down in the deep ravine. In his mind, a crack filled with dark thoughts opens.

The phone rings, as if from a distance. Hörður drives over the bridge, over the deep abyss of the ravine—and then he answers the phone. Not because he wants to, but to break the vicious circle that has engulfed his thoughts.

The bridge is behind him, and ahead is a short section of road ending at the highway.

"Am I interrupting?"

"No, no," Hörður manages to groan. He's all numb, and feels like he's trapped under a heavy load.

"How have you been today?"

"Just, so-so," says Hörður. He doesn't want to talk; he doesn't have the energy for it, but doesn't want to cause his friend unnecessary worry. He clears his throat and tries to sound normal. "I've interviewed the witnesses. But not much came of it. Barbara is still missing and I'm actually no closer to determining her fate. If she's dead, then ... "

For a moment, his vision goes black.

"That's enough of that! Give me a summary of what you've found out today. Every little detail can make a difference. Two eyes are better than one and all that."

"Found out?" Hörður heaves a sigh as he slows down and turns left. He's at the intersection with the highway. "Well, Björgvin lied to me, though I don't know why. He said he didn't know what the girls were talking about in his car, after he picked them up in Hvolsvöllur. But his mother just told me that he speaks fluent German. I don't know if this matters."

"Of course it matters! If a witness is lying, he's hiding something, right?"

"Yes, probably." Seeing that there's no oncoming traffic, Hörður drives onto the highway, heading eastward, back toward Klaustur. "But it's a pretty innocent lie. Björgvin is suspicious, but I don't have anything on him."

"I understand. But what about his dad and the older cases?"

"I actually did discover one thing today," says Hörður. "Lieutenant Steingrímur isn't dead, as I had thought. He's in a nursing home in Klaustur."

"Oh?"

"He had a stroke and is more or less a vegetable, unless he's pretending," says Hörður. He puts on his sunglasses and gradually speeds up. The sunshine is glaring, and mirages waver over the road in the distance.

"You tried talking to him?"

"There's more," says Hörður. He shifts into fifth gear and drives at a hundred kilometers per hour on the sun-baked asphalt.

"Tell me."

"He's Geirharður's older brother; in other words, Björgvin's uncle," says Hörður. He holds the steering wheel with both hands and stares at the road ahead.

"That matters."

"It does," says Hörður. "Geirharður was apparently in Kleppur at the time that Johanna Schmitz disappeared. He was admitted due to depression. In other words, he has an alibi, though it's unconfirmed."

"I'll check it out. Maybe there's some data on it."

"If it turns out to be true, then it's more likely that Steingrímur had something to do with the disappearance of those girls than Geirharður," says Hörður. "Apparently, he's been a bully since childhood—a sadist, some say."

"Could he even have had something to do with Barbara's disappearance?"

Hörður sighs. "I don't know. I doubt it. He's very old, and in bad shape. The girls' belongings were removed from the scene and buried, and Barbara is probably being held captive somewhere. The perpetrator therefore presumably has access to a car and housing off the beaten path, probably a sheep shed. Which should narrow the search, but around here, of course, there are sheep sheds everywhere—nothing but countryside everywhere you look."

"Why a sheep shed?"

"Because ..." Hörður is overwhelmed, and feels as if he's in free fall. The SUV rushes along the highway, while he himself sinks into the darkness of despair and surrender. He sees a fuel truck approaching from the opposite direction, a hundred-ton diesel tanker on eighteen wheels.

Hörður goes numb, and without exactly wanting to or making a conscious decision, he gets the vague idea that maybe he should turn onto the wrong side of the road and drive straight into the steel meteorite that's flying toward him—to steer the SUV, and thus himself, into oblivion...

"Hörður?"

He starts and blinks, and simultaneously, the fuel truck's driver blows its horn. The hair rises on the back of the lieutenant's neck and he just manages to jerk the steering wheel to avoid a terrible collision.

"Are you there?"

Hörður exhales, takes his foot off the gas pedal and stares in disbelief at the empty road. What was he thinking?

"I'm here," he says.

"What happened? What horn was that?"

What happened? He isn't sure... Hörður wipes beads of sweat off his forehead. His mouth is dry and his heart is pounding in his chest.

"Hörður? What's going on?"

The red-haired giant clears his throat. "Axel called earlier."

"And?"

"Two CID detectives are coming here late tonight," says Hörður in a broken voice. "They'll check into the hotel and start work early in the morning."

"I don't quite understand. Is Axel sending you assistants or...?"

Hörður slumps in his seat. "No. They're taking over the investigation. I've been sidelined. I've screwed it up."

He drives on without knowing exactly where he's going, and feels as if he's rushing backward.

The Murderer's Memorabilia

Monday—Second Part

Hörður Grímsson is standing as if petrified inside the police station. It's ten minutes to six in the evening. Outside, the sun is shining, but the curtains are drawn before the windows and the station is dark and silent. The lieutenant is holding his folder and is still wearing his jacket and cap. He's pale, his beard is unkempt, and his eyes are empty. Piled on the desk next to the computer are the old reports. There are also sheets of paper covered with hand-written questions, speculations, and notes. He'd put a lot of work into investigating this case and digging up older, similar cases. He'd organized searches and coordinated operations, interviewed witnesses, made countless phone calls, and driven all over the place. He'd hiked around Systravatn Lake, found clues in Fjaðrárgljúfur Canyon and evidence at the Stjórnarsandur landfill site. He asked questions, turned over stones and tried to find a clearing in a dark forest, but in the end, got lost among the trees. He had eaten little, slept little, and was on edge, was plagued by worries and suffered persistent headaches and stomachaches. Minutes have turned into hours and hours into long days and nights, yet he still hasn't found Barbara Hoffmann, much less the person responsible for her disappearance and the death of Hertha Meier.

All the work and all the trouble has been in vain, and to add insult to injury, he's been sidelined.

He came, saw, and screwed up.

"Damn it," Hörður whispers, on the verge of tears. He takes off his cap and jacket. Then he throws the folder toward the desk. He'd intended for it to land with elegant, dramatic flair, but instead, it slides along the desktop and ends up on the floor on the other side, taking with it two pens and a half-empty coffee mug. The pens shoot here and there, while the coffee mug lands with a clunk on the floor and the cold coffee splashes all over.

The red-haired giant twitches at the unexpected noise, and then it's as if something breaks inside him. He screams, attacks the desk, and overturns it. The computer screen breaks, pages of reports glide through the air, and the keyboard, mouse, and all sorts of smaller items skip along the floor.

"What's going on here?"

Hörður starts and looks over his shoulder. Adam Knútsson is standing in the doorway to the vestibule, dressed in beige camouflage clothing from head to toe and with his rifle in a camouflage-colored bag on his shoulder.

"I…" begins Hörður, but he doesn't know what he was going to say and stops mid-sentence. He looks down, sheepishly, like a child who's been caught doing something wrong.

"Has something happened?" Adam asks cautiously. He takes the gun off his shoulder and props it in the corner by the window, then turns on the overhead lights.

Hörður shrugs. "No…or yes…apparently, I'll no longer be investigating this case. There are people coming from the south to take over."

He takes a deep breath before uttering the words he fears most. "It isn't even certain that I'll be returning to the CID. Maybe I'll just be stuck here for the rest of my life, in this damn backwoods."

"People from the south," says Adam. "You've started speaking like a local. Maybe you just belong here after all."

Is he trying to be funny? Hörður glares at his neighbor. Then he notices that the hiking boots he's wearing are muddy and covered with bits of grass. "Where have you been?"

"I took my six-wheeler up to the heath," Adam replies. "To look around for the girl or clues about her whereabouts. A search team from the Scouts is up there, but two eyes are better than one. I can cover ground quickly on the six-wheeler, and know the area pretty well."

"Why did you take your gun?" Hörður asks skeptically.

Adam shrugs. "I always take it with me. If I happen to see a mink or fox. Just a habit, I suppose."

Hörður clears his throat. He still doesn't know what to think about this gun-loving teacher. But he has no real reason to distrust him.

"Um…" Adam smiles a crooked smile as he points at the chaos on the floor. "Shouldn't we clean this up before those southerners arrive? So this… what should I call it… *insurrection* of yours doesn't go beyond these walls."

Hörður sneers. "I really just feel like leaving it as it is. Then I'll just be fired."

"Yes, but…" Adam throws up his hands. "You can't expect those people to have to start by cleaning up after you? They have work to do. *You* have work to do. The girl is still missing, and as long as those people from the south aren't here, you're still in charge of investigating the case, right?"

"Yes, or…" Hörður sighs. "I don't know anything anymore. I've done my best, but…"

His voice breaks and his eyes fill with tears. He can't stop thinking about the dream or vision or whatever it was. If Barbara is really somewhere in captivity, locked in some fucking cage, then he's *got to* find her before it's too late.

But how?

"Sorry, I…" the red-haired giant splutters. Is he crying? What the hell! He hurriedly wipes the tears from his cheeks.

"Listen, pal." Adam pats him on the back. "Go and freshen up a little. I'll tidy this mess in the meantime. Then we'll review the situation. Okay?"

"Fine," mutters Hörður. He ambles dejectedly into the bathroom and closes the door behind him. He turns on the cold water, bends down, and splashes a few handfuls of water in his face. Then he drinks the refreshing water from the tap before turning it off. He wipes his face with a towel, then faces himself in the mirror above the sink.

It's as if he's aged about ten years in a few days. His untrimmed, full beard appears thicker than it is because of his sunken, pale cheeks. There are dark circles under his bloodshot eyes, and his lips are dry and cracked.

Hörður heaves a sigh, sits down on the closed toilet and blows his nose on toilet paper. He still has a headache and a sick feeling in his stomach, yet he does feel a tiny bit better. He's glad Adam has stopped in. He's so tired of being alone. Alone with all these responsibilities and the world on his shoulders.

He props his elbows on his knees, leans forward, and hides his face in his hands. He has to get hold of himself; that's what he has to do. He can't allow himself to crack or give up.

But he doesn't have the energy to keep it together, let alone keep going. He's so tired that he hardly knows his own name.

The lieutenant blows his nose again and takes a deep breath before getting to his feet and going back to the office.

Adam is in the break room, looking over the newspaper clippings on the corkboard. He's put water and ground coffee in the coffee machine and pressed start—freshly brewed coffee trickles into the glass pot. Out in the office, everything is as it was before, or nearly so. The desk is upright again and in its place, and Adam has put everything back on it in tidy order. He has even wiped up the splattered coffee.

"Is the computer out of action?" Hörður asks softly.

"Just the screen," Adam replies, without taking his eyes off the corkboard. "Do you think these disappearances are related, the older and more recent ones? That those older deaths may not have been accidental, and there's a villain here among us?"

"A villain here among us?" Hörður exclaims annoyedly. "Who talks like that? Are you on stage, or what?"

Adam blushes. "I teach literature and drama, among other things. But ignoring that—are you willing to tell me what you've come up with? About your suspicions and speculations on this case? *These* cases, rather."

Hörður takes a seat. "Why should I do that? Not that I've come up with anything, mind you. I've been sidelined, after all."

Adam points at the corkboard. "These aren't just names and faces; it's not just yellowed paper. They're dead girls. Five in all. The sixth is still missing and could be alive. Are you really going to sit on your ass and wait for some people from the south to take over? The least you can do is write a kind of summary of the investigation over the past few days, so they don't have to start from scratch. But…"

"But the computer is broken," mutters the red-haired giant.

"The screen, yes," says Adam. "I have a computer at home. You're welcome to use it, if you want."

"Thanks, I'll think about it," says Hörður. He knows very well that Adam is right. Of course he should write such a summary. He was going to do it anyway. But he's just had enough; he's confused and unable to think clearly any longer. The last few days are a haze in his mind—they've disappeared into a fog in which he himself long since became hopelessly lost.

"The coffee's ready." Adam pours them cups of hot coffee and sits down next to the lieutenant.

"Thanks." Hörður takes a sip of the strong coffee. It's refreshing and gets his blood flowing.

"Tell me something," Adam says after a short silence.

Hörður sighs wearily. But then nods. "Fine. I think Barbara Hoffmann is being held against her will somewhere. Probably on a farm or in an outbuilding: more specifically, in a sheep shed. Wool and sheep dung were found on Hertha Meier's body."

"I see," says Adam thoughtfully.

Hörður hesitates, but decides to go on. "Björgvin Geirharðsson is at the top of my list of suspects. Barbara and Hertha got a ride from him here to Klaustur, from Hvolsvöllur. Lena Nilsson was Björgvin's girlfriend when she died. She supposedly fell to her death in Hörgsárgljúfur Canyon, close to the farm where Björgvin lives now. When Lena died, Björgvin was supposedly bedridden at his mother's home at Heiðarsel, where he lived at the time. He was supposedly having an affair with Juliette Vermeulen, who was found at the estuary of the Skaftá river. Björgvin also had an alibi in that instance—that is, he was on a drinking binge at the home of Júlíus, the garbage man."

Adam takes a deep breath. "Those can hardly be considered strong alibis. A mother and a mentally challenged, drunken loner. Has anyone else confirmed these alibis, or what?"

Hörður shakes his head. "In my opinion, the investigations of all those older deaths were deficient. And the person who investigated them is Björgvin's uncle, as you know. He sometimes had help from Reykjavík, but it was probably just pro forma, as there was nothing, at a glance, to indicate anything other than that the deaths had been accidental. And maybe they *were* accidental—that can't be ruled out."

"But if not," says Adam, looking at the newspaper clippings. "If, for example, Klara Zimmerman and Johanna Schmitz didn't die accidentally, who is responsible for their deaths?"

"Klara was Geirharður's fiancée," says Hörður. "And Johanna was working for him and Sigrún at Heiðarsel. So my suspicion quickly turned to him. I saw him as a cold-blooded misogynist who tormented and murdered young women—a violent and distant father who one day shares his sadistic secrets with his only son, who then follows in his footsteps, under compulsion or willingly."

"But…?" Adam asks after a short silence.

"But it seems that Geirharður was in Kleppur when Johanna drowned in Eldvatn," says the red-haired giant. "In fact, I'm having someone check on that to confirm it—Þóra Sverrisdóttir, my colleague in Reykjavík. But whether it's true or not, I'm not convinced that Geirharður was a murderer. He doesn't seem to have been that type of person. Unlike…"

Hörður looks at Adam.

"His brother Steingrímur," says his neighbor.

The lieutenant nods. "I'd already told you about the locked room in the house at Efri-Vík. I broke into it. There I found, among other things, the reports on these old deaths. They weren't here in the filing cabinet, but hidden at the home of Steingrímur, the man who was in charge of investigating those same cases."

Adam whistles softly.

"There was more there, in the room," says Hörður hesitantly.

"Oh?"

"For example, old photographs of Steingrímur," says the lieutenant. "With other men, you see. Leather and straps and so on."

Adam nods. "I can't say that surprises me. So he was into BDSM or whatever it's called? Maybe he hated women because he despised his own urges? Did he take revenge on them because he couldn't enjoy them?"

"How should I know?" says Hörður. "But it appears that someone used those photos against him. To blackmail him or extort money from him."

"I see," says Adam thoughtfully.

For a few moments, they say nothing, just sip their coffee and stare into space.

"What about Barbara and Hertha?" Adam finally asks. "I highly doubt that old Steingrímur had something to do with their disappearance. At least, he could hardly have done it alone."

Hörður clears his throat. "I really don't know what happened to them, unfortunately. Björgvin was alone at home with his son, according to him. Of course, he could have gone out, because the baby was sleeping. But I've got nothing on him, no evidence and no witnesses who saw one thing or another. Where would he have gone with the girls? I took a look at his stable today and saw nothing suspicious. But that doesn't mean he's innocent."

"What about Hallgrímur Olsen?" asks Adam. "Or Júlli, the garbage man?"

"Júlíus is more or less a child, isn't he?" says Hörður. "But the girls' tent and other belongings were found at the landfill site down here on the sands. Someone had buried the stuff there."

"Really?" says Adam.

Hörður nods. "But of those two, Hallgrímur is definitely more likely to have something really bad on his conscience. But I've got nothing on him, any more than anyone else."

"It's no wonder you're exhausted," says Adam. "You've taken on so much, but have reaped so little."

"The worst thing is…" the lieutenant sips his coffee. "The worst thing is that I have the feeling that I've been overlooking something the whole time. That there's someone I still have to interview. Someone I've seen and spoken to, yet not in connection with this investigation but something entirely different."

"Who could that be?" asks Adam.

Hörður glares at him. "I don't *know. That's* the problem. Are you a bit dense?"

Adam reddens. "Sorry. I was just thinking out loud."

Hörður sighs. He realizes that he was brusque, but doesn't feel like apologizing for it. "Do you know whether Hallgrímur or Júlíus have access to outbuildings, preferably sheep sheds?"

Adam shakes his head. "Not that I know of. But there are sheep sheds all over the place, both new and old, and some of them are on abandoned farms. Theoretically, everyone in the area has access to outbuildings, so to speak."

"Yes," mutters Hörður pensively. "Like the ones at Systravatn. The Sel outbuildings, as I understand they're called. I took a look at them on Saturday and found a cigarette butt that the German girls might have left there. But it's a stable there, not a sheep shed, and I found nothing suspicious there, either."

"A cigarette butt?" Adam asks. "Wouldn't it be possible to take a DNA sample from it to determine whether it belongs to the girls or not? It would make a difference as far mapping their movements is concerned, right?"

"Yes, that's right," says Hörður. "But it was Barbara who smoked, not Hertha. And since Barbara is still missing, we have no genetic material from her to compare with a saliva sample from the butt."

"She must have relatives in Germany," says Adam. "It shouldn't be much trouble getting a DNA sample from one of them."

"Sure," mutters Hörður. Adam is right. He himself is too tired and confused to be able to think clearly. Maybe it's not so surprising that he was sidelined.

"Maybe we should go up to Systravatn and take a better look at the old buildings," says Adam. "The Sel outbuildings. Who knows, maybe the searchers overlooked something yesterday. We could take the six-wheeler."

Hörður nods sharply. "But you were one of those who searched there yesterday. The Torch search-and-rescue unit searched the area around Systravatn and the heath north of it. You're in Torch, right? Didn't you go into the buildings?"

Adam's face reddens. "No, but the team from Lifesave must have."

Hörður looks firmly at him. "What are you talking about? I remember very well who searched where. Lifesave was assigned the area around Fjaðrárgljúfur Canyon and the heath north of it."

"That's right. But…" Adam smiles awkwardly.

"But what?" the lieutenant asks gruffly.

"They switched," says Adam.

"Who switched?" Hörður asks. "What are you talking about?"

Adam swallows. "Björgvin asked Úlfar to switch areas with him. And they did. So it was Lifesave, and not Torch, that searched around Systravatn yesterday."

"So Björgvin wanted to switch areas," mutters Hörður pensively. "Why?"

Adam shrugs. "I'm not sure. But he of course knows the area north of Fjaðrárgljúfur like the back of his hand."

Hörður stares into space, lost inside his own head. He recalls his visit to Heiðarból. He envisions the track that led away from the farmyard and disappeared into the fog to the north, and the sign with the name of the farm. There were other brackets on the pole, as if there had once been two signs on it.

"Heiðarsel," whispers the red-haired giant. "Of course."

"What's that?" asks Adam.

Hörður blinks, then gets to his feet and marches out of the break room. "There's a deserted farm on the heath north of Heiðarból. Heiðarsel, where Björgvin's mother Sigrún grew up. An old smallholding."

"I know," Adam calls out after him. "We passed by it on Saturday."

"But not yesterday?" Hörður asks as he walks back into the break room. He's holding his notepad, which he went and got from his jacket.

Adam shakes his head. "No, yesterday we searched other areas, farther west than on Saturday."

"Are any buildings still standing at Heiðarsel?" Hörður asks. He hunches over the notepad and leafs back a few pages in search of his notes from when he last spoke to Reverend Páll.

Adam nods. "Outbuildings, yes. But they're pretty dilapidated—maybe on the verge of collapse. And it looked as if lightning struck them during the storm on Friday. Part of one roof was black and there was a strong burnt smell in the air."

"There was soot on Hertha Meier's body," says Hörður without looking up from his notepad. "Did you go into the building?"

Adam swallows; his throat is dry. "Yes, or…Björgvin went in. He didn't want to put any of the rest of us in danger. As I said, they're in bad shape, and…Do you think Barbara is being held there?"

"Here it is!" Hörður declares triumphantly. He looks up, but keeps his finger on one line in the book. "This was one of the things that Reverend Páll told me last Saturday. Listen. *Sigrún grew up on a smallholding, Heiðarsel, a small sheep farm—I guess you'd call it a croft, actually.* End of quotation. Heiðarsel was a sheep farm! So one of those outbuildings is a sheep shed. And yes, I consider it highly likely that Barbara Hoffmann is there."

"And what do we do?" says Adam. "Are we going there, or…?"

"Yes, but…" Hörður drums the table with his fingertips.

"But what?" asks Adam.

"First, I've got to find out where Björgvin is," says Hörður. "What if he's there, maybe armed? It would be nuts to wind up in a fight with that man. He's capable of anything. Best of all would be to…"

The lieutenant stops. His expression is distant.

"Yes?" Adam asks hesitantly.

"I'll call him and ask him to come here," says Hörður. "Then we'll arrest him and lock him up."

"We?" exclaims Adam, in a voice shrill with stress.

"Yes, we," Hörður replies irritably. "Aren't you the deputy lieutenant?"

"Yes, but I've never come anywhere near anything like this," says Adam. "Do you think he'll resist, or … ?"

"We'll see," Hörður mutters, as he searches for Björgvin's phone number. "But the chances decrease if there are two of us. Don't worry too much about it. I've grappled with people more dangerous, and I'm not dead yet."

"I understand, but … "

Hörður holds out the palm of his left hand, interrupting Adam. Having dialed the number, he holds his phone to his ear and listens to the ringing at the other end.

"Hello?"

"Björgvin?" says the red-haired giant. "This is Hörður, the lieutenant here. Are you busy?"

"What do you need?"

"I was finishing typing our conversation into the computer," says Hörður. "Could you come to the station? I have two other quick questions for you, and then I'll need you to sign the report, after I print it out."

The lieutenant winks at Adam, who listens pale-faced to the conversation.

"Can't it wait?"

"No, I'm under time pressure here," Hörður answers. "It won't take long. Could you be here in five minutes?"

"All right, then. I'll be there in ten, max."

"See you then," says Hörður. He removes the phone from his ear and hangs up. "Well, that worked out … "

He stops when Adam utters a half-stifled cry. The camouflage-colored deputy runs to the bathroom and throws up.

Hörður looks at his watch. It's been seven minutes since he spoke to Björgvin. Is the bastard on his way? Or is he destroying evidence? Or has he maybe even gone on the lam? If the lieutenant had one or two officers, they would be monitoring the highway on both sides of Klaustur at that moment. But he doesn't have any; just a teddy-bearish assistant recruited from the locals. A deputy who's trying to recompose himself after puking from stress. Hörður decides to use the time to speak to Þóra.

"Hi, hi! Anything new?"

"As a matter of fact," Hörður says into his phone, and then he tells her about his discovery, and how the suspect is expected at the station at any time now. *"Aren't you afraid that he'll take off, instead, or do something awful?"*

Hörður grunts. "Of course. But it's not like I have a police force at my disposal here. I'm by myself, damn it!"

"Sorry, I know. But have you informed the chief of police in the South? He could send officers to you, right?"

"No, not yet," mutters Hörður. In the first place, he can't bear that man, and in the second place, he hadn't thought of that possibility. "I'll do that, if Björgvin doesn't show up in the next three minutes."

"What are you going to do, arrest the suspect?"

"Yes," says the lieutenant. "I can hold him for twenty-four hours while I gather more evidence. I'm going to start by checking the outbuildings at Heiðarsel. If I'm lucky, I'll find Barbara there."

"Do you have a search warrant?"

Hörður scoffs. He has neither the time nor the patience for paperwork at the moment. "It's a deserted farm! I don't need any damn warrant to look around there, do I?"

"Yes, I would think so. There's always someone who handles matters involving abandoned farms, presumably the magistrate or district manager. Do you know who the last occupant was?"

"No, but…" Hörður stops at the loud sound of a diesel engine outside, followed by the crackling of gravel under large car tires. "Björgvin's pulling up; I've got to go now!"

"Okay. Keep in contact, okay? I'm going to go into the system and see if I can find anything about Geirharður's admission to Kleppur. I've been out, but have a free moment here at the station now."

"No problem, and don't worry about it," says Hörður quickly. "It doesn't matter at the moment. We'll take a better look at those old cases later. Finding Barbara is top priority right now."

Out in the parking lot, Björgvin shuts off his truck's engine, then steps out of it and slams the door.

"Of course, but it pays to think ahead…"

"Later!" Hörður hangs up, and then knocks on the bathroom door. "Are you coming, man?"

The door opens and Adam walks out of the bathroom, deathly pale and with glossy eyes.

Hörður gestures to him to hurry up. "Björgvin has arrived. Pull yourself together and…"

"Hello?" comes a call from the vestibule.

"Coming!" Hörður calls out, before turning back to Adam and lowering his voice to a whisper. "You don't have to do anything. Just be visible, and for God's sake, try to act normal."

Adam nods.

Hörður goes to the office. Björgvin is waiting in the vestibule.

"Just a moment," says the lieutenant. He opens the smallest drawer in his desk and is relieved to see what he was looking for. It's a key ring with two keys on it. He puts the key ring in his trouser pocket, and then lets the suspect into the police station.

"What is *he* doing here?" Björgvin asks coldly when he sees Adam, who is standing there at the door to the break room, looking awkward. The blond giant is in the same checkered shirt as earlier in the day, but has changed from his jeans into work trousers with countless pockets, and from his rubber boots into work boots with steel toes.

"We were just discussing the situation," says Hörður as he closes the vestibule door. "Adam was searching all day, but with no result."

The blond giant nods curtly. His blue eyes, suspicious and cold, wander about the police station. Hörður watches his every move. Björgvin is like an animal that senses something is going on. He appears calm but every muscle is tense, and his nerves are taut.

"Wasn't I supposed to sign something?" he asks.

Hörður takes a deep breath. "Björgvin Geirharðsson. You're under arrest, on suspicion of causing the death of Hertha Meier and holding Barbara Hoffmann against her will."

"What?" Björgvin barks. His whole body expands and his eyes shoot sparks. Adam's face pales even more and he takes a tiny step backward.

"You heard what I said," says Hörður in a grave voice, simultaneously pulling his nightstick from his equipment belt. "Empty your pockets on the desk; no quick movements."

Björgvin clenches his fists, but suddenly relaxes and sneers sarcastically. "Is that the reason the fat teacher's here? Was he supposed to stop the fight if I resisted? What a joke!"

"Do as I ask," says the lieutenant firmly.

"What fucking idiots you are!" growls Björgvin. He tosses his car keys, cell phone, and wallet on the desk. "I'm innocent, as you surely know. What evidence do you claim to have? None, that's obvious!"

"No pocketknife?" Hörður asks.

Björgvin shakes his head.

"Search him," says the lieutenant.

"Me?" Adam asks in a shrill voice.

"Who else?" says Hörður irritably. The sooner he can lock Björgvin up, the better.

Adam steps hesitantly toward the blond giant, who stares at him contemptuously.

"Raise your arms and spread your legs," the deputy lieutenant orders.

Björgvin stubbornly hesitates, but then does as he's asked.

"Sorry," mutters Adam, before lightly patting down the suspect.

"Easy with your groping," says the blond giant, sneering and turning halfway round.

Adam hurriedly finishes the pat down and nods at the lieutenant. "He's got nothing on him, I think."

"Come on, then," says Hörður as he pulls out the key ring holding the cell keys. He signals Björgvin to walk ahead of him into the hallway behind the desk. "Open the first cell and sit on the bed."

Björgvin pulls open the barred door, bends down as he steps into the cell, and sits down on the narrow cot at its far wall. His face is like a thundercloud.

Without hesitation, Hörður slams the door shut and turns the key in the lock.

"What a fucking great show this is!" Björgvin exclaims. "What are you going to do now? Search my place? I'd have allowed you to do that, if you'd just asked! Seeing as how I've got nothing to hide. Do you have a search warrant? If not, I'll press charges, you stupid redhead."

"I'm not on my way to your house," says Hörður through the bars. He breathes lighter now, as this blue-eyed lunatic no longer poses a threat. "I know very well that I'll find nothing there. But the same might not go for the abandoned farm, Heiðarsel."

Björgvin twitches, as if shocked by an electric current. "You wouldn't dare!"

"Maybe you want to confess right away?" asks Hörður cockily. The suspect's reactions suggest that this investigation is finally on the right track.

"I'll kill you!" growls Björgvin. With a shout, he jumps to his feet, grabs the bars, and shakes the door.

Hörður starts in alarm and throws himself backwards, causing the back of his head to hit the concrete wall separating the hallway from the interrogation room. His vision darkens and he nearly loses his balance.

"Are you okay?" asks Adam, who is keeping a safe distance. Björgvin stops shaking the door and laughs crazily at the lieutenant's mishap.

"I think so," groans Hörður. He goes into the office and rubs his aching head.

"Let me out and I'll go with you to Heiðarsel!" Björgvin calls from his cell. "I promise I'll be peaceful. Don't leave me here!"

Hörður pretends not to hear him. He hands Adam the cell keys. "Take these, just in case. But don't listen to him and don't let him out, no matter what he says."

Adam backs away and refuses to accept the keys. "You're not going to leave me here, with him?"

"I can't leave him here alone, can I?" says Hörður irritably. He lays the key ring on the desk and puts on his cap. "I'll lock up the station. All you have to do is be here and maybe answer the phone, nothing else."

"Let me out!" Björgvin shouts. He clenches the bars and shakes the door. The hinges and lock creak.

Adam swallows. "You won't be long, will you?"

"No longer than I need to be," Hörður answers dryly. With a grimace, he puts on his jacket and hat; his head is so sore.

"Are you taking a gun?" asks Adam.

Hörður glances at the gun cabinet. "No, it's unnecessary."

Parked on the lot in front of the police station are three vehicles. The police SUV, Adam's six-wheeler, and Björgvin's pickup truck. The lieutenant peeks into the suspect's car. Björgvin has left his dog at home, but in the back seat of the car are a shotgun and a pack of shells. Hörður is thankful that the blond giant didn't bring the weapon into the station. The situation would probably be very different now. He grabs the handle of the truck's back door, but it's locked.

Hörður gets into the SUV and starts the engine. The back of his head is aching and has started to swell—he'll probably have a nice bump there. He opens the glove compartment and finds a packet of painkillers. He crunches two tablets between his teeth and swallows them with saliva, as there's nothing to drink in the car. He drives off, and after a few moments is out on the highway. It's a quarter to eight, the sun is still high in the sky, and the countryside is bright. He drives west along the empty road.

Should he call someone? Axel, for example? He isn't sure. The head of the CID would no doubt want to know about the changed situation. But since Axel is no longer Hörður's boss, he really has no obligation to inform him of anything. He also wants to solve the case and close it before the CID detectives arrive. Just to prove himself and win back the favor of old Steppenwolf.

Hörður has driven up to the heathlands and is about ten minutes out from Heiðarból when his phone rings. He looks at the screen and sees that it's Þóra who is trying to reach him. What does she want? He swerves around several deep potholes in the road before answering via the hands-free system.

"Hi!"

"Hörður, where … ?"

"Are you there?" he asks after a short silence.

No answer.

Hörður slows down and looks again at the phone's screen. The call has been cut off, as there's no phone connection there on the heath, any more than the day before. He'll just have to call back later.

The heath is as desolate as ever, but the fog is gone and the lieutenant sees the farmhouse at Heiðarból at the end of the road. But old Sigrún doesn't appear to be at home. At least her Land Rover is nowhere to be seen.

"Let me out, damn it!" roars Björgvin. He holds the bars with both hands and shakes the door from time to time. "If you let me out, I won't hurt you. But if you don't, then … !"

He lets out a brutish howl and shakes the door so violently that the floor and walls tremble.

Adam is standing in the office, struggling not to hyperventilate. He's white as a corpse, has a buzzing in his ears and a dry mouth, and feels so sick that he's on the verge of fainting. His dream of taking part in a real police investigation has turned into a nightmare.

He's a teacher, he reminds himself. He's a teacher and he loves teaching children and teenagers. He's not a policeman, not a soldier, not a hero, just a teacher who enjoys the outdoors and hunting.

"Let. Me. Out!"

Adam swallows. All he wants is to get out of this horrendous situation as soon as possible. He longs to get out of there, to get away, to get home…

He starts when the desk phone starts ringing. Should he answer? When the phone rings for the third time, Björgvin stops shaking the door. The suspect listens, doubtless wondering who is calling and whether his fat guard will answer or not.

He has to answer, doesn't he? Adam takes a deep breath, then sits down at the desk and answers the lieutenant's phone.

"The police station, Adam speaking." His voice is so high-pitched from stress that her sounds like a confirmation boy.

"Is Hörður there?" asks a woman's voice unceremoniously.

"No, not at the moment," Adam replies. He looks around for a piece of paper and a pen. "Can I take a message?"

"This is Þórhildur Sverrisdóttir, Hörður's colleague in the police in Reykjavík. Where is he, might I ask?"

Adam looks over his shoulder. He notices that Björgvin is no longer holding the bars, but otherwise, can't see what he's doing. From the cell come strange noises, as if something is being dragged along the floor. "Hello, Þóra. Hörður is out doing fieldwork. He thinks he knows where Barbara Hoffmann is."

"Where did he go?"

Adam lowers his voice. "To an old farm called Heiðarsel. The suspect is in custody here. Hörður asked me to look after him."

"He has his phone turned off!"

Adam starts at a heavy blow that comes from the prison cell. "He's probably outside the service area. There's no telephone connection on the heath."

"Does he have a radio?"

"He should have…" Adam stops when he spies the lieutenant's walkie-talkie hanging on a hook at the exit. "He doesn't have his walkie-talkie, but there's a radio in the car. Do you want me to try to contact him?"

"Yes! Tell him that Geirharður was definitely at Kleppur when Johanna Schmitz disappeared. He was admitted the same day."

Adam searches for and finds a pen and paper. Another blow comes from the cell, so heavy that the floor vibrates. "Wait. I'm going to write that down."

He writes down the message with a trembling hand. "Does this matter now?"

"There's more! The one who took Geirharður to Kleppur to have him admitted was his brother, Steingrímur."

"Steingrímur had him admitted," Adam mutters as he writes this down. A third blow comes from the cell, followed by a screechy metallic sound. What the hell is Björgvin doing?

"So Steingrímur also has an alibi!"

"Which means?" asks Adam, who is under too much pressure to think clearly.

"Try to contact Hörður and ask him to turn back immediately and contact me, okay?"

"Will do," says Adam. Just as he hangs up, Björgvin emits a deep-voiced howl, and a heavy, fourth blow comes from the prison cell, followed by a loud screeching of iron and some sort of rumbling.

Adam gets up from the desk. His forehead is dripping with sweat and he's half-paralyzed with stress. He breathing is rapid and shallow, his heart is pounding in his chest, and his legs are numb. Shouldn't he go and see what Björgvin is doing before he calls the lieutenant on the radio?

Or what?

When Hörður Grímsson drives in through the gate at Heiðarból, he sees the front end of the householder's Land Rover peeking out from behind the southeast corner of the house. Sigrún has apparently backed it behind the house and is perhaps unloading it, after buying fertilizer or something like that. So the old woman is home after all, probably working in her vegetable garden.

The housewife's worldview is doubtless peaceful and innocent at the moment, Hörður thinks—but it's about to break into a thousand pieces. He isn't exactly looking forward to delivering the old woman the news that her son is in custody, suspected of serious crimes. But now is not the time for that. He doesn't stop in the farmyard, but turns left onto the track that runs north, farther and higher into the heathlands.

Hörður drives rather slowly, as the track is little more than deep wheel ruts. The ruts are littered with both potholes and rocks, and grass tufts regularly brush the undercarriage of the SUV, which rocks to and fro in low drive. The red-haired giant grimaces at the pain in the back of his head. He tries, however, not to let it get to him, having more to think about than his own well-being. He hopes to find Barbara Hoffmann—and alive, preferably. At the same time, he fears discovering only a stiff corpse, or nothing at all—which would in fact be worst. He longs for nothing more than to end the search, to close the case. One more loose end would probably break him down permanently, or drive him insane. He simply can't think that thought to the end...

The lieutenant drives over a low hill, and then the track turns down to the right. In front of him he catches a glimpse of old outbuildings—a sheep shed and adjacent barn, and at the same time, his heart starts beating faster in his chest. The track ends in something of a hollow, above a few small fields that probably haven't been mown in decades.

Hörður drives off the track and stops. So this is the smallholding, Heiðarsel. Or *was*, rather. The outbuildings are old, dilapidated, and weathered, but it's an exaggeration to say that they're on the verge of collapse, as Adam had suggested. The corrugated iron is colorless and rusty, but black around a big hole on the far gable of the barn roof. Covering the narrow windows are decaying boards, and the buildings are surrounded by weeds and knee-high grass. Next to a closed door, a white X has been painted. To the south of the haunted outbuildings is a crumbling foundation where the farmhouse used to stand. The house was clearly quite small.

The lieutenant steps down from the SUV, with his cap on his head and a large flashlight in hand. It's bright outside, but cooler than down in the lowlands. Down from the highlands streams a cold breeze, the breath of glaciers and sandy wastes. He walks over tussocks and dry grass, past the ruins of the farmhouse and over to the gloomy outbuildings. He notices recent wheel ruts in the grass, as if someone turned an SUV around there in the old farmyard, and more than once. Around the old foundation of the house are piles of rubble, rotten boards, and rusty iron scraps. He sees window frames with broken panes, enameled bowls and wooden crates containing rusty cans, nails, and broken bottles.

There's an awkward silence over everything and all around, as if this old abandoned farm is holding its breath. But the silence isn't complete. A fly buzzes as it shoots past; the breeze creates whispers among the tall blades of grass and a faint rustle is heard as Hörður strides through it. He stops before the door of the outbuildings. It's made of washed-out planks of wood and hangs on rough hinges, and the lock is a string wrapped around a stout nail. Hörður hesitates, though he can hardly wait to get into that cursed sheep shed. A burnt smell irritates his nose.

Hörður unwraps the string from the nail and pulls the door open. Inside the sheep shed it's nearly pitch black, and much damper and cooler than out in the sun. The only light comes in through a small window that's so grimy it does no good. Hörður switches on the flashlight before stepping carefully over the high threshold. Inside the door is a narrow corridor that ends at another door, which presumably leads to the barn. Another corridor runs along the wall separating the barn and the sheep shed. To the right is the buildings' south gable, and to the left is the sheep shed—a crib reaching from end to end, and on both sides of it, empty pens that were once full of sheep that gobbled down hay and feed enhancers from the crib. But it's been quite a long time since there were sheep here. The woodwork is decaying, dust covers everything, and there's a musty smell in the air—mingled with another newer, more unpleasant smell, a dull yet rather aggressive odor that Hörður has smelled before. It's an odor that he associates mainly with prisons: a combination of sweat, feces, urine, and blood.

In the small window is a spider web and a buzzing bluebottle. Hörður hears a soft gurgle of water. He gets the strange feeling that he's been in this place before. Yet he knows that's not the case. Was it in a dream, maybe?

"Barbara?" says the lieutenant loudly—but there's no answer. He sets off down the corridor. Behind him, the door starts closing under its own weight; the rusty hinges creak and it shuts with a low bang.

Hörður has come to the barn door. He shines his flashlight down the corridor to his left. There he sees a kind of concrete bathtub, with steps at each end. The tub is overflowing with water, which trickles from a tap protruding from the wall above it. The floor around the bathtub is wet. As a young boy, Hörður spent time in the countryside, and he remembers when the sheep were bathed in the spring in such a tub, done in order to rid them of some sort of vermin—lice or something similar.

Outside in the SUV, the radio crackles, and Adam's voice breaks the silence of the heath. *"Police station calling lieutenant, police station calling lieutenant! Are you there, boss? Answer if you hear me, over… Police station calling lieutenant, police station calling lieutenant!"*

But the lieutenant doesn't hear the call.

"Fuck," Adam mutters in a tremulous voice. He lays the walkie-talkie on the desk and pulls himself together before walking hesitantly into the prisoners' corridor and peeking into the cell. He can hear Björgvin panting, but doesn't see him. Facing him is the mattress that ought to have been on the bed. Björgvin has torn it up and is standing behind it; all that can be seen of the prisoner are his long fingers holding onto the edges of the mattress.

"What are you…?" Adam is unable to finish the question. Björgvin howls once more, and then runs with the mattress in his arms and throws himself with all his might at the door. The blow is terribly heavy, and something seems to give way. Adam is so startled that he loses his balance and falls on his rear end. At the same time, the barred door comes loose at the top; there's a creaking and cracking and concrete dust rains down.

"No, no!" shouts Adam. He tries to escape before the door comes completely free, but isn't fast enough. Björgvin jumps and stomps and pounds violently on the door, which falls like a domino from its frame onto the deputy, who squirms on the floor and stares in terror through the bars, straight into the eyes of the prisoner who lies sneering on top of the door.

Hörður opens the door and steps over the threshold. The barn is almost completely empty, it appears to him, apart from small quantities of old hay and a couple of piles of wooden boards. The air has the same unpleasant human odor as the sheep shed, only stronger and more aggressive. The sun is shining through the hole in the roof at the far end. He walks slowly in that direction. On the floor below the hole lie several corrugated iron sheets and one of the rafters that previously held up the roof. The rafter is black with soot and broken at one end. Hörður looks up. Several corrugated-iron sheets hang by a seeming thread over him, like leaves on a tree branch. If one of them happened to break free, it could easily cut off his head.

Lightning struck the outbuildings on Friday night, Hörður thinks. It blows a hole in the barn roof, which partially collapses. The rafter lands on ... he looks around inquisitively and finally sets eyes on a black gash in the wooden floor. He takes a closer look. On the floor is a rect-angular patch the size of a shower base, as if something had been standing there on the barn floor. At a distance of around five meters is another such rectangular patch. What was standing here on the barn floor? And where are those things now?

Hörður looks around, simultaneously shining his flash-light into every nook and cranny. His attention soon turns to the piles of boards. They don't seem to have been there long. The boards are thick and strong and all of similar length, maybe one-and-a-half meters. In them are nail holes, and on one of them are imprints of hinges.

Hinges? Hörður blinks. Why hinges? Then he remembers his dream, the vision he saw. The hair rises on the back of his neck and the blood in his veins goes cold. Cages! They were locked in cages.

Hörður kicks at one of the piles of boards, scattering them, and takes a closer look. Nausea and malaise wash over him. Some of the boards are scratched, and even have a few broken fingernails stuck to them. On others there are dark splotches of blood, and in some of the splotches, he sees hair—light and long. The red-haired giant's heart beats faster in his chest; he can smell the bitter odor of blood, and echoing in his mind is a piercing scream of terror that no one outside these walls could have heard. He straightens up, takes a deep breath, and looks again at the rectangular patches on the floor. Two small cages had stood there. The girls were locked inside them, between being pulled out and … he tries not to think this thought to the end. In the storm, lightning strikes the barn, the roof collapses and the rafter breaks open one of the cages. It's the cage that Hertha was locked in. She escapes. She tries, maybe, to free Barbara from her cage, but can't open it. Instead, she decides to try to reach others, to get help.

And she almost succeeded.

Adam is lying on the floor with the jail-cell door on top of him, listening. He hears a door slam, and then the roar of a powerful car engine. Björgvin has gotten out and into his pickup truck. He backs up and then peels out before speeding away from the police station. Adam breathes a sigh of relief. He feared that Björgvin would harm him, even kill him. He starts wriggling to and fro, pushing on the heavy door until he finally manages to crawl out from under it. He gets stiffly to his feet and brushes off concrete dust. He limps to the office, his legs and back aching from his fall.

The first thing he needs to do is warn Hörður. If only the lieutenant had his radio switched on!

But where is…? Adam searches for the walkie-talkie but doesn't find it. Didn't he put it on the table? Yes, next to…He feels a chill when he realizes where it is. Björgvin has taken it.

That bastard! Adam feels sick with stress. What should he do? Doesn't he need to call for help?

Yes, of course…

He picks up the handset and dials 112.

"Emergency center, how can I help?"

"This is Kirkjubæjarklaustur, the police station," says Adam breathlessly. "There was a man here in custody—a dangerous man, suspected of murder—but he escaped and I'm afraid our lieutenant is in danger. He's up on the heaths, there's no telephone connection, and he's not answering the radio. He was on his way to an abandoned farm called Heiðarsel…in connection with the girls who disappeared…"

Adam is forced to stop. He can barely catch his breath; his legs feel weak and he's lightheaded.

"Who are you, might I ask?"

Adam plunks onto the desk chair. "You've got to send help right away! The SWAT team, by helicopter. Björgvin is extremely dangerous. How long would a take a helicopter to get here? And an ambulance, of course…more than one."

"Who is Björgvin? What's your name?"

Adam blinks. How long will it take Björgvin to drive to Heiðarsel? Fifteen minutes? Less? Could he be armed? "Fuck, fuck, fuck!"

"Will you please calm down."

Adam takes a deep breath. He can't just sit on his ass and do nothing, can he? No, he's got to do something! "Sorry, but I've got to go now. Send the SWAT team here! I just hope it's not too late."

"Wait, no … !"

Adam hangs up. Then he gets to his feet, grabs his rifle, and hurries out.

Hörður is downcast and has a bad taste in his mouth. He sits hunched in the driver's seat, holding the steering wheel with both hands and staring pensively at the road as he drives away from Heiðarsel, that cursed place. He was right, but came too late and found nothing. Where did Björgvin go with Barbara's body? The last thing the lieutenant did before he left the outbuildings was shine his flashlight into the concrete tub of water. At its bottom lay the nails, hinges, and locks from the two cages, as well as a hammer, a large pair of pincers, old-fashioned sheep shears, and a pocket knife. Hörður doesn't want to know what horrors took place in those godforsaken outbuildings, but it's clearer than daylight that the Forensics team will have more than enough on its plate when it shows up.

Worst is that he couldn't save the poor girl …

Sad and angry at himself, Hörður shakes his head. He decides to turn on the radio, in the vague hope that music can break the vicious cycle of disappointment, self-criticism, and negative thinking that he's stuck in. But no music comes from the speakers, just a loud buzz. This annoys him, but then he remembers the cassette in the glove compart-ment—the *Top of the Pops* collection from 1963. He opens the glove compartment, takes the cassette out of its case and inserts it into the device. After a few seconds, the old pop song "The End of The World" by Skeeter Davis starts sound-ing in the SUV. Hörður remembers this song well, as it was a favorite of his mother's. He turns up the player and croons along:

Why does the sun go on shining?
Why does the sea rush to shore?
Don't they know it's the end of the world?
'Cause you don't love me anymore…

Hörður sighs as he turns off the music. This may not have been quite the right song to lift him up. He drives back over the low hill, with sorrow in his heart and his head full of dark thoughts. Ahead of him are the sloping heathlands, colorless and homogeneous under a blue sky. The dull track winds downhill to the left and ends at the farmyard of Heiðarból, where Sigrún's Land Rover is back in its place in front of the stately farmhouse. Beyond it, to the east, is the hilly Klausturheiði Heath. At the house's northern gable are shrubs and buxom trees that provide shade from the sun, and at the same time shelter the vegetable garden from the north wind on cold days.

He wonders if Sigrún was fertilizing the vegetable beds—or what was it that she was watering? thinks the lieutenant, without the answer mattering at all. If only the world were as harmless and predictable as the life the old woman lives, the policeman's job would be simpler, more straightforward, that much is sure.

Hörður sighs. What he would give to be retired and spending his days pulling weeds and digging up rutabagas, without worries and free. But anyway—doesn't he have to stop in to see the old woman? If only to tell her that her son has been arrested and to request that she keep away from Heiðarsel, so that she doesn't contaminate the scene. He was also going to ask her about something, although he doesn't remember just now what it was.

She probably also has hot coffee. He could certainly use a bit of a refreshment.

He drives into the farmyard, parks the SUV next to the Land Rover and shuts off the engine. His head still hurts, but that's irrelevant. What's tormenting him most is that he was unable to save Barbara. He was so close, but… He shuts his eyes for just a second, but sees the tools at the bottom of the concrete tub and hurriedly opens them again. In any case, he can take comfort in the fact that the sadist who built the cages and tormented the girls is behind bars. That's something, although the terrible fate of the German girls weighs heavier in the big picture.

Has Adam calmed down? Hörður wonders. He takes out his phone, but then remembers that there's no cell-phone connection on the heath. But there's the radio in his car, of course. He takes the handset from it and clears his throat.

"Lieutenant calling police station, lieutenant calling police station! Are you there, deputy?" he calls into the radio.

No answer.

Strange, thinks Hörður. He calls again, but Adam doesn't answer. Is the walkie-talkie turned off, or what? He didn't think it was, but maybe the battery is dead. Maybe he should hurry back to the station?

Hörður restarts the car, but then remembers that there's a landline phone at Heiðarból. He could ask Sigrún if he could use it to call the station. He nods, shuts off the engine again, and steps out into the sunshine and silence.

He goes to the front door and knocks. When no one comes to the door, he grabs the handle and opens the door slightly.

"Hello?" he calls in through the gap. No answer.

Hörður looks at the Land Rover. The old woman must be at home. He opens the door all the way and walks uninvited into the house. "Hello? Sigrún, are you home?"

Still no answer. The house is dead silent. Is she taking a nap? Or a bath? He hesitates, not quite knowing what to do. It's probably best for him just to leave. But then he sets eyes on the telephone table at the bottom of the stairs.

Should he?

Hörður goes to the table, lifts the handset, and holds it to his ear. The dial tone is clear and strong—the phone works. He dials the number of the police station. It rings on the other end. As the lieutenant waits for Adam to answer, he fiddles distractedly with the crocheted tablecloth. On the table is the case for the old woman's hearing aids, with the devices on top of it. Hörður flips distractedly through the housewife's telephone/address book, and then notices that the table has a small drawer.

Why doesn't Adam answer?

He pulls out the drawer. In it are pens, pins, and various other small items, including an old-fashioned key.

"Answer!" mutters Hörður. He lets it ring a bit longer, then gives up and hangs up the phone. He gets an uncomfortable feeling, as if something isn't as it should be.

He curses in silence and heads for the door. But then he suddenly remembers the locked chest in the room upstairs. And the key that's in the telephone-table drawer. Should he . . . ?

Hörður goes back, pulls out the drawer again, and takes the key from it. His curiosity overwhelms everything else. He walks up the creaking stairs and opens the door of the room that was probably once Björgvin's, but is now used for storage. The chest is in its place, on the floor beneath the dormer window. The lieutenant goes down on his knees, sticks the key in the keyhole and turns it.

There's a low click, and the red-haired giant shudders with relief. He opens the trunk and opens his eyes wide—he can hardly believe what he sees.

Adam tears off on his six-wheeler out of the parking lot in front of the police station and onto the highway. Björgvin's pickup truck is nowhere to be seen. How far has he gone? Far enough so that Adam won't catch up with him before her reaches his destination, that much is certain.

But what if…?

Adam slows down in the roundabout east of the bridge-head. Then he makes a quick decision and turns onto Klausturvegur Road, instead of driving over the bridge and out onto the highway to the west. Björgvin certainly has a good head start, but since Adam is on a six-wheeler, he can shorten his route. And the shortest route between two points is always a straight line, even if the line is dotted with slopes, countless tussocks, dells, boulders, gullies, and streams.

Or what?

He'll see…Adam tears into the village and through it, past the fish farm and out onto the country road beyond it. Where the country road ends, he takes his chance and heads diagonally up the mountainside—the straightest way up to the heaths. He opens up the throttle, lifts his rear end off the seat and shoots on six soft tires over everything in his path.

"Fucking hell," Hörður mutters. He holds the lid open with one hand and looks wide-eyed into the chest. In it are various items, including black-and-white negatives in specially made plastic sleeves and several reprints—more compromising photos of Lieutenant Steingrímur having sex with foreign men. Topmost are a number of recent newspaper clippings, two German passports, a pink watch with a black dial, a necklace made of turquoise stones, and two locks of hair—one light and the other dark.

On one of the recent newspaper clippings are black splotches. Dried blood? Hörður swallows, but his throat is dry. Farther down in the chest are other, yellowed newspaper clippings, more jewelry, including a silver necklace with a green stone, and various small items, from hair clips and buttons to bras, a camera, and a few CDs.

Hörður wants desperately to go through everything in the chest, but he doesn't have disposable gloves with him, besides the fact that he's there without authorization. His heart pounds behind the rib cage. He's convinced that he's found something that might be called the murderer's memorabilia—a gruesome collection of things that were either in the possession of his victims or, in the case of the locks of hair, simply cut from them. At first, the chest and its horrible secrets doubtless belonged to Lieutenant Steingrímur, then to him and his apprentice, and finally solely to the fully trained apprentice, Björgvin Geirharðsson, who for some reason turned against his master and threatened him with the photographs.

But threatened him with what? The red-haired giant takes a deep breath. He isn't sure. But Björgvin has no doubt come here from time to time, locked himself in his old room and relived the atrocities in peace and quiet, while his mother made crepes for him downstairs. Then he locked the chest, strolled whistling down to the kitchen and stuffed himself with the treats as if nothing were more natural.

Hörður nods, as if distracted. But then his brow furrows and his expression hardens.

But why didn't he take ... ?

A noise from outside breaks Hörður's concentration; it's from the backyard, below the dormer window. He closes the chest, gets stiffly to his feet, and pulls the crocheted curtain aside. He sees Sigrún from behind; she's wearing boots and a wool sweater, and is digging a big hole in the corner of the vegetable garden. The sound he heard was probably a shovel blade hitting rocks. The old woman tosses a shovelful of earth onto a growing pile and sticks the shovel back in the hole. Lying on the ground close to the pile is something that looks to the lieutenant like a pinch bar. The housewife is clearly doing some serious excavation work. Between the hole she's digging and the garden shed lie two canvas bags side by side, full of something he's unsure of.

Maybe seed potatoes?

Hörður lets go of the curtain and leaves the room. He needs to have a word with Sigrún before he leaves—to ask her not to go upstairs at all. It's bad enough that he opened the chest without a search warrant and disposable gloves. But if the old woman also starts rummaging through the evidence, there's a risk of her contaminating it, and she may also be tempted to make it disappear, in an attempt to protect her only son.

Maybe she also knows more about what is and has been going on than she's letting on, Hörður thinks as he walks down the creaking wooden stairs. At the bottom of them, he stops, having the strong feeling that something wasn't as it should be in the room upstairs.

He knits his brow and tries to recall his previous visit to it. Wasn't something missing now? Something that was there before.

Yes, he thinks so, but can't pinpoint what it might be. Slightly irritated, he shakes his head and hurries to the front door. Whatever it was, it will have to wait. No doubt nothing important. In any case, he doesn't have time for details just now.

The main thing first, as Axel M. Axelsson likes to say.

Hörður opens the door onto the sunshine. The light is white and unsparing, like freshly washed linen. From a distance comes the faint rumble of an engine, which he hardly notices. He walks around the south corners to the back of the house, which casts a shadow over the backyard. At the same time, a statement of Goethe's flashes through the lieutenant's mind:

Where the light is brightest, the shadows are deepest.

Sigrún's back is turned to him. She tosses one more shovelful of earth from the hole onto the pyramid-shaped pile, then sticks the shovel into the pile and wipes sweat off her forehead. The hole is probably deep enough.

It's cooler in the shade, and the air smells of moist soil and something more powerful, maybe some kind of fertilizer. Two starlings squabble over an earthworm before one of them takes it and flies away. The clotheslines are hung with white laundry, mainly bedclothes, but also towels and washcloths. Water drips from the tap into the watering can—*drip, drip.*

Hörður walks slowly up to the old woman from behind. He doesn't want to startle her, but doesn't know how to avoid it. She's probably not expecting anyone, is half-deaf and clearly deeply immersed in her work, and will no doubt be deathly startled when she finally notices the troll creeping up on her. He just hopes she doesn't have a heart attack or a stroke.

"Hello? Sigrún?" he says loudly.

Sigrún starts in alarm. "What the hell!"

"I'm sorry, I…" The lieutenant stops, throws up his hands, and smiles apologetically.

"What…? What are you doing here?" The old woman stares furiously at him, in between glancing at the hole she was digging and the plump canvas bags lying on the ground behind her. There are dark patches on the bags, as if their contents are moist.

"I was just passing by, so to speak." Hörður scratches his head. "I needed to use the phone, was up at Heiðarsel and…"

The lieutenant stops; what he found in the outbuildings weighs so heavily on him. There, horrors had taken place that he will never understand.

"At Heiðarsel?" exclaims the old woman. Not having her hearing aids on, she speaks loudly.

"Yes, I…" In his mind's eye, Hörður sees the cages that had been taken apart, the dried blood, and the tools at the bottom of the concrete tub. He shudders with angst and disgust. He has discovered what happened to Hertha and Barbara, but hasn't yet found the body of the latter.

Shouldn't he be getting back to the station? To question Björgvin and contact Axel?

"What were you doing there?" Sigrún asks suspiciously.

"Just, my work," mutters Hörður. He was going to tell the old woman that her son was in custody and ask her not to go to Heiðarsel or up to Björgvin's old room, but somehow, he doesn't have the energy for it.

But wasn't he going to ask her about something?

"Your work, yes," says Sigrún dryly. She looks away, at the pinch bar lying in the grass a short distance from her boot-clad feet. Hörður is clearly keeping her from her gardening.

"I see that you're busy," says the lieutenant. "Are you planting seed potatoes, or…?"

Sigrún blinks. "Seed potatoes?"

"Yes, or…" Hörður says distractedly, as a bluebottle shoots past his head. He's trying to remember what he was going to ask Sigrún about. Then he suddenly remembers it and snaps his fingers. "Listen, tell me, who's Hallbera?"

"Hallbera?" asks Sigrún. "She was my mother. Why do you ask?"

"Your mother?" Hörður frowns. What did Steingrímur say again? *It was Hallbera,* right? It was she who what?

"Why are you asking about her?" Sigrún asks coldly. From a distance comes the engine noise—it's drawing closer, but neither of them pays it much attention, as they both have their minds on other matters.

"Because…" Hörður mutters, before disappearing into his own thoughts. He envisions the trunk in the bedroom on the upper floor of the house, and the key that was in the drawer of the telephone table.

Why did Björgvin keep the key there, of all places? Why didn't he take the key home with him?

Because…

A paralyzing numbness comes over Hörður, and the hairs rise on the back of his neck. Between him and the old woman, a black haze appears—a hovering shadow. The air cools, the colors fade, and for a few seconds everything becomes dark and gloomy. *It was Hallbera who marked Sigrún. She treated her daughter like an animal, broke her down and gradually transformed her into…* Seconds become like an eternity in the lieutenant's mind.

Then the death shadow disappears like dew before the sun. Hörður catches his breath and blinks. Who is doomed to die? The old woman? Or he himself?

Sigrún is staring belligerently at him. He looks away, at the deep hole in the corner of the vegetable garden and the two canvas bags at its edge. He finally realizes that there aren't two bags, as it appeared to him, but one large one—and suddenly the bag moves slightly, as if its contents are alive.

And at the same time, everything clicks in the lieutenant's head. Can it be? The answer is yes. But he can hardly believe it, even though two hateful eyes are staring at him. Sick with envy and jealousy, Sigrún had first killed Klara and then Johanna. When Björgvin started having eyes for girls, the insanity flared up again. How could he have been so blind?

"Barbara?" Hörður grunts as he steps closer to the hole. A hole that's wide and deep enough to accommodate the canvas bag and what's in it.

"Help!" the girl answers in German. Her voice is fragile, but desperate. "Help me!"

Sigrún turns and reaches down for the pinch bar.

Was she going to bury the girl alive? Is it Barbara who's doomed? Hörður takes another step toward the hole, simultaneously answering the girl in English. "Keep calm, I'm…!"

"Don't move!" barks Sigrún. The lieutenant obeys, because the tool she's aiming at him isn't a pinch bar at all, as he'd thought, but the old shotgun that was in the upstairs bedroom when he first looked in it. He'd noticed earlier that *something* was missing from the room, but hadn't figured out what it was.

Not until now…

"Easy," says Hörður, raising his hands. At the same moment, the engine noise that had grown steadily stops. The ensuing silence is heavy and uncomfortable. "The game is over. Lower your gun. Then we can talk, you and I."

"Men don't tell me what to do!" hisses the old woman. Her eyes are pitch-black and merciless. "You know too much, and aren't leaving here alive. I don't mind digging another grave."

Hörður swallows. Is she serious? Probably. She doesn't seem quite sane. "Let's keep calm, okay?"

Sigrún cocks the gun and points it at the red-haired giant, whose face pales.

Had he seen his own death shadow? Hörður feels a stitch in his chest, as if his heart is breaking. He's never feared death, but that doesn't mean he's prepared to die.

"Hello, Mom," says a depressed-sounding male voice.

Hörður stiffens, then looks over his shoulder. Björgvin comes walking into the backyard. He's holding his shotgun and appears to be aiming it at back of the lieutenant's head.

"Bjöggi!" says Sigrún. "What are you doing here?"

"What I should have done a long time ago," says the blond giant, in his expressionless voice.

"I want you to leave," says Sigrún.

Björgvin shakes his head, and then pumps the shotgun. Hörður doesn't like the look of things. Can't he try to buy himself some time?

"How did you get out?" he asks with his hands in the air. "What did you do to Adam?"

"Shut up," Björgvin mutters, and then he pulls the trigger. The deafening shot echoes over the wide expanse of the heath.

Adam drives the six-wheeler as fast as he can over the heath. There's still a slope ahead of him, but as far as he recalls, it's the last one, and from the top of it, he'll have a view all the way to Heiðarból. He floors it, tears over tussocks and gravel and doesn't slow down until he's reached the top of the slope. There he stops and shades his eyes to take a look around. The house at Heiðarból is a white spot in the distance. It's still about one and a half kilometers away, over uncultivated land. The distance from Heiðarból to the abandoned farm Heiðarsel is about the same.

Adam peers into the distance. He sees that there are cars in front of the house, but can't tell if it's two or three. But he thinks he recognizes Björgvin's pickup truck. Is Hörður's SUV there, too?

He isn't sure, but he fears that Hörður is in trouble.

"Fuck!" Adam barks. He gets off the six-wheeler, takes the rifle out of its bag and lies down with it on the grass. He adjusts the scope and looks through it at the farm. He sees now that there are three cars in front of the house: Sigrún's Land Rover, the lieutenant's SUV, and Björgvin's pickup truck.

A chill runs down Adam's spine. He hasn't managed to warn Hörður or come to his aid. Looking through the scope, he sees no one in front of the house.

Are they inside?

He's about to get up again when he notices movement behind the house, where light and shadow meet.

Is that…?

Adam positions himself better, holds his breath, and adjusts the scope's focus. Then the hair rises on the back of his neck. He sees Björgvin and Hörður from behind. The former is pointing his shotgun at the lieutenant's neck. Adam starts to tremble, but tightens his grip on the rifle so as not to lose the focus. Within the shadow is a third person, presumably old Sigrún. But he can't see her clearly.

But he's not going to…? Adam starts in alarm when Björgvin moves suddenly and smoke erupts. Moments later, a shot echoes over the heath.

Adam goes numb.

The loudness dies out but the air still smells of gunpowder.

Hörður fell to his knees when the shot was fired—it was as if his legs had been yanked out from under him. His eyes are pinched shut, he has a pain in his chest, and he hears nothing but a high-pitched whine. He moves his hands to the nape of his neck but hardly dares to touch his head.

He's in a kind of shock and is convinced that he's been shot in the back of the head. What if his fingers find nothing but bone chips and splotches of brain?

But if he can think, isn't he alive? He tries moving his jaws, and then it's as if a bubble bursts; his hearing returns and he hears himself breathing. He opens his eyes and sees grass and earth and the booted feet of Sigrún, who is lying on her back on the ground with her arms out to the sides, the gun in her right hand and…

"What the hell!" Hörður yells, startled. Where the old woman's face was, there is now just tattered flesh, bones, and blood.

"Don't move," Björgvin mutters as he walks in front of the lieutenant. He pumps the shotgun again and aims it at the red-haired giant, who crouches in the grass and looks up at him.

"Don't do anything stupid," says Hörður, hoarse with stress. He's often gotten himself into tight spots, but has never experienced a situation like this before. Towering over him is a depressed giant who has just murdered his mother in cold blood—an old woman who had just finished digging a grave for a girl who is wriggling inside a canvas bag on the grave's edge, terrified and no doubt closer to death than life.

"I'm sorry," says the blond giant. In his blue eyes there's no hope, no light. They look most like the eyes of a shark.

Hörður goes numb. "Don't do this! You saved my life. That will help to mitigate your sentence. But if you murder a policeman, you'll be given a harsh sentence. You won't see your son for decades. At least not outside the prison walls. You don't want that, do you?"

"There will be no trial," says Björgvin sadly. "I'm going to kill you and then myself. It all ends here and now."

"But…?" Hörður is desperate. "But what about the girl? We've got to help her! Get her to a doctor and…!"

"Goodbye," Björgvin mutters. He aims the gun at the lieutenant and places his right index finger on the trigger.

"No!" Hörður instinctively throws his hands over his head. But just when he expects the gun to fire and his life to be over, something else happens. A swish is heard, and something heavy but invisible hits Björgvin's left shoulder—something that strikes him so hard that he whirls in a semicircle. He groans loudly as he falls to the ground at his mother's feet, dropping the gun at the same time. Below his left shoulder, a dark blotch appears on his work shirt.

A few seconds later, a muffled sound carries across the expanse of the heath. It's the report from a powerful rifle.

Hörður looks over his shoulder. At first, he sees nothing, but then something glints in the distance, up on a far-off ridge.

"Adam," mutters the lieutenant. The glint he saw was a ray of sunlight reflecting off the lens of a gun scope.

Björgvin lies still, with his eyes closed and his mouth open. He appears to be unconscious, perhaps in shock.

His cotton work shirt absorbs the blood trickling from the wound on his shoulder—slowly but surely, the blotch grows in size and darkens.

"Help me," comes a whimper in German. The canvas bag wriggles as if full of kittens.

Hörður shakes off the numbness that had poured over him like cold concrete. He thought he was going to die, but is now suddenly so very much alive that he has a hard time believing it. He would probably laugh and dance if the circumstances were different.

"I'm coming," says the lieutenant in English. He gets to his feet and takes a few staggering steps. His legs are weak and his hands tremble. His heart is pounding and he's panting from stress.

Hörður tries not to look at Sigrún's body, but concentrates on coming to Barbara's aid. He's halfway around the grave when Björgvin gasps for breath. The lieutenant stops. The blond giant, regaining consciousness, fumbles for the shotgun, which is just out of reach. The bloodstain is now just over hand-size and is still growing.

"Keep calm," Hörður calls to the girl, then he grabs Björgvin's legs and pulls him over to the back of the house, where he handcuffs his right hand to the railing of the steps leading to the laundry-room door.

"What are you doing?" murmurs Björgvin.

"Shut up," Hörður snaps. He hurries over to Barbara, pulls out a pocketknife, and rips open the grimy canvas bag.

A stench erupts from it. The face that is revealed is so filthy and battered that he hardly recognizes the German girl he's been searching for for three days. Her hair has been cut with sheep shears, leaving little of it but tufts here and there. Her ears are torn and bloody, with pieces missing in some places. Her skin is pale, dirty, and bruised, her lips are cracked, and her eyes bloodshot and glossy. The girl's forehead is burning hot and she is clearly dehydrated.

"Wait!" Hörður runs and grabs the watering can with one hand, and a towel and sheet from off the clotheslines with the other. He squats next to Barbara and carefully washes her face before giving her a sip of water. She tries to swallow it and starts coughing.

"There, that's enough…for now," says Hörður, who knows that it's not good for her to drink too much to begin with. He cuts the bag free from Barbara and wipes most of the dirt off her naked body with a damp towel before wrapping her in the sheet. Then he takes her in his arms, carries her out of the shadows, and lays her down gently in a sunny spot on the soft grass.

"I'm in such pain," cries Björgvin, who has sat up and leaned his back against the stairs. "I'm bleeding, I…"

"It's not your turn," snaps Hörður, before giving Barbara a little more water to drink. She stares at him with an anxiety-tinged glimmer of hope in her feverish eyes. He tries to smile at her reassuringly, but since he fears that she won't survive this calamity, he doesn't know how convincing his smile is.

"It's going to be okay," he says in a hoarse voice. "Help is on the way…I think. Soon, I'll get you out of here and…"

Hörður is interrupted by Björgvin, crying out in pain and rage.

"Wait here, and try to relax," Hörður says to the girl. He gets up, takes off his jacket and spreads it over her. Then he goes back to the clotheslines, takes another sheet off of them and tears it into three pieces.

"I'm bleeding out," Björgvin whines. His face is paler than usual and he struggles to free himself, making the handcuffs rattle. "Let me go; I promise not to try anything. I'm just in so much pain!"

"Shut up and keep still," Hörður orders. "If you try anything, you'll have me to deal with—you understand?"

"Yes, I ... " Björgvin falls silent and hangs his head in surrender. Hörður kneels down next to him. The bloodstain reaches all the way down to his left breast pocket, which is bulging from a pack of Prince cigarettes and a lighter. The lieutenant takes the pack from Björgvin's pocket, shakes a cigarette from it, and lights it.

"Nothing ever happens here, huh?" Hörður mutters irritably, and then he inhales the smoke and holds it in for a long time before blowing it contentedly out his nostrils.

"Can I have one?" Björgvin asks in a weak voice.

"Shut up," Hörður mutters, holding the burning cigarette between his lips. He wraps a long strip of the sheet around Björgvin's wounded shoulder, then makes a sling out of another strip and supports his left arm with it.

Björgvin looks at Sigrún's body. He blinks his blue eyes, which are filled with disgust and shame. "Will you cover her with something?"

Hörður nods. He goes and gets the cut-open canvas bag that the old woman stuffed Barbara into. The bag is damp and dirty and smells bad. Hörður forces himself to look at Sigrún's disfigured head. Her hair is bloody and plastered backward, revealing her eyes, distorted and crumpled. Her upper denture is lying on the ground a short distance from the corpse. Her mouth is a gaping, black, disgusting cavity. Her face is little more than a mess of blood, as Björgvin shot his mother in the head from a short distance. The flesh is tattered, the nose and upper lips are pretty much gone, and the eyes are just dark red balls. The woman's white skull is revealed through the torn flesh of her forehead.

It's as if the horror and foulness that always simmered inside the old woman's head have finally welled out through all the holes in it, like pus from a huge boil. Hörður shudders before throwing the canvas bag over that inhuman face.

"Thanks," Björgvin mutters in a broken voice. He sits with his knees bent and his head hanging, no doubt in great physical pain, but probably psychologically broken, first and foremost.

Hörður is relieved to hear the popping noises of an engine break the silence. Adam has finally left the heath behind. He drives the six-wheeler through the gate at Heiðarból and then back behind the house, where he shuts off the engine and dismounts. Hörður takes one more drag off the cigarette before tossing it away.

"Is he … ?" Adam asks hesitantly.

Hörður glances at Björgvin. "Alive? Yes. You hit him in the shoulder. Darned good shot, I must say."

"Thanks," says Adam, both humble and proud. "I decided just to go for it. The chances of hitting anything from such a long distance are actually…"

Hörður silences the deputy by patting him on the back. "We'll write a report on this later, okay? Now it's imperative that we get Barbara into the hands of a doctor as soon as possible."

"Barbara? Is she…?" Adam gasps when he sees the girl, lying in the grass close by and wrapped in a kind of swaddling.

"She's alive, yes." Hörður takes his jacket off of Barbara before bending down and taking her in his arms. "Have you called for help?"

Adam nods quickly. "An ambulance and the police are on their way, presumably from Vík in Mýrdalur; hopefully the Coast Guard helicopter as well—I requested the SWAT team."

"The SWAT team's too late," mutters the red-haired giant. He walks off with the girl in his arms and Adam at his heels. "But the ambulance will hopefully arrive in time."

"Your friend Þóra called the station, see," says Adam awkwardly. "She tried to reach you first, but you were outside the service area, of course. I tried to call you on the radio, but that didn't work. Didn't you have it on? What Þóra discovered was that…"

"We'll talk about this later, okay?" says Hörður irritably. He walks to the front of the house and stops beside the SUV.

"Okay, but I…"

"Open the door, man!" orders Hörður.

"Sorry, yes, I'll…" splutters Adam. He opens the SUV's back door and Hörður slides Barbara into the back seat. She's conscious, but not much more than that. He gets the wool blanket from the trunk and spreads it over her.

"Thank you," Barbara whispers in Icelandic. Her eyes are half-closed, and she manages to squeeze out a faint smile.

"Don't die," Hörður whispers back in English, husky-voiced with emotion. He clumsily strokes her clammy cheek before closing the door.

He clears his throat and pats Adam on the back. "You take the SUV and her to meet the ambulance. We can't waste any time."

"But…?"

"But nothing!" Hörður pushes the deputy. "The keys are in the ignition. Get going! I'll wait here with Björgvin. We'll talk later."

"Okay." Adam gets behind the wheel, starts the engine, and drives off. Hörður stands there in the farmyard, watching. In the distance, he sees flashing lights. Help is on the way. He's hugely relieved. He shakes out another cigarette from Björgvin's pack, lights it, and walks back behind the house.

Björgvin is sitting there staring into space, his expression empty. The bloodstain on his shirt has grown quite large, but has probably stopped expanding.

"The cavalry is on its way," says Hörður.

"Shoot me, please," says Björgvin, who isn't actually staring into space, but at his shotgun—the lieutenant sees that now.

Hörður shakes his head. "The last time I shot a man, I was punished by being sent here to Klaustur. I can't imagine where I'd be sent if I shot you, too."

"I'm not kidding," says Björgvin, in his melancholy, robotic voice.

"I know," says the lieutenant. "But can I offer you a cigarette instead? Then we can talk while we wait."

"I've got nothing to say," mutters Björgvin.

"I'm not so sure about that," says Hörður. He sticks a cigarette between Björgvin's lips and lights it. The blond giant responds by inhaling the smoke.

Hörður sits down on the grass at the feet of the handcuffed man and has a long-awaited smoke. "Let's talk a bit about your mom."

THE SOURCE OF EVIL

July

What a summer! The weather has been the same for a long time—clear, calm, and comfortably warm. Hörður sits lightly dressed on his deck, drinking beer in the shade. His face is swollen, his beard is unkempt, and his eyes are bloodshot. Next to the lawn chair is a half-empty cigarette carton, an overflowing ashtray, and a washtub of beer cans floating in ice water. In the yard are garbage bags full of empty cans. Loud music blares through the half-open door. It's been two weeks since he received a telegram from the parents of Barbara Hoffmann, thanking him for saving her life. It could just as well have been two minutes or two years ago. Time has both stood still and rushed along. The summer has been numbness; a strange dream.

Hörður lights a cigarette.

He thinks about Sigrún Arnkelsdóttir, who was both an old woman and the face of evil. It's remarkable, in fact research material, that a malignant tumor of that magnitude could have been hidden in such a small community as this. In such a beautiful and peaceful place as Kirkjubæjarklaustur, and for such a long time. The inhabitants of this village lived in the belief that nothing ever happens here, while young girls regularly disappeared before their eyes. Actually, at quite long intervals, but still. Young girls who were tormented, humiliated, and tortured until the moment of death and then thrown over cliffs or into the nearest glacial river.

Lieutenant Steingrímur must have suspected something. But it's hard to say when he woke from his Cinderella sleep. Probably no warning bells rang when Klara Zimmerman fell to her death in Fjaðrárgljúfur Canyon. When Johanna Schmitz was found dead in the Eldvatn river, he may have thought it a tragic accident. But Hörður can't really say. When Lena Nilsson, however, was found lifeless in Hörgsárgljúfur Canyon, his predecessor in this job must surely have scratched his head rather vigorously. First, two women connected to his brother Geirharður die, and then a young woman connected to Björgvin, Geirharður's son. The death of Juliette Vermeulen must have removed all doubt.

But the widow in Heiðarból was prepared for everything. She'd somehow gotten hold of those photographs of her brother-in-law and used them to coerce him. Probably threatened to let the photos get out. To reveal to everyone that he was a disgusting pervert.

But would anyone cover for a murderer, for someone who had already committed more than one murder, just to avoid personal discomfort?

Hörður nods. First of all, the circulation of those photographs would have resulted in more than just personal discomfort. Steingrímur's reputation was at stake, as were his job and his entire existence here in Klaustur. He is of a generation that views homosexuality as a sin, as something abnormal and unhealthy. Steingrímur is an old-fashioned man, a kind of cliché. The big and strong lieutenant. He never came out of the closet and was probably ashamed of his urges, or at least kept them completely secret. Besides, the photos are quite hardcore. Many people would have been offended or shocked, others would have laughed at him. His reputation would have been ruined; the respect that he had, gone.

Secondly, the murderer was his sister-in-law. His brother's wife and nephew's mother. She was part of his immediate family, and she was *evil*. Not just temperamental, manipulative, and difficult to deal with, but also evil itself, in the flesh. Of course, she was of retirement age by the time her and Hörður's paths coincided, but considering the strength and acrimony she still possessed, he can just imagine how cruel and ruthless she was in her younger years. She was a genuine murderess; he saw that when her mask fell off and her true nature was revealed. Hatred shone from her eyes, and Hörður would be dead if Björgvin hadn't intervened. So he has no doubt that all who knew her feared her, too, and did everything in their power to keep her *happy*. She was like a sleeping dragon in a fairy tale—a terrible creature that everyone tiptoes around, so as not to wake it.

Third, the girls were foreign. Which means that Steingrímur wasn't under direct pressure from desperate relatives or worried neighbors when one of them didn't return home. That's the bleak reality. A foreign girl disappears and the people in the village are alarmed, of course; the matter is disturbing and everyone is ready and willing to search and the like. Then the girl is found dead; it's tragic and all that, but life goes on and the consequences for the local community are minimal. The girl wasn't *one of us*. Few knew her; she's gradually forgotten, and after a few weeks it's as if she never existed. And even though the same thing happens a few years later, it isn't considered suspicious or in fact unnatural; the area is dangerous, of course, and those foreigners are always doing reckless things out in the wilderness, which leads to accidents. At least there are no suspicions of foul play, and the police reports gradually gather dust.

Hörður takes a drag from his cigarette.

Björgvin had talked, fortunately. At first, he was stubborn, but the lieutenant got him to tell him the whole story. His mother, Sigrún Arnkelsdóttir, grew up on the smallholding Heiðarsel, the only child of a poor couple who made a meager living from sheep farming. Her father was hardworking but quiet, one of those people who works all the time yet never accumulates anything and is stuck in the same rut all his life. Heiðarsel isn't at all suitable for farming; there's little to no flat land there, just a few small, poor hayfields; spring arrives late and autumn early. Heiðarból isn't a particularly good farm, either, but Róbert, the father of Geirharður and Steingrímur, had with enthusiasm and diligence managed to put together a herd of fine saddle horses, which he bred and tamed. He had a decent income from selling horses, both domestically and to Germany. This success of his awoke both admiration and envy in the community. One person, however, literally hated the horse farmer, and that was Hallbera from Heiðarsel, Arnkell's wife and Sigrún's mother. It wasn't enough that the people of Heiðarból lived in semi-luxury, in her opinion, while they were practically starving, but they also had to pay those landowners a sky-high rent for their measly croft. Hallbera had an unhealthy obsession with the people at Heiðarból, and cursed them day in and out. She said that Róbert was nothing more than a sadist who was deliberately tormenting them and starving them to death. But it was Hallbera who was a sadist, not Róbert. Hallbera appears to have been very mentally ill, with a shockingly sadistic bent. She spoke down to her husband and called him weak and servile, even in front of others, but it was her daughter, Sigrún, who bore the brunt of the housewife's toxic venom at Heiðarsel. It appears that Hallbera despised her just for being a girl. Maybe she longed to have a son whom she imagined would take care of her in her old age or suchlike, but maybe she was just evil-minded and would have been as cruel to a son as she was to her daughter. Maybe her mistreatment of the girl had been a kind of transferred self-loathing; Hörður can't be sure. But as far as he understands, she humiliated and tormented her daughter endlessly, systematically breaking her down and gradually turning her into a hateful monster. To underscore the girl's position, Hallbera marked her with the smallholding's sheep earmark: over-half-crop right, under-bit left. She cut into her ears with a knife, so that she understood that she was of no more worth than any other ewe lamb, and that she would never be anything more or more important than someone's property.

As far as Hörður can determine, Sigrún never attended school with other children. At least not until adolescence. She was home-schooled, as her mother thought she wasn't healthy enough to attend school. She claimed she had bad asthma. Whether any doctors examined her, Hörður doesn't know, but it appears that Hallbera managed to keep her daughter more or less at home, without the authorities interfering. At first, the only children she met were the boys at Heiðarból, Steingrímur and Geirharður. But when Sigrún finally started to go to school and meet other people, she was careful not to let anyone else see her disfigured ears.

Sometimes Sigrún played with the boys at Heiðarból, and probably quite early on developed a crush on the younger one, Geirharður. Hallbera was unhappy with this contact between the children. But she also saw a certain opportunity in the situation. If Sigrún ended up with one of the brothers, she would inherit a share in the land. Hallbera saw her chance to acquire something through her daughter, and at the same time, free herself from bondage, because the folk at Heiðarból would hardly charge rent from the parents of their daughter-in-law. But at the same time, Hallbera highly doubted that Sigrún would manage to snag either boy—she was so ugly and paltry, after all. So Hallbera teased her daughter about her crush, and reminded her every day of the fact that she wasn't good enough for that handsome boy, Geirharður. Steingrímur, on the other hand, showed little or no interest in girls.

Time passes. Then what Sigrún feared most, and what Hallbera always knew would happen, does indeed happen. Geirharður falls in love with a girl and plans to marry her. It's a German girl, Klara Zimmerman, who came to Iceland because of her love of Icelandic horses. It's a huge blow to Sigrún. Something inside her probably breaks. But maybe she was already broken. Whether Hallbera encouraged her to do so or not, Sigrún gets rid of Klara. Pushes her over a cliff. At Klara's death, Geirharður's will to live is extinguished, and he simply can't get out of bed. He never really recovers from this event. It's then that Sigrún seizes her opportunity. She nurses Geirharður, becomes his savior, and doesn't stop until she manages to drag Geirharður out of bed. Then they got married, but their marriage was probably not based on love. He always mourned Klara, the love of his life, and Sigrún never trusted him. Especially when it came to foreign girls.

Geirharður may at that point have started to have suspicions about Johanna Schmitz's disappearance, possibly earlier. He slipped back into a depression after her death, as she'd been working for him as a hired hand. Maybe there had been something between them; Hörður can't say. But at some point, he sneaks a peek into his wife's chest. There he finds locks of hair from Klara and Johanna, as well as some of their personal items. Hörður can't imagine how much of a shock this would have been for Geirharður. The fact that Geirharður didn't go to the police with this evidence seems to him to suggest that he didn't find it until after Björgvin came into the world.

Was he supposed to subject the mother of his young son to life imprisonment?

Björgvin was born two years after Johanna's death, and then it seemed that Sigrún calmed down; at least she didn't murder anyone for nearly twenty years—not that Hörður knows. Maybe Geirharður lived in the hope that something had changed for the better and the nightmare was over. He himself had lost the will to live. But before he died, he hid evidence in a portable cassette player that Johanna had owned. His conscience had clearly been gnawing at him, so he left behind those vague clues, which gathered dust for decades.

Geirharður dies in a sandstorm, the years go by and the evil lies dormant—the dragon sleeps. But as soon as little Björgvin, the apple of his mother's eye, reaches puberty and begins to show interest in girls, it's as if the insanity flares up again in Sigrún. A sort of mixture of hatred and jealousy. She wants Björgvin for herself; he should stay at home with his mother and rest in her deep and suffocating embrace.

Soon after Lena Nilsson's disappearance, Björgvin discovers the truth. Sigrún behaved strangely both before and after the girl's disappearance, was away from home quite a bit and/or distracted, and so on. He was, however, more or less in denial, as often happens when the truth is too painful. But he does recall certain things, such as the days and weeks after his father died. Björgvin was then only ten years old. Shortly before Geirharður died, he'd not only taken Johanna's cassette player to Reverend Páll, but also given his son an old black and white photograph—*half* a photograph, rather. It shows Geirharður standing in front of the farm Heiðarból as a young boy. When Sigrún sees the photo, she becomes agitated and asks her son where he got it and where the other half of it is. He tells her the truth; that his father gave him the photo, but that he doesn't know what she's talking about regarding the other half of it. He does, however, see that she's right; the photo has clearly been cut in two. He doesn't understand his mother's agitation, and naturally begins to wonder what on earth happened to the lost half of the photo.

Sigrún was so upset about the photo because in it, her ears can be seen. That's why she hid it. She realizes that Geirharður has gotten into the chest. So when he died, he knew the truth. Not only was the photograph gone, but also the locks of hair from Klara and Johanna, as well as the ring and earrings that belonged to them. She asks Björgvin repeatedly whether his father let him have anything besides this half-photo, doesn't believe him when he says no, and turns everything upside down in her search for something of which her son has no clue. It isn't until Lena's body is found that he begins to suspect that that nine-year-old flare-up of his mother's may have been related to the girls who disappeared decades earlier. He'd actually given Lena a necklace that she never took off, silver, with a green stone. But she apparently didn't have it with her when she fell into the canyon; it was found neither there nor in her room.

Someone had taken it...

Hörður blows smoke out his nostrils.

Of course, Sigrún was in trouble as soon as Hertha Meier appeared in the rain. Then the search began for Barbara Hoffmann, which meant search-and-rescue teams all over the heaths and the police snooping about day after day. So she had to wait and trust in God and luck, as well as her son Björgvin. He made sure that no one searched the outbuildings at Heiðarsel. Of course, she couldn't wait indefinitely to get rid of Barbara. Still, she couldn't bury the girl at Heiðarsel or somewhere on the heath, because signs of the burial would have been visible. It was a sticky situation. When Hörður visited her on the Monday, she realized that he'd picked up the scent and the game would soon be over. When he left, she probably went over to Heiðarsel to destroy the evidence there. She stuffed Barbara in a canvas bag and put it in the back of the Land Rover—Forensics confirmed that. She must have wanted to bring the girl somewhere else, but it was too much of a risk. It was a bright day and people were out and about, including the lieutenant. So she decided to dig a grave in her own vegetable garden, which was actually an ingenious idea. Afterward, she could have just sown carrots or something in the soil.

No one would have noticed anything.

But now, the old witch is dead…

Hörður knocks the ashes off his cigarette. He finished writing his final report on the investigation three days ago. Since then, he's done pretty much nothing but slack off, listen to Kansas, and drink beer. The atmosphere in Klaustur is both dull and oppressive. The media frenzy has fizzled away, for the most part. But the locals can't get any peace from the curious tourists, who, however, hardly dare to get out of their cars. Sigrún Arnkelsdóttir's funeral was held inconspicuously. Björgvin Geirharðsson is waiting to be tried. The few times the lieutenant has ventured to Kjarval or the liquor store, he's been met with silence, aloofness, and cold glances. He isn't a hero who cleansed the village of an old disease, but a disgraced newcomer who turned over stones he had no business turning over. In the minds of his countrymen, Kirkjubæjarklaustur is no longer a historically rich natural pearl and a peaceful friend, but a bloody crime scene and the home of an insane murderess, thanks to him.

"The world rewards benevolence with ill will," mutters the red-haired giant, quoting from Hallgrímur Pétursson's *Passion Hymns.* He has hardly uttered the words when a red compact car drives into the lot.

Hörður starts from his numbness. Is he dreaming? Is it really Saturday? Is she *here?* He blinks and watches in amazement as his partner steps out of her car and walks toward the house.

"Bíbí?" he says, as husky-voiced as an old blues singer. He can hardly believe his own eyes, but it certainly is her. Bíbí is tanned and fresh-looking, dressed in bright, light summer clothes, and has clearly lost a little weight. She opens the trunk of the car and takes a suitcase from it.

Is she going to be here for a whole week, or what? Hörður stubs out his cigarette. He gets to his feet to welcome her, and at the same time becomes self-conscious about his appearance and dress. He looks and smells like a bum. She looks him over, but says nothing. Still, he can see the disappointment in her eyes. Or is it sadness?

"You're here," he says, embarrassed.

"Nice to see you, too." Bíbí smiles faintly as she puts her suitcase down on the deck. She kisses him on the cheek. He hugs her clumsily.

"Sit down," says Hörður. "You must be tired after your trip."

Bíbí sits down in the other lawn chair. She's strangely silent—not the way she usually is.

"You're like a caveman," she says.

Hörður scratches his beard. "Yeah."

Bíbí looks around. "So this is the house you've told me about. A shack, more or less. High time for some maintenance, it seems to me."

"Would you like a beer?" he asks, half-offended. Did she call his house a shack? Of course, it isn't *his* house, really—but still.

"Maybe I would," she says.

Hörður opens a can of beer and hands it to her. He himself was halfway through one. They sit side by side and drink in silence. He doesn't feel well. It's been so long since they've seen each other. Of course, they'd spoken by phone, but it's not the same. Something has changed. They haven't been together for so long.

It's been so long since they've slept together. Uncomfortably long.

"You've started smoking again," says Bíbí.

"Just by accident," he says.

They fall silent.

"A girl died in Borgarnes last night," she then says. "I heard about it on the radio. A drug overdose. Very sad."

"I'm sorry to hear it," Hörður mutters. But he couldn't care less. He's just glad it happened somewhere besides Klaustur. So he doesn't have to interview witnesses and write a report on the case.

Silence again.

"Axel says you've accrued summer-vacation time," says Bíbí. "He says you can take your vacation at any time and then return to the CID after that."

"Apparently so," says Hörður. He hadn't known that he'd accrued any vacation time. But Axel had informed him of these things. He knows that old Steppenwolf wishes him well. Hörður also wants to get out of Klaustur as soon as possible. But for some reason, he hasn't yet agreed to this plan.

"Are you worried about coming back?" asks Bíbí cautiously.

Hörður gets a knot in his stomach. "Yes, a little. I've been here so long. I've gotten used to it, though I don't necessarily like it. And everything's a bit strange now, between us."

"I know," she says. "It isn't easy to be in a long-distance relationship. All closeness disappears…intimacy and warmth. And you've always had difficulty with changes. Even the ones that are beneficial."

Hörður nods. She understands him, knows how he is. But what he doesn't understand is why she wants to be with him, knowing how he is. She's a mystery, that's for sure.

With a distant expression, Bíbí sips her beer. "What do you say about just jumping into bed together?"

Hörður does a double take. "Huh?"

She shrugs. "This conversation just gets more awkward with each passing minute."

"Yes, it does," Hörður admits.

With a smile, she stands up. "Come on."

"Okay," says Hörður. He's relieved, as always when she decides matters. Sometimes he can just be so stiff, like a troll turned to stone.

They go in and shut the door behind them.

The door doesn't open until noon the next day. It's Hörður Grímsson who opens it and walks tall out under the bare sky, with his duffel bag in one hand. His hair is still damp from his morning shower, he's smooth-shaven and smells of shampoo and aftershave. His green eyes glow like emeralds in his rough-hewn, pale face. Despite the heat, he's wearing a black shirt and black trousers, and has laced on his combat boots. Over it all, he's wearing his special, beloved leather coat—heavy and black as a winter's night.

What a night, what a morning! Hörður breathes in the aroma of green, growing things. He's in such a good mood that he feels like whistling. But he settles for munching his nicotine gum. He walks over to Bíbí's car and unlocks it with the key fob, opens the car, and throws his duffel bag into the back seat.

Bíbí comes out after him. She's holding her suitcase, which is considerably lighter than the day before, as there had been almost nothing in it apart from Hörður's leather coat. She wanted to surprise her partner by bringing him his coat, and she succeeded. They'd had a joyous reunion, the red-haired giant and the gothic garment.

"Is that everything?" She hands Hörður the suitcase.

"I think so." He opens the trunk and puts the suitcase in it. Then he looks up and listens. A sound he doesn't recognize is coming from the teacher's residence. A kind of rhythmic squeaking.

"Is everything okay, babe?" asks Bíbí.

"Yes, I'm just going to…" Hörður stops mid-sentence and starts walking away, so distracted that he has disappeared into himself.

Bíbí sighs. She's seen that distant expression many times before and knows that there's no way she'll connect with her giant at the moment. He's thinking, the dear man. Instead of getting annoyed at his lack of attention, she just sits down behind the wheel, rolls down the side window, switches on the radio, and waits quietly.

Hörður ambles over to the teacher's residence. Adam's pickup truck is in the driveway, along with the six-wheeler. In the sunny garden, something swings to and fro, in rhythm with the high-pitched sound that cuts through the silence. It's the swing. In it sits a little girl. The squeaking comes from the chains rubbing against the fasteners. Adam is standing in the middle of the yard, watching the girl glide back and forth. He's wearing Bermuda shorts, a T-shirt and house shoes, his face is sunburned and he's smiling out to his ears.

"Has your wife come back?" asks the red-haired giant cheerfully.

"No-oo, actually not," says Adam, and at the same time, his smile turns into a painful grimace. "But this is my daughter's first weekend with her divorced dad. That's something, huh?"

"Sorry, man," mutters Hörður, who never seems to be able to read situations correctly, let alone have the sense to keep quiet instead of saying something that makes things worse.

"No problem," says Adam. "You're looking dapper. What's up?"

"I'm leaving," says Hörður.

Adam's face pales. "What? So where are you going?"

Hörður shrugs and smiles apologetically. "South, home…my partner came to pick me up. *My work here is done*, as they say."

"Oh, I…" Adam clears his throat. "This is unexpected. And what? Have you come to say goodbye now?"

Feeling awkward, Hörður hesitates. Is that bastard going to start crying, or what? "Yes, actually…no reason to wait."

"Oh, okay," Adam mutters. He seems to be hurt or offended or something. Hörður isn't sure. "I would have liked to say goodbye to you properly. We could have had a barbecue or something. You know. Had a bit of fun. After all that we've been through together. The outsiders."

"Yeah." Hörður doesn't know what to say or how to act. Adam is right, of course. Hörður hadn't even thanked him for his help—for saving his life—let alone the rest. But it's too late now to do anything. Or what? Well, Bíbí is waiting in the car and …

The red-haired giant furrows his brow.

Unless …

Adam smiles reassuringly. "Don't let me hold you up. I'll just say *bon voyage* and … "

Hörður interrupts him. "Wait a minute!" He lifts his index finger, then turns on his heel and marches back to the car. He opens his duffel bag and rummages through it. Now where did he put … ?

"What are you doing?" asks Bíbí.

"Found it!" Hörður clenches something in his right hand.

"Found what?" Bíbí asks, but she gets no answer. Hörður saunters back to the teacher's residence, where Adam stands awkwardly inside the fence.

"What's that you've got there?" he asks hesitantly, suspicious of the mischievous, crazy gleam in the eyes of the red-haired giant.

"*Ten-hut!*" Hörður barks at him. Adam responds involuntarily by straightening his back, lifting his chin, and pressing his arms to the sides, knowing, as he does, this American military slang, which is an abbreviation of *a-ten-hut*, which is easier for officers to shout than *come to attention*, if they want the undivided attention of their subordinates.

Hörður can't help but smile. Then he reaches over the fence and pins a medal onto Adam's T-shirt, over his chest on the right. It's a five-pointed star hanging from a white, red, and blue ribbon that is now crumpled and discolored. In the center of the star is a small diamond star within a gold laurel wreath.

Adam stares wide-eyed at the medal. "Is this…?"

"An American military Silver Star, yes," replies Hörður. "Awarded for outstanding courage in battle. Wear it with pride and dignity, soldier."

"But…? I can hardly believe it." Tears well in Adam's eyes. "For me? Where did you get…?"

"*At ease, soldier,*" says the red-haired giant, grinning and patting Adam on the shoulder. "Thanks for all the help, neighbor."

"You're welcome," Adam mutters tearfully, and the two men shake hands. "It was nice to get to know you, Hörður Grímsson. A real honor."

"Likewise, friend." Hörður smiles a crooked smile. He's feeling a bit embarrassed, and would prefer to get this farewell over as soon as possible. He nods abruptly and hurries away before Adam says anything more.

Hörður stuffs himself into the compact car and fastens his seat belt. "Right, then. We can finally get going."

"Who was that?" asks Bíbí. She backs out of the parking lot, and then drives away from the house.

"My neighbor," mutters the red-haired giant. Out of the corner of his eye, he sees Adam standing at the fence, watching them.

They'll probably never meet again.

"A great guy," he adds.

The End

About the Author

The Dark Prince of Nordic Noir: Stefán Máni was raised in the rural fishing village Ólafsvík, on the Snaefellsnes peninsula in western Iceland. At the age of twenty-six, he put all his belongings in an old car and moved to the capital city of Reykjavík to publish his first book. For the first ten years as a writer, he was working full or half time as a construction worker, a dishwasher, in a printing press and in a home for the insane. His first major success, at home and abroad, was the haunting thriller *The Ship*. Since then, he has been writing the hugely popular Grímsson detective series, along with occasional thrillers and other work. In 2012 the movie *Black's Game* premiered, based on his bestselling thriller by the same title. The movie is the second most popular and second highest grossing film in Icelandic history.

About the Publisher

This book is published on behalf of the author by the Ethan Ellenberg Literary Agency.

https://ethanellenberg.com

Email: agent@ethanellenberg.com

Facebook: https://www.facebook.com/EthanEllenberg LiteraryAgency/

www.ingramcontent.com/pod-product-compliance
Lightning Source LLC
Chambersburg PA
CBHW060618100726
47907CB00006B/1672